"Harlan Ellison is the cult writer ...
—*The Village Voice*

"Jorge Luis Borges' stories dovetail with Ellison's and provide the key to the theme underlying ANGRY CANDY. The similarities between Borges' and Elison's work are obvious. They both have built reputations primarily on the short-story form. They both use fantastic themes and ideas. Both authors enjoy an exploration of infinite possibilities. Ellison has demonstrated in a painfully personal way that he and Borges are one, in risking the solitary death of the author in the name of art."
—*The Bloomsbury Review*

"Ellison's writing is so willful, so bizarre, that one is not sure whether to be offended or impressed. It has chutzpah. It is about as far removed from the classical style as is possible within the boundaries of the English language. But it is *always* brilliant, *always* full of emotional power."
—*Washington Post Book World*

"When it comes to our contemporary writers, when he's working at the top of his form, they really don't get much better than Ellison. You really should check out ANGRY CANDY for yourself."
—*Mystery Scene*

"Intoxicating stuff. Rage and venom and hurt and the bitterness of someone who wanted to believe in a fair universe, who still wants to live in a fair universe, simply boils off the page . . . a tidy and emotionally moving structure. Ellison's technique is superb, as we expect. His words, his sentences, his stories are all top-notch."
—*San Diego Tribune*

---

HARLAN ELLISON has won more awards than any other living fantasist. The Silver Pen from P.E.N. for journalism in defense of the First Amendment. Two Edgars of the Mystery Writers of America. Eight and a half Hugos, three Nebulas, the Bram Stoker award for horror, the British Fantasy Award; the Georges Méliès film award twice, the Milford Award for Lifetime Achievement in Editing, the Jupiter award twice. And he is the only writer ever to win the Writers Guild of America Most Outstanding Teleplay award *four* times for solo work. He is the author of 45 Books, more than 1200 stories, essays, articles and newspaper columns. As a TV critic his two *Glass Teat* books are taught in hundreds of university media classes. As a film critic, his recently published collection, HARLAN ELLISON'S WATCHING, has raised shrieks of fury. Asimov calls him "the best damned writer in the world,"

A PLUME BOOK

PLUME
Published by the Penguin Group
Penguin Books USA Inc., 375 Hudson Street, New York, New York 10014, U.S.A.
Penguin Books Ltd, 27 Wrights Lane, London W8 5TZ, England
Penguin Books Australia Ltd, Ringwood, Victoria, Australia
Penguin Books Canada Ltd, 2801 John Street, Markham, Ontario, Canada L3R 1B4
Penguin Books (N.Z.) Ltd, 182-190 Wairau Road, Auckland 10, New Zealand

BOOKS ARE AVAILABLE AT QUANTITY DISCOUNTS WHEN USED TO PROMOTE PRODUCTS OR SERVICES. FOR INFORMATION PLEASE WRITE TO PREMIUM MARKETING DIVISION, PENGUIN BOOKS USA INC., 375 HUDSON STREET, NEW YORK, NEW YORK 10014.

Penguin Books Ltd, Registered Offices: Harmondsworth, Middlesex, England



The stories in this collection originally appeared in the following anthologies and magazines: THE BLACK LIZARD ANTHOLOGY OF CRIME FICTION and UNIVERSE 15; *The Best of Omni #6, Galaxy Magazine, Gallery, The Magazine of Fantasy and Science Fiction, Midnight Graffiti, The Mystery Scene Reader, Omni, The Twilight Zone Magazine, Shayol,* and *Weird Tales*. "Broken Glass" was originally published as a broadside by The Avenue Victor Hugo Bookstore, Boston.



*Published by arrangement with Houghton Mifflin Company.*

REGISTERED TRADEMARK—MARCA REGISTRADA

Library of Congress Cataloging-in-Publication Data

Ellison, Harlan.
Angry candy / Harlan Ellison.
p. cm.
ISBN 0-452-26335-2
I. Title.
[PS3555.L62A87 1989]
813′.54—dc20

89-35100
CIP

First Plume Printing, December, 1989

8 9

PRINTED IN THE UNITED STATES OF AMERICA

*And this little box of bon-bons*
*is for the only other man I know*
*who enjoys poisoned chocolates . . .*

*my friend*

ROBERT BLOCH

# ACKNOWLEDGMENTS

They've been at it again. The ones who encourage me in these efforts. The ones you can blame for making it easier to write the words. It's *their* fault: I'm merely a victim of the fever, or as Heinrich Von Kleist put it, "I write only because I cannot stop." So you see, it's all depositable at the feet of:

Dottie Amblin, Georgie Auld, Kevin Avery, Sophie & Stan Barets, Michael Bernstein, Franco & Carol Betti, Bob Booth, Alan Brennert, Sharon Buck, Jody Clark, Sarah Coatts, James Crocker, Richard Curtis, Ellen Datlow, Phil DeGuere, Judy-Lynn del Rey, Lance A. Diernback, Bart Di Grazia, Gardner Dozois, Diane Duane, Susan Ellison (wife-person), James Ellroy, Jack Gaughan, David Gerrold, Ed Gorman, the Grand Forks (North Dakota) Public Library, Ellie Grossman, Mike Hodel, Ejler Jakobsson, Tom Kafka, Alan Kay, Ann Knight, Grant Kornberg, Gil Lamont, Michele D. Malamud, Vincent McCaffrey, Patrice Messina, Don Myrus, Larry Niven, Rockne O'Bannon, Austin Olney, Otto Penzler, Frederik Pohl, Barry J. Post, Eric Protter, Robert J. Randisi, Kathleen Roché-Zujko, Charles C. Ryan, Robert Silverberg, Dr. C. D. Spangler, Jr., Michael Toman, Glynn Turman, Mark Valenti, Bill Warren, and Sheila Williams.

They're all in this with me. If I gotta swing for it, I'll take 'em all with me.

Incidentally, just to quash the rumors, neither Ronald Reagan and Ed Meese, nor Jerry Falwell, turned a hand to help me.

CONTENTS

# INTRODUCTION: THE WIND TOOK YOUR ANSWER AWAY

WE WENT TO THE funeral on a pleasantly cool but very sunny Sunday afternoon in February. I'm not sure I'd ever been to Redondo Beach before that Sunday, though I've lived in Southern California since 1962, and we had some small difficulty finding the Church of Religious Science. We: my wife, Susan, my old friend Norman Spinrad, who had been Emily's lover, and I, who had been her friend. I parked the car a few blocks away, and we got out and, without talk, we went back up the street to the friendly-looking, modern church where Emily's spirit was to be honored.

Saturday a week, Emily had been at home, changing clothes to meet her daughter for dinner. I'd talked to her that morning. I couldn't remember what we'd discussed, perhaps something about the business of copyediting and proofreading that she shared with Gil Lamont. She was planning to come by to see Susan and me early the next week.

I never knew she had epilepsy. She never mentioned it. If I had known, maybe I might have . . .

No, that isn't anything. You think it; but it isn't anything.

She was all dressed up, looking as she always looked, like a million bucks tax-free, and she must have been checking herself out in the mirror one last moment before leaving, because they found her lying beside her bed, composed and well-dressed, dead from a stroke or cardiac arrest or a thrombosis — I can never figure out how they differ, I'm sorry — and I always feel the trembling start when I try to make a picture in my head that will tell me if she was lying looking up or face down. There is no reason in the world why I should need to know that, but I still feel as helpless and lost as I did then, when I think of Emily dying all alone like that, and I keep thinking if I knew whether she was prostrate or supine it would help stop the loneliness. But that isn't anything, either. I know that.

She had had a seizure, and her heart had stopped, and she had gone away without anyone knowing, or even hearing a sound.

They found Emily the following Monday.

**April 1985**
Larry Shaw
Tom Sherred

**May 1985**
Ted Sturgeon

**July 1985**
Jack Gaughan

**October 1985**
Bernard Wolfe

**December 1985**
Walter Gibson
Howard Rodman

**January 1986**
L. Ron Hubbard
Emily Austin

**February 1986**
Bob Mills
Frank Herbert
Judy-Lynn del Rey
DeeDee Lavender

**April 1986**
Manly Wellman
Terry Kirgo
Tom Scortia

**May 1986**
Mike Hodel

**June 1986**
Benny Goodman
Jorge Luis Borges

**July 1986**
Stan Ellin

**September 1986**
Jerry Jacks

**November 1986**
Glenn Wright

And now it was Sunday a week, and we were going to the funeral. We didn't know anyone there. Emily's life was very compartmented, and she had wide circles of friendship in half a dozen social settings. Both Norman and I had been asked to speak about her, because we had known her during this last part of her life, when she was getting things together again and having a fine old time, and feeling more alive than she had in years, but we felt like outsiders, like intruders coming in for the big show who weren't bearing the proper credentials.

We sat through the early part of the service, and we perhaps heard the remarks and sentiments from the minister, Mr. Richelieu. Then he called on me, and everything I'd wanted to say about Emily, about her warmth and decency and flawless friendship and personal strength, all of it fled, and I was angry. There is no other word, I was just goddamed *angry*!

Richelieu had done that standard number about the deceased going on to a better place, that Emily was at peace at last, that we could all take heart in the sure and certain knowledge that she was watching us from on high, and smiling at us.

And I began speaking, and I'm not sure exactly what I said, but it was like this:

It's not seemly to speak harshly at the funeral of someone you loved, and who's gone away, and you miss so much it squeezes your chest when you think about them. It's not right to make a big scene and cry about how it hurts when you ask that lost friend a question, and she's not there to answer, as if the wind took her answer away, and if you listen hard enough you can still hear her voice receding, getting thinner and smaller and more transparent. We're not supposed to do that. We're supposed to reassure one another, and say dumb things like, "Well, she couldn't have suffered much." And I *want* to say things like that, because ceremonies like this are for the living, and not the dead, because the dead are gone and can't hear what we say, and I can't even take any solace in that, because it isn't a new thought. And the truth of it is, I can't take any solace *at all*, because Emily is dead. She's just gone, and we won't hear her cleverness ever again, and we won't see the way she gave that wry smile, as she turned half-away so you could enjoy what she'd said without having to worry about her reaction. No one allows us to be angry. It isn't fitting, it isn't seemly. But that's how I feel. I'm just pure and deeply angry that she's gone. That she died when her life was so good. That's cruel. It's like some kind of old Arabian Nights revenge, where the djinn waits till you're happiest to slice you down. And in the compassion that we try to show each other, we won't let ourselves be angry, won't let ourselves scream at the world that is now minus that special part.

*You can be angry!* "Do not go gentle into that good night, old age should burn and rave at close of day; rage, rage against the dying of the light." It will be a brief enough time before our daily measure softens the edges of memory, and Emily, and all that she was, and all the places in which she resided in our hearts will have closed over like the Red Sea, and we won't *feel* like being angry. We'll just be miserable, and lonely for her, and we'll never have taken the opportunity to let the stupid nasty world that took her know how much we miss her and how just goddamed *angry* we are!

And I sat down, and could feel that these people were angry, but not at Emily's death. They were angry because I hadn't played the game. And I felt awful, just awful, and I hung my head. And Susan touched my hand, and I cried.

And Norman got up, and he climbed the risers to the platform filled with flowers, and he stood behind the lectern, and he spoke so well. He believed as I believed, that it is better to send off the loved one with rage, to show at least for a moment to the empty sky and the sunny day that you *cared*, enough to look cranky and unseemly, that the loved one deserved at least *that* much, but he was saner that I. He said (and this is just a part, just the best part that I remember), "Don't expect justice. Emily being taken like

**December 1986**
John D. MacDonald

**January 1987**
Dick Sapir

**February 1987**
Ted Cogswell
Jimmy Coco

**March 1987**
Dick Levinson
Arch Oboler
Bea Mahaffey
Dick Wilson

**April 1987**
Catherine Moore
Ejler Jakobsson
Terry Carr
Dick Shawn

**May 1987**
Joey Lo Brutto
Ali Sheldon
Frank Andrasovsky

**June 1987**
Fred Astaire
Matt Morrell

**August 1987**
John Huston
Lee Marvin

**September 1987**
Alfy Bester

**October 1987**
Richard Delap

**November 1987**
Ron Smith

this, is not fair. It is not just. She never deserved to die so soon. There is no justice inherent in the universe . . . except what we put there. All the justice that exists, is what we make. So let us show compassion and sense and courage, in Emily's name."

Oh, that was *so much* better. I wish I'd had the wit or the skill or the clear head to say that. Because it was what lay at the core of my anger. It was something that could keep you busy while mourning. It could kill the guilt at not having been there to save her. Of not having said to her the things you now realized she needed to hear from a friend. Of not feeling adequate to face death. It was wise and sane and correct.

And then Richelieu got up and — gently but firmly — debunked what we had said. With oleaginous sincerity, he told his flock the same fable all over again, pushing the philosophy of that particular House of God and House of Men.

When the ceremony was ended, we three stood alone for a time, and no one came to speak to us, except for one woman who approached us and, smiling as Richelieu had been smiling, advised us that Emily *was* above, and she hoped and prayed for us that we would be able to let the sun into our hearts. She meant well, but I wanted to slug her.

And we walked back to the car, and we got in and drove away from Redondo Beach; and there hasn't been a day since February of 1986 that I haven't thought about Emily, and how much I miss my friend.

This is the twenty-second or -third or -fifth book of stories I've done. I'd like to be more precise, but what with "retrospectives" and larger collections broken in half for British publication, and suchlike, it's 22 or 23 or 25. In that neighborhood. And most of them seem to have a thread running through them unifying the diverse tales. One book was mostly about love, and the forms it takes. Another was made up of stories written during the Years of the Movement in the late '60s–early '70s, stories about social conscience and civil rights and censorship and working to stop the Viet Nam War. Another collection contained stories about the "new gods" we worship: the gods of neon, freeways, street violence, big money.



I never seem to plan these unifying aspects.

They just happen, and I'm more surprised than anyone that the linkages exist. Till now, I've always found that extra added attraction a salutary gift to give the reader. Till now.

With some trepidation I discover, now that ANGRY CANDY is an assembled artifact, that in large measure it deals with death. Enough to scare away the casual reader.

If it does any good, I never planned it to be so.

But even though I thought, during the recent years in which I've written these seventeen works, that they were about the things I've usually worried and chewed and tried to understand — the nature of courage, the parameters of genuine friendship, what it takes to be strong in a world that prefers we be weak and frightened — when I looked over the totality here assembled, the unifying thread was the end of life, personal and universal. I never planned it to be so.

When the book was completed, there were sixteen stories here. After I perceived the thread, I knew I had to write one more. So I wrote "The Function of Dream Sleep" maybe possibly to tie it all together. Because what I realized, what this book brought home to me, was how much unchanneled and free-floating pain I was suffering . . . from the deaths of my friends.

It started getting really bad in April of 1985, when Larry Shaw died. You'd have liked Larry a lot. Apart from being one of my oldest friends, he was the guy who bought my first story back in 1955. Once he wrote an article or a story or something and signed the pseudonym "N.R. DeMexico" to it. I asked him what the N.R. stood for. He said, "Not Really."

There had been the usual number of passings any adult gets in his/her life. Both my parents were long gone. Phil Seuling died unexpectedly. But they went away with enough time in between so I could catch my breath. But in April of '85 it started getting awful. Old Tom Sherred died, wonderful T.L. Sherred who had written only a handful of yarns, but each one was a radiant gem, polished and shining. He was a gentle, sweet man with a mordant sense of humor; and it was only about two weeks after Larry that I got the news on Tom. And the beginning of the second week in May, Ted Sturgeon died.

And I began the almost full-time job of writing obituaries for major pieces of my past. Here's what I said about Ted:



• • •

It began raining in Los Angeles tonight at almost precisely the minute Ted Sturgeon died in Springfield, Oregon. Edward Hamilton Waldo would have cackled at the cosmic silliness of it; but I didn't. It got to me; tonight, May 8th.

It had been raining for an hour, and the phone rang. Jayne Sturgeon said, "Ted left us an hour ago, at 7:59."

I'd been expecting it, of course, because I'd talked to him — as well as he could gasp out a conversation with the fibrosis stealing his breath — early in March, long distance to Haiku, Maui, Hawaii. Ted had written his last story for me, for the *Medea* project; and we'd sent him the signature plates for the limited edition. He said to me, "I want you to write the eulogy."

I didn't care to think about that. I said, "Don't be a pain in the ass, Ted. You'll outlive us all." Yeah, well, he *will*, on the page; but he knew he was dying, and he said it again, and insisted on my promise. So I promised him I'd do it, and a couple of weeks ago I came home late one night to find a message on my answering machine: it was Ted, and he'd come home, too. Come home to Oregon to die, and he was calling to say goodbye. It was only a few words, huskily spoken, each syllable taking it out of him, and he gave me his love, and he reminded me of my promise; and then he was gone.

Now I have to say important words, extracted from a rush of colliding emotions. About a writer and a man who loomed large, whose faintest touch remains on everyone he ever met, whose talent was greater than the vessel in which it was carried, whose work influenced at least two generations of the best young writers, and whose brilliance remains as a reminder that this poor genre of dreams and delusions can be literature.

Like a very few writers, his life was as great a work of artistic creation as the stories. He was no myth, he was a legend. Where he walked, the ether was disturbed by his passage.

For some he was the unicorn in the garden; for others he was a profligate who'd had ten hot years as the best writer in the country, regardless of categorizations (even the categorization that condemned him to the ghetto); for young writers he was an icon; for the old hands who'd lived through stages of his unruly life he was an unfulfilled promise. Don't snap at me for saying this: he liked the truth, and he wouldn't care to be remembered sans limps and warts and the hideous smell of that damned grape-scented pipe tobacco he smoked.

But who the hell needs the truth when the loss is still so painful? Maybe you're right: maybe we shouldn't speak of that.

It's only been an hour and a half since Jayne called, as I write this, and my promise to Ted makes me feel like the mommy who has to clean up her kid's messy room. I called CBS radio, and I called the *Herald-Examiner*, and that will go a ways toward getting him the hail-and-farewell I think he wanted, even though I know some headline writer will say SCI-FI WRITER STURGEON DEAD AT 67.

And the kid on the night desk at the newspaper took the basics — Ted's age, his real name, the seven kids, all that — and then he said, "Well, can you tell me what he was known for? Did he win any awards?" And I got crazy. I said, with an anger I'd never expected to feel, "Listen, sonny, he's only gone about an hour and a half, and he was as good as you get at this writing thing, and no one who ever read *The Dreaming Jewels* or *More Than Human* or *Without Sorcery* got away unscathed, because he could squeeze your heart till your life ached; and he was one of the best writers of the last half a century; and the tragedy of his passing is that *you* don't know who the fuck he was!" And then I hung up on him, because I was angry at his ignorance, but I was *really* angry at Ted's taking off like that, and I'm angry that I'm trying to write this when I don't know what to write, and I'm furious as hell that Ted made me promise to do this unthinkable thing, which is having to write a eulogy for a man who could have written his own — or any other damned thing — better than I or any of the rest of us could do it.

Theodore Sturgeon, 1918–1985. You begin to see the pattern emerging? Death was intruding in a way I'd never permitted it to obsess me. One cannot write about what Faulkner called "the human heart in conflict with itself," the only thing, he said, that was worth the blood and sweat and anguish of writing, without dealing with death. And anyone who has read my work knows I never shirked that part of the job. There is death in plenitude in my stories. But I was starting to learn that there is death . . . and there is death. The kind one uses as a story element, and the kind that wakes you shivering in the night, listening to the wind carrying away the answers.

The necrology began growing. Funny Jack Gaughan, the artist; and Bernie Wolfe, who was one of the greatest writers this country produced and whose books are almost all out of print, and most of you have never even heard his name, much less read a word he wrote, which is the worst punishment after death you can visit on a writer; and dear old Walter Gibson, who created The Shadow; and the brilliant and fiery Howard Rodman, who taught me to fight the television censors, who said to me when I was wet behind the ears in Hollywood, "When they want to change your words, don't let them send you to lawyers, don't let them run their rationalizations, don't let them scare you . . . *hit them.*"

And that was only December.

But do you see what was happening? I was getting angrier and angrier. I couldn't stop it. I'd go to bed angry, and get up angrier the next morning. Death was consuming me. Nothing was safe. I was living on the edge of the slide area.

Ron Hubbard and Emily went in January of '86. I hadn't seen Ron in decades, but we'd exchanged a few letters; and despite the looneytunes scene his Dianetics and Scientology had become, he was always still just Ron Hubbard, who'd written *To the Stars* and *Final Blackout* and *Fear* and *Typewriter in the Sky* and *Slaves of Sleep*, all of which great pulp fiction I can still reread with pleasure; and he was not some sort of mysterious recluse with a worldwide following of dippy "clears" who are so scared someone will let light into their cultish religion that they sue people who talk in their sleep, one supposes, rather than suffer any negative comment. He was just Ron, and I kinda liked him, mostly because he wrote well, and I never felt he took all that Scientology nonsense seriously but knew how to make a good buck, and he liked me, and . . . well, he was a friend who died. As Emily was a friend who died.

Then, all in one month, the very next month through which I was reeling at Emily's sudden death . . . Bob Mills, who had been my agent and friend for more than twenty years . . . just at that moment in his long life when he'd gotten out of the literary game and had come to California to retire and start to enjoy his years without having to babysit the lives of a buncha writers who always needed an advance on some story they'd sold . . . and Judy-Lynn del Rey, who had been very good and very encouraging to me for a long time till we had a falling out . . . and DeeDee Lavender . . . who died leaving

Roy all alone . . . and I remembered all the good times we'd had when I was a teenaged science fiction fan back in Ohio in the early Fifties . . . and then, in a moment, Frank Herbert was gone.

Oh, I writ a real eloquent 3,000 words about Frank, you can be sure. Hell, I can almost read that obit today without falling apart. I'm getting good at this death business. Maybe I'll join a M.A.S.H. unit. Just shovel the dead at me, I can take it, sarge.

In April, I was half an hour late to the deathbed of Manly Wade Wellman. And again had to sit down to write of it:

And now Manly is gone. I know it's the way, the way it's always been; but my god how it goes on and on till we cannot bear it a moment longer. Now Manly, gone: along with Ted and Frank, Bob Mills and Judy-Lynn, John Ciardi and Ron Hubbard, Jerry Paris and Howard Rodman, DeeDee Lavender and dear Emily Austin. And more of whom we've heard . . . soon, too soon.

Like you, I fear to lift the receiver when the phone rings, I fear what dread announcement will come next.

This one was just a trifle more awful for me than the unbearable pains of the other old friends who have left in the past few months. I was in Chapel Hill to speak at the university, having accepted the engagement chiefly because it provided a chance to spend some time with Manly and Frances. Manly's fall in June of 1985, and the resultant loss of his legs due to gangrene in September, had left that fine man in a terrible state of depression. We had talked several times, and Karl Edward Wagner had told me everyone was working very hard at getting Manly to rally, to try and make a comeback. They said a visit from someone Manly and Frances felt affection for, might do some good. And so I came to Chapel Hill.

I missed him by less than an hour. I had spoken the night before, and to my shame I dawdled. I am always late, and most of the time it doesn't matter. This time it mattered very much. When Danny Reid and I drove up to the house, Karl came to meet us. He was crying. "You missed him by half an hour," he said. I have to live with that one.

But he and Frances had wanted some Chinese food, and I'd sent some over earlier that day with Eva McKenna; and she told me he had been eating my Chinese food just a little while before he had the cardiac arrest. Eva said he liked scallops and had enjoyed it. Only that slender thread permits me to bear the guilt, because I fear I have no more tears in me. It has been too terrible a year.

So there will be no more stories of John the Ballad Singer and his guitar with the silver strings, no more tales of John Thunstone, no more miraculous prose, no more sly and sensitive reminders that we are all carried on the wind by forces we cannot control. Manly's voice is silenced, and the books remain, which is some consolation but not much. And another empty place in our lives is fitted into the jigsaw scheme of our days.

Karl was closer, and he will write of Manly's charm and grace and goodwill and courage and overwhelming humanity; and David Drake and Julie Schwartz and Bob Bloch and Gerry de la Ree and I will have the memories of his kindnesses, the pure treasure of having been permitted to know him; but for those of you who never knew him, who know only the words he wrote, for you the loss is greater. We have the stories, but we also had the privilege of touching his hand and seeing his smile.

The recollection of meeting him in Chicago, the letters we exchanged, that now-terribly-important sack of Chinese food . . . these become the urgent inconsequentialities that I can share with you in tribute to Manly. Did I ever tell you that his was the very first science fiction name I ever knew? Yes. It was on the cover of an issue of *Startling Stories* that I bought in the Forties, before I even knew there was something called scientifiction. It was the byline under a story titled "Twelve Hours to Live" but that was a silly proofreader's error, because inside the magazine that Hall of Fame reprint was bylined Jack Williamson. But Manly's was the first name I remembered.

What I tell you in memoriam is trivial. It is here to establish a fragile link with a man I admired and enjoyed, a man who expressed affection for me, which was reciprocated in full measure. It is not significant data; and it is as self-serving as anything any of us says about someone who is gone, whom we miss. The words are for the living. Manly knew who loved him, he doesn't need this affirmation. We do it for ourselves, perhaps to remind ourselves that we haven't been in touch with the few who matter to us, we haven't written that letter or made that phone call.



The wind blows. Don't be half an hour late.

. . .

Nor did it stop. The exquisitely witty wife of my friend George Kirgo, dear Terry, died in April, soon after Manly. And then Tom Scortia, who had literally saved my ass from being courtmartialed back in 1958 when I was waging my PFC war with the U.S. Army at Fort Knox, he died. He called a week or so before the end, to tell me, and to say he was sorry we'd had such coolness between us for the last ten years. He said he wanted to died with us as friends again. Oh, that was a swell telecon, that was. And in May, it was Mike Hodel:

First, and always, there was that voice. For more than fifteen years, if one lived in Los Angeles, tuning in to 90.7 on the FM dial, one heard that voice. Warm and kind and instantly the sound of a friend speaking to no one but you. Every Friday night from ten o'clock till midnight on KPFK, Pacifica's station in the City of the Angels, there was Mike Hodel hosting the (literally) world-famous *Hour 25* program.

It remains the longest-running science fiction show on radio; and though imitators came and went, it remains the only show of its kind in America. A forum and meeting place for writers and fans, publishers and readers of the genre.

For fifteen years there was no writer of significance who was not interviewed by Mike, no topic of interest he did not address, no cause of merit he did not champion. For a decade and a half, *Hour 25* was the foremost forum providing publicity for writers coming into L.A. to promote their books. Mike Hodel took it as a personal responsibility to keep people reading. His anti-illiteracy campaign, under the title READ/SF, fought the forces of obscurantism and illogic by providing audio cassettes of sf writers reading their stories. And on the air, week after week, he brought serious thinkers and noble madmen to the microphone in that tiny, squalid control booth at KPFK . . . to champion the space program, to recommend new writers whose work had reached him, to feed what he called "the group mind." He was the voice of reason and decency and friendship, for those who needed a community of like souls.

He had no enemies. To make enemies one must be suspected of having unkind thoughts or petty purposes. Mike was free of such thoughts and purposes; and so he was the recipient of a free-floating affection that all of us envy but seldom achieve.

In January of this year he seemed to have come down with a case of the flu he could not shake. So his wife, Nancy, a registered nurse, took him into the hospital for X-rays. They discovered thoracic cancer, and subsequently learned it had metastasized in the brain. Malignant melanoma, the worst possible scenario, became the reality. Mike knew, and with the grace and kindness that were his trademarks, he set about ordering his last days.

The program was his chief concern, and he took steps to insure its continued life, even if his personal existence was to be ended. He has left *Hour 25* in the hands of Terry Hodel and his long-time friend, Demon Engineer Burt Handelsman, and this writer. The show will continue, unaltered, save it will now be known at *Mike Hodel's Hour 25*. The work that Mike carried on for fifteen years will continue.

He died at 9:27 P.M. on Tuesday, May 6th, in room 4802 of Cedars-Sinai Medical Center in Los Angeles. The disease came and took him so quickly that it permitted him to spend his last few months with dignity. He even hosted the show two weeks before his death, though the magnificent voice was furry and thin. But he did it. And he even tried to spare his listeners the pain of knowing he was about to leave. He mentioned casually that he had a small medical problem, about which many of them had heard; but they were not to worry; it wasn't anything very important or troublesome.

He was our friend, and so we mourn his passing; but he was also the voice of our community for fifteen years, and the evening air will not sound as safe and friendly and worth the breathing without him.

Mike Hodel is gone and there is little comfort in saying well, his was as good a death as we're permitted. No death is good because it robs us of the only treasures that matter, the companionship and closeness of a friend who mattered. Perhaps others will find consolation in remembering that we had him with us for forty-six years, fifteen of which enriched all of us, and the literature he loved so much.

Good night, Michael.

I did the radio show for a year, but it didn't help much. I still miss Mike. The litter of his pipe ashes around my office. Funny how many of my friends smoke pipes. I smoke a pipe, too. That probably isn't anything, but it occurred to me.

The necrology went on, gathering names. Most of them close friends, others I'd only known as important icons in my world, with whom I'd had minimal personal contact. Benny Goodman and Jorge Luis Borges. I wrote the last liner notes on a Benny Goodman album. Wrote them for the *Musical Heritage Review*, and Benny had to approve them. And when he read them he told Bob Nissim at the Musical Heritage Society, "These are terrific. Use them on the album, too. This kid can write."

I thought I'd fuckin' die!

And I met Borges once. For a second. After a lecture. But he was my father in what he wrote. He is the pinnacle always before me, the reminder that no matter how arrogant I get about what I write, at my tip-top finest I'm not fit to sweep up his shadow. That he died, never having received the Nobel Prize for Literature that he deserved, crushed me and sent me deeper into melancholia.

When we entered his room at the hospital, I smelled the smell war correspondents talk about: the odor of impending death. I'd always thought that was hyperbole, an old wive's tale that inadequate talents perpetuate when they need a bit of emotional manipulation for a desensitized audience. Because death has never been arcane to me, and because *I* had never smelled that smell, I chuckled at the mendacity of those who thought they could put such a scam over on anyone with common sense and a bit of experience with the world.

I can't tell you his name, because his family still refuses to admit—to themselves or anyone else—that he died of AIDS. He was a friend of mine, and when I got the call that he was in the hospital, though we hadn't seen each other in a number of years, my wife and I went immediately.

What magnified terror I felt, pushing open that lockless door in the white corridor, and being cudgeled by the smell I'd taken for a cheap metaphor. It was everything they'd said of it. Thick and warm, as if the walls had been papered with old flannel. Sickly sweet like the odor of a gangrenous leg, like the scent in some sections of the Everglades that oozes through the air into open water, that you discern long before the flatboat pushes into the area of rotting vegetation. The heady, evil miasma of rotting gardenias. And it tracked through the tiny hospital room, swirling like a tide, even in that place with windows tightly closed and blinded and draped. In the dusk of the room at midday, the evil breeze roiled the air and made my spine hurt.

It was just that: the smell of death coming for my friend and announcing its ETA as soon, very soon.

My friend lay there, in pain, half-blind, attended by his forlorn mother and sister, whose every word and movement spoke of their fear and helplessness. Without the shrieking, they were hysterical. What used to be called "beside themselves." The fear was in the air, magnified and validated by the odor of what was coming.

In the air, as much and as paralyzingly as had been the unreasoning fear of other friends of mine who'd warned me not to go see him. If it's AIDS, they'd said, you could get it. Their warnings echoed all the ghost alerts that resounded between the lines of every article I'd read since the terrible plague had been named. Echoed the fibrillations of horror in even the sanest and most recondite news reports. This was the unseen killer come again. The spore carried in the air. The Black Death and typhus and polio and leprosy and tertiary syphilis.

And when, during that long visit, with his mother and sister taking a needed break from the deathwatch to get a cup of coffee and a cruller, and my wife off wandering through the hospital, when he had to go to the toilet, I helped his wasted body to the cubicle, and after a few minutes I heard the sound of something hitting the floor, and I called in to him, "Are you okay? Do you need some help?"

His voice came back weakly through the door, "No, I'm all right . . . I just can't . . ." And I waited, as sounds of cloth and flesh scraping the floor came to me faintly. Until I had to open the door; and he had fallen, because his left side was paralyzed. He was wedged between toilet and wall, his hospital gown tangled around his blue shanks.

It took a nurse and an attendant to help me get him up and back to bed.

And very soon thereafter, I fled.

I didn't just leave, I ran away.



I told myself that it was because I'd been a damned fool to expose my wife, whom I love more than anything or anyone in the world, to even the scent of the unseen killer. And I almost believed that noble sentiment for five minutes. Because it was true, I *had* been a damned fool for taking her there. But in truth, the fear was my own.

The fear that is in the air. Like that smell. The fear that paralyzes us all, and commits us to less-than-humane acts toward those who have been cudgeled by this new Black Death.

I hated myself for my cowardice, for my inability to go that extra moment into terror for a friend. And I came, finally, to the only bit of sustaining knowledge such an encounter can offer. And it is this:

We are fragile things, tormented by the dark and by the fearful things coming toward us through the dark. It is not just the death, which is an abstract till it cudgels, but the vessels in which that terrible smell takes up residence. It is a fear that swirls in the air until we choke, and it drives us to cowardice and brutality and flight. And all we have to keep us human in the face of it, is the sure and certain knowledge that we are all one. We must reject actively the meanspirited suggestions of lunatics and those with secret agendas, that this is some sort of "divine judgment."

Any god responsible for such terror and plague death, is no god we should consider worthy of our attention.

Those who spread such deranged explanations of what we're going through serve *no* god, but an evil entity of our own making. We are as one, all together in fragility, and terribly susceptible to bad behavior. We learn from these awful deaths the one fact that sustains us:

Only kindness and rational thinking permit us to weather the plague. Eventually, one day not too far off, some lone virologist will find the answer. And like whooping cough or infantile paralysis, this monster will be driven away. But when that day comes, and we confront the ways in which we comported ourselves—as I did that Sunday driving away from the hospital—will we be able to say that the monster offered itself and we refused to become one with it because we were nobler and saner than the mere alibi "I'm only human" provides?

If we don't resist the fear in the air, if we don't stand up to the monster of our own creating, then when the odor of death has passed will any of us be able to draw an untainted breath?



* * *

The list mounted. You'll find the necrology printed as side-runners near the beginning of this rumination. You may recognize some of the names. Trust me on this, they were all extraordinary people. I still can't believe I live in a world that doesn't have Alfred Bester and Terry Carr somewhere over there, out of sight, still saying and writing nifty stuff.

Alfy got the book I dedicated to him and Ray Bradbury, just a week before he died. He told the day nurse to go back to the phone and tell me I was the best there is. That was bullshit, of course, but coming from the best there was, it made all the work worth the effort. And Terry Carr. Jeezus, he couldn't bear it when someone used "hopefully" the wrong way. Or "viable."

And so I went a little more than a little bit mad about all the deaths. And the stories started reflecting it. "Paladin of the Lost Hour" and "Eidolons" and "The Avenger of Death" and "Laugh Track" and I saw the thread, and one day actually had the strange dream that opens "The Function of Dream Sleep" and I knew I had to write that story to make some sense of all this misery and loneliness and aching.

Now it's done, and it was never my intention to sadden the reader, but if a writer is what he writes, then perhaps anyone who picks up this book needs to know that the footsteps in which we walk are deep. There is little anyone can say that makes sense and doens't read as arrant foolishness. Dead is dead, and we all feel as if we've driven cross-country without any sleep or break, when someone we need is taken away.

Like Jack London, Jack Black, Josiah Flynt and Jim Tully, I was a road kid who found a way to get off the road. I learned how to write. It was mostly time alone. But there have always been friends and lovers who brought me back to the understanding that when it is all written, there remains nothing more important than the lives you touch, and that touch you. You are not alone.

This is a book of stories that you may think of as angry candy. They will please and entertain, I really and truly hope they will entertain (and a few of them are supposed to do no more than that), but they are also stories that I hope leave a bittersweet taste in your mind, like a jalapeño-laced cinnamon bear. They are stories I wrote because my friends are gone, a lot of them, and if you can't be angry about it, how the hell much did you care to begin with?

It's something. At last, it *is* something.

# ANGRY CANDY:

There is no memory
with less satisfaction
in it than the memory
of some temptation
we resisted.

JAMES BRANCH CABELL

# PALADIN OF THE LOST HOUR

THIS WAS AN OLD MAN. Not an incredibly old man; obsolete, spavined; not as worn as the sway-backed stone steps ascending the Pyramid of the Sun to an ancient temple; not yet a relic. But even so, a *very* old man, this old man perched on an antique shooting stick, its handles open to form a seat, its spike thrust at an angle into the soft ground and trimmed grass of the cemetery. Gray, thin rain misted down at almost the same angle as that at which the spike pierced the ground. The winter-barren trees lay flat and black against an aluminum sky, unmoving in the chill wind. An old man sitting at the foot of a grave mound whose headstone had tilted slightly when the earth had settled; sitting in the rain and speaking to someone below.

"They tore it down, Minna.

"I tell you, they must have bought off a councilman.

"Came in with bulldozers at six o'clock in the morning, and you *know* that's not legal. There's a Municipal Code. Supposed to hold off till at least seven on weekdays, eight on the weekend; but there they were at six, even *before* six, barely light for godsakes. Thought they'd sneak in and do it before the neighborhood got wind of it and call the landmarks committee. Sneaks: they come on *holidays*, can you imagine!

"But I was out there waiting for them, and I told them, 'You can't do it, that's Code number 91.03002, subsection E,' and they lied and said they had special permission, so I said to the big muckymuck in charge, 'Let's see your waiver permit,' and he said the Code didn't apply in this case because it was supposed to be only for grading, and since they were demolishing and not grading, they could start whenever they felt like it. So I told him I'd call the police, then, because it came under the heading of Disturbing the Peace, and he said . . . well, I know you hate that kind of language, old girl, so I won't tell you what he said, but you can imagine.

"So I called the police, and gave them my name, and of course they didn't get there till almost quarter after seven (which is what makes me think they bought off a councilman), and by then those 'dozers had leveled most of it. Doesn't take long, you know that.

"And I don't suppose it's as great a loss as, maybe, say, the Great Library of Alexandria, but it was the last of the authentic Deco design drive-ins, and the carhops still served you on roller skates, and it was a landmark, and just about the only place left in the city where you could still get a decent grilled cheese sandwich pressed very flat on the grill by one of those weights they used to use, made with real cheese and not that rancid plastic they cut into squares and call it 'cheese food.'

"Gone, old dear, gone and mourned. And I understand they plan to put up another one of those mini-malls on the site, just ten blocks away from one that's already there, and you know what's going to happen: this new one will drain off the traffic from the older one, and then that one will fail the way they all do when the next one gets built, you'd think they'd see some history in it; but no, they never learn. And you should have seen the crowd by seven-thirty. All ages, even some of those kids painted like aborigines, with torn leather clothing. Even they came to protest. Terrible language, but at least they were concerned. And nothing could stop it. They just whammed it, and down it went.

"I do so miss you today, Minna. No more good grilled cheese." Said the *very* old man to the ground. And now he was crying softly, and now the wind rose, and the mist rain stippled his overcoat.

Nearby, yet at a distance, Billy Kinetta stared down at another grave. He could see the old man over there off to his left, but he took no further notice. The wind whipped the vent of his trenchcoat. His collar was up but rain trickled down his neck. This was a younger man, not yet thirty-five. Unlike the old man, Billy Kinetta neither cried nor spoke to memories of someone who had once listened. He might have been a geomancer, so silently did he stand, eyes toward the ground.

One of these men was black; the other was white.

Beyond the high, spiked-iron fence surrounding the cemetery two boys crouched, staring through the bars, through the rain; at the men absorbed by grave matters, by matters of graves. These were not really boys. They were legally young men. One was nineteen, the other two months beyond twenty. Both were legally old enough to vote, to drink alcoholic beverages, to drive a car. Neither would reach the age of Billy Kinetta.

One of them said, "Let's take the old man."

The other responded, "You think the guy in the trenchcoat'll get in the way?"

The first one smiled; and a mean little laugh. "I sure as shit hope so." He wore, on his right hand, a leather carnaby glove with the fingers cut off, small round metal studs in a pattern along the line of his knuckles. He made a fist, flexed, did it again.

They went under the spiked fence at a point where erosion had created a shallow gully. "Sonofabitch!" one of them said, as he slid through on his stomach. It was muddy. The front of his sateen roadie jacket was filthy. "Sonofabitch!" He was speaking in general of the fence, the sliding under, the muddy ground, the universe in total. And the old man, who would now *really* get the crap kicked out of him for making this fine sateen roadie jacket filthy.

They sneaked up on him from the left, as far from the young guy in the trenchcoat as they could. The first one kicked out the shooting stick with a short, sharp, downward movement he had learned in his tae kwon do class. It was called the *yup-chagi*. The old man went over backward.

Then they were on him, the one with the filthy sonofabitch sateen roadie jacket punching at the old man's neck and the side of his face as he dragged him around by the collar of the overcoat. The other one began ransacking the coat pockets, ripping the fabric to get his hand inside.

The old man commenced to scream. "Protect me! You've got to protect me . . . it's necessary to protect me!"

The one pillaging pockets froze momentarily. What the hell kind of thing is that for this old fucker to be saying? Who the hell does he think'll protect him? Is he asking *us* to protect him? I'll protect you, scumbag! I'll kick in your fuckin' lung! "Shut 'im up!" he whispered urgently to his friend. "Stick a fist in his mouth!" Then his hand, wedged in an inside jacket pocket, closed over something. He tried to get his hand loose, but the jacket and coat and the old man's body had wound around his wrist. "C'mon loose, motherfuckah!" he said to the very old man, who was still screaming for protection. The other young man was making huffing sounds, as dark as mud, as he slapped at the rain-soaked hair of his victim. "I can't . . . he's all twisted 'round . . . getcher hand outta there so's I can . . ." Screaming, the old man had doubled under, locking their hands on his person.

And then the pillager's fist came loose, and he was clutching — for an instant — a gorgeous pocket watch.

What used to be called a turnip watch.

The dial face was *cloisonné*, exquisite beyond the telling.

The case was of silver, so bright it seemed blue.

The hands, cast as arrows of time, were gold. They formed a shallow V at precisely eleven o'clock. This was happening at 3:45 in the afternoon, with rain and wind.

The timepiece made no sound, no sound at all.

Then: there was space all around the watch, and in that space in the palm of the hand, there was heat. Intense heat for just a moment, just long enough for the hand to open.

The watch glided out of the boy's palm and levitated.

"Help me! You *must* protect me!"

Billy Kinetta heard the shrieking, but did not see the pocket watch floating in the air above the astonished young man. It was silver, and it was end-on toward him, and the rain was silver and slanting; and he did not see the watch hanging free in the air, even when the furious young man disentangled himself and leaped for it. Billy did not see the watch rise just so much, out of reach of the mugger.

Billy Kinetta saw two boys, two young men of ratpack age, beating someone much older; and he went for them. Pow, like that!

Thrashing his legs, the old man twisted around — over, under — as the boy holding him by the collar tried to land a punch to put him away. Who would have thought the old man to have had so much battle in him?

A flapping shape, screaming something unintelligible, hit the center of the group at full speed. The carnaby-gloved hand reaching for the watch grasped at empty air one moment, and the next was buried under its owner as the boy was struck a crackback block that threw him face first into the soggy ground. He tried to rise, but something stomped him at the base of his spine; something kicked him twice in the kidneys; something rolled over him like a flash flood.

Twisting, twisting, the very old man put his thumb in the right eye of the boy clutching his collar.

The great trenchcoated maelstrom that was Billy Kinetta whirled into the boy as he let loose of the old man on the ground and, howling, slapped a palm against his stinging eye. Billy locked his fingers and delivered a roundhouse wallop that sent the boy reeling backward to fall over Minna's tilted headstone.

Billy's back was to the old man. He did not see the miraculous pocket watch smoothly descend through rain that did not touch it, to hover in front of the old man. He did not see the old man reach up, did not see the timepiece snuggle into an arthritic hand, did not see the old man return the turnip to an inside jacket pocket.

Wind, rain and Billy Kinetta pummeled two young men of a legal age that made them accountable for their actions. There was no thought of the knife stuck down in one boot, no chance to reach it, no moment when the wild thing let them rise. So they crawled. They scrabbled across the muddy ground, the slippery grass, over graves and out of his reach. They ran; falling, rising, falling again; away, without looking back.

Billy Kinetta, breathing heavily, knees trembling, turned to help the old man to his feet; and found him standing, brushing dirt from his overcoat, snorting in anger and mumbling to himself.

"Are you all right?"

For a moment the old man's recitation of annoyance continued, then he snapped his chin down sharply as if marking end to the situation, and looked at his cavalry to the rescue. "That was very good, young fella. Considerable style you've got there."

Billy Kinetta stared at him wide-eyed. "Are you sure you're okay?" He reached over and flicked several blades of wet grass from the shoulder of the old man's overcoat.

"I'm fine. I'm fine but I'm wet and I'm cranky. Let's go somewhere and have a nice cup of Earl Grey."

There had been a look on Billy Kinetta's face as he stood with lowered eyes, staring at the grave he had come to visit. The emergency had removed that look. Now it returned.

"No, thanks. If you're okay, I've got to do some things."

The old man felt himself all over, meticulously, as he replied, "I'm only superficially bruised. Now if I were an old woman, instead of a spunky old man, same age though, I'd have lost considerable of the calcium in my bones, and those two would have done me some mischief. Did you know that women lose a considerable part of their calcium when they reach my age? I read a report." Then he paused, and said shyly, "Come on, why don't you and I sit and chew the fat over a nice cup of tea?"

Billy shook his head with bemusement, smiling despite himself. "You're something else, Dad. I don't even know you."

"I like that."

"What: that I don't know you?"

"No, that you called me 'Dad' and not 'Pop.' I *hate* 'Pop.' Always makes me think the wise-apple wants to snap off my cap with a bottle opener. Now *Dad* has a ring of respect to it. I like that right down to the ground. Yes, I believe we should find someplace warm and quiet to sit and get to know each other. After all, you saved my life. And you know what that means in the Orient."

Billy was smiling continuously now. "In the first place, I doubt very much I saved your life. Your wallet, maybe. And in the second place, I don't even know your name; what would we have to talk about?"

"Gaspar," he said, extending his hand. "That's a first name. Gaspar. Know what it means?"

Billy shook his head.

"See, already we have something to talk about."

So Billy, still smiling, began walking Gaspar out of the cemetery. "Where do you live? I'll take you home."

They were on the street, approaching Billy Kinetta's 1979 Cutlass. "Where I live is too far for now. I'm beginning to feel a bit peaky. I'd like to lie down for a minute. We can just go on over to your place, if that doesn't bother you. For a few minutes. A cup of tea. Is that all right?"

He was standing beside the Cutlass, looking at Billy with an old man's expectant smile, waiting for him to unlock the door and hold it for him till he'd placed his still-calcium-rich but nonetheless old bones in the passenger seat. Billy stared at him, trying to figure out what was at risk if he unlocked that door. Then he snorted a tiny laugh, unlocked the door, held it for Gaspar as he seated himself, slammed it and went around to unlock the other side and get in. Gaspar reached across and thumbed up the door lock knob. And they drove off together in the rain.

Through all of this the timepiece made no sound, no sound at all.

Like Gaspar, Billy Kinetta was alone in the world.

His three-room apartment was the vacuum in which he existed. It was furnished, but if one stepped out into the hallway and, for all the money in all the numbered accounts in all the banks in Switzerland, one was asked to describe those furnishings, one would come away no richer than before. The apartment was charisma poor. It was a place to come when all other possibilities had been expended. Nothing green, nothing alive, existed in those boxes. No eyes looked back from the walls. Neither warmth nor chill marked those spaces. It was a place to wait.

Gaspar leaned his closed shooting stick, now a walking stick with handles, against the bookcase. He studied the titles of the paperbacks stacked haphazardly on the shelves.

From the kitchenette came the sound of water running into a metal pan. Then tin on cast iron. Then the hiss of gas and the flaring of a match as it was struck; and the pop of the gas being lit.

"Many years ago," Gaspar said, taking out a copy of Moravia's *The Adolescents* and thumbing it as he spoke, "I had a library of books, oh, thousands of books — never could bear to toss one out, not even the bad ones — and when folks would come to the house to visit they'd look around at all the nooks and crannies stuffed with books; and if they were the sort of folks who don't snuggle with books, they'd always ask the same dumb question." He waited a moment for a response and when none was forthcoming (the sound of china cups on sink tile), he said, "Guess what the question was."

From the kitchen, without much interest: "No idea."

"They'd always ask it with the kind of voice people use in the presence of large sculptures in museums. They'd ask me, 'Have you read all these books?' " He waited again, but Billy Kinetta was not playing the game. "Well, young fella, after a while the same dumb question gets asked a million times, you get sorta snappish about it. And it came to annoy me more than a little bit. Till I finally figured out the right answer.

"And you know what that answer was? Go ahead, take a guess."

Billy appeared in the kitchenette doorway. "I suppose you told them you'd read a lot of them but not all of them."

Gaspar waved the guess away with a flapping hand. "Now what good would that have done? They wouldn't know they'd asked a dumb question, but I didn't want to insult them, either. So when they'd ask if I'd read all those books, I'd say, 'Hell, no. Who wants a library full of books you've already read?' "

Billy laughed despite himself. He scratched at his hair with idle pleasure, and shook his head at the old man's verve. "Gaspar, you are a wild old man. You retired?"

The old man walked carefully to the most comfortable chair in the room, an overstuffed Thirties-style lounger that had been reupholstered many times before Billy Kinetta had purchased it at the American Cancer Society Thrift Shop. He sank into it with a sigh. "No sir, I am not by any means retired. Still very active."

"Doing what, if I'm not prying?"

"Doing ombudsman."

"You mean, like a consumer advocate? Like Ralph Nader?"

"Exactly. I watch out for things. I listen, I pay some attention; and if I do it right, sometimes I can even make a little difference. Yes, like Mr. Nader. A very fine man."

"And you were at the cemetery to see a relative?"

Gaspar's face settled into an expression of loss. "My dear old girl. My wife, Minna. She's been gone, well, it was twenty years in January." He sat silently staring inward for a while, then: "She was everything to me. The nice part was that I knew how important we were to each other; we discussed, well, just *everything*. I miss that the most, telling her what's going on.

"I go to see her every other day.

"I used to go every day. But. It. Hurt. Too much."

They had tea. Gaspar sipped and said it was very nice, but had Billy ever tried Earl Grey? Billy said he didn't know what that was, and Gaspar said he would bring him a tin, that it was splendid. And they chatted. Finally, Gaspar asked, "And who were you visiting?"

Billy pressed his lips together. "Just a friend." And would say no more. Then he sighed and said, "Well, listen, I have to go to work."



"Oh? What do you do?"

The answer came slowly. As if Billy Kinetta wanted to be able to say that he was in computers, or owned his own business, or held a position of import. "I'm night manager at a 7-Eleven."

"I'll bet you meet some fascinating people coming in late for milk or one of those slushies," Gaspar said gently. He seemed to understand.

Billy smiled. He took the kindness as it was intended. "Yeah, the cream of high society. That is, when they're not threatening to shoot me through the head if I don't open the safe."

"Let me ask you a favor," Gaspar said. "I'd like a little sanctuary, if you think it's all right. Just a little rest. I could lie down on the sofa for a bit. Would that be all right? You trust me to stay here while you're gone, young fella?"

Billy hesitated only a moment. The very old man seemed okay, not a crazy, certainly not a thief. And what was there to steal? Some tea that wasn't even Earl Grey?

"Sure. That'll be okay. But I won't be coming back till two A.M. So just close the door behind you when you go; it'll lock automatically."

They shook hands, Billy shrugged into his still-wet trenchcoat, and he went to the door. He paused to look back at Gaspar sitting in the lengthening shadows as evening came on. "It was nice getting to know you, Gaspar."

"You can make that a mutual pleasure, Billy. You're a nice young fella."

And Billy went to work, alone as always.

When he came home at two, prepared to open a can of Hormel chili, he found the table set for dinner, with the scent of an elegant beef stew enriching the apartment. There were new potatoes and stir-fried carrots and zucchini that had been lightly battered to delicate crispness. And cupcakes. White cake with chocolate frosting. From a bakery.

And in that way, as gently as that, Gaspar insinuated himself into Billy Kinetta's apartment and his life.

As they sat with tea and cupcakes, Billy said, "You don't have any-place to go, do you?"

The old man smiled and made one of those deprecating movements of the head. "Well, I'm not the sort of fella who can bear to be homeless, but at the moment I'm what vaudevillians used to call 'at liberty.'"

"If you want to stay on a time, that would be okay," Billy said. "It's not very roomy here, but we seem to get on all right."

"That's strongly kind of you, Billy. Yes, I'd like to be your roommate for a while. Won't be too long, though. My doctor tells me I'm not long for this world." He paused, looked into the teacup, and said softly, "I have to confess . . . I'm a little frightened. To go. Having someone to talk to would be a great comfort."

And Billy said, without preparation, "I was visiting the grave of a man who was in my rifle company in Vietnam. I go there sometimes." But there was such pain in his words that Gaspar did not press him for details.

So the hours passed, as they will with or without permission, and when Gaspar asked Billy if they could watch television, to catch an early newscast, and Billy tuned in the old set just in time to pick up dire reports of another aborted disarmament talk, and Billy shook his head and observed that it wasn't only Gaspar who was frightened of something like death, Gaspar chuckled, patted Billy on the knee and said, with unassailable assurance, "Take my word for it, Billy . . . it isn't going to happen. No nuclear holocaust. Trust me, when I tell you this: it'll never happen. Never, never, not ever."

Billy smiled wanly. "And why not? What makes *you* so sure . . . got some special inside information?"

And Gaspar pulled out the magnificent timepiece, which Billy was seeing for the first time, and he said, "It's not going to happen because it's only eleven o'clock."

Billy stared at the watch, which read 11:00 precisely. He consulted his wristwatch. "Hate to tell you this, but your watch has stopped. It's almost five-thirty."

Gaspar smiled his own certain smile. "No, it's eleven."

And they made up the sofa for the very old man, who placed his pocket change and his fountain pen and the sumptuous turnip watch on the now-silent television set, and they went to sleep.

One day Billy went off while Gaspar was washing the lunch dishes, and when he came back, he had a large paper bag from Toys "R" Us.



Gaspar came out of the kitchenette rubbing a plate with a souvenir dish towel from Niagara Falls, New York. He stared at Billy and the bag. "What's in the bag?" Billy inclined his head, and indicated the very old man should join him in the middle of the room. Then he sat down crosslegged on the floor, and dumped the contents of the bag. Gaspar stared with startlement, and sat down beside him.

So for two hours they played with tiny cars that turned into robots when the sections were unfolded.

Gaspar was excellent at figuring out all the permutations of the Transformers, Starriors and GoBots. He played well.

And they went for a walk. "I'll treat you to a matinee," Gaspar said. "But no films with Karen Black, Sandy Dennis or Meryl Streep. They're always crying. Their noses are always red. I can't stand that."

They started to cross the avenue. Stopped at the light was this year's Cadillac Brougham, vanity license plates, ten coats of acrylic lacquer and two coats of clear (with a little retarder in the final "color coat" for a slow dry) of a magenta hue so rich that it approximated the shade of light shining through a decanter filled with Château Lafite-Rothschild 1945.

The man driving the Cadillac had no neck. His head sat thumped down hard on the shoulders. He stared straight ahead, took one last deep pull on the cigar, and threw it out the window. The still-smoking butt landed directly in front of Gaspar as he passed the car. The old man stopped, stared down at this coprolitic metaphor, and then stared at the driver. The eyes behind the wheel, the eyes of a macaque, did not waver from the stoplight's red circle. Just outside the window, someone was looking in, but the eyes of the rhesus were on the red circle.

A line of cars stopped behind the Brougham.

Gaspar continued to stare at the man in the Cadillac for a moment, and then, with creaking difficulty, he bent and picked up the smoldering butt of stogie.

The old man walked the two steps to the car — as Billy watched in confusion — thrust his face forward till it was mere inches from the driver's profile, and said with extreme sweetness, "I think you dropped this in our living room."

And as the glazed simian eyes turned to stare directly into the pedestrian's face, nearly nose to nose, Gaspar casually flipped the butt with its red glowing tip, into the back seat of the Cadillac, where it began to burn a hole in the fine Corinthian leather.

Three things happened simultaneously:

The driver let out a howl, tried to see the butt in his rearview mirror, could not get the angle, tried to look over his shoulder into the back seat but without a neck could not perform that feat of agility, put the car into neutral, opened his door and stormed into the street trying to grab Gaspar. "You fuckin' bastid, whaddaya think you're doin' tuh my car you asshole bastid, I'll kill ya . . ."

Billy's hair stood on end as he saw what Gaspar was doing; he rushed back the short distance in the crosswalk to grab the old man; Gaspar would not be dragged away, stood smiling with unconcealed pleasure at the mad bull rampaging and screaming of the hysterical driver. Billy yanked as hard as he could and Gaspar began to move away, around the front of the Cadillac, toward the far curb. Still grinning with octogeneric charm.

The light changed.

These three things happened in the space of five seconds, abetted by the impatient honking of the cars behind the Brougham; as the light turned green.

Screaming, dragging, honking, as the driver found he could not do three things at once: he could not go after Gaspar while the traffic was clanging at him; could not let go of the car door to crawl into the back seat from which now came the stench of charring leather that could not be rectified by an inexpensive Tijuana tuck-'n-roll; could not save his back seat and at the same time stave off the hostility of a dozen drivers cursing and honking. He trembled there, torn three ways, doing nothing.

Billy dragged Gaspar.

Out of the crosswalk. Out of the street. Onto the curb. Up the side street. Into the alley. Through a backyard. To the next street from the avenue.

Puffing with the exertion, Billy stopped at last, five houses up the street. Gaspar was still grinning, chuckling softly with unconcealed pleasure at his puckish ways. Billy turned on him with wild gesticulations and babble.

"You're *nuts*!"



"How about that?" the old man said, giving Billy an affectionate poke in the bicep.

"Nuts! Looney! That guy would've torn off your head! What the hell's wrong with you, old man? Are you out of your boots?"

"I'm not crazy. I'm responsible."

"Responsible!?! Res*pon*sible, fer chrissakes? For what? For all the butts every yotz throws into the street?"

The old man nodded. "For butts, and trash, and pollution, and toxic waste dumping in the dead of night; for bushes, and cactus, and the baobab tree; for pippin apples and even lima beans, which I despise. You show me someone who'll eat lima beans without being at gunpoint, I'll show you a pervert!"

Billy was screaming. "What the hell are you talking about?"

"I'm also responsible for dogs and cats and guppies and cockroaches and the President of the United States and Jonas Salk and your mother and the entire chorus line at the Sands Hotel in Las Vegas. Also their choreographer."

"Who do you think you are? God?"

"Don't be sacrilegious. I'm too old to wash your mouth out with laundry soap. Of course I'm not God. I'm just an old man. *But I'm responsible.*"

Gaspar started to walk away, toward the corner and the avenue and a resumption of their route. Billy stood where the old man's words had pinned him.

"Come on, young fella," Gaspar said, walking backward to speak to him, "we'll miss the beginning of the movie. I hate that."

Billy had finished eating, and they were sitting in the dimness of the apartment, only the lamp in the corner lit. The old man had gone to the County Art Museum and had bought inexpensive prints — Max Ernst, Gérôme, Richard Dadd, a subtle Feininger — which he had mounted in Insta-Frames. They sat in silence for a time, relaxing; then murmuring trivialities in a pleasant undertone.

Finally, Gaspar said, "I've been thinking a lot about my dying. I like what Woody Allen said."

Billy slid to a more comfortable position in the lounger. "What was that?"

"He said: I don't mind dying, I just don't want to be there when it happens."

Billy snickered.

"I feel something like that, Billy. I'm not afraid to go, but I don't want to leave Minna entirely. The times I spend with her, talking to her, well, it gives me the feeling we're still in touch. When I go, that's the end of Minna. She'll be well and truly dead. We never had any children, almost everyone who knew us is gone, no relatives. And we never did anything important that anyone would put in a record book, so that's the end of us. For me, I don't mind; but I wish there was someone who knew about Minna . . . she was a remarkable person."

So Billy said, "Tell me. I'll remember for you."

Memories in no particular order. Some as strong as ropes that could pull the ocean ashore. Some that shimmered and swayed in the faintest breeze like spiderwebs. The entire person, all the little movements, that dimple that appeared when she was amused at something foolish he had said. Their youth together, their love, the procession of their days toward middle age. The small cheers and the pain of dreams never realized. So much about him, as he spoke of her. His voice soft and warm and filled with a longing so deep and true that he had to stop frequently because the words broke and would not come out till he had thought away some of the passion. He thought of her and was glad. He had gathered her together, all her dowry of love and taking care of him, her clothes and the way she wore them, her favorite knickknacks, a few clever remarks: and he packed it all up and delivered it to a new repository.

The very old man gave Minna to Billy Kinetta for safekeeping.

Dawn had come. The light filtering in through the blinds was saffron. "Thank you, Dad," Billy said. He could not name the feeling that had taken him hours earlier. But he said this: "I've never had to be responsible for anything, or anyone, in my whole life. I never belonged to anybody . . . I don't know why. It didn't bother me, because I didn't know any other way to be."

Then his position changed, there in the lounger. He sat up in a way that Gaspar thought was important. As if Billy were about to open the secret box buried at his center. And Billy spoke so softly the old man had to strain to hear him.

"I didn't even know him.

"We were defending the airfield at Danang. Did I tell you we were 1st Battalion, 9th Marines? Charlie was massing for a big push out of

Quang Ngai province, south of us. Looked as if they were going to try to take the provincial capital. My rifle company was assigned to protect the perimeter. They kept sending in patrols to bite us. Every day we'd lose some poor bastard who scratched his head when he shouldn't of. It was June, late in June, cold and a lot of rain. The foxholes were hip-deep in water.

"Flares first. Our howitzers started firing. Then the sky was full of tracers, and I started to turn toward the bushes when I heard something coming, and these two main-force regulars in dark blue uniforms came toward me. I could see them so clearly. Long black hair. All crouched over. And they started firing. And that goddam carbine seized up, wouldn't fire; and I pulled out the banana clip, tried to slap in another, but they saw me and just turned a couple of AK-47's on me . . . God, I remember everything slowed down . . . I looked at those things, seven-point-six-two-millimeter assault rifles they were . . . I got crazy for a second, tried to figure out in my own mind if they were Russian-made, or Chinese, or Czech, or North Korean. And it was so bright from the flares I could see them starting to squeeze off the rounds, and then from out of nowhere this lance corporal jumped out at them and yelled somedamnthing like, 'Hey, you VC fucks, looka here!' except it wasn't that . . . I never could recall what he said actually . . . and they turned to brace him . . . and they opened him up like a baggie full of blood . . . and he was all over me, and the bushes, and oh god there was pieces of him floating on the water I was standing in . . ."

Billy was heaving breath with impossible weight. His hands moved in the air before his face without pattern or goal. He kept looking into far corners of the dawn-lit room as if special facts might present themselves to fill out the reasons behind what he was saying.

"Aw, geezus, he was *floating* on the water . . . aw, Christ, *he got in my boots!*" Then a wail of pain so loud it blotted out the sound of traffic beyond the apartment; and he began to moan, but not cry; and the moaning kept on; and Gaspar came from the sofa and held him and said such words as *it's all right*, but they might not have been those words, or *any* words.

And pressed against the old man's shoulder, Billy Kinetta ran on only half sane: "He wasn't my friend, I never knew him, I'd never talked to him, but I'd seen him, he was just this guy, and there wasn't any reason to do that, he didn't know whether I was a good guy or a shit or anything, so why did he do that? He didn't need to do that. They wouldn't of seen him. He was dead before I killed them. He was gone already. I never got to say thank you or thank you or . . . *anything!*

"Now he's in that grave, so I came here to live, so I can go there, but I try and try to say thank you, and he's dead, and he can't hear me, he can't hear anything, he's just down there, down in the ground, and I can't say thank you . . . oh, geezus, geezus, why don't he hear me, I just want to say thanks . . ."

Billy Kinetta wanted to assume the responsibility for saying thanks, but that was possible only on a night that would never come again; and this was the day.

Gaspar took him to the bedroom and put him down to sleep in exactly the same way one would soothe an old, sick dog.

Then he went to his sofa, and because it was the only thing he could imagine saying, he murmured, "He'll be all right, Minna. Really he will."

When Billy left for the 7-Eleven the next evening, Gaspar was gone. It was an alternate day, and that meant he was out at the cemetery. Billy fretted that he shouldn't be there alone, but the old man had a way of taking care of himself. Billy was not smiling as he thought of his friend, and the word *friend* echoed as he realized that, yes, this was his friend, truly and really his friend. He wondered how old Gaspar was, and how soon Billy Kinetta would be once again what he had always been: alone.

When he returned to the apartment at two-thirty, Gaspar was asleep, cocooned in his blanket on the sofa. Billy went in and tried to sleep, but hours later, when sleep would not come, when thoughts of murky water and calcium night light on dark foliage kept him staring at the bedroom ceiling, he came out of the room for a drink of water. He wandered around the living room, not wanting to be by himself even if the only companionship in this sleepless night was breathing heavily, himself in sleep.

He stared out the window. Clouds lay in chiffon strips across the sky. The squealing of tires from the street.



Sighing, idle in his movement around the room, he saw the old man's pocket watch lying on the coffee table beside the sofa. He walked to the table. If the watch was still stopped at eleven o'clock, perhaps he would borrow it and have it repaired. It would be a nice thing to do for Gaspar. He loved that beautiful timepiece.

Billy bent to pick it up.

The watch, stopped at the V of eleven precisely, levitated at an angle, floating away from him.

Billy Kinetta felt a shiver travel down his back to burrow in at the base of his spine. He reached for the watch hanging in air before him. It floated away just enough that his fingers massaged empty space. He tried to catch it. The watch eluded him, lazily turning away like an opponent who knows he is in no danger of being struck from behind.

Then Billy realized Gaspar was awake. Turned away from the sofa, nonetheless he knew the old man was observing him. And the blissful floating watch.

He looked at Gaspar.

They did not speak for a long time.

Then: "I'm going back to sleep," Billy said. Quietly.

"I think you have some questions," Gaspar replied.

"Questions? No, of course not, Dad. Why in the world would I have questions? I'm still asleep." But that was not the truth, because he had not been asleep that night.

"Do you know what 'Gaspar' means? Do you remember the three wise men of the Bible, the Magi?"

"I don't want any frankincense and myrrh. I'm going back to bed. I'm going now. You see, I'm going right now."

" 'Gaspar' means master of the treasure, keeper of the secrets, paladin of the palace." Billy was staring at him, not walking into the bedroom; just staring at him. As the elegant timepiece floated to the old man, who extended his hand palm-up to receive it. The watch nestled in his hand, unmoving, and it made no sound, no sound at all.

"You go back to bed. But will you go out to the cemetery with me tomorrow? It's important."

"Why?"

"Because I believe I'll be dying tomorrow."

It was a nice day, cool and clear. Not at all a day for dying, but neither had been many such days in Southeast Asia, and death had not been deterred.

They stood at Minna's gravesite, and Gaspar opened his shooting stick to form a seat, and he thrust the spike into the ground, and he settled onto it, and sighed, and said to Billy Kinetta, "I'm growing cold as that stone."

"Do you want my jacket?"

"No. I'm cold inside." He looked around at the sky, at the grass, at the rows of markers. "I've been responsible, for all of this, and more."

"You've said that before."

"Young fella, are you by any chance familiar, in your reading, with an old novel by James Hilton called *Lost Horizon*? Perhaps you saw the movie. It was a wonderful movie, actually much better than the book. Mr. Capra's greatest achievement. A human testament. Ronald Colman was superb. Do you know the story?"

"Yes."

"Do you remember the High Lama, played by Sam Jaffe? His name was Father Perrault?"

"Yes."

"Do you remember how he passed on the caretakership of that magical hidden world, Shangri-La, to Ronald Colman?"

"Yes, I remember that." Billy paused. "Then he died. He was very old, and he died."

Gaspar smiled up at Billy. "Very good, Billy. I knew you were a good boy. So now, if you remember all that, may I tell you a story? It's not a very long story."

Billy nodded, smiling at his friend.

"In 1582 Pope Gregory XIII decreed that the civilized world would no longer observe the Julian calendar. October 4th, 1582 was followed, the next day, by October 15th. Eleven days vanished from the world. One hundred and seventy days later, the British Parliament followed suit, and September 2nd, 1752 was followed, the next day, by September 14th. Why did he do that, the Pope?"

Billy was bewildered by the conversation. "Because he was bringing it into synch with the real world. The solstices and equinoxes. When to plant, when to harvest."

Gaspar waggled a finger at him with pleasure. "Excellent, young fella. And you're correct when you say Gregory abolished the Julian calendar because its error of one day in every one hundred and twenty-eight years had moved the vernal equinox to March 11th. That's what the history books say. It's what *every* history book says. But what if?"

"What if *what*? I don't know what you're talking about."

"What if: Pope Gregory had the knowledge revealed to him that he *must* readjust time in the minds of men? What if: the excess time in 1582 was eleven days and one hour? What if: he accounted for those eleven days, vanished those eleven days, but that one hour slipped free, was left loose to bounce through eternity? A very special hour . . . an hour that must *never* be used . . . an hour that must never toll. What if?"

Billy spread his hands. "What if, what if, what if! It's all just philosophy. It doesn't mean anything. Hours aren't real, time isn't something that you can bottle up. So what if there *is* an hour out there somewhere that . . ."

And he stopped.

He grew tense, and leaned down to the old man. "The watch. Your watch. It doesn't work. It's stopped."

Gaspar nodded. "At eleven o'clock. My watch works; it keeps very special time, for one very special hour."

Billy touched Gaspar's shoulder. Carefully he asked, "Who are you, Dad?"

The old man did not smile as he said, "Gaspar. Keeper. Paladin. Guardian."

"Father Perrault was hundreds of years old."

Gaspar shook his head with a wistful expression on his old face. "I'm eighty-six years old, Billy. You asked me if I thought I was God. Not God, not Father Perrault, not an immortal, just an old man who will die too soon. Are you Ronald Colman?"

Billy nervously touched his lower lip with a finger. He looked at Gaspar as long as he could, then turned away. He walked off a few paces, stared at the barren trees. It seemed suddenly much chillier here in this place of entombed remembrances. From a distance he said, "But it's only . . . what? A chronological convenience. Like daylight saving time; Spring forward, Fall back. We don't actually *lose* an hour; we get it back."

Gaspar stared at Minna's grave. "At the end of April I lost an hour. If I die now, I'll die an hour short in my life. I'll have been cheated out of one hour I want, Billy." He swayed toward all he had left of Minna. "One last hour I could have with my old girl. That's what I'm afraid of, Billy. I have that hour in my possession. I'm afraid I'll use it, god help me, I want so much to use it."

Billy came to him. Tense, and chilled, he said, "Why must that hour never toll?"

Gaspar drew a deep breath and tore his eyes away from the grave. His gaze locked with Billy's. And he told him.

The years, all the days and hours, exist. As solid and as real as mountains and oceans and men and women and the baobab tree. Look, he said, at the lines in my face and deny that time is real. Consider these dead weeds that were once alive and try to believe it's all just vapor or the mutual agreement of Popes and Caesars and young men like you.

"The lost hour must never come, Billy, for in that hour it all ends. The light, the wind, the stars, this magnificent open place we call the universe. It all ends, and in its place — waiting, always waiting — is eternal darkness. No new beginnings, no world without end, just the infinite emptiness."

And he opened his hand, which had been lying in his lap, and there, in his palm, rested the watch, making no sound at all, and stopped dead at eleven o'clock. "Should it strike twelve, Billy, eternal night falls; from which there is no recall."

There he sat, this very old man, just a perfectly normal old man. The most recent in the endless chain of keepers of the lost hour, descended in possession from Caesar and Pope Gregory XIII, down through the centuries of men and women who had served as caretakers of the excellent timepiece. And now he was dying, and now he wanted to cling to life as every man and woman clings to life no matter how awful or painful or empty, even if it is for one more hour. The suicide, falling from the bridge, at the final instant, tries to fly, tries to climb back up the sky. This weary old man, who only wanted to stay one brief hour more with Minna. Who was afraid that his love would cost the universe.

He looked at Billy, and he extended his hand with the watch waiting for its next paladin. So softly Billy could barely hear him, knowing that he was denying himself what he most wanted at this last place in his life, he whispered, "If I die without passing it on . . . it will begin to tick."

"Not me," Billy said. "Why did you pick me? I'm no one special. I'm not someone like you. I run an all-night service mart. There's nothing special about me the way there is about you! I'm *not* Ronald Colman! I don't want to be responsible, I've *never* been responsible!"

Gaspar smiled gently. "You've been responsible for me."

Billy's rage vanished. He looked wounded.

"Look at us, Billy. Look at what color you are; and look at what color I am. You took me in as a friend. I think of you as worthy, Billy. Worthy."

They remained there that way, in silence, as the wind rose. And finally, in a timeless time, Billy nodded.

Then the young man said, "You won't be losing Minna, Dad. Now you'll go to the place where she's been waiting for you, just as she was when you first met her. There's a place where we find everything we've ever lost through the years."

"That's good, Billy, that you tell me that. I'd like to believe it, too. But I'm a pragmatist. I believe what exists . . . like rain and Minna's grave and the hours that pass that we can't see, but they *are*. I'm afraid, Billy. I'm afraid this will be the last time I can speak to her. So I ask a favor. As payment, in return for my life spent protecting the watch.

"I ask for one minute of the hour, Billy. One minute to call her back, so we can stand face-to-face and I can touch her and say goodbye. You'll be the new protector of this watch, Billy, so I ask you please, just let me steal one minute."

Billy could not speak. The look on Gaspar's face was without horizon, empty as tundra, bottomless. The child left alone in darkness; the pain of eternal waiting. He knew he could never deny this old man, no matter what he asked, and in the silence he heard a voice say: "*No!*" And it was his own.

He had spoken without conscious volition. Strong and determined, and without the slightest room for reversal. If a part of his heart had been swayed by compassion, that part had been instantly overridden. No. A final, unshakable no.

For an instant Gaspar looked crestfallen. His eyes clouded with tears; and Billy felt something twist and break within himself at the sight. He knew he had hurt the old man. Quickly, but softly, he said urgently, "You know that would be wrong, Dad. We mustn't . . ."

Gaspar said nothing. Then he reached out with his free hand and took Billy's. It was an affectionate touch. "That was the last test, young fella. Oh, you know I've been testing you, don't you? This important item couldn't go to just anyone.

"And you passed the test, my friend: my last, best friend. When I said I could bring her back from where she's gone, here in this place we've both come to so often, to talk to someone lost to us, I knew you would understand that *anyone* could be brought back in that stolen minute. I knew you wouldn't use it for yourself, no matter how much you wanted it; but I wasn't sure that as much as you like me, it might not sway you. But you wouldn't even give it to *me*, Billy."

He smiled up at him, his eyes now clear and steady.

"I'm content, Billy. You needn't have worried. Minna and I don't need that minute. But if you're to carry on for me, I think you *do* need it. You're in pain, and that's no good for someone who carries this watch. You've got to heal, Billy.

"So I give you something you would never take for yourself. I give you a going-away present . . ."

And he started the watch, whose ticking was as loud and as clear as a baby's first sound; and the sweep-second hand began to move away from eleven o'clock.

Then the wind rose, and the sky seemed to cloud over, and it grew colder, with a remarkable silver-blue mist that rolled across the cemetery; and though he did not see it emerge from that grave at a distance far to the right, Billy Kinetta saw a shape move toward him. A soldier in the uniform of a day past, and his rank was Lance Corporal. He came toward Billy Kinetta, and Billy went to meet him as Gaspar watched.

They stood together and Billy spoke to him. And the man whose name Billy had never known when he was alive, answered. And then he faded, as the seconds ticked away. Faded, and faded, and was gone. And the silver-blue mist rolled through them, and past them, and was gone; and the soldier was gone.

Billy stood alone.

When he turned back to look across the grounds to his friend, he saw that Gaspar had fallen from the shooting stick. He lay on the ground. Billy rushed to him, and fell to his knees and lifted him onto his lap. Gaspar was still.



"Oh, god, Dad, you should have heard what he said. Oh, geez, he let me go. He let me go so I didn't even have to say I was sorry. He told me he didn't even *see* me in that foxhole. He never knew he'd saved my life. I said thank you and he said no, thank *you*, that he hadn't died for nothing. Oh, please, Dad, please don't be dead yet. I want to tell you . . ."

And, as it sometimes happens, rarely but wonderfully, sometimes they come back for a moment, for an instant before they go, the old man, the very old man, opened his eyes, just before going on his way, and he looked through the dimming light at his friend, and he said, "May I remember you to my old girl, Billy?"

And his eyes closed again, after only a moment; and his caretakership was at an end; as his hand opened and the most excellent timepiece, now stopped again at one minute past eleven, floated from his palm and waited till Billy Kinetta extended his hand; and then it floated down and lay there silently, making no sound, no sound at all. Safe. Protected.

There in the place where all lost things returned, the young man sat on the cold ground, rocking the body of his friend. And he was in no hurry to leave. There was time.

A blessing of the 18th Egyptian Dynasty:

*God be between you and harm in*
*all the empty places you walk.*

The Author gratefully acknowledges the importance of a discussion with Ms. Ellie Grossman in the creation of this work of fiction.

# FOOTSTEPS

FOR HER, darkness never fell in the City of Light. For her, nighttime was the time of life, the time filled with moments of light brighter than all the cheap neon sullying the Champs-Élysées.

Nor had night ever fallen in London; nor in Bucharest; nor in Stockholm; nor in any of the fifteen cities she had visited on this holiday. This gourmet tour of the capitals of Europe.

But night had come frequently in Los Angeles.

Precipitating flight, necessitating caution, producing pain and hunger, terrible hunger that could not be assuaged, pain that could not be driven from her body. Los Angeles had become dangerous. Too dangerous for one of the children of the night.

But Los Angeles was behind her, and all the headlines about the INSANE SLAUGHTER, about the RIPPER, about the TERRIBLE DEATHS. All that was behind her . . . and so were London, Bucharest, Stockholm, and a dozen other feeding grounds. Fifteen wonderful banquet halls.

Now she was in Paris for the first time, and night was coming with all its light and all its promise.

In the Hôtel des Saints Pères she bathed at great length, taking the time she always took before she went out to dine, before she went out to find passion.

She had been startled to find the hotels in France did not provide washcloths. At first she had thought the chambermaid had forgotten to leave one, but when she called down to the reception desk, the girl who answered the phone could not understand what she was asking for. The receptionist's English was not good; and French was almost incomprehensible to Claire. Claire spoke Los Angeles very well: which was of no use in Paris. It was fortunate language was no barrier for Claire when she was ordering a meal. No problem at all.

They made querulous sounds at one another for ten minutes till the receptionist *finally* understood she was asking for a washcloth.



"Ah! *Oui, mademoiselle,*" the receptionist said, *"le gant de toilette!"*

Instantly, Claire knew she had hit it. "Yes, that's right . . . *oui* . . . *gant*, uh . . . *gant* whatever you said . . . *oui* . . . a washcloth . . ."

And after *another* ten minutes she understood that the French thought the cloth with which one washed one's body was too personal to leave in a hotel room, that the French carried their own *gants de toilette* when they traveled.

She was amazed. And somehow mildly pleased. It bespoke a foreign way of life that promised new tastes, new thrills, possibly new highs of love. What she thought of as transports of ecstasy. In the night. In the bright light of darkness.

She lingered a long time in the bath, using the shower head on a flexible metal cord to wash her long blonde hair. The extremely hot bath water around her lower body, between her thighs, the cascade of hot water pouring down over her, eased the tension of the plane trip from Zurich, washed away the first signs of jet-lag that had been creeping up on her since London. She lay back in the tub and let the water flow over her. Rebirth. Rejuvenation.

And she was ferociously hungry.

But Paris was world-renowned for its cuisine.

She sat at a table outside Les Deux Magots, the café on the Boulevard St.-Germain where Boris Vian and Sartre and Simone de Beauvoir had sat in the Forties and Fifties, thinking their thoughts and sometimes writing their words of existential loneliness. They sat there drinking their *pastis*, their Pernod, and they were filled with a sense of the oneness of humanity with the universe. Claire sat and thought of her impending oneness with selected parts of humanity . . . And the universe was of no concern to her. For the children of the night, loneliness was born in the flesh. It lay at the core of the bones, it swam in the blood. For her, the idea of existential solitude was not an abstract theory; it was her way of life. From the first moment of awareness.

She had dressed for effect. Tonight the blue sky silk, slit high in the front. She sat at the edge of the crowd, facing the sidewalk, her legs crossed high, a simple glass of Perrier *avec citron* before her. She had not ordered *pâté* or *terrine*: never taint the palate before indulging in a gourmet repast. She had avoided snacking all day, keeping herself on the trembling edge of hunger.

And the movable feast walked past.

He was in his early forties, stuffy-looking, holding himself erect like Marshal Foch in the guidebook history of France she had bought. This man wore a sincere gray suit, double-breasted, pompously cut to obscure the fact that the quality was not that good.

The man — whom Claire now thought of as Marshal Foch — walked past, caught a flicker of nylon as she crossed her legs for his benefit, glanced sidewise and met the stare of her green eyes, and bumped into an old woman with a string bag filled with greens and bread. They did a little dance trying to avoid each other, and the old woman elbowed him aside roughly, muttering an obscenity under her breath.

Claire laughed brightly, warmly, disarmingly.

Marshal Foch looked embarrassed.

"Old women have very sharp elbows," she said to him. "They stay at home with pumice stone and sharpen them every day." He stared at her, and the expression that passed over his face assured her she had him hooked.

"Do you speak English?"

He took a long moment to shift linguistic gears and took a step closer. He nodded. "Yes, I do." His voice was deep, but measured: the voice of a man who watched the sidewalk as he walked, watched to make certain he did not filthy his shoes with dog droppings.

"I'm sorry I don't speak French," she said, drawing a deep breath so the blue sky silk parted slightly at her bosom. Making certain he didn't miss it, she let a pale, slim hand drift to her breasts as if in apology. He followed the movement with his narrowed eyes. Hooked, oh yes, hooked.

"You are American?"

"Yes. From Los Angeles. You've been there?"

"Yes, oh of course. I have been in America many times. My business."

"What is your business?"

Now he stood before her table, his briefcase hanging from his left hand, his chest pulled up to conceal the soft opulence gravity and age had brought to his stomach.

"I could sit down perhaps?"

"Oh, yes, of course. Certainly. How rude of me. Do sit down."



He pulled out the metal chair beside her, pushed the briefcase under, and sat down. He crossed his legs very carefully, like Marshal Foch, making certain the creases were sharp and straight. He sucked in his stomach and said, "I am dealing in artists' prints. Very fine work of new painters, graphic artists, airbrush persons. I travel very much in the world."

*Not by foot,* Claire thought. *By 747, by Trans Europ Express, by chic tramp steamers carrying only a dozen curried passengers as supercargo. Not by foot. You haven't a stringy inch on your succulent body, Marshal Foch.*

"I think that sounds wonderful," Claire said. Enthusiasm. Heady wine. Doors standing open. Invitations on stiff cockleshell vellum, embossed with elegant script. And, as always, since the morning of the world — spiders and flies.

"Oh, yes, I think so," he said, chuckling with pride. He did not say *think*; he pronounced it *sink*.

Sink. Down and down into the green water of her fine cool eyes.

He offered her a drink, she said she had a drink, he offered her *another* drink, some other kind of drink, some *stronger* drink. But she said no, she had a drink, thank you. Thus did she let him know she was not a prostitute. It was always the same, in any great city. Strong drink.

She hoped he could not hear her stomach growling.

"Have you had dinner?" she asked.

He did not answer immediately. *Ah, you have a wife and children waiting for you, waiting to start dinner, perhaps in Neuilly,* she thought. *Why, you dirty middle-aged man.*

Then he said, "Ah, *non.* But I must make the phone call to break engagement of a business nature. You would care to have dinner with me, perhaps?"

"I think that would be lovely," she said, showing him, by a turn of her head, the precise angle that highlighted her excellent cheekbones. Before she had finished the sentence he was out of the chair and heading for the *cabines téléphoniques.*

She sat and sipped her Perrier, waiting for dinner to return.

*That was quick,* she thought, as he hustled back to her. *Let me guess what you said, darling: something important has come up . . . a buyer from Doubleday shops in America . . . he is interested in the Kawalerowicz and the Meynard prints . . . you know I hate staying in the city so late . . . but I must . . . ah,* non, *Françoise, don't be like zat . . . tell the children I bring them a* tarte . . . *stop! stop! I must stay longer . . . I will come as soon as I can . . . eat without me . . . I will not argue with you . . . goodbye* . . . au revoir . . . salut . . . à bientôt . . . *gimme a break, will you, I want to get laid . . . I can hear you saying it now, my dear Marshal Foch.*

And she thought one thing more: *I hope they don't try to keep your dinner hot for you.*

He smiled at her but there was strain in his face. It wasn't all that good a face to contain strain. But he tried valiantly not to show the effect of the phone call. "Now we go, yes?"

She stood up slowly, letting the parts assemble in the most esthetic manner, and the smile on his face grew more placid. Oh yes: hooked.

They began walking. She had already done some walking in the area. Be prepared, that's the Girl Scouts' marching song.

She steered him into the Rue St. Benoît, thinking she could have dinner there without attracting a crowd. But it was still too early in the evening. The night life of Paris flows through the streets till well after two A.M., and dining *alfresco* is next to impossible. Claire never liked to hurry through a meal.

There were two restaurants at the end of Rue St. Benoît, and he suggested both of them. She made a charming move and said, "Why don't we walk a little farther. I want someplace more . . . romantic." He did not argue. Down Rue St. Benoît.

Left into Rue Jacob. Too busy.

Right onto Rue des Saints Pères. Still too busy. But up ahead . . . the river. The dark Seine, in the evening.

"Can we walk down to the river?"

He looked confused. "You want dinner, yes?"

"Oh, sure. Of course. But first let's walk down to the river. It's so beautiful, so lovely at night; this is my first time in Paris; it's so *romantic.*" He did not argue.

On their right the bulk of a large building lay in darkness. She looked up at it and past it to the sky, in which the full moon shone like a waiting message.

Dining under the full moon was always nice.

He said, "This building is l'École des Beaux-Arts. Very famous." He pronounced it *fay*-moose. She laughed.

Dark. Always light. Sweet full moon riding through the heavens. Dinner warm and waiting. And then there was a bridge sweeping across the dark river. And steps leading down to the bank. Ah.

"Le Pont Royal," Marshal Foch said, indicating the bridge. "Very *fay*-moose." They walked across the quay and she led him down the steps. On the bank, two meters above the languid Seine, she turned and looked to left and right. Now she leaned against him and stood on her toes and kissed him. He sucked in his stomach, but it was not to hide the rotundity. She took him by the hand and led him toward the Pont Royal.

"Under the bridge," she said.

The sound of his breathing.

The sound of her high heels on the ancient stones.

The sound of the city above them.

The sound of the full moon glowing golden and getting larger in the sky.

And there, under the bridge, swathed in darkness, she leaned against him again and took his thick head between her slim, pale hands and put her mouth against his and let the sweet smell of her wash over him. She kissed him for a long moment, nipping at his lips with her teeth, and he made a small sound, like a tiny animal being stroked. But she was ahead of him. Her passion was already aroused.

And now Claire went away, to be replaced by something else.

A child of the night.

Child of loneliness.

With the last flickering awareness of her departing humanity she perceived the instant he knew he was in the love embrace of something else, the child of the night.

It was the instant she changed.

But that instant was too short for him to free himself. Now her spine had curved, and now her mouth had filled with fangs, and now the claws had grown, and now the body beneath the blue sky silk was matted with fur, and now she was dragging him down, and now she was on top of him, and now the claws were ripping the sincere gray suit from his flesh, and now one blackened claw sliced a line through his throat so he could not scream; and now it was dinnertime.

It had to be done carefully and quickly.

He was erect, his penis swollen with arrested lust. Now she had him naked and on his back, and she was on him, and settling down over him; and he entered her, even as he gurgled his life away. She rode him, bucking and sweating, while his mouth worked futilely and his eyes grew large and surrounded by white.

Her orgasm was accompanied by a howl that rose up over the Seine and was lost in the night sky above Paris where the golden sovereign of the full moon swallowed it, glowing just a bit brighter with passion.

And down in the dark, surfeited with passion, she dined elegantly.

The food in Berlin had been too starchy; in Bucharest the blood had run too thin and the taste had not risen; in Stockholm the dining was too bland; in London too stringy; in Zurich too rich, she had been ill. Nothing to compare with the hearty fare in Los Angeles.

Nothing to compare with home cooking . . . until Paris.

The French were justly famous for their cuisine.

And she ate out every night.

It was a very good week, her first week in Paris. An elegant older man with bristling white moustaches who spoke of the military, right up to the end. A shampoo girl from a chic shop, who wore a kind of fluorescent purple jumpsuit and red candy-apple cowboy boots. An American student from Westfield, New York, studying at the Sorbonne, who told her he was in love with her, until the end when he said nothing. And others. Quite a few others. She was afraid her figure was going to hell.

And now it was Saturday again. *Samedi.*

She had felt like dancing. She was a good dancer. All the right rhythms at just the right times. One of her meals had said the most interesting boîte, at the moment, was a bar and restaurant combined with a discothèque called Les Bains-Douches, which translated as "the bath and shower" because it had formerly been a bath and shower house since the nineteenth century.

She had come to the Rue du Bourg l'Abbé and had stood before the large glass in the heavy door. A man and a woman were behind the glass, selecting who could come in and who could not. In Paris, the more one is kept out of the club, the more one wishes to enter.

The man and the woman looked at her. Both reached to unlock the door. Claire knew what she looked like; the appeal was evident to male and female alike. She had never worried for a moment about gaining access. Inside.

And now, all around her, the excitement and the color and the firm strong young flesh of Paris moved in stately passion like underwater plants.

She danced a little, she drank a little, she waited.

But not for long.

He wore a very tight T-shirt with the words 1977 NCAA Soccer Champions on it. But he was not an American, nor an Englishman. He was French and his jeans, like his shirt, were very tight. He wore motorcycle boots with little chains banding the toe. His hair was long and waved back carelessly, but he did not have the sloe eyes of a punk. The eyes were sharp and blue and too intelligent for the face in which they rested. He stared down at her.

For a few moments she was unaware of him standing there, even though he was directly in front of her table. She was watching a particularly elegant couple performing lifts at the far right side of the dance floor; and he stood there, watching her without interference.

But when she looked up and he did not turn away, when his eyes did not narrow and he did not grow nervous as she turned the full power of her personality on him, she knew tonight would very likely be the best gourmet dining she had ever had.

His name was Patrick. He was a good dancer; they danced well together; and he held her tighter than a stranger had any right to hold her. She smiled at the thought because they would not be strangers for long; soon, if the night filled with light, they would be very intimate. Eternally intimate.

And when they left he suggested his apartment in Le Marais.

They went over the river to the old section, now quite fashionable. He lived on the top floor, but he was not wealthy. He told her that. She found him quite charming.

Inside, he turned on a soft blue light and another that was recessed in the wall behind a long chrome planter box filled with fat, healthy plants.

He turned to her and she reached out to take his head between her hands. He reached up and stopped her hands, and he smiled and said, in French she could understand, "You would eat some food?" She smiled. Yes, she *was* hungry.

He went into the kitchen and came back with a tray of carrots and asparagus and shredded beets and radishes.

They sat and talked. He talked, for the most part. In a French manner that posed no problems for her. She couldn't understand that. He spoke as fast and with as much complexity as all other Frenchmen, but when others spoke to her, in the hotel, in the street, in the disco, it was gibberish; when he spoke, she understood perfectly. She thought he might have learned English somewhere and was speaking partially in her native tongue. But when her mind tried to halt one of the words she thought might be in English, it was gone too fast. But after a while she stopped worrying about it and just let him talk.

And when she leaned toward him, finally, to kiss him on the mouth, he reached across and put his hand up under her long blonde hair, up to the nape of the neck, and brought her face close.

Through the window she could see the waning moon. She smiled faintly within the kiss: it was not necessary to have a full moon. It never had been. That was where the legends were wrong. But the legend was correct about silver bullets. Silver of any kind. And therein lay the reason a vampire cast no reflection. (Except that was merely *another* legend. There were no vampires. Only children of the night who had been badly observed.) Because Jesus had been betrayed by Judas for thirty pieces of silver, the metal had been put to an evil purpose and was therefore, thereafter, invested with the power to turn away evil. So it was not the *mirror* that cast no reflection of the children of the night, it was the silver backing. Claire could be seen in a mirror of polished steel or aluminum. She could bathe in the river and see her reflection.

But never in a silver-backed mirror.

Such as the one over the fireplace just across from where she sat on the sofa with Patrick.

A *frisson* of warning went through her.

She opened her eyes. He was looking past her.

Into the mirror.

Where he sat alone, embracing nothing.

And Claire began to leave, to be replaced by the child of the night.

Fast. She moved very fast.

Spine curves, fur mats, teeth lengthen, teeth sharpen, claws grow.

And her hand that was no longer a hand came up as she shoved him away from her, raking the razoring claws across his throat.

The throat opened wide.

And the green sap flowed out. For a moment. And then the wound magically puckered, drew together, formed a white line of scar, and then vanished altogether.

He watched her as she watched him heal.

For the first time in her life she was frightened.

"Would you like me to put on some music?" he asked. But he did not speak. His mouth did not move.

And she understood why his French had not been incomprehensible to her. He was speaking inside her head, without sound.

She could not answer.

"If not music, then perhaps you'd like something to eat," he said. And he smiled.

Her hands moved in vagrant ways, without purpose. Fear and total confusion commanded her. He seemed to understand. "It's a very large world," he said. "The spirit moves in many ways, in many forms. You think you're alone, and you are. There are many of us, one of each, last of our kind, perhaps, and each of us is alone. The mists part and the children emerge, and after a while the old ones die, leaving the last of the children motherless and fatherless."

She had no idea what he was saying. She had always known she was alone. That was simply the way it was. Not the foolish concept of loneliness of Sartre or Camus, but *alone*, all alone in a universe that would kill her if it knew she existed.

"Yes," he said, "and that's why I have to do something about you. If you are the last of your kind, then this life of chances, just to satisfy your needs, must end."

"You're going to kill me. Then do it quickly. I always knew that would happen. Just do it fast, you weird son of a bitch."

He had read her thoughts.

"Don't be a fool. I know it's hard not to be paranoid; what you've been all your life programs that into you. But don't be a fool if you can stop. There's nothing of survival in stupidity. That's why so many of the last of their kind are gone."



"What the hell *are* you?!?" she demanded to know.

He smiled and offered her the tray of vegetables.

"You're a carrot, a goddam carrot!" she yelled.

"Not quite," said the voice in her head. "But from a different mother and father than you; from a different mother and father than everyone else out on the streets of Paris tonight. And neither of us will die."

"Why do you want to protect *me*?"

"The last save the last. It's simple."

"For what? For what will you protect me?"

"For yourself . . . for me."

He began to remove his clothes. Now, in the blue light, she could see that he was very pale, not quite the shade that facial makeup had lent him; not quite white. Perhaps the faintest green tinge surging along under the firm, hard skin.

In all other respects, and superbly constructed, he was human; and tumescently male. She felt herself responding to his nakedness.

He came to her and carefully, slowly — because she did not resist — he removed her clothes; and she realized that she was Claire again, not the matted-fur child of the night. When had she changed back?

It was all happening without her control.

Since the time a very *long* time ago when she had gone on her own, she had controlled. Her life, the lives of those she met, her destiny. But now she was helpless, and she didn't mind giving over control to him. Fear had drained out of her, and something quicker had replaced it.

When they were both naked, he drew her down onto the carpet and began to make slow, careful love to her. In the planter box above them she thought she could detect the movement of the hearty green things trembling slightly, aching toward them and the power they released as they spasmed together in a ritual at once utterly new because theirs was the meeting of the unfamiliar, yet ancient as the moon.

And as the shadow of passion closed around her she heard him whisper, "There are many things to eat."

For the first time in her life, she could not hear the sound of footsteps following her.

# ESCAPEGOAT

SIXTY FEET ABOVE the smooth surface of the North Atlantic, next to the forward rail of the *Titanic*'s main deck, a rippling slit opened in the darkness of the night. A scintillant orange mist swirled through the slit, and the three Time Commandos stepped through onto the deck of the luxury liner.

Even before he had emerged completely from riptime Sgt. Ratliff was complaining. "Why me? Why is it always me? Why the hell don't one of *you* smartapples ever volunteer? Just once! Why's it always me has to do the dangerous stuff?"

It was 11:27 P.M. on April 14, 1912. The orange mist sucked itself back into the slit, the egress into riptime vanished, and the raiding patrol from the far future stood in the darkness.

The *Titanic* rode a surface of saintly calm. That millennium's *Oberstgruppenführer* of Time Commandos, "Blackjack" Alec de la Ree, fished among the shaped charges in a bandolier pocket, came up with a nasty stub of cigar, wetted it and wedged it in the left corner of his mouth. "Because, Ratlips," he said, grinding Ratliff's gears with the hated nickname, "you know damned well you've got the highest probability distribution quotient of anybody on the team." The words *probability*, *distribution*, and *quotient* were almost unintelligible around the cigar butt. He lit up with a wooden kitchen match endemic to the phenomenological year in which this raid was being staged. "Just once is there a chance we can pull off a patrol without you piss and moan? Try to fix your pea-brain on the idea, Sergeant: we're here in service of humanity! Bernoulli equations picked *you*, chum, not us. You're the one stays behind so the rest of us get back through riptime. That's what you draw your pay for."

The third Time Commando, Corporal Cicero, chimed in with agreement and annoyance that Ratliff was sturmdranging again. "You're a fast pain in the fundament, y'know that?"

"Okay, okay," Ratliff said. "But I'm gonna register a beef when we get back to Chronobase."

"Let's just correct this node in the Phenom Flow, save the future again, and go home," de la Ree said. "Then you can squeal all you want."

He glanced down at the fingernail of his left thumb, where the subjective hour of this year in the Phenom Flow strobed crimson in digital readout. They were crossing the Grand Banks. "It's eleven-forty their time." He stared off the starboard bow. "There it is!"

A gigantic, menacing hulk of ice loomed up fifty feet from the flat surface of the sea.

"Move fast!" de la Ree hissed. The trio of Time Commandos rushed to complete their assigned tasks. Within two minutes they were back at the bow rail.

"Everything set?" de la Ree asked. The cigar was out; he was winded from his activities. Ratliff and Cicero nodded it was all set. De la Ree smiled. "In thirty seconds the future'll be set right, humanity'll be okay for another thousand years, and we get some relief time."

He opened the slit into riptime, shooed Cicero into the pulsing orange mist, and took a step toward the egress. "I still think it's chickendoo," Ratliff said. "What if I get caught in the Flow?"

De la Ree gave him one last look of disgust as he relit the cigar stub, blew a cloud of noxious smoke at the noncom, and said, "Up yours, Ratlips. Just save humanity and we'll see ya at Chronobase." As he placed one foot into the mist, he looked back and added, "An' try not to drag a decade along with ya, y'wanna listen to me?" Then he was gone.

At that moment, still doing twenty-two knots, the great liner began slipping to port as the First Officer yelled to the Wheelman that a berg was drifting in on their starboard side. The Wheelman reacted instantly. The ship slid slowly toward safety.

So Ratlips ensured the future of humanity by triggering the charges as he leaped into the orange mist of the riptime, and sank the *Titanic*.

Thinking, crankily, *There's gotta be an easier way to make a living. A guy could get* hurt *like this!*

# WHEN AULD'S ACQUAINTANCE IS FORGOT

"THAT'S A FEDERAL OFFENSE you're suggesting, Mr. Auld. It's not just my job, it's the whole franchise. The auditors come in, they fall over it — because *I* don't know how to cover it — and the people who own this Bank lose everything they sank into it." The young woman stared at Jerry Auld till he looked away. She wasn't trying to be kind, despite the look of desperation on his face. She was telling him in as flat and forthright a manner as she could summon — just in case he was a field investigator for the regulatory agency looking for bootleg Banks — possibly wired for gathering evidence — so he would understand that *this* Memory Bank was run strictly along the lines of the Federal directives.

"Is that what you want, Mr. Auld? To get us in the most serious kind of trouble?"

He was pale and thin, holding his clasped hands in his lap, rubbing one thumb over the other till the skin was raw. His eyes had desperation brimming in them. "No . . . no, of course not. I just thought . . ."

She waited.

"I just thought there might be *some* way you could make an exception in this case. I really . . . have to get rid of this one last, pretty *awful* memory. I know you've gone as far as you can by the usual standards; but I felt if you just looked in the regulations, maybe you'd find some legitimate way to . . ."

"Let me stop you," she said. "I've monitored your myelin sheathing, and the depletion level is absolutely at maximum. There is no way on earth, short of a Federal guideline being relaxed, that we can leach one more memory out of your brain." She let a mildly officious — some might say nasty — smile cross her lips. "Simply put, Mister Auld: you are overdrawn at the Memory Bank."

He straightened in the formfit and his voice went cold. "Lady, I'm about as miserable as a human being can be. I've got a head full of stuff that makes sex with spiders and other small, furry things seem like a happy alternative, and I don't need you to make me feel like a fool."

He stood up. "I'm sorry I asked you to do something you can't do. I just hope you don't come to where I am some day and need someone to help."

She started to reply, but he was already walking toward the iris. As it dilated, he turned to look at her once more. "You don't look anything like her. I was wrong."

Then he was gone.

It took her some time to unravel the meaning of his last words; but she decided she had no time to feel sorry for him. She wondered who "her" was; then she forgot it.

The little man with the long nose and the cerise caftan spotted Auld as he left the Memory Bank. He had been sitting on a bench in the mall, sipping at a bulb of Flashpoint Soda, watching the Bank. He recognized Auld's distressed look at once, and he punctiliously deposited the bulb in a nearby incinerator box and followed him.

When Jerry Auld wandered into a showroom displaying this year's models of the Ford hoverpak, the little man sauntered around the block once, strolled into the showroom, and sidled up to him. They stood side-by-side, looking at the pak.

"They say it's the same design the aircops use, just less juice," the little man said, not looking at Auld.

Jerry looked down at him, aware of him for the first time. "That so? Interesting."

"You look to me," the little man said, in the same tone of voice he had used to comment on the Ford pak, casual, light, "like a man with some bad memories."

Jerry's eyes narrowed. "Something I can do for you, chum?"

The little man shrugged and acted nonchalant. "For me? Hell, no. I'm fuzz-free and frilly, friend. What I thought, I might be able to do something upright for you."

"Like what?"

"Like get you to a clean, precise Bank that could leach off some bad stains."



Jerry looked around. The showroom grifters were busy with live customers. He turned to face the little man.

"Why me?"

The little man smiled. "Saw you hobble out of the Franchise Bank in the mall. You looked rocky, friend. Mighty rocky. Carrying a freightload of old movies in your skull. Figured they turned you down for one reason or another. Figured you could use a friendly steer."

Jerry had been expecting something like this. The Bank in the mall had not been his first stop. There had been the Memory Bank in the Corporate Tower and the Bank in the Longacre Shopping Center and the Bank at Mount Sinai. They had all turned him down, and from recent articles he'd read on bootleg memory operations, he'd suspected that maintaining a visible image would put the steerers on to him.

"You got a name, chum?"

"Do I gotta have a name?"

"Just in case I go around a dark corner with you and get a sap upside my head. I want to be able to remember a tag to go with the face."

The little man grinned nastily. "Remember the nose. My friends call me Pinocchio."

"Let's go see the man," Jerry Auld said.

"Woman," Pinocchio said.

"Woman," Jerry Auld said. "Let's go see the woman."

The bootleg Bank was on an air-cushion yacht anchored beyond the twelve-mile limit. They reached it using hoverpaks, and by the time the strung lights of the vessel materialized out of the mist, it was night. They put down on the forecastle pad and racked their units. Pinocchio kept up a line of useless chatter, intended to allay Auld's fears. It served to draw him up tighter than he'd been before the little man had braced him.

Jerry saw guards with weapons on the flying bridge.

Pinocchio caught his glance and said, "Precautions."

"Sure."

Pinocchio didn't move. Jerry said, "Are we doing something here or just taking the night air?" He didn't like being under the guns.

Pinocchio kept his eyes on the flying bridge as he said, "They're making us: reporting. It'll only be a minute."



"What kind of trouble do these people get?" Jerry asked.

"Hijackers sometimes. You know: pirates. The market's lively right now. A lot of jockeying for territory, getting good product to push . . ." One of the armed guards motioned with his weapon, and Pinocchio said, "Come on."

They went belowdecks. The yacht was handsomely appointed. Flocked-velvet wallpaper in the companionways, burnished metal banisters, thick carpets. Pinocchio knocked at an inlaid teak door. The door was opened by an unexceptional-looking woman. She smiled, pro forma, and walked back into the cabin, permitting Auld and the little man to enter.

The room was a spacious saloon, fitted to the walls with the memory-leaching devices Auld recognized from his many trips to legitimate Banks in the city.

"Ms. Keogh, I'd like to introduce Mr. Jerry Auld. Met him in the city, thought we could do a little business . . . ."

She waved him to silence. "Do you have your own transportation, Mr. Auld? Or did you come with Mr. Timiachi?"

Auld said, "I have my own pak."

"Then you can go, Mr. Timiachi," she said to the little man. "Stop by the office and get a check."

Obsequious, Pinocchio bobbed his head and smiled a goodbye at Jerry. Then, sans forelock-tugging, he bowed himself out of the saloon. Ms. Keogh waved at a formfit. Jerry sat down.

"How close are you to maximum depletion?" she said.

He decided not to fence. He was in too much pain. They were both here for the same thing. "I'm at the limit."

She walked around the saloon, thinking. Then she came and sat down beside him in the other formfit. Through the open porthole Auld heard the mournful sound of something calling to its mate across the night water. "Let me tell you several things," she said.

"I want to get rid of some bad stains," Auld said. "I know what I need to know."

She raised a hand to silence him. "Probably. Nonetheless, this is not a bucket shop. Bootleg, yes; but not a crash and burn operation."

He indicated he'd listen.

"The 'holographic' memory model postulates that a memory is stored in a manner analogous to a hologram — not sited in any specific area, but stored all over the brain. To remove one certain memory, it is always necessary to break molecules of myelin all over the brain . . . from the densely packed myelin of the corpus callosum —"

"The white matter," Auld said. She nodded. "I've heard all this before."

"— from the white matter right down the spinal cord; perhaps even down into the peripheral nerves." She finished on a tone of dogged determination.

"Now tell me about the weak point in the long-chain myelin molecule. The A-1 link. Tell me how easily the molecule breaks there. The point at which muscular dystrophy and other neurodegenerative diseases attack the molecule. Tell me how I might become a head of lettuce if I go past the max. I've heard it all before. I'm surprised you're trying to discourage me. I'm also annoyed, lady."

She looked at him with resignation. "We don't push anyone; and we don't lie. It's bad enough we're outside the law. I don't want anyone's life on my hands. Your choice, fully informed."

He stood up. "Put me in the drain and let's get this over with."

"It must be nasty."

"I pity the poor sonofabitch you sell these stains to."

"Would you like to meet the head that will be receiving what you'll be losing?"

"Not much."

"He's a very old man whose life has been bland beyond the telling. He wants action, danger, adventure, romance. He wants to settle into his twilight years with a head filled with wonder and experience."

"I'm touched." He made his fists. "Goddammit, lady, *get this shit out of my head!*"

She waved him to the leaching unit on the wall. He followed her as she opened out the wings. She folded down the formfit with its probe helmet, and he sat without waiting for instructions. He had been in that seat before. Perhaps too many times.

"This won't hurt," Ms. Keogh said.

"That's not true," he replied.

"You're right. It's not true," she said, and the helmet dropped and the probes fastened to his skull and she turned on the power. The universe became a whirlpool.



. . .

Lucy spat blood and he touched her chin with the moist cloth. "Jerry, please."

"No. Forget it."

"I'm in terrible pain, Jerry."

"I'll call the medic."

"You know it won't do any good. You know what you have to do."

He turned away. "I can't, kid. I just can't."

"I trust you, Jerry. If *you* do it, I won't be afraid. I know it'll be okay."

It wasn't going to be okay, no matter how it happened. For a moment he hated her for wanting to share it with him, for needing that last terrible measure of love no one should be asked to give.

"Don't let them put me in the ground, Jerry. Nobody can talk to worms. Send me to the fire. I wouldn't mind that, not if you were with me . . ."

She was rambling. He understood about her fear of the dark; down there forever in the cold; with things moving toward her. Yes, he could guarantee the clean fire would have what remained . . . after. But she was rambling, talking about things she was seeing on the other side —

"I know they're over there, past the crossover, Jerry. They were there before, when I thought I was going. Don't let me die alone. Be there to keep them at bay till I can run, honey. Please."

She coughed blood again, and her eyes closed. He held the moist cloth and reached down and lifted her head from the pillow and placed it over her face. "I love you, kiddo."

After a very long time he took the pillow away. It was heavily stained.

Ms. Keogh called two deckhands to help him onto the forecastle. They strapped his pak on him. The mist was heavier now, had slipped into fog. If there were stars somewhere beyond the yacht, they could not be seen.

"Can you travel?" she said. He was looking off to starboard. She took his head in her hands. "Can you travel?"

"Yes. Of course. I'm fine." He looked away again.



"Set the auto for the city," she said to one of the deckhands. She spoke softly. "Do you remember Lucy?"

"Yes."
"Do you remember the fire?"
"What fire?"
"Lucy."
"Yes. She smiled at me."
They sent him aloft and he hovered for a moment. Then the autopilot cut in and he moved slowly off into the fog.
She watched for a time, but there were no stars visible.
Then she went belowdecks to purify the stain that had been stored in the unit.
Later that night an old man sat in the unit's formfit, and the balance of pain in the universe was restored.

The Author wishes to acknowledge the assistance of Ms. Dottie Amlin, Ms. Diane Duane, Mr. Mark Valenti and Mr. David Gerrold in the creation of this piece of fiction.

# BROKEN GLASS

DANA WAS SITTING in the window seat on the left side of the bus, eyes closed, breathing shallowly, having the teak fantasy, when she became aware of the peeping tom in her mind.

She had reconciled the teak fantasy years before: what it might say about the basic nature of her sexuality had no bearing on its potency: as a lubricating daydream when she was in a place where she could do nothing physical to bring herself off, the teak fantasy was the best.

She fantasized herself as a cocktail waitress in a small restaurant frequented almost exclusively by beautiful, slim-hipped models seen repeatedly on television commercials, who worked out of an agency in the building just across the street. She was wearing a very short miniskirt and smoke-colored pantyhose that had a small rip in the crotch. In the fantasy she always reminded herself to repair the rip before someone noticed. In the fantasy her breasts were larger than in real life, and they stood out prominently against the white-and-blue peasant blouse. In the fantasy she wore a wide patent leather wristband, shiny black against her pale left wrist.

She was serving two exquisite models, one of them certainly Eurasian, the other a black woman with incredible high cheekbones. As she bent over the table to place the dishes of food, she felt a hand steal up her thighs and over her buttocks from behind. She looked over her shoulder and a blonde who wore her hair in a highly styled Gibson Girl coiffure was leaning away from the table behind her, a slim hand up under Dana's skirt. She heard herself gasp.

The old man in the bus seat beside her looked up from his copy of *The National Review*, then looked away quickly, as though he had been caught eavesdropping. She was unaware of him. The blonde had found the rip in her pantyhose.

In the fantasy, the two models she was serving had moved their plates to an empty table, and now they were gently, but forcefully, bending her forward. The edge of the table pressed tightly into her stomach, her cheek lay against the warm teak of the tabletop. There was no peripheral sound in the fantasy, just sounds of voices dimly heard, her own murmuring down in her throat. The blonde had flipped up her little skirt, exposing Dana's upper thighs and buttocks. She had her finger inside the rip, exploring.

The Eurasian and the black model were stroking Dana's long brown hair, her ears, her cheek, her neck. The Eurasian was pushing down the elastic top of the peasant blouse, revealing Dana's smooth back. In the fantasy she had no moles on her back, it was all smooth and white, now turning faintly rose-colored as blood rushed through her body.

Now the blonde was on her knees behind Dana; and Dana could feel the woman's hands on the hemispheres of her ass, spreading her slightly. Then something moist and ever so quick touched her vagina and she squeezed her eyes shut with pleasure.

The models were saying things she could not understand as their faces came down and their tongues ran over her neck and cheek. She felt herself breathing with difficulty; short, mouth-drying breaths, splendid little gasps.

And then she realized someone else was watching.

She *saw* a pair of eyes, as black as marbles, surrounded by dark shadows; the kind of circular darkening of the skin she sometimes saw around her own eyes when she had been working long hours, when she was tired, when she accidentally caught her reflection in a mirror; surrounding the eyes, not merely beneath them.

They were the eyes of a man. She had no way of knowing that; but she knew it. There was a man watching her and the three models as she lay bent over the table on her stomach, as they worked at her body, the blonde's face buried between her legs, the Eurasian and the black woman licking her smooth, pink and white, unblemished back.

She began to tremble, but this time it was not the secret and contained trembling the fantasy always brought. It was the trembling of the fear she experienced every time she walked down a dark and unfamiliar street. She was being *watched*!

Then she heard the man's voice: *Is that nice? Does it feel especially nice?*



The gentle silences and warm teak security of the fantasy were suddenly disrupted by the sound of a sustained, keening whine: metallic, shocking, like biting down on a piece of tin foil. The whine of a giant generator going wild. It climbed and climbed and Dana shuddered like a patient on a shock table.

"Get out of my head!"

The old man with the magazine jumped away from her, dropping a box of doughnuts that had been resting on his lap. Everyone on the bus turned to stare at her. Dana was shaking, moving her hands in front of her eyes, batting at invisible cobwebs, pulling her hair away from the sides of her face as if to provide openings through which the peeping tom could escape.

Then she opened her eyes, and she was still on the bus.

Everyone was staring. The old man was standing in the aisle, looking terrified. And she *knew* one of these people, one of these men had been inside her fantasy, watching everything.

And it was a long bus ride.

The driver's voice, distorted by the intercom system, echoed through the bus. "Everything okay back there?" They had been on the Interstate for several hours and he was clearly trying to make time despite the rain lashing the divided highway: he neither pulled over nor turned around. Dana could see only the back of his head . . . and his eyes in the enormous rearview mirror. They *seemed* to be black.

The terribly thin, elderly woman in the right-side aisle seat in front of Dana looked concerned. "Are you all right, dear?"

Dana's mouth was dry. She couldn't get her lips to form the words. She nodded quickly and heard herself croak, "Bad dream . . ."

The elderly woman raised her voice to the driver. "It's all right, Driver. She just had a bad dream."

The intercom squawked. "What?"

The florid man beside the old woman cupped his meaty hands and shouted, "It's okay, okay; lady back here had a bad dream. It's okay . . . just watch the road!"

Everyone laughed. Not long, and not loud. But the passengers settled down and turned around. The old man retrieved his doughnuts and looked at her querulously before resuming his seat. She smiled up at him quickly, shyly, trying to allay his fear. He seemed timid and nervous, and when he sat down it was not all the way back in the padded seat. His battered hat shaded his eyes, concealed their color.



The bus hurtled on through the night.

Out there in the darkness cut by the slanting lines of silvery rain, a smash of lightning fractured the sky and lit nothing discernible.

And here, inside and warm, Dana shivered, knowing that she was not alone. The feeling was not merely fear. Horror came with the knowledge that one of these men could wander unchecked through her most private thoughts. Once, while living in Boston, her apartment had been robbed. It had not been the theft of her stereo and camera and portable television set and even her best clothes — her leather car coat and other marketable goods carried away in the new parachute-fabric luggage — that had sent her to the bathroom to be sick in the sink. It had been the eerie certainty that someone had *touched* the apartment. Had walked the rooms. Had opened the drawers where her private life was neatly ranked. Had exposed her most intimate secrets. Had walked across her grave. The place had been defiled. Shadows and alien odors now lay across the planes and angles where she had stood naked. She had moved out three days later.

Now the last private refuge in the world had been soiled. The far, secret grotto no one could ever visit had been invaded. There were footprints other than her own in the sand of that hidden cavern at the center of her life. Now there was nothing safe, nothing sacred, nothing inviolate. When the newspaper stories of deranged street violence became too much for her, when the radio's endless dotage on slaughter and dismemberments made her gag with fear, when the six o'clock news bore loving eyewitness to the fragility of the human spirit . . . now there was no place to run. The door that never needed locks and bars and keys could not be closed.

The one mundane aspect of the Boston robbery that had induced screaming in her soul, that had left her no choice but to move, had been waiting for her in the bathroom when she went to vomit. The burglar had used the toilet. He had urinated and had left the seat up. Nothing brought home to her more forcefully than that inconsequential difference in sexes that it had been a man, a strange man, an unknown and faceless man, who had invaded her universe. Men leave the seat up on the toilet after pissing.

She felt that same inarticulate alarm now.

And he spoke to her again. *You show me your kink and I'll show you mine.*



Then he was there again, the black eyes surrounded by fatigued, discolored skin. There, again, and filling the grotto of her mind with his own fantasy.

She whimpered and huddled against the window, pressing her face to the bitterly cold pane. Rain pelted the glass and a shellburst sound she realized dimly was thunder out there in the night commanded her attention but could not dim the clarity of the peeping tom's vile fantasy. He had appropriated her fantasy image of herself, and was using it to his own purpose.

Dana buried the heels of her palms in her closed eyes, trying with the pressure to drive the vision away. But he was strong, he had been visiting women's minds for a very long time — she knew that, she knew it — and he had anchored himself for as long as the pleasure would take.

He was experienced at it. It was sharp and clear and there was sound — moist, wrenching, meaty sounds — and the sounds of bone cracking — and the sound of suction — and most disgusting of all there was the smell of him.

She heard herself mewling like a small animal, and she drew her knees up from the floor, into the seat.

Beside her, the old man quietly got up and moved to the back of the bus. Across from Dana a woman in her forties stole a sidewise glance, trying to discern what was troubling the writhing figure in the shadows against the window.

Then the invader reached orgasm after orgasm and there was the sinking feeling of a falling elevator, with the certain knowledge that the cable had parted; and there was the hard, thin feel of a sharp wire cutting the soft inside of her cheek, with the certain knowledge that needles would have to stitch it up; and there was the shrieking horror of a car crash, with the certain knowledge that someone she loved was being pulped to garbage behind the wheel; and there was the pressure of vomit burning its track up into her mouth, with the certain knowledge that the poison was still in her belly and the track of acid would come again and again; and there was the overwhelming feeling of his pleasure as he came and came and came . . .

When she regained her composure, the woman from across the aisle and the thin old lady who had called to the driver were bending over her. The younger woman was holding a paper cup of water to Dana's lips. "Here . . . sip at this . . . are you all right . . . should we tell the driver to take the next exit and maybe find you a doctor . . . are you all right . . . ?"

Dana pushed at the cup of water, spilling some down the front of her jacket. The tweed absorbed it at once. "No, I'm fine, I'm *fine*," she said huskily. She wanted to bathe. She wanted to stand under a shower for a long time, though she knew it was the worst thing to do after rape.

And the word was there, for the first time. She had been raped. No different than the lumbering shape with a knife in the alley. No different than the lurker on the landing who had unscrewed the light bulb, throwing the stairwell into darkness. No different than the disembodied hand on her breast in the crowded theater lobby. No different.

*Wasn't that nice?* His voice was emotionless. If she had been presented with a dozen police voiceprints of possible assailants she would not have been able to pick him out of the pack. However he was doing it, coming and going in her mind, he was shrouding himself absolutely.

*If you like that,* he said, *wait until I start the variations.* And he showed her a moment of what was to come.

Dana felt her eyes rolling up in her head, and then she fainted.

Half-world. Iron colored. Misty.

Semiconscious, she knew she had found another level; one from which he was excluded. Half-aware, she willed herself not to sharpen her senses, secure down there under the swirling cloud cover, like a primordial beast swimming in murky waters. Now she felt another emotion: fury.

The assault had been more effective than he could have known. Dana had moved through nights and days of her life, and felt the power for her existence outside herself, had been manipulated and had exercised free will. But she had never been moved as now.

This creature could not be allowed to live.

She felt herself regaining total consciousness. She fought it. She needed time down here beneath the surface, drifting languidly in the gray and swirling waters, learning what it took to kill. This is how we came out of the sea, she thought. Out of the sea and into the street. No more fear of alleys.

The concept of fangs grew in her mind.

Not fangs: the *concept* of fangs.

Slowly, kindly, painstakingly, arming herself, she came back to the world.

The driver, the old woman, and the woman with the water were waiting for her. Yes, the driver's eyes were black. But he wasn't the one who roamed at will through the grotto of her thoughts. Because the invader was there, too.

*You missed the fun*, he said. *I had to start without you.*

He had left the area foul from his pleasures.

Like a picnic ground overrun by barbarians, he had left the evidence of his passion. She felt the sickness rising in her again.

"I'll be all right now," she said to the concerned faces hanging over her. She said it in a strong, controlled voice, and she looked at them directly. "I said: I'll be just fine now. Really. You can start the bus." They were parked on the shoulder. Cars shushed and swept past in the rain.

She smiled at the driver. "I'm fine."

He looked at her. "You sure?"

"I'm okay now. Just motion sickness . . . and bad dreams."

*You tell him, kid*, the rapist said.

The driver and the two concerned women returned to their seats, the bus heaved an asthmatic sigh and pulled out onto the Interstate again.

Dana got up and walked to the front of the bus.

She began walking back slowly, looking into the face of each passenger. There were many men here. Some were awake, and they looked back at her. She was the weirdo in the rear. Others were asleep — or pretending to be asleep. She looked at every one of them. With the overhead lights out, they *all* had black eyes. Dark circles under brow ridges. No way of selecting him from the mass of male passengers.

*I see you but you don't see me*, he said.

She walked all the way to the rear, causing the old man with the box of doughnuts to scrunch down in the back seat. Then she resumed her place. *Well, which one am I?* he asked.

She spoke to him. Silently. There in the grotto.



*Well, whichever one you are, you haven't seen anything yet, dar-*

*lin'*. Like his, her voice was emotionless. Fangs.

Then she went to that part of her secret grotto where the dreams she feared to dream were kept. In there, in that walled-off section, was all the broken glass.

She began clawing at the mortar binding the bricks together, and it came away much more easily than she'd expected. Her fingers bloodied quickly, but she was able to prise out one of the kiln-dried rectangles. She clutched at the top of the next brick below the opening in the wall . . . and wrenched it loose. Then another. And another. The wall came away quickly, and as the rows of bricks dropped, the horrors inside were revealed.

The rapist seemed fascinated. *Oh, yeah. The good stuff. I knew you were too squeaky clean to be true.*

She pulled out the nearest awfulness and let it expand in the sweet but now polluted air of her secret grotto. Like a fine mist, it spread and there they were together, Dana and the rapist, in a special fantasy.

The dog was a German shepherd. She got down on her knees. The dog stood waiting. She looked over her shoulder but it did not move. Then she put two fingers inside herself and moistened them and, on hands and knees, went to the dog and touched the fingers to its muzzle. She turned her back again and the dog came to her.

The rapist watched. The black eyes were lit with a malevolent fire. And the skin around the eyes darkened. And now Dana could see the shadow of a nose below the eyes, as he watched her . . . while the dog mounted.

Before the fantasy could end, Dana let another loose from behind the brick enclosure. It was the gynecology examination.

She was naked on her back on the table, feet up in the stirrups. But she was taped down, bands of shipping filament tape strapped across her stomach and her thighs, holding her arms and shoulders and neck to the table. And in the examination fantasy she conceived the thick, inserting rod with the razored spines. And the rapist's hand and arm and the left side of his body could be seen, and he took the rod and he came to her there on the table. She screamed and begged, but he used it nonetheless.

And then the water fantasy.

And then the wax fantasy.

And then the fantasy of cutting small holes in one's love partner and putting that certain part of his body — which now could be seen by Dana — in the terrible little holes.

And then the meat fantasy without laughter.

And then . . .

While he worked, while he worked fascinated, while he worked fascinated to the point of obliviousness, she began creating walls. Not bricks this time, because unlike the initial sealing-off of the horrors that she might one day wish to experience again, this was to be an enclosure from which no escape was possible.

And she bound him there with her fantasy body. No *vagina dentata*, no castratory pleasure of his secret self-hatred. She bound him with a muscular lock that no amount of struggling could ease. She spasmed once, a vise-grip wrench that locked together with a crushing pressure that would not permit withdrawal.

And she raised the steel walls around him, leaving him in there in a darkness with that now-discarded fantasy female who could never be used again, not even by herself.

And the only light would come from the horrors that would escape from behind the brick enclosure, for time without end, and which would eventually present themselves so bent and diseased and horrible that not even he, alien Visigoth marauder, not even he could derive joy from them.

And she left her fantasy grotto.

When the bus pulled into Philadelphia, she was the first one off. She hurried away from the station, knowing that she had lost the only secret place anyone ever *really* has to hide in. She had lost the ability to dream those private dreams; and what that would mean to her she could not say. Worse, she now knew what horrors she had kept entombed, knew that she was one with the rest of the human race, each member of which had grotesqueries beyond belief merely waiting to claw their way out from behind insufficient brickwork.

She was not sure she could bear to be Dana, knowing what had always lived, breathing deeply, behind those walls.

But she also knew that this animal would never walk the streets again.

When the bus was emptied, one passenger would still be sitting there, hollow-eyed and with a recognizable expression of demented agony on his face. And no matter where they took him, from that bus and from that station, no matter where they took things that had once been human and were now vegetables . . . no matter where that final passenger came to rest, he would spend the number of his days locked away from the real world where he could do harm.

He, like Dana, would spend his days and nights alone.

The difference was only broken glass.

# ON THE SLAB

LIGHTNING WAS DRAWN to the spot. Season after season, August to November, but most heavily in September, the jagged killing bolts sought out George Gibree's orchard.

Gibree, a farmer with four acres of scabrous apple trees whose steadily diminishing production of fruit would drive him, one year later, to cut his throat with a rabbit-skinning knife and to bleed to death in the loft of his barn in Chepachet, near Providence, Rhode Island, *that* George Gibree found the dismal creature at the northeast corner of his property late in September. In the season of killing bolts.

The obscenely crippled trees — scarred black as if by fireblight — had withstood one attack after another; splintering a little more each year; withering a little more each year; dying a little more each year. The McIntoshes they produced, hideous and wrinkled as thalidomide babies. Night after night the lightning, drawn to the spot, cracked and thrashed, until one night, as though weary of the cosmic game, a monstrous forked bolt, sizzling with power, uncovered the creature's graveplace.

When he went out to inspect the orchard the next morning, holding back the tears till he was well out of sight of Emma and the house, George Gibree looked down into the crater and saw it stretched out on its back, its single green eye with the two pupils glowing terribly in the morning sunlight, its left forearm — bent up at the elbow — seeming to clutch with spread fingers at the morning air. It was as if the thing had been struck by the sky's fury as it was trying to dig itself out.

For just a moment as he stared down into the pit, George Gibree felt as if the ganglia mooring his brain were being ripped loose. His head began to tremble on his neck . . . and he wrenched his gaze from the impossible titan, stretched out, filling the thirty-foot-long pit.

In the orchard there could be heard the sounds of insects, a few birds, and the whimpering of George Gibree.



• • •

Children, trespassing to play in the orchard, saw it; and the word spread through town, and by stringer to a free-lance writer who did occasional human-interest pieces for the Providence *Journal.* She drove out to the Gibree farm and, finding it impossible to speak to George Gibree, who sat in a straight-back chair, staring out the window without speaking or even acknowledging her presence, managed to cajole Emma Gibree into letting her wander out to the orchard alone.

The item was small when published, but it was the beginning of October and the world was quiet. The item received interested attention.

By the time a team of graduate students in anthropology arrived with their professor, pieces of the enormous being had been torn away by beasts of the field and by curious visitors. They sent one of their group back to the University of Rhode Island, in Kingston, advising him to contact the University's legal representatives, readying them for the eventual purchase of this terrifying, miraculous discovery. Clearly, it was not a hoax; this was no P. T. Barnum "Cardiff Giant," but a creature never before seen on the Earth.

And when night fell, the professor was forced to badger the most amenable of the students into staying with the thing. Coleman lanterns, down jackets, and a ministove were brought in. But by morning all three of the students had fled.

Three days later, a mere six hours before the attorneys for the University could present their offer to Emma Gibree, a rock concert entrepreneur from Providence contracted for full rights to, and ownership of, the dead giant for three thousand dollars. Emma Gibree had been unable to get her husband to speak since the morning he had stood on the lip of the grave and stared down at the one-eyed being; she was in a panic; there were doctors and hospitals in her future.

Frank Kneller, who had brought every major rock group of the past decade to the city, rented exposition space in the Providence Civic Center at a ridiculously low rate because it was only the second week in October . . . and the world was quiet. Then he assigned his public relations firm the task of making the giant a national curiosity. It was not a difficult task.

It was displayed via minicam footage on the evening news of all three major networks. Frank Kneller's flair for the dramatically staged was not wasted.

The thirty-foot humanoid, pink-skinned and with staring eye malevolently directed at the cameraman's lens, was held in loving close-up on the marble slab Kneller had had hewn by a local monument contractor.

Pilbeam of Yale came, and Johanson of the Cleveland Museum of Natural History, and both the Leakeys, and Taylor of Riverside came with Hans Seuss from the University of California at La Jolla. They all said it was genuine. But they could not say where the thing had come from. It was, however, native to the planet: thirty feet in height, Cyclopean, as hard as rhinoceros horn . . . but human. And they all noticed one more thing.

The chest, just over the place where the heart lay, was hideously scarred. As though centurions had jammed their pikes again and again into the flesh when this abomination had been crucified. Terrible weals, puckered skin still angrily crimson against the gentle pink of the otherwise unmarred body.

Unmarred, that is, but for the places where the curious had used their nail files and penknives to gouge out souvenirs.

And then Frank Kneller made them go away, shaking their heads in wonder, mad to take the creature back to their laboratories for private study, but thwarted by Kneller's clear and unshakable ownership. And when the last of them had departed, and the view of the Cyclops on its slab could be found in magazines and newspapers and even on posters, *then* Frank Kneller set up his exposition at the Civic Center.

There, within sight of the Rhode Island State House, atop whose dome stands the twelve-foot-high, gold-leafed statue of the Independent Man.

The curious came by the thousands to line up and pay their three dollars a head, so they could file past the dead colossus, blazoned on life-sized thirty-foot-high posters festooning the outer walls of the Civic Center as *The 9th Wonder of the World!* (Ninth, reasoned Frank Kneller with a flash of wit and a sense of history uncommon to popularizers and entrepreneurs, because King Kong had been the Eighth.) It was a gracious *hommage* that did not go unnoticed by fans of the cinematically horrific; and the gesture garnered for Kneller an acceptance he might not have otherwise known from the cognoscenti.



And there was an almost symphonic correctness to the titan's having been unearthed in Providence, in Rhode Island, in that Yankee state so uncharacteristic of New England; that situs founded by Roger Williams for "those distressed for cause of conscience" and historically identified with independence of thought and freedom of religion; that locale where the odd and the bizarre melded with the mundane: Poe had lived there, and Lovecraft; and they had had strange visions, terrible dreams that had been recorded, that had influenced the course of literature; the moral ownership of the city by the modern coven known as the Mafia; these, and uncountable reports of bizarre happenings, sightings, gatherings, beliefs that made it seem the Providence *Journal* was an appendix to the writings of Charles Fort . . . provided a free-floating ambience of the peculiar.

The lines never seemed to grow shorter. The crowds came by the busloads, renting cassette players with background information spoken by a man who had played the lead in a television series dealing with the occult. Schoolchildren were herded past the staring green eye in gaggles; teenagers whose senses had been dulled by horror movies came in knots of five and ten; young lovers needing to share stopped and wondered; elderly citizens from whose lives had been leached all wonder smiled and pointed and clucked their tongues; skeptics and cynics and professional debunkers stood frozen in disbelief and came away bewildered.

Frank Kneller found himself involved in a way he had never experienced before, not even with the most artistically rewarding groups he had booked. He went to bed each night exhausted, but uplifted. And he awoke each day feeling his time was being well-spent. When he spoke of the feeling to his oldest friend, his accountant, with whom he had shared lodgings during college days, he was rewarded with the word *ennobled*. When he dwelled on the word, he came to agree.

Showing the monstrosity was *important*.

He wished with all his heart to know the reason. The single sound that echoed most often through the verdant glade of his thoughts was: *why?*

"I understand you've taken to sleeping in the rotunda where the giant is on display?" The host of the late-night television talk show was leaning forward. The ash on his cigarette was growing to the point where it would drop on his sharply creased slacks. He didn't notice.

Kneller nodded. "Yes, that's true."

"Why?"

"*Why* is a question I've been asking myself ever since I bought the great man and started letting people see him . . ."

"Well, let's be honest about it," the interviewer said. "You don't *let* people see the giant . . . you charge them for the privilege. You're showing an attraction, after all. It's not purely an humanitarian act."

Kneller pursed his lips and acceded. "That's right, that's very true. But I'll tell you, if I had the wherewithal, I'd do it free of charge. I don't, of course, so I charge what it costs me to rent space at the Civic Center. That much; no more."

The interviewer gave him a sly smile. "Come *on* . . ."

"No, really, honest to God, I mean it," Frank said quickly. "It's been eleven months, and I can't begin to tell you how many hundreds of thousands of people have come to see the great man; maybe a million or more; I don't know. And everybody who comes goes away feeling a little bit better, a little more important . . ."

"A religious experience?" The interviewer did not smile.

Frank shrugged. "No, what I'm saying is that people feel *ennobled* in the presence of the great man."

"You keep calling the giant 'the great man.' Strange phrase. Why?"

"Seems right, that's all."

"But you still haven't told me why you sleep there in the place where he's on display every day."

Frank Kneller looked straight into the eyes of the interviewer, who had to live in New York City every day and so might not understand what peace of mind was all about, and he said, "I like the feeling. I feel as if I'm worth the trouble it took to create me. And I don't want to be away from it too long. So I set up a bed in there. It may sound freaky to you, but . . ."

But if he had not been compelled to center his life around the immobile figure on the marble slab, then Frank Kneller would not have been there the night the destroyer came.

Moonlight flooded the rotunda through the enormous skylights of the central display areas.



Kneller lay on his back, hands behind his head, as usual finding sleep a long way off, yet at peace with himself, in the presence of the great man.

The titan lay on his marble slab, tilted against the far wall, thirty feet high, his face now cloaked in shadows. Kneller needed no light. He knew the single great eye was open, the twin pupils staring straight ahead. They had become companions, the man and the giant. And, as usual, Frank saw something that none of the thousands who had passed before the colossus had ever seen. In the darkness up there near the ceiling, the scars covering the chest of the giant glowed faintly, like amber plankton or the minuscule creatures that cling to limestone walls in the deepest caverns of the earth. When night fell, Frank was overcome with an unbearable sadness. Wherever and however this astounding being had lived . . . in whatever way he had passed through the days and nights that had been his life . . . he had suffered something more terrible than anyone merely human could conceive. What had done such awesome damage to his flesh, and how he had regenerated even as imperfectly as this, Kneller could not begin to fathom.

But he knew the pain had been interminable, and terrible.

He lay there on his back, thinking again, as he did every night, of the life the giant had known, and what it must have been for him on this Earth.

The questions were too potent, too complex, and beyond Frank Kneller's ability even to pose properly. The titan defied the laws of nature and reason.

And the shadow of the destroyer covered the skylight of the rotunda, and the sound of a great wind rose around the Civic Center, and Frank Kneller felt a terror that was impossible to contain. Something was coming from the sky, and he knew without looking up that it was coming for the great man on the slab.

The hurricane wind shrieked past the point of audibility, vibrating in the roots of his teeth. The darkness outside seemed to fall toward the skylight, and with the final sound of enormous wings beating against the night, the destroyer splintered the shatterproof glass.

Razor-edged stalactites struck the bed, the floor, the walls; one long spear imbedded itself through the pillow where Frank's head had lain a moment before, penetrating the mattress and missing him by inches where he cowered in the darkness.

Something enormous was moving beyond the foot of the bed.

Glass lay in a scintillant carpet across the rotunda. Moonlight still shone down and illuminated the display area.

Frank Kneller looked up and saw a nightmare.

The force that had collapsed the skylight was a bird. A bird so enormous he could not catalog it in the same genus with the robin he had found outside his bedroom window when he was a child . . . the robin that had flown against the pane when sunlight had turned it to a mirror . . . the robin that had struck and fallen and lain there till he came out of the house and picked it up. Its blood had been watery, and he could feel its heart beating against his palm. It had been defenseless and weak and dying in fear, he could feel that it was dying in fear. And Frank had rushed in to his mother, crying, and had begged her to help restore the creature to the sky. And his mother had gotten the old eyedropper that had been used to put cod-liver oil in Frank's milk when he was younger, and she had tried to get the robin to take some sugar-water.

But it had died.

Tiny, it had died in fear.

The thing in the rotunda was of that genus, but it was neither tiny nor fearful.

Like no other bird he had ever seen, like no other bird that had ever *been* seen, like no other bird that had ever existed. Sinbad had known such a bird, perhaps, but no other human eyes had ever beheld such a destroyer. It was gigantic. Frank Kneller could not estimate its size, because it was almost as tall as the great man, and when it made the hideous watery cawing sound and puffed out its bellows chest and jerked its wings into a billowing canopy, the pinfeathers scraped the walls of the rotunda on either side. The walls were seventy-five feet apart.

The vulture gave a hellish scream and sank its scimitar talons in the petrified flesh of the great man, its vicious beak in the chest, in the puckered area of scars that had glowed softly in the shadows.

It ripped away the flesh as hard as rhinoceros horn.

Its head came away with the beak locked around a chunk of horny flesh. Then, as Kneller watched, the flesh seemed to lose its rigidity, it softened, and blood ran off the carrion crow's killer beak. And the great man groaned.

The eye blinked.

The bird struck again, tossing gobbets of meat across the rotunda.

Frank felt his brain exploding. He could not bear to see this.

But the vulture worked at its task, ripping out the area of chest where the heart of the great man lay under the scar tissue. Frank Kneller crawled out of the shadows and stood helpless. The creature was immense. *He* was the robin: pitiful and tiny.

Then he saw the fire extinguisher in its brackets on the wall, and he grabbed the pillow from the bed and rushed to the compartment holding the extinguisher and he smashed the glass with the pillow protecting his hand. He wrenched the extinguisher off its moorings and rushed the black bird, yanking the handle on the extinguisher so hard the wire broke without effort. He aimed it up at the vulture just as it threw back its head to rid itself of its carrion load, and the virulent Halon 1301 mixture sprayed in a white stream over the bird's head. The mixture of fluorine, bromine, iodine, and chlorine washed the vulture, spurted into its eyes, filled its mouth. The vulture gave one last violent scream, tore its claws loose, and arced up into the darkness with a spastic beating of wings that caught Frank Kneller across the face and threw him thirty feet into a corner. He struck the wall; everything slid toward gray.

When he was able to get to his knees, he felt an excruciating pain in his side and knew at once several ribs had been broken. All he could think of was the great man.

He crawled across the floor of the rotunda to the base of the slab, and looked up. There, in the shadows . . .

The great man, in terrible pain, was staring down at him.

A moan escaped the huge lips.

*What can I do?* Kneller thought, desperately.

And the words were in his head. *Nothing. It will come again.*

Kneller looked up. Where the scar tissue had glowed faintly, the chest was ripped open, and the great man's heart lay there in pulsing blood, part of it torn away.

*Now I know who you are,* Kneller said. *Now I know your name.*

The great man smiled a strange, shy smile. The one great green eye made the expression somehow winsome. *Yes,* he said, *yes, you know who I am.*

*Your tears mingled with the earth to create us.*

*Yes.*

*You gave us fire.*

*Yes; and wisdom.*

*And you've suffered for it ever since.*

*Yes.*

"I have to know," Frank Kneller said, "I have to know if *you* were what *we* were before we became what we are now."

The sound of the great wind was rising again. The destroyer was in the night, on its way back. The chemicals of man could not drive it away from the task it had to perform, could not drive it away for long.

*It comes again,* the great man said in Kneller's mind. *And I will not come again.*

"Tell me! Were you what we were . . . ?"

The shadow fell across the rotunda and darkness came down upon them as the great man said, in that final moment, *No, I am what you* would *have become . . .*

And the carrion crow sent by the gods struck him as he said one more thing . . .

When Frank Kneller regained consciousness, hours later, there on the floor where the scissoring pain of his broken ribs had dropped him, he heard those last words reverberating in his mind. And heard them endlessly all the days of his life.

No, I am what you *would* have become . . . *if you had been worthy.*

And the silence was deeper that night across the face of the world, from pole to pole, deeper than it had ever been before in the life of the creatures that called themselves human.

But not as deep as it would soon become.

# PRINCE MYSHKIN, AND HOLD THE RELISH

IT'S NOT *ONLY* that Pink's has the best hot dogs in what we have come to accept as the civilized world (and that *includes* Nathan's, the original stand out at Coney Island, not those fast-shuffle mickey-mouse surrogates they've opened up from time to time all the way from Broadway to the San Fernando Valley, which, in a less enlightened era, I thought was the dispenser of the *ne plus ultra* of frankfurters), it is also that Michael, who works at Pink's, is one of the best conversationalists on the subject of Dostoevsky in what we have come to accept as the civilized world (and that includes the academic-turned-screenwriter from New York who did a sorta kinda Dostoevskian film about an academic-turned-gambler, back in 1974).

Which double incentive explains why I was down there at 711 N. La Brea Avenue, almost at the corner of Melrose, at Pink's, founded in 1939 by Paul Pink with a pushcart at that very same location where a heavensent hot dog cost a decent 10¢, what now sets one back a hefty dollar-and-a-quarter punch under the heart, even if the quality of dog has not diminished one iota, or even a random scintilla . . . quality and Michael Bernstein who knows what there is to know about the Fabulous Fyodor were the double incentives to drag me out at dead midnight.

Because I had been lying there in my bed, all the way out on the top of the Santa Monica Mountains in the middle of the Mulholland Scenic Corridor, overlooking the twinkling lights of the bedroom communities of the San Fernando Valley which, I have been led to believe, each one represents a broken heart that couldn't make it to Broadway, unable to sleep, tossing and turning, turning and tossing, widdershins and tormented, backing and filling in my lightly starched bedsheets, and of a sudden visions, not of sugar plums, but of dancing hot dogs, fandango'ing frankfurters, waltzing wienies, gavotted through my restless head. Eleven-thirty, for god's sake, and all I could think about was sinking my fangs into a Pink's hot dog and discussing a little Karamazov hostility with this Israeli savant who ladles up chili dogs on the graveyard shift behind the steam table. Go figure it. Facts are definitely facts.

So at midnight I'm pulling into the parking spaces beside Pink's, right next door to that shoe store that sells funny Italian disco shoes the heels of which fall off if you spin too quickly on the misguided belief that you are the reincarnation of Valentino or merely just the latest Travoltanoid to turn female heads, and I'm slouching up to the counter, and Michael sees me coming even before I'm out of the car and he's got a hot one working, ready to hand me as I lean up against the clean but battered stainless steel counter.

Just a dog, light on the mustard, hold the relish. No chili, yuchhh the chili; I'm a purist.

And as the front four sink into that strictly kosher nifty, Michael opens with the following: "It wasn't his fault he was so mean to women. Dostoevsky was a man swayed by passions. Two of these, his lamentable love for Paulina Suslova and his obsession for gambling, overlapped."

I'm halfway finished with the first frank as Michael is building the second, and I respond, "You see how you are? You, like everyone else, are ready to condemn a genius simply because he was a liar, a cheat, a pathological gambler who borrowed from his friends and never paid them back, a man who deserted his wife and children, an epileptic existentialist who merely wrote at least half a dozen of the greatest works of fiction the world has ever seen. If he brutalized women it was simply another manifestation of his tormented soul and give me another dog, light on the mustard, hold the relish."

Having now defined the parameters of our evening's discussion, we could settle down to arguing the tiniest, most obscure points; as long as the heartburn didn't start and the hungry hookers and junkies coming in for sustenance didn't distract Michael too much.

"Ha!" Michael shouted, aiming his tongs at my head. "Ha! and Ha again! You fall into the trap of accepted cliché. You mythologize the Russian soul, several thousand years' retroactive *angst*. When the simple truth that *every man in Dostoevsky's novels treats women monstrously* invalidates your position. The canon itself says you are wrong!

"Name one exception of substance. Not a minor character, a major one; a moving force, an image, an icon . . . name one!"

I licked my fingers, nodded for my third sally of the night and said, with the offensive smugness of one who has lured his worthy opponent hipdeep into quicksand, "Prince Myshkin."

Michael was shaken. I could tell, shaken: he slathered too much mustard onto the dog. Shaken, he wiped off the excess with a paper napkin and, shaken, he handed it across to me. "Well . . . yes . . . of course, *Myshkin* . . ." he said slowly, devastated and groping for intellectual balance. "Yes, of course, *he* treated women decently . . . but he was an *idiot*!"

And the six-foot-two pimp with the five working girls at the far end of the counter started screaming about sleazy kike honkie muthuhfuckuh countermen who let their Zionist hatred of Third World peoples interfere with the speedy performance of their duties. "But . . . the image of the brutalizer of women was the one with which Dostoevsky identified . . ." He started toward the other end of the counter where black fists were pounding on stainless steel.

"Myshkin was his model," I called after him. "Some men are *good* for women . . ."

He held up a chili-stained finger for me to hold that place in the discussion, and rushed away to quell the lynch tenor in the mob.

As I stood there, I looked across La Brea Avenue. The street was well-lit and I saw this guy standing at the curb right in front of the Federated Stereo outlet, all dressed up around midnight in a vanilla-flavored ice-cream suit as pale and wan as the cheek of a paperback heroine, his face ratty and furtive under a spectacular Borsalino hat that cast a shadow across his left eye. Natty and spiffy, but something twitchoid and on the move about him. And as I stood there, waiting for Michael to come back so I could tell him how good some men are for some women, this ashen specter comes off the curb, looking smartly left and right up and down La Brea, watching for cars but also watching for typhoons, sou'westers, siroccos, monsoons, khamsins, Santa Anas and the fall of heavy objects. And as I stood there, he came straight across the avenue and onto the sidewalk there at the front of Pink's, and he slouched to a halt right beside me, and leaned up close with one elbow on the counter just touching my sleeve, and he thumbed back the Borsalino so I could see both of his strange dark little eyes, set high in his feral, attractive, strange dark little face, and this is what he said to me:

"Okay. This is it. Now listen up.

"The first girl I ever fell in love with was this raven-tressed little beauty who lived down the block from me when I was in high school in Conshohocken, Pennsylvania. She was sixteen, I was seventeen, and her father owned an apple orchard. Big deal, I said; big fucking deal. An apple orchard. We're not talking here the Sudetenland. Nonetheless, he thought he was landed gentry, my old man worked with his hands over in Kutztown. So we ran away. Got all the way to Eunice, New Mexico, walking, hitching, slipping and sliding, sleeping out in the rain, she comes down with pneumonia and dies at a lying-in hospital over at Carlsbad.

"I'm shook. I'm ruined. What I'm sayin' here, I was distraught.

"Next thing I know I'm signed up with the Merch Marine, shipped out to Kowloon. Twenty minutes in town on shore leave I fall across this little transistor girl named Orange Blossom. I don't ask questions. Maybe her name was Sun Yung Sing, how'm I to know? She likes me, I like her, we go off hand in hand to make a little rice music, if you catch my drift. Sweet, this was sweet, two young kids, okay so it's miscegenation, a little intermingling of the Occidental with the Oriental, so what? It was purely sweet, and we're talking here about cleaning up some bad leftover feelings. I treat her good, she has respect for an innocent young man, everything's going only terrific until we're walking up Three Jade Lacquer Box Road looking for this swell little dimsum joint that's been recommended to us, when some nut case off a harbor junk that caught fire and killed his wife and three kids comes running down the street brandishing a kukri, this large knife used for hunting and combat purposes by the Nepalese Gurkhas, and he sticks it right through this sweet little kid possibly named Orange Blossom, and the next thing I know she's lying in a pool of it, right at my feet as this maniac goes screaming up Three Jade Lacquer Box Road.

"Well, let me tell you. I'm devastated. Freaked out of my mind. I'm down on my knees wailin' and cryin', what else was there to do?

"So I get myself shipped back home to recuperate, try to blow it all away, try to forget my sorrow, they put me up in a VA hospital even though I'm not a vet, they figure, you know, the Merch Marine's as good as the service. Well, I'm not in the hospital three days when I meet this terrific candy striper name of Henrietta. Blonde hair, blue eyes, petite little figure, a warm and winning personality.

"She takes a real fancy to me, sees I'm in need of extensive chicken soup therapy, slips in late at night when the ward's quiet and gets under the covers with me. We fall desperately in love, I'm on the mend, we go out to lightweight pizza dinners and G-rated movies. Move in with me, she says, when my time is up at the hospital. Move in with me and we'll whistle a jaunty tune forevermore. Okay, says I, okay you got it. So I move in all my worldly possessions, I'm not there three weeks when she slips boarding a number 10 uptown bus, the doors close on her left foot and she's dragged half a city block before the driver realizes the thumping sound is her head hitting the street.

"So I'm left with the lease on a four-room apartment in San Francisco, you might think that's a neat thing to have, what with the housing shortage, but I'm telling you friend, without love even the Taj Mahal is a cold water flat. So I can't take it, I'm whipped, really downtrodden, sorrowful and in misery.

"I know I shouldn't, but I get involved with this older woman on the rebound. She's sixty-one, I'm twenty, and all she can do is do for me. All right, I admit it, this wasn't such straight thinking, but I'm crippled, you know what I mean? I'm a fledgling bird with a crippled wing. I need some taking care of, some bringing out of myself. She's good medicine, maybe a little on the wrinkled side but who the hell says a sixty-one-year-old woman ain't entitled to a little affection, too?

"Everything's going great, strictly great; I move in with her on Nob Hill, we go for long walks, take in Bizet operas, Hungarian goulash in Ghirardelli Square, open and frank discussions about clitoral stimulation and the Panama Canal. All good, all fine, until one night we go a little too deeply into the Kama Sutra and she has this overwhelming uplifted celestial experience which culminates in massive cardiac infarction, so I'm adrift again, all alone on the tides of life, trying to find a soul mate with whom I can traverse the desert of loneliness.

"Then in rapid succession I meet Rosalinda, who gets polio and refuses to see me because she's going to be an invalid the rest of her life; Norma, whose father kills her because she's black and I'm white and he's disappointed she'd rather be just a housewife for some white guy than the world's first black female heart transplant specialist;

Charmaine, who was very high on me till she got hit by a cinderblock dropped from a scaffold on a construction job where she was architect in training, working during her summer college session toward a degree in building stuff; Olive, who was a stewardess who got along fine with me even though our political orientation was very different, until her dinner flight to Tucson came in a little too low and they sent me what was left of her in a very nice imitation Sung dynasty vase from the Federal Aeronautics Administration; and then Fernanda and Erwina and Corinne, all of whom wound up in destructive relationships with married men; and finally I meet Theresa, we'll call her Terry, she preferred Terry, I meet her at the track, and we're both on the same horse, a nice little two-year-old name of Leo Rising, and we get to the window at the same time and I ask her what's her sign, because I overhear what horse she's betting, and she says Virgo, and I say I'm a Virgo, and I ask her what's her rising sign and she says, of course Leo, and I say so's mine, and the next thing I know we're dating heavily, and she's gifted me with a sterling silver ID bracelet with my name on the front and WITH LOVE FROM TERRY on the reverse, and I've gifted her with a swell couple strands genuine natural simulated pearls, and we name the date, and we post the bands whatever that means, and I meet her family and she can't meet mine because I haven't seen mine in about twenty years, and everything is going just swell when she's out in Beverly Hills going to select her silver pattern, something simple but eloquent in Gorham, and they left a manhole cover off a sewer thing, and she slips and falls in and breaks her back in eleven places, her neck, and both arms.

"Sweet kid never comes out of the coma, they keep her on the machine nine months, one night her father slips in there on all fours and chews off the plug on the electrical connection, she goes to a much-needed peace.

"So that's it. That's the long and the short of it. Here I am, deeply distressed, not at all settled in my mind, at sixes and sevens, dulled and quite a bit diminished, gloomy, apathetic, awash in tribulation and misery, confused and once more barefoot on the road of life.

"Now what do you think of that?"



And he looks at me.

I look back at him.

"Hmmmpf," he snorts. "Try and find a little human compassion."

And he walks off, crosses La Brea at the corner, turns left onto Melrose, and disappears.

I'm still standing there, staring at where he'd been, when Michael comes over, having served the pimp and his staff. It had been three minutes; three minutes tops.

"What was that all about?" he asks.

I think I focused on him.

"On the other hand," I say, "there are *some* guys who are strictly *no god damned good for a woman.*"

Michael nods with satisfaction and hands me a frankfurter. Light on the mustard, pleasantly devoid of relish.

# THE REGION BETWEEN

DESIGN AND GRAPHICS BY JACK GAUGHAN

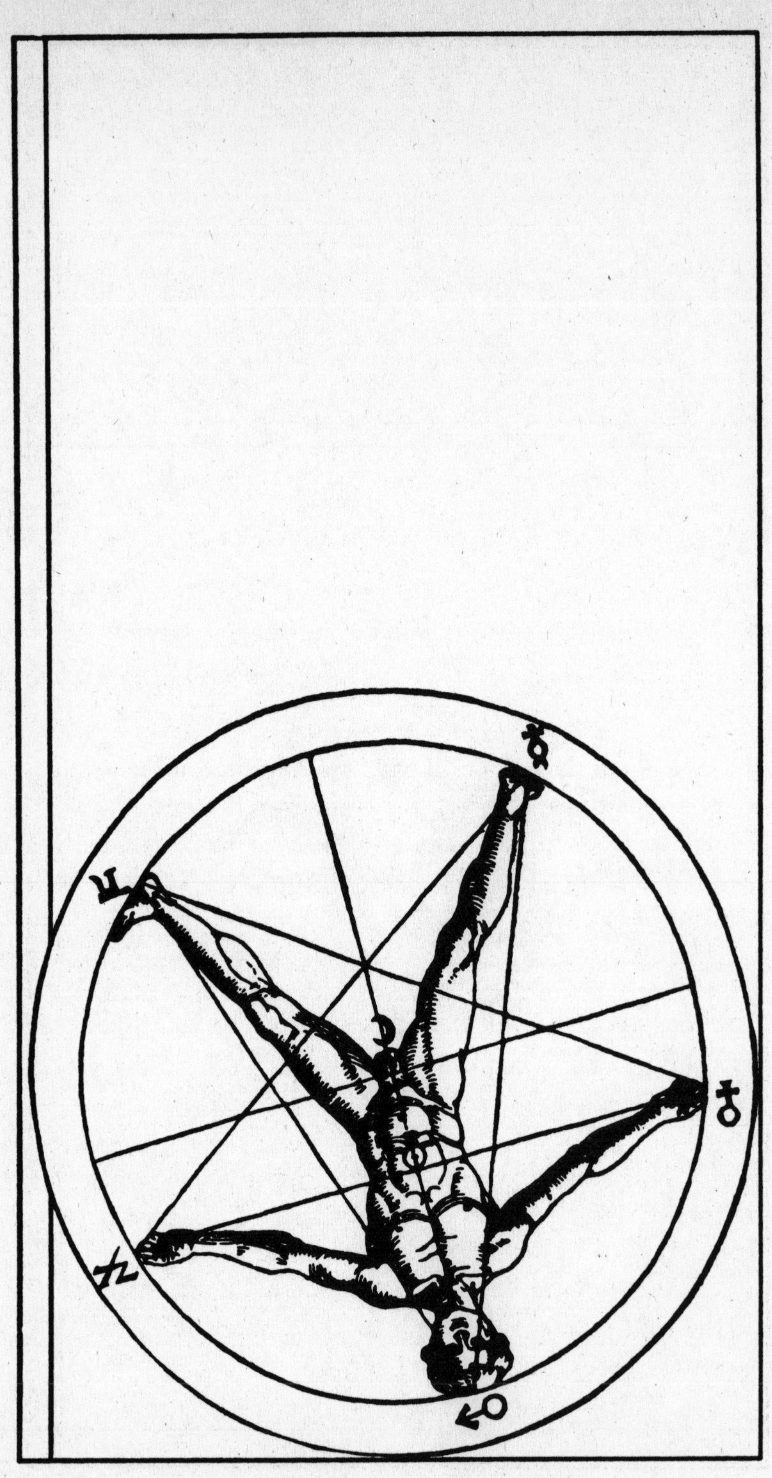

"Left hand," the thin man said tonelessly. "Wrist up."

William Bailey peeled back his cuff; the thin man put something cold against it, nodded toward the nearest door.

"Through there, first slab on the right," he said, and turned away.

"Just a minute," Bailey started. "I wanted—"

"Let's get going, buddy," the thin man said. "That stuff is fast."

Bailey felt something stab up under his heart. "You mean—you've already . . . that's all there is to it?"

"That's what you came for, right? Slab one, friend. Let's go."

"But—I haven't been here two minutes—"

"Whatta you expect—organ music? Look, pal," the thin man shot a glance at the wall clock, "I'm on my break, know what I mean?"

"I thought I'd at least have time for . . . for . . ."

"Have a heart, chum. You make it under your own power, I don't have to haul you, see?" The thin man was pushing open the door, urging Bailey through into an odor of chemicals and unlive flesh. In a narrow, curtained alcove, he indicated a padded cot.

"On your back, arms and legs straight out."

Bailey assumed the position, tensed as the thin man began fitting straps over his ankles.

"Relax. It's just if we get a little behind and I don't get back to a client for maybe a couple hours and they stiffen up . . . well, them issue boxes is just the one size, you know what I mean?"

A wave of softness, warmness swept over Bailey as he lay back.

"Hey, you didn't eat nothing the last twelve hours?" The thin man's face was a hazy pink blur.

"I awrrr mmmm," Bailey heard himself say.

"OK, sleep tight, paisan. . . ." The thin man's voice boomed and faded. Bailey's last thought as the endless blackness closed in was of the words cut in the granite over the portal to the Euthanasia Center:

". . . send me your tired, your poor, your hopeless, yearning to be free. To them I raise the lamp beside the brazen door. . . ."

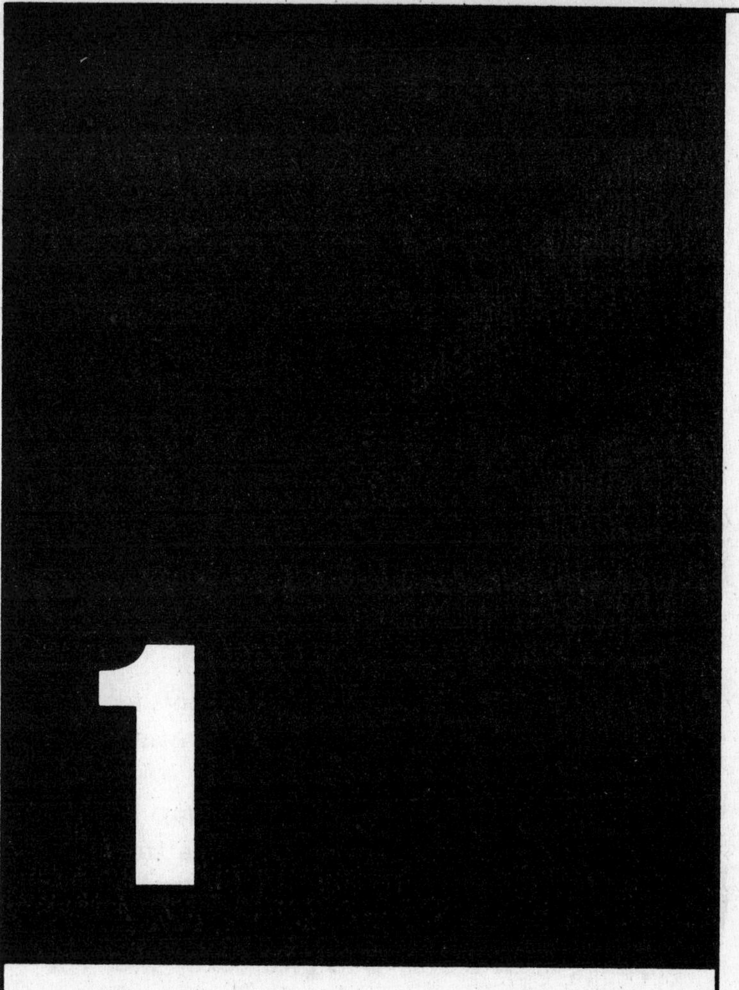

Death came as merely a hyphen. Life, and the balance of the statement, followed instantly. For it was only when Bailey died that he began to live.

Yet he could never have called it "living"; no one who had ever passed that way could have called it "living." It was something else. Something quite apart from "death" and something totally unlike "life."

Stars passed through him as he whirled outward.

Blazing and burning, carrying with them their planetary systems, stars and more stars spun through him as though traveling down invisible wires into the dark behind and around him.

Nothing touched him.

They were as dust motes, rushing silently past in incalculable patterns, as Bailey's body grew larger, filled space in defiance of the Law that said two bodies could not coexist in the same space at the same instant. Greater than Earth, greater than its solar system, greater than the galaxy that contained it, Bailey's body swelled and grew and filled the universe from end to end and ballooned back on itself in a slightly flattened circle.

His mind was everywhere.

A string cheese, pulled apart in filaments too thin to be measurable, Bailey's mind was there and there and there. And there.

It was also in the lens of the Succubus.

Murmuring tracery of golden light, a trembling moment of crystal sound. A note, rising and trailing away infinitely high, and followed by another, superimposing in birth even as its predecessor died. The voice of a dream, captured on spiderwebs. There, locked in the heart of an amber perfection, Bailey was snared, caught, trapped, made permanent by a force that allowed his Baileyness to roam unimpeded anywhere and everywhere at the instant of death.

Trapped in the lens of the Succubus.

[Waiting: empty. A mindsnake on a desert world, frying under seven suns, poised in the instant of death; its adversary, a fuzzball of cilia-thin fibers, sparking electrically, moving toward the mindsnake that a moment before had been set to strike and kill and eat. The mindsnake, immobile, empty of thought and empty of patterns of light that confounded its victims in the instants before the killing strike. The fuzzball sparked toward the mindsnake, its fibers casting about across the vaporous desert, picking up the mole sounds of things moving beneath the sand, tasting the air and feeling the heat as it pulsed in and away. It was improbable that a mindsnake would spend all that light-time, luring and intriguing, only at the penultimate moment to back off—no, not back off: shut down. Stop. Halt entirely. But if this was not a trap, if this was not some new tactic only recently learned by the ancient mindsnake, then it had to be an opportunity for the fuzzball. It moved closer. The mindsnake lay empty: waiting.]

Trapped in the lens of the Succubus.

[Waiting: empty. A monstrous head, pale blue and veined, supported atop a swan-neck by an intricate latticework yoke-and-halter. The Senator from Nougul, making his final appeal for the life of his world before the Star Court. Suddenly plunged into silence. No sound, no movement, the tall, emaciated body propped on its seven league crutches, only the trembling of balance—having nothing to do with life—reminding the assembled millions that an instant before this husk had contained a pleading eloquence. The fate of a world quivered in a balance no less precarious than that of the Senator. What had happened? The amalgam of wild surmise that grew in the Star Court was scarcely less compelling than had been the original circumstances bringing Nougul to this place, in the care of the words of this Senator. Who now stood, crutched, silent, and empty: waiting.]

Trapped in the lens of the Succubus.

[Waiting: empty. The Warlock of Whirrl, a power of darkness and evil. A force for chaos and destruction. Poised above his runic symbols, his bits of offal, his animal bones, his stringy things without names, quicksudden gone to silence. Eyes devoid of the pulverized starlight that was his sight. Mouth abruptly slack, in a face that had never known slackness. The ewe lamb lay still tied to the obsidian block, the graven knife with its unpleasant figures rampant, still held in the numb hand of the Warlock. And the ceremony was halted. The forces of darkness had come in gathering, had come to their calls, and now they roiled like milk vapor in the air, unable to go, unable to do, loath to abide. While the Warlock of Whirrl, gone from his mind stood frozen and empty: waiting.]

Trapped in the lens of the Succubus.

[Waiting: empty. A man on Promontory, fifth planet out from the star Proxima Centauri, halted in mid-step. On his way to a bank of controls and a certain button, hidden beneath three security plates. This man, this inestimably valuable kingpin in the machinery of a war, struck dumb, struck blind, in a kind of death—not even waiting for another moment of time. Pulled out of himself by the gravity of non-being, an empty husk, a shell, a dormant thing. Poised on the edges of their continents, two massed armies waited for that button to be pushed. And would never be pushed, while this man, this empty and silent man, stood rooted in the sealed underworld bunker where precaution had placed him. Now inaccessible, now inviolate, now untouchable, this man and this war stalemated frozen. While the world around him struggled to move itself a fraction of a thought toward the future, and found itself incapable, hamstrung, empty: waiting.]

Trapped in the lens of the Succubus.

And . . .

[Waiting: empty. A subaltern, name of Pinkh, lying on his bunk, contemplating his fiftieth assault mission. Suddenly gone. Drained, lifeless, neither dead nor alive. Staring upward at the bulkhead ceiling of his quarters. While beyond his ship raged the Montag–Thil War. Sector 888 of the Galactic Index. Somewhere between the dark star Montag and the Nebula Cluster in Thil Galaxy. Pinkh, limbo-lost and unfeeling, needing the infusion of a soul, the filling up of a life-force. Pinkh, needed in this war more than any other man, though the Thils did not know it . . . until the moment his essence was stolen. Now, Pinkh, lying there one shy of a fifty-score of assault missions. But unable to aid his world. Unable, undead, unalive, empty: waiting.]

While Bailey . . .

Floated in a region between. Hummed in a nothingness as great as everywhere. Without substance. Without corporeality. Pure thought, pure energy, pure Bailey. Trapped in the lens of the Succubus.

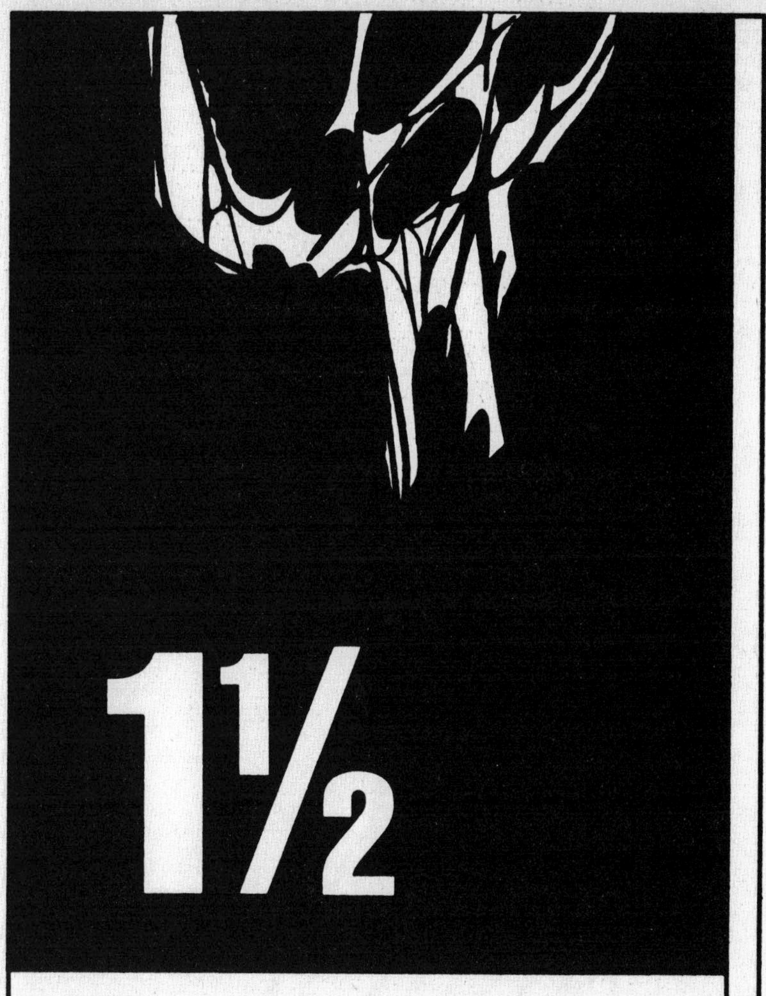


More precious than gold, more sought-after than uranium, more scarce than yinyang blossom, more needed than salkvac, rarer than diamonds, more valuable than force-beads, more negotiable than the vampyr extract, dearer than 2038 vintage Chateau Luxor, more lusted after than the twin-vagina'd trollops of Kanga . . .

Souls.

Thefts had begun in earnest five hundred years before. Random thefts. Stolen from the most improbable receptacles. From beasts and men and creatures who had never been thought to possess "souls." Who was stealing them was never known. Far out somewhere, in reaches of space (or not-space) (or the interstices between space and not-space) that had no names, had no dimensions, whose light had never even reached the outmost thin edge of known space, there lived or existed or *were* creatures or things or entities or forces—*someone*—who needed the life-force of the creepers and walkers and lungers and swimmers and fliers who inhabited the known universes. Souls vanished, and the empty husks remained.

Thieves they were called, for no other name applied so well, bore in its single syllable such sadness and sense of resignation. They were called Thieves, and they were never seen, were not understood, had never given a clue to their nature or their purpose or even their method of theft. And so nothing could be done about their depredations. They were as Death: handiwork observed, but a fact of life without recourse to higher authority. Death and the Thieves were final in what they did.

So the known universes—the Star Court and the Galactic Index and the Universal Meridian and the Perseus Confederacy and the Crab Complex—shouldered the reality of what the Thieves did with resignation, and stoicism. No other course was open to them. They could do no other.

But it changed life in the known universes.

It brought about the existence of soul-recruiters, who pandered to the needs of the million billion trillion worlds. Shanghaiers. Graverobbers of creatures not yet dead. In their way, thieves, even as the Thieves. Beings whose dark powers and abilities enabled them to fill the tables-of-organization of any world with fresh souls from worlds that did not even suspect *they* existed, much less the Court, the Index, the Meridian, the Confederacy or the Complex. If a key figure on a fringe world suddenly went limp and soulless, one of the soul-recruiters was contacted and the black traffic was engaged in. Last resort, final contact, most reprehensible but expeditious necessity, they stole and supplied.

One such was the Succubus.

He was gold. And he was dry. These were the only two qualities possessed by the Succubus that could be explicated in human terms. He had once been a member of the dominant race that skimmed across the sand-seas of a tiny planet, fifth from the star-sun labeled Kappel-112 in Canes Venatici. He had long since ceased to be anything so simply identified.

The path he had taken, light-years long and several hundred Terran-years long, had brought him from the sand-seas and a minimum of "face"—the only term that could even approximate the one measure of wealth his race valued—to a cove of goldness and dryness near the hub of the Crab Complex. His personal worthiness could now be measured only in terms of hundreds of billions of dollars, unquenchable light sufficient to sustain his offspring unto the nine thousandth generation, a name that could only be spoken aloud or in movement by the upper three social sects of the Confederacies races, more "face" than any member of his race had ever possessed

. . . more, even, than that held in myth by Yaele.

Gold, dry, and inestimably worthy: the Succubus.

Though his trade was one publicly deplored, there were only seven entities in the known universes who were aware that the Succubus was a soul-recruiter. He kept his two lives forcibly separated.

"Face" and graverobbing were not compatible.

He ran a tidy business. Small, with enormous returns. Special souls, selected carefully, no seconds, no hand-me-downs. Quality stock.

And through the seven highly placed entities who knew him—Nin, FawDawn, Enec-L, Milly(Bas)Kodal, a Plain without a name, Cam Royal, and Pl—he was channeled only the loftiest commissions.

He had supplied souls of all sorts in the five hundred years he had been recruiting. Into the empty husk of a master actor on Bolial V. Into the waiting body of a creature that resembled a plant aphid, the figurehead of a coalition labor movement, on Wheechitt Eleven and Wheechitt Thirteen. Into the unmoving form of the soul-emptied daughter of the hereditary ruler of Golaena Prime. Into the untenanted shape of an arcane maguscientist on Donadello III's seventh moon, enabling the five hundred-zodjam religious cycle to progress. Into the lusterless spark of light that sealed the tragic laocoönian group-mind of Orechnaen's Dispassionate Bell-Silver Dichotomy.

Not even the seven who functioned as go-betweens for the Succubus's commissions knew where and how he obtained such fine, raw, unsolidified souls. His competitors dealt almost exclusively in the atrophied, crustaceous souls of beings whose thoughts and beliefs and ideologies were so ingrained that the souls came to their new receptacles already stained and imprinted. But the Succubus . . .

Cleverly contrived, youthful souls. Hearty souls. Plastic and ready-to-assimilate souls. Lustrous, inventive souls. The finest souls in the known universe.

The Succubus, as determined to excel in his chosen profession as he was to amass "face," had spent the better part of sixty years roaming the outermost fringes of the known universe. He had carefully observed many races, noting for his purpose only those that seemed malleable, pliant, far removed from rigidity.

He had selected, for his purpose:

The Steechii
Amassanii
Cokoloids
Flashers
Griestaniks
Bunanits
Condolis
Tratravisii
and Humans.

On each planet where these races dominated, he put into effect subtle recruiting systems, wholly congruent with the societies in which they appeared:

The Steechii were given eterna dreamdust.

The Amassanii were given doppelgänger shifting.

The Cokoloids were given the Cult of Rebirth.

The Flashers were given proof of the Hereafter.

The Griestaniks were given ritual mesmeric trances.

The Bunanits were given (imperfect) teleportation.

The Condolis were given an entertainment called Trial by Nightmare Combat.

The Tratravisii were given an underworld motivated by high incentives for kidnapping and mind-blotting. They were also given a wondrous narcotic called Nodabit.

The Humans were given Euthanasia Centers.

And from these diverse channels the Succubus received a steady supply of prime souls. He received Flashers and skimmers and Condolis and ether-breathers and Amassanii and perambulators and Bunanits and gill creatures and . . .

William Bailey.

Trapped in the lens of the Succubus.

# 1¾

Bailey, cosmic nothingness, electrical potential spread out to the ends of the universe and beyond, nubbin'd his thoughts. Dead. Of that, no doubt. Dead and gone. Back on Earth, lying cold and faintly blue on a slab in the Euthanasia Center. Toes turned up. Eyeballs rolled up in their sockets. Rigid and gone.

And yet alive. More completely alive than he had

ever been, than *any* human being had ever conceived of being. Alive with all of the universe, one with the clamoring stars, brother to the infinite empty spaces, heroic in proportions that even myth could not define.

He knew everything. Everything there had ever been to know, everything that was, everything that would be. Past, present, future . . . all were merged and met in him. He was on a feeder line to the Succubus, waiting to be collected, waiting to be tagged and filed even as his alabaster body back on Earth would be tagged and filed. Waiting to be cross-indexed and shunted off to a waiting empty husk on some far world. All this he knew.

But one thing separated him from the millions of souls that had gone before him.

He didn't want to go.

Infinitely wise, knowing all, Bailey knew every other soul that had gone before had been resigned with soft acceptance to what was to come. It was a new life. A new voyage in another body. And all the others had been fired by curiosity, inveigled by strangeness, wonder-struck with being as big as the known universe and going *somewhere else.*

But not Bailey.

He was rebellious.

He was fired by hatred of the Succubus, inveigled by thoughts of destroying him and his feeder-lines, wonder-struck with being the only one—the *only* one!—who had ever thought of revenge. He was somehow, strangely, not tuned in with being rebodied, as all the others had been. *Why am I different?* he wondered. And of all the things he knew . . . he did not know the answer to that.

Inverting negatively, atoms expanded to the size of whole galaxies, stretched out membraned, osmotically breathing whole star systems, inhaling blue-white stars and exhaling quasars, Bailey the known universe asked himself yet another question, even more important:

*Do I* WANT *to do something about it?*

Passing through a zone of infinite cold, the word came back to him from his own mind in chill icicles of thought:

*Yes.*

"I see here, during the month of September, that you worked overtime at least . . . what is it . . . uh . . . eleven hours."

"Is there a law against that?"

"Oh, no . . . no, of course not. It just seems to us here at the block that you're perhaps, uh, over*do*ing it a bit."

"Working."

"Yes. Working."

"Has my block steward complained? Has my EEG been erratic? Am I being *accused* of something?"

"No, of *course* not! My lord, man, there's no need to be so defensive! We're only trying to find out if something is, well, disturbing you."

If I'd been able to, I'd have killed the sonofabitch; right then and right there. In his conversation grouping. It would have made fine conversation for his office staff. Come in and find him brained to death with his own coffee urn.

"Nothing's disturbing me."

"Then you'll pardon me if I feel it apropos to ask why you aren't taking your proper relaxation periods, Mr. Bailey."

"I feel like keeping busy."

"Ah, but all work and no play—"

And borne on comets plunging frenziedly through his cosmic body, altering course suddenly and traveling at right angles in defiance of every natural law he had known when "alive," the inevitable question responding to a *yes* asked itself:

*Why should I?*

Life for Bailey on Earth had been pointless. He had been a man who did not fit. He had been a man driven to the suicide chamber literally by disorientation and frustration.

I was called to the office of the Social Director of my residence block. Frankly, I was frightened. I knew I hadn't done anything to be afraid about, but ever since I'd been a child, ever since I'd been called to the office of the school principal, just the being *summoned* had made my gut tight, made me feel like I wanted to go to the bathroom.

He made me wait half an hour, on a bench, damn him, with a gaggle of weirdos who looked like they hadn't had their heads scrubbed and customized in seven months.

Finally, the box called my name and I dropped to his office, and he was sitting in one of those informal conversation-groupings of chairs and coffee table that instantly put me off.

"Mr. Bailey," he said. Smiled. Hearty bastard. I walked over and sat down even before he suggested I sit. He didn't drop the smile for a second. He was up to anything.

"Why don't we get right to it," he said. I smiled back at him, but I felt trapped, really hemmed-in.

"I've been looking at your tag-chart, Mr. Bailey, and well, I hesitate to make any jump conclusions here, but it *appears* you've been neglecting your relaxation periods."

Damn him! Damn him!

The omnipresent melancholy that had consumed him on an Earth bursting with overpopulation was something to which he had no desire to return. Then why this frenzy to resist being shunted into the body of a creature undoubtedly living a life more demanding, more exciting—*anything* had to be better than what he'd come from—more *alive*? Why this fanatic need to track back along the feeder-lines to the Succubus, to destroy the one who had saved him from oblivion? Why this need to destroy a creature who was merely fulfilling a necessary operation-of-balance in a universe singularly devoid of balance?

In that thought lay the answer, but he did not have the key. He turned off his thoughts. He was Bailey no more.

And in that instant the Succubus pulled his soul from the file and sent it where it was needed. He was certainly Bailey no more.

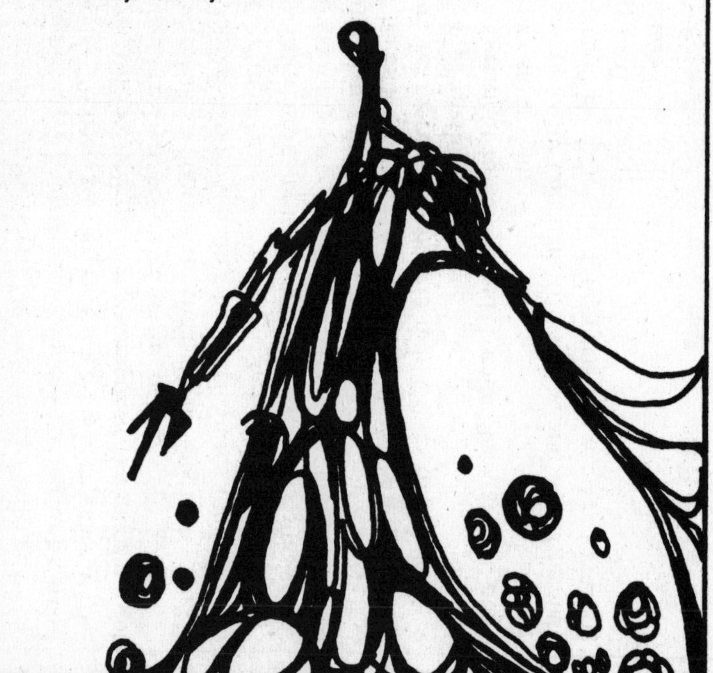

Subaltern Pinkh squirmed on his spike-palette, and opened his eye. His back was stiff. He turned, letting the invigorating short-spikes tickle his flesh through the heavy mat of fur. His mouth felt dry and loamy.

It was the morning of his fiftieth assault mission. Or was it? He seemed to remember lying down for a night's sleep . . . and then a very long dream without substance. It had been all black and empty; hardly something the organizer would have programmed. It must have malfunctioned.

He slid sidewise on the spike-palette, and dropped his enormous furred legs over the side. As his paws touched the tiles a whirring from the wall preceded the toilet facility's appearance. It swiveled into view, and Pinkh looked at himself in the full-length mirror. He looked all right. Dream. Bad dream.

The huge, bearlike subaltern shoved off the bed, stood to his full seven feet, and lumbered into the duster. The soothing powders cleansed away his sleep-fatigue and he emerged, blue pelt glistening, with bad dreams almost entirely dusted away. Almost. Entirely. He had a lingering feeling of having been . . . somewhat . . . *larger* . . .

The briefing colors washed across the walls, and Pinkh hurriedly attached his ribbons. It was informalwear today. Three yellows, three ochers, three whites and an ego blue.

He went downtunnel to the briefing section, and prayed. All around him his sortie partners were on their backs, staring up at the sky dome and the random (programmed) patterns of stars in their religious significances. Montag's Lord of Propriety had programmed success for today's mission. The stars swirled and shaped themselves and the portents were reassuring to Pinkh and his fellows.

The Montag–Thil War had been raging for almost one hundred years, and it seemed close to ending. The dark star Montag and the Nebula Cluster in Thil Galaxy had thrown their might against each other for a century; the people themselves were weary of war. It would end soon. One or the other would make a mistake, the opponent would take the advantage, and the strike toward peace would follow immediately. It was merely a matter of time. The assault troops—especially Pinkh, a planetary hero—were suffused with a feeling of importance, a sense of the relevance of what they were doing. Out to kill, certainly, but with the sure knowledge that they were working toward a worthwhile goal. Through death, to life. The portents had told them again and again, these last months, that this was the case.

The sky dome turned golden and the stars vanished. The assault troops sat up on the floor, awaited their briefing.

It was Pinkh's fiftieth mission.

His great yellow eye looked around the briefing room. There were more young troopers this mission. In fact . . . he was the only veteran. It seemed strange.

Could Montag's Lord of Propriety have planned it this way? But where were Andakh and Melnakh and Gorekh? They'd been here yesterday.

*Was it just yesterday?*

He had a strange memory of having been—asleep?—away?—unconscious?—what?—something. As though more than one day had passed since his last mission. He leaned across to the young trooper on his right and placed a paw flat on the other's. "What day is today?" The trooper flexed palm and answered, with a note of curiosity in his voice, "It's Former. The ninth." Pinkh was startled. "What cycle?" he asked, almost afraid to hear the answer.

"Third," the young trooper said.

The briefing officer entered at that moment, and Pinkh had no time to marvel that it was *not* the next day, but a full cycle later. Where had the days gone? What had happened to him? Had Gorekh and the others been lost in sorties? Had he been wounded, sent to repair, and only now been remanded to duty? Had he been wounded and suffered amnesia? He remembered a Lance Corporal in the Throbbing Battalion who had been seared and lost his memory. They had sent him back to Montag, where he had been blessed by the Lord of Propriety himself. What had happened to him?

Strange memories—not his own, all the wrong colors, weights and tones wholly alien—kept pressing against the bones in his forehead.

He was listening to the briefing officer, but also hearing an undertone. Another voice entirely. Coming from some other place he could not locate.

**■■■■■ You great ugly fur-thing, you! Wake up, look around you. One hundred years, slaughtering. Why can't you see what's being done to you? How dumb can you be? The Lords of Propriety; they set you up. Yeah, *you,* Pinkh! Listen to me. You can't block me out . . . you'll hear me. Bailey. You're the one, Pinkh, the special one. They trained you for what's coming up . . . no, don't block me out, you imbecile . . . don't blot me out ■■■■■ I'll be here, you can't blot me out ■■■■■**

The background noise went on, but he would not listen. It was sacrilegious. Saying things about the Lord of Propriety. Even the Thil Lord of Propriety was sacrosanct in Pinkh's mind. Even though they were at war, the two Lords were eternally locked together in holiness. To blaspheme even the enemy's

Lord was unthinkable.

*Yet he had thought it.*

He shuddered with the enormity of what had passed in his thoughts, and knew he could never go to release and speak of it. He would submerge the memory, and pay strict attention to the briefing officer who was

"This cycle's mission is a straightforward one. You will be under the direct linkage of Subaltern Pinkh, whose reputation is known to all of you."

Pinkh inclined with the humbleness movement.

"You will drive directly into the Thil labyrinth, chivvy and harass a path to Groundworld, and there level as many targets-of-opportunity as you are able, before you're destroyed. After this briefing you will reassemble with your sortie leaders and fully familiarize yourselves with the target-cubes the Lord has commanded to be constructed."

He paused, and stared directly at Pinkh, his golden eye gone to pinkness with age and dissipation. But what he said was for all of the sappers. "There is one target you will *not* strike. It is the Maze of the Thil Lord of Propriety. This is irrevocable. You will not, repeat *not* strike near the Maze of the Lord."

Pinkh felt a leap of pleasure. This was the final strike. It was preamble to peace. A suicide mission; he ran eleven thankfulness prayers through his mind. It was the dawn of a new day for Montag and Thil. The Lords of Propriety were good. The Lords held all cupped in their holiness.

*Yet he had thought the unthinkable.*

"You will be under the direct linkage of Subaltern Pinkh," the briefing officer said again. Then, kneeling and passing down the rows of sappers, he palmed good death with honor to each of them. When he reached Pinkh, he stared at him balefully for a long instant, as though wanting to speak. But the moment passed, he rose, and left the chamber.

They went into small groups with the sortie leaders and examined the target-cubes. Pinkh went directly to the briefing officer's cubicle and waited patiently till the older Montagasque's prayers were completed.

When his eye cleared, he stared at Pinkh.

"A path through the labyrinth has been cleared."

"What will we be using?"

"Reclaimed sortie craft. They have all been outfitted with diversionary equipment."

"Linkage level?"

"They tell me a high six."

"They *tell* you?" He regretted the tone even as he spoke.

The briefing officer looked surprised. As if his desk had coughed. He did not speak, but stared at Pinkh with the same baleful stare the subaltern had seen before.

"Recite your catechism," the briefing officer said, finally.

Pinkh settled back slowly on his haunches, ponderous weight downdropping with grace. Then:

"Free flowing, free flowing, all flows
"From the Lords, all free, all fullness,
"Flowing from the Lords.
    "What will I do
    "What will I do
"What will I do without my Lords?

"Honor in the dying, rest in honor, all honor
"From the Lords, all rest, all honoring,
"To honor my Lords.
"This I will do
"This I will do
"I will live when I die for my Lords."

And it was between the First and Second Sacredness that the darkness came to Pinkh. He saw the briefing officer come toward him, reach a great palm toward him, and there was darkness . . . the same sort of darkness from which he had risen in his own cubicle before the briefing. Yet, not the same. *That* darkness had been total, endless, with the feeling that he was . . . somehow . . . larger . . . greater . . . as big as all space . . .

And this darkness was like being turned off. He could not think, could not even think that he was unthinking. He was cold, and not there. Simply: not there.

Then, as if it had not happened, he was back in the briefing officer's cubicle, the great bearlike shape was moving back from him, and he was reciting the Second Sacredness of his catechism.

What had happened . . . he did not know.

"Here are your course coordinates," the briefing officer said. He extracted the spool from his pouch and gave it to Pinkh. The subaltern marveled again at how old the briefing officer must be: the hair of his chest pouch was almost gray.

"Sir," Pinkh began. Then stopped. The briefing officer raised a palm. "I understand, Subaltern. Even to the most reverent among us there come moments of confusion." Pinkh smiled. He *did* understand.

"Lords," Pinkh said, palming the briefing officer with fullness and propriety.

"Lords," he replied, palming honor in the dying.

Pinkh left the briefing officer's cubicle and went to his own place.

As soon as he was certain the subaltern was gone, the briefing officer, who was *very* old, linked-up with someone else, far away; and he told him things.

# 3

First, they melted the gelatin around him. It was hardly gelatin, but it had come to be called jell by the sappers, and the word had stuck. As the gelatin stuck. Face protected, he lay in the ten troughs, in sequence, getting the gelatinous substance melted around him. Finally, pincers that had been carefully padded lifted him from the tenth trough, and slid him along the track to his sortie craft. Once inside the pilot country, stretched out on his stomach, he felt the two hundred wires insert themselves into the jell, into the fur, into his body. The brain wires were the last to fix.

As each wire hissed from its spool and locked onto the skull contacts, Pinkh felt himself go a little more to integration with the craft. At last, the final wire tipped on icily and so Pinkh was metalflesh, bulkheadskin, eyescanners, bonerivets, plasticartilege, artery / ventricle / capacitors / molecules / transistors,

BEASTC<br>
C      R<br>
R      A<br>
    i<br>
A      F<br>
F      T<br>
TBEAST

all of him as one, totality, metal-man, furred-vessel, essence of mechanism, soul of inanimate, life in force-drive, linkage of mind with power plant. Pinkh the ship. Sortie Craft 90 named Pinkh.

And the others: linked to him.

Seventy sappers, each encased in jell, each wired up, each a mind to its sortie craft. Seventy, linked in telepathically with Pinkh, and Pinkh linked into his own craft, and all of them instrumentalities of the Lord of Propriety.

The great carrier wing that bore them made escape orbit and winked out of normal space.

Here■Not Here.

In an instant gone.

(Gone where!?!)

Inverspace.

Through the gully of inverspace to wink into existence once again at the outermost edge of the Thil labyrinth.

Not Here•Here.

Confronting a fortified tundra of space criss-crossed by deadly lines of force. A cosmic fireworks display. A cat's cradle of vanishing, appearing and disappearing threads of a million colors; each one receptive to all the others. Cross one, break one, interpose . . . and suddenly uncountable others home in. Deadly ones. Seeking ones. Stunners and drainers and leakers and burners. The Thil labyrinth.

Seventy-one sortie craft hung quivering—the last of the inverspace coronas trembling off and gone. Through the tracery of force-lines the million stars of the Thil Galaxy burned with the quiet reserve of ice crystals. And there, in the center, the Nebula Cluster. And there, in the center of the Cluster, Groundworld.

"Link in with me."

Pinkh's command fled and found them. Seventy beastcraft tastes, sounds, scents, touches came back to Pinkh. His sappers were linked in.

"A path has been cleared through the labyrinth for us. Follow. And trust. Honor."

"In the dying," came back the response, from seventy minds of flesh-and-metal.

They moved forward. Strung out like fish of metal with minds linked by thought, they surged forward following the lead craft. Into the labyrinth. Color burned and boiled past, silently sizzling in the vacuum. Pinkh detected murmurs of panics, quelled them with a damping thought of his own. Images of the still pools of Dusnadare, of deep sighs after a full meal, of Lord-worship during the days of First Fullness. Trembling back to him, their minds quieted. And the color beams whipped past on all sides, without up or down or distance. But never touching them.

Time had no meaning. Fused into flesh/metal, the sortie craft followed the secret path that had been cleared for them through the impenetrable labyrinth.

Pinkh had one vagrant thought: *Who cleared this for us?*

And a voice from somewhere far away, a voice that

was his own, yet someone else's—the voice of a someone who called himself a bailey—said, *That's it! Keep thinking what they don't want you to think.*

But he put the thoughts from him, and time wearied itself and succumbed, and finally they were there. In the exact heart of the Nebula Cluster in Thil Galaxy.

Groundworld lay fifth from the source star, the home sun that had nurtured the powerful Thil race till it could explode outward.

"Link in to the sixth power," Pinkh commanded.

They linked. He spent some moments reinforcing his command splices, making the interties foolproof and trigger-responsive. Then he made a prayer, and they went in.

*Why am I locking them in so close,* Pinkh wondered, damping the thought before it could pass along the lines to his sappers. *What am I trying to conceal? Why do I need such repressive control? What am I trying to avert?*

Pinkh's skull thundered with sudden pain. Two minds were at war inside him, he knew that. He *SUDDENLY* knew it.

*Who is that?*

*It's me, you clown!*

*Get out! I'm on a mission . . . it's import—*

*It's a fraud! They've prog—*

*Get out of my head listen to me you idiot I'm trying to tell you something you need to know I won't listen I'll override you I'll block you I'll damp you no listen don't do that I've been someplace you haven't been and I can tell you about the Lords oh this can't be happening to me not to me I'm a devout man fuck that garbage listen to me they lost you man they lost you to a soul stealer and they had to get you back because you were their specially programmed killer they want you to Lord oh Lord of Propriety hear me now hear me your most devout worshipper forgive these blasphemous thoughts I can't control you any more you idiot I'm fading fading fading Lord oh Lord hear me I wish only to serve you. Only to suffer the honor in the dying.*

*Peace through death. I am the instrumentality of the Lords. I know what I must do.*

*That's what I'm trying to* tell *you. . . .*

And then he was gone in the mire at the bottom of Pinkh's mind. They were going in.

They came down, straight down past the seven moons, broke through the cloud cover, leveled out in a delta wing formation and streaked toward the larger of the two continents that formed ninety percent of Groundworld's land mass. Pinkh kept them at supersonic speed, blurring, and drove a thought out to his sappers: "We'll drop straight down below a thousand feet and give them the shock wave. Hold till I tell you to level off."

They were passing over a string of islands—causeway-linked beads in a pea-green sea—each one covered from shore to shore with teeming housing dorms that commuted their residents to the main continents and the complexes of high-rise bureaucratic towers.

"Dive!" Pinkh ordered.

The formation angled sharply forward, as though it was hung on puppet strings, then fell straight down.

The metalflesh of Pinkh's ship-hide began to heat.

Overlapping armadillo plates groaned; Pinkh pushed their speed; force-bead mountings lubricated themselves, went dry, lubricated again; they dropped down; follicle-thin fissures were grooved in the bubble surfaces; sappers began to register fear, Pinkh locked them tighter; instruments coded off the far right and refused to register; the island-chain flew up toward them; pressure in the gelatin trough flattened them with g's; now there was enough atmosphere to scream past their sortie craft and it whistled, shrilled, howled, built and climbed; gimbal-tracks rasped in their mountings; down and down they plunged, seemingly bent on thundering into the islands of Groundworld; "Sir! Sir!"; "Hold steady, not yet . . . not yet . . . I'll tell you when . . . not yet . . ."

Pushing an enormous bubble of pressurized air before them, the delta wing formation wailed straight down toward the specks of islands that became dots, became buttons, became masses, became everything as they rushed up and filled the bubble sights from side to side—

"Level out! *Now*! Do it, do it, *level now*!"

And they pulled out, leveled off and shot away. The bubble of air, enormous, solid as an asteroid, thundering down unchecked . . . hit struck burst broke with devastating results. Pinkh's sortie craft plunged away, and in their wake they left exploding cities, great structures erupting, others trembling, shuddering, then caving in on themselves. The shock wave hit and spread outward from shore to shore. Mountains of plasteel and lathite volcano'd in blossoms of flame and flesh. The blast-pit created by the air bubble struck to the core of the island-chain. A tidal wave rose like some prehistoric leviathan and boiled over one entire spot of land. Another island broke up and sank almost at once. Fire and walls of plasteel crushed and destroyed after the shock wave.

The residence islands were leveled as Pinkh's sortie craft vanished over the horizon, still traveling at supersonic speed.

They passed beyond the island-chain, leaving in their wake dust and death, death and ruin, ruin and fire.

"Through death to peace," Pinkh sent.

"Honor," they responded, as one.

(Far away on Groundworld, a traitor smiled.)

(In a Maze, a Lord sat with antennae twined, waiting.)

(Flesh and metal eased.)

(In ruins, a baby whose exoskeleton had been crushed, crawled toward the pulsing innards of its mother.)

(Seven moons swung in their orbits.)

(A briefing officer on Montag knew it was full, golden.)

*Oh, Lords, what I have done, I have done for you.*

*Wake up. Will you wake up, Pinkh! The mission is—*

The other thing, the bailey, was wrenching at him, poking its head up out of the slime. He thrust it back down firmly. And made a prayer.

"Sir," the thought of one of his sappers came back along the intertie line, "did you say something?"

"Nothing," Pinkh said. "Keep in formation."

He locked them in even tighter, screwing them down with mental shackles till they gasped.

The pressure was building.

A six-power linkup, and the pressure was building.

*I am a hero,* Pinkh thought, *I can do it.*

Then they were flashing across the Greater Ocean and it blurred into an endless carpet of thick heaving green; Pinkh felt sick watching it whip by beneath him; he went deeper into ship and the vessel felt no sickness. He fed the stability of nausea-submerged along the interties.

They were met by the Thil inner defense line over empty ocean. First came the sea-breathers but they fell short when Pinkh ordered his covey to lift for three thousand feet. They leveled off just as the beaks swooped down in their land-to-sea parabolas. Two of them snouted and perceived the range, even as they were viciously beamed into their component parts by Pinkh's outermost sappers. But they'd already fed back the trajectories, and suddenly the sky above them was black with the blackmetal bodies of beaks, flapping, dropping, squalling as they cascaded into the center of the formation. Pinkh felt sappers vanish from the linkup and fed the unused power along other lines, pulling the survivors tighter under his control. "Form a sweep," he commanded.

The formation regrouped and rolled in a graceful gull-wing maneuver that brought them craft-to-craft in a fan. "Plus!" Pinkh ordered, cutting in—with a thought—the imploding beam. The beams of each sortie craft fanned out, overlapping, making an impenetrable wall of deadly force. The beaks came whirling back up and careened across the formation's path. Creatures of metal and mindlessness. Wheels and carapaces. Blackness and berserk rage. Hundreds. Entire eyries.

When they struck the soft pink fan of the overlapping implosion beams, they whoofed in on themselves, dropped instantly.

The formation surged forward.

Then they were over the main continent. Rising from the exact center was the gigantic mountain atop which the Thil Lord of Propriety lived in his Maze.

"Attack! Targets of opportunity!" Pinkh commanded, sending impelling power along the linkup. His metal hide itched. His eyeball sensors watered. In they went, again.

"Do not strike at the Lord's Maze," one of the sappers thought

AND PINKH<br>
THREW UP!!<br>
A WALL OF<br>
THOUGHT!!!<br>
THAT DREW<br>
THE!!!!!!!!!!!<br>
THOUGHT!!!<br>
OFF THE!!!!! do not strike at the lords maze . :<br>
LINKUP SO<br>
IT DID!!!!!!!!<br>
NOT REACH<br>
THE OTHER<br>
SAPPERS!!!!!<br>
BUT HIT!!!!<br>
THE WALL!!!<br>
AND BROKE!<br>
LIKE FOAM!

Why did I do that? We were briefed not to attack the Lord's Maze. It would be unthinkable to attack the Lord's Maze. It would precipitate even greater war than before. The war would *never* end. Why did I stop my sapper from reiterating the order? And why haven't *I* told them not to do it? It was stressed at the briefing. They're linked in so very tightly, they'd obey in a moment—anything I said. What is happening? I'm heading for the mountain! Lord!

*Listen to me, Pinkh. This war has been maintained by the Lords of Propriety for a hundred years. Why do you think it was made heresy even to* think *negatively about the opposing Lord? They keep it going, to feed off it. Whatever they are, these Lords, they come from the same pocket universe and they live off the energy of men at war. They* must *keep the war going or they'll die. They programmed you to be their secret weapon. The war was reaching a stage where both Montag and Thil want peace, and the Lords can't have that. Whatever they are, Pinkh, whatever kind of creature they are, wherever they come from, for over a hundred years they've held your two galaxies in their hands, and they've used you. The Lord isn't in his Maze, Pinkh. He's safe somewhere else. But they planned it between them. They knew if a Montagasque sortie penetrated to Groundworld and struck the Maze, it would keep the war going indefinitely. So they programmed you, Pinkh. But before they could use you, your soul was stolen. They put my soul in you, a man of Earth, Pinkh. You don't even know where Earth is, but my name is Bailey. I've been trying to reach through to you. But you always shut me out—they had you programmed too well. But with the linkup pressure, you don't have the strength to keep me out, and I've got to let you know you're programmed to strike the Maze. You can stop it, Pinkh. You can avoid it all. You can end this war. You have it within your power, Pinkh. Don't strike the Maze. I'll redirect you. Strike where the Lords are hiding. You can rid your galaxies of them, Pinkh. Don't let them kill you. Who do you think arranged for the path through the labyrinth? Why do you think there wasn't more effective resistance? They* wanted *you to get through. To commit the one crime they could not forgive.*

The words reverberated in Pinkh's head as his sortie craft followed him in a tight wedge, straight for the Maze of the Lord.

"I—no, I—" Pinkh could not force thoughts out to his sappers. He was snapped shut. His mind was aching, the sound of straining and creaking, the buildings on the island-chain ready to crumble. Bailey inside, Pinkh inside, the programming of the Lords inside . . . all of them pulling at the fiber of Pinkh's mind.

For an instant the programming took precedence. "New directives. Override previous orders. Follow me in!"

They dove straight for the Maze.

*No, Pinkh, fight it! Fight it and pull out. I'll show you where they're hiding. You can end this war!*

The programming phasing was interrupted, Pinkh abruptly opened his great golden eye, his mind synched in even more tightly with his ship, and at that instant he knew the voice in his head was telling him the truth. He *remembered*:

Remembered the endless sessions.

Remembered the conditioning.

Remembered the programming.

Knew he had been duped.

Knew he was not a hero.

Knew he had to pull out of this dive.

Knew that at last *he* could bring peace to both galaxies.

He started to think *pull out, override* and fire it down the remaining linkup interties . . .

And the Lords of Propriety, who left very little to chance, who had followed Pinkh all the way, contacted the Succubus, complained of the merchandise they had bought, demanded it be returned . . .

Bailey's soul was wrenched from the body of Pinkh. The subaltern's body went rigid inside its jell trough, and, soulless, empty, rigid, the sortie craft plunged into the mountaintop where the empty Maze stood. It was followed by the rest of the sortie craft.

The mountain itself erupted in a geysering pillar of flame and rock and plasteel.

One hundred years of war was only the beginning.

Somewhere, hidden, the Lords of Propriety—umbilicus-joined with delight shocks spurting softly pink along the flesh-linkage joining them—began their renewed gluttonous feeding.

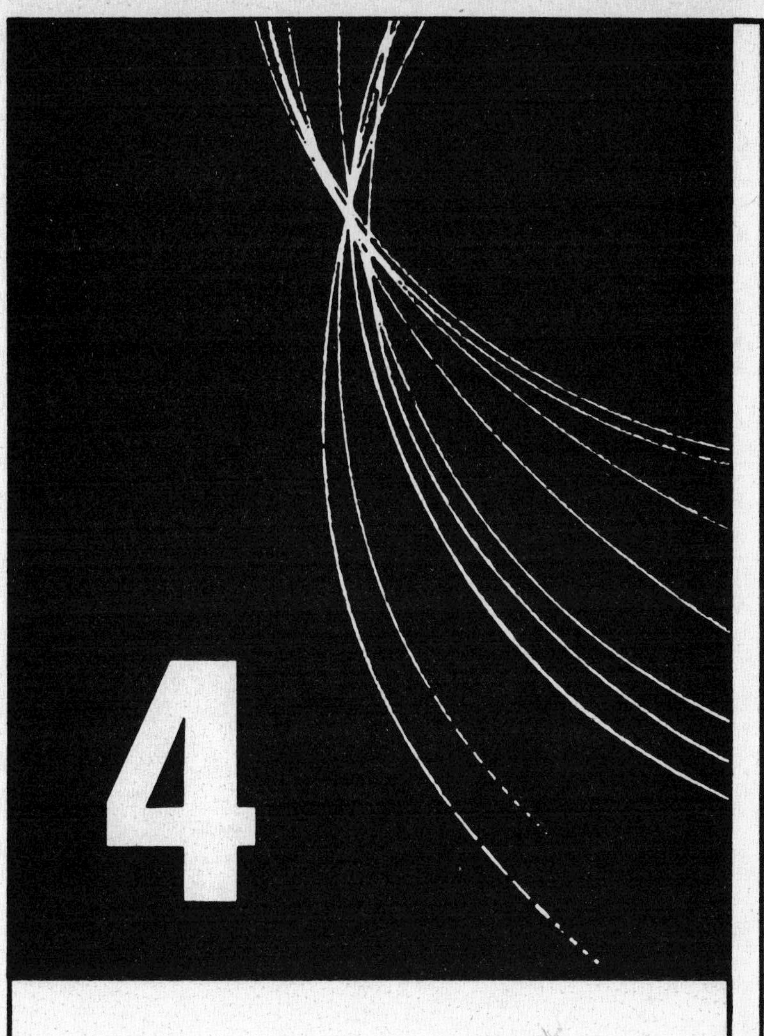

Bailey was whirled out of the Montagasque subaltern's body. His soul went shooting away on an asymptotic curve, back along the feeder-lines, to the soul files of the Succubus.

This is what it was like to be in the soul station.

Round. Weighted with the scent of grass. Perilous in that the music was dynamically contracting: souls had occasionally become too enriched and had gone flat and flaccid.

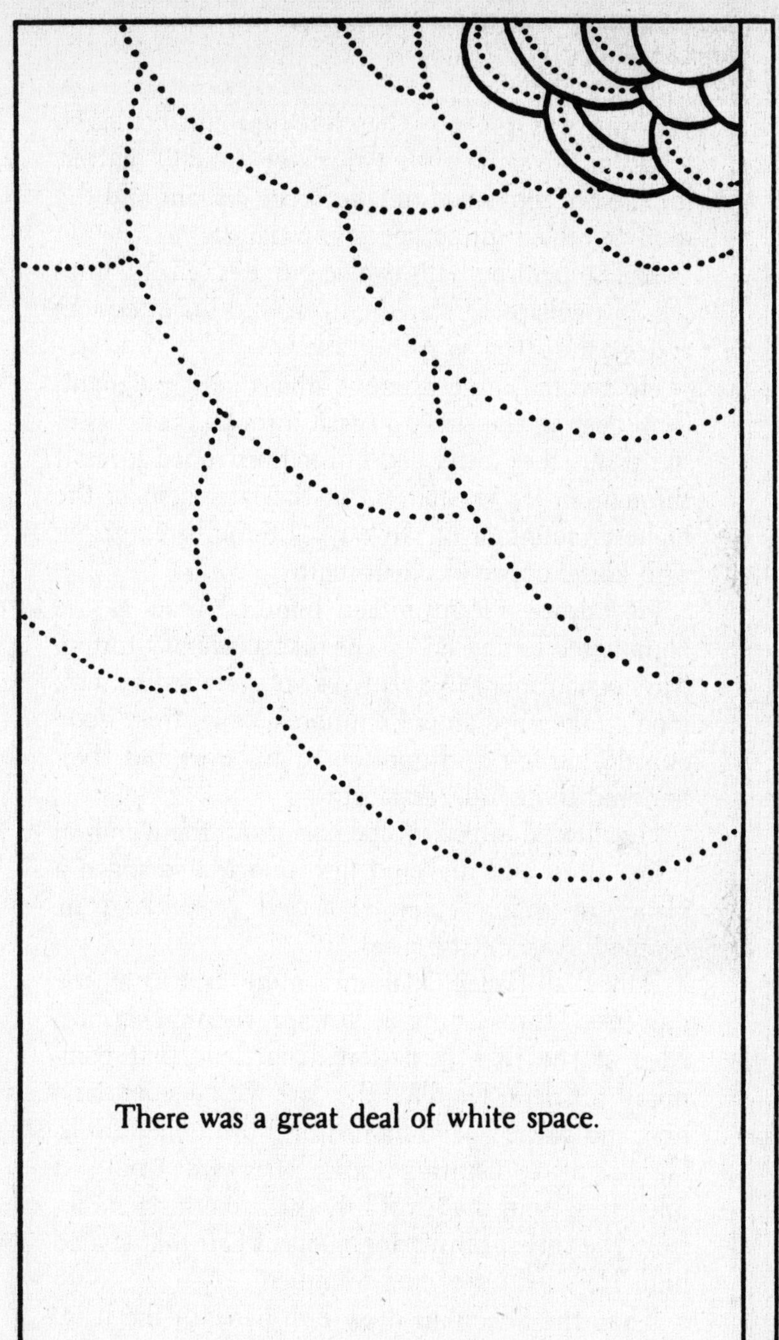

There was a great deal of white space.

Nothing was ranked, therefore nothing could be found in the same place twice; yet it didn't matter, for the Succubus had only to focus his lens and the item trembled into a special awareness.

Bailey spent perhaps twelve minutes reliving himself as a collapsing star then revolved his interfaces and masturbated as Anne Boleyn.

He savored mint where it smells most poignant, from deep in the shallow earth through the roots of the plant, then extended himself, extruded himself through an ice crystal and lit the far massif of the highest mountain on an onyx asteroid—recreating The Last Supper in chiaroscuro.

He burned for seventeen hundred years as the illuminated letter "B" on the first stanza of a forbidden enchantment in a papyrus volume used to summon up the imp James Fenimore Cooper then stood outside himself and considered his eyes and their hundred thousand bee-facets.

He allowed himself to be born from the womb of a tree sloth and flickered into rain that deluged a planet of coal for ten thousand years. And he beamed. And he sorrowed.

Bailey, all Bailey, soul once more, free as all the universes, threw himself toward the farthermost edge of the slightly flattened parabola that comprised the dark. He filled the dark with deeper darkness and bathed in fountains of brown wildflowers. Circles of coruscating violet streamed from his fingertips, from the tip of his nose, from his genitals, from the tiniest fibrillating fibers of hair that coated him. He shed water and hummed.

Then the Succubus drew him beneath the lens.

And Bailey was sent out once more.

Waste not, want not.

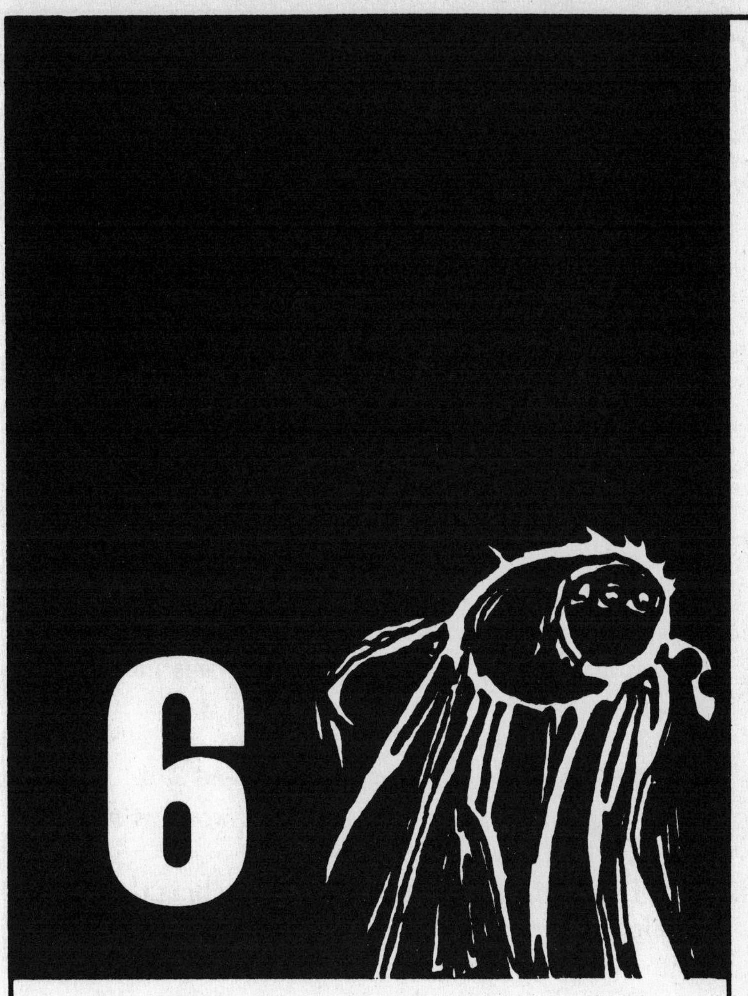

# 6

He was just under a foot tall. He was covered with blue fur. He had a ring of eyes that circled his head. He had eight legs. He smelled of fish. He was low to the ground and he moved very fast.

He was a stalker-cat, and he was first off the survey ship on Belial. The others followed, but not too soon. They always waited for the cat to do its work. It was safer that way. The Filonii had found that out in ten thousand years of exploring their universe. The cats did the first work, then the Filonii did theirs. It was the best way to rule a universe.

Belial was a forest world. Covered in long continents that ran from pole to pole with feathertop trees, it was ripe for discovery.

Bailey looked out of his thirty eyes, seeing around himself in a full 360° spectrum. Seeing all the way up into the ultra-violet, seeing all the way down into the infra-red. The forest was silent. Absolutely no sound. Bailey, the cat, would have heard a sound, had there been a sound. But there was no sound.

No birds, no insects, no animals, not even the whispering of the feathertop trees as they struggled toward the bright hot-white sun. It was incredibly silent.

Bailey said so.

The Filonii went to a condition red.

*No* world is silent. And a forest world is *always* noisy. But this one was silent.

They were out there, waiting. Watching the great ship and the small stalker-cat that had emerged from it.

Who they were, the cat and the Filonii did not know. But they were there, and they were waiting for the invaders to make the first move. The stalker-cat glided forward.

Bailey felt presences. Deep in the forest, deeper than he knew he could prowl with impunity. They were in there, watching him as he moved forward. But he was a cat, and if he was to get his fish, he would work. The Filonii were watching. *Them*, in there, back in the trees, *they* were watching. *It's a bad life,* he thought. *The life of a cat is a nasty, dirty, bad one.*

Bailey was not the first cat ever to have thought that thought. It was the litany of the stalker-cats. They knew their place, had always known it, but that was the way it was; it was the way it had always been. The Filonii ruled, and the cats worked. And the universe became theirs.

Yet it wasn't shared. It was the Filonii universe, and the stalker-cats were hired help.

The fine mesh cap that covered the top and back of the cat's head glowed with a faint but discernible halo. The sunbeams through which he passed caught at the gold filaments of the cap and sent sparkling radiations back toward the ship. The ship stood in the center of the blasted area it had cleared for its prime base.

Inside the ship, the team of Filonii ecologists sat in front of the many process screens and saw through the eyes of the stalker-cat. They murmured to one another as first one, then another, then another saw something of interest. "Cat, lad," one of them said softly, "still no sound?"

"Nothing yet, Brewer. But I can feel them watching."

One of the other ecologists leaned forward. The entire wall behind the hundred screens was a pulsing membrane. Speak into it at any point and the cat's helmet picked up the voice, carried it to the stalker. "Tell me, lad, what does it feel like?"

"I'm not quite sure, Kicker. I'm getting it mixed. It feels like the eyes staring . . . and wood . . . and sap . . . and yet there's mobility. It can't be the trees."

"You're sure."

"As best I can tell right now, Kicker. I'm going to go into the forest and see."

"Good luck, lad."

"Thank you, Driver. How is your goiter?"

"I'm fine, lad. Take care."

The stalker-cat padded carefully to the edge of the forest. Sunlight slanted through the feathertops into the gloom. It was cool and dim inside there.

Now, all eyes were upon him.

The first paw in met springy, faintly moist and cool earth. The fallen feathers had turned to mulch. It smelled like cinnamon. Not overpoweringly so, just pleasantly so. He went in . . . all the way. The last the Filonii saw on their perimeter screens—twenty of the hundred—were his tails switching back and forth. Then the tails were gone and the seventy screens showed them dim, strangely-shadowed pathways between the giant conifers.

"Cat, lad, can you draw any conclusions from those trails?"

The stalker padded forward, paused. "Yes. I can draw the conclusion they aren't trails. They go fairly straight for a while, then come to dead ends at the bases of the trees. I'd say they were drag trails, if anything."

"What was dragged? Can you tell?"

"No, not really, Homer. Whatever was dragged, it was thick and fairly smooth. But that's all I can tell." He prodded the drag trail with his secondary leg on the left side. In the pad of the paw were tactile sensors.

The cat proceeded down the drag trail toward the base of the great tree where the trail unaccountably ended. All around him the great conifers rose six hundred feet into the warm, moist air.

Sipper, in the ship, saw through the cat's eyes and pointed out things to his fellows. "Some of the qualities of *Pseudotsuga Taxifolia*, but definitely a conifer. Notice the bark on that one. Typically *Eucalyptus Regnans* . . . yet notice the soft red spores covering the bark. I've never encountered that particular sort of thing before. They seem to be melting down the trees. In fact . . ."

He was about to say the trees were *all* covered with the red spores, when the red spores attacked the cat.

They flowed down the trees, covering the lower bark, each one the size of the cat's head, and when they touched, they ran together like jelly. When the red jelly from one tree reached the base of the trunk, it fused with the red jelly from the other trees.

"Lad . . ."

"It's all right, Kicker. I see them."

The cat began to pad backward: slowly, carefully. He could easily outrun the fusing crimson jelly. He moved back toward the verge of the clearing. Charred, empty of life, blasted by the Filonii hack-shafts, not even a stump of the great trees above ground, the great circles where the trees had stood now merely reflective surfaces set flush in the ground. Back.

Backing out of life . . . backing into death.

The cat paused. What had caused *that* thought?

"Cat! Those spores . . . whatever they are . . . they're forming into a solid . . ."

*Backing out of life . . . backing into death*

my name is

bailey and i'm in
here, inside you.
i was stolen from
my called is wants—
body the some somewhere. he
by succubus. kind there in the stars
a he, of recruiter from out
creature *it* puppeteer, a sort of

The blood-red spore thing stood fifteen feet high, formless, shapeless, changing, malleable, coming for the cat. The stalker did not move: within him, a battle raged.

"Cat, lad! Return! Get back!"

Though the universe belonged to the Filonii, it was only at moments when the loss of a portion of that universe seemed imminent that they realized how important their tools of ownership had become.

Bailey fought for control of the cat's mind.

Centuries of conditioning fought back.

The spore thing reached the cat and dripped around him. The screens of the Filonii went blood-red, then went blank.

The thing that had come from the trees oozed back into the forest, shivered for a moment, then vanished, taking the cat with it.

The cat focused an eye. Then another. In sequence he opened and focused each of his thirty eyes. The place where he lay came into full luster. He was underground. The shapeless walls of the place dripped with sap and several colors of viscous fluid. The fluid dripped down over bark that seemed to have been formed as stalactites, the grain running long and glistening till it tapered into needle tips. The surface on which the cat lay was planed wood, the grain exquisitely formed, running outward from a coral-colored pith in concentric circles of hues that went from coral to dark teak at the outer perimeter.

The spores had fissioned, were heaped in an alcove. Tunnels ran off in all directions. Huge tunnels twenty feet across.

The mesh cap was gone.

The cat got to his feet. Bailey was there, inside, fully awake, conversing with the cat.

"Am I cut off from the Filonii?"

"Yes, I'm afraid you are."

"Under the trees."

"That's right."

"What is that spore thing?"

"I know, but I'm not sure you'd understand."

"I'm a stalker; I've spent my life analyzing alien life-forms and alien ecology. I'll understand."

"They're mobile symbiotes, conjoined with the bark of these trees. Singly, they resemble most closely anemonic anaerobic bacteria, susceptible to dichotomization; they're anacusic, anabiotic, anamnestic, and feed almost exclusively on ancyclostomiasis."

"Hookworms?"

"Big hookworms. Very big hookworms."

"The drag trails?"

"That's what they drag."

"But none of that makes any sense. It's impossible."

"So is reincarnation among the Yerbans, but it occurs."

"I don't understand."

"I told you you wouldn't."

"How do *you* know all this?"

"You wouldn't understand."

"I'll take your word for it."

"Thank you. There's more about the spores and the trees, by the way. Perhaps the most important part."

"Which is?"

"Fused, they become a quasi-sentient gestalt. They can communicate, borrowing power from the tree-hosts."

"That's even *more* implausible!"

"Don't argue with me, argue with the Creator."

"First Cause."

"Have it your way."

"What are you doing in my head?"

"Trying very hard to get out."

"And how would you do that?"

"Foul up your mission so the Filonii would demand the Succubus replace me. I gather you're pretty important to them. Rather chickenshit, aren't they?"

"I don't recognize the term."

"I'll put it in sense form."

£■■■■■]

"Oh. You mean ••◖[–."

"Yeah. Chickenshit."

"Well, that's the way it's always been between the Filonii and the stalkers."

"You like it that way."

"I like my fish."

"Your Filonii like to play God, don't they? Changing this world and that world to suit themselves.

Reminds me of a couple of other guys. Lords of Propriety they were called. And the Succubus. Did you ever stop to think how many individuals and races like to play God?"

"Right now I'd like to get out of here."

"Easy enough."

"How?"

"Make friends with the Tszechmae."

"The trees or the spores?"

"Both."

"One name for the symbiotic relationship?"

"They live in harmony."

"Except for the hookworms."

"No society is perfect. Rule 19."

The cat sat back on his haunches and talked to himself.

"Make friends with them you say."

"Seems like a good idea, doesn't it?"

"How would you suggest I do that?"

"Offer to perform a service for them. Something they can't do for themselves."

"Such as?"

"How about you'll get rid of the Filonii for them. Right now that's the thing most oppressing them."

"Get rid of the Filonii."

"Yes."

"I'm harboring a lunatic in my head."

"Well, if you're going to quit before you start . . ."

"Precisely *how*—uh, do you have a name?"

"I told you. Bailey."

"Oh. Yes. Sorry. Well, Bailey, precisely *how* do I rid this planet of a star-spanning vessel weighing somewhere just over thirteen thousand tons, not to mention a full complement of officers and ecologists who have been in the overlord position with my race for more centuries than I can name? I'm conditioned to respect them."

"You sure don't sound as if you respect them."

The cat paused. That was true. He felt quite different. He disliked the Filonii intensely. Hated them, in fact; as his kind had hated them for more centuries than he could name.

"That *is* peculiar. Do you have any explanation for it?"

"Well," said Bailey, humbly, "there *is* my presence. It may well have broken through all your hereditary conditioning."

"You wear smugness badly."

"Sorry."

The cat continued to think on the possibilities.

"I wouldn't take too much longer, if I were you," Bailey urged him. Then, reconsidering, he added, "As a matter of fact, I *am* you."

"You're trying to tell me something."

"I'm trying to tell you that the gestalt spore grabbed you, to get a line on what was happening with the invaders, but you've been sitting here for some time, musing to yourself—which, being instantaneously communicative throughout the many parts of the whole, is a concept they can't grasp—and so it's getting ready to digest you."

The stalker blinked his thirty eyes very rapidly. "The spore thing?"

"Uh-uh. All the spores eat are the hookworms. The bark's starting to look at you with considerable interest."

"Who do I talk to? Quick!"

"You've decided you don't respect the Filonii so

much, huh?"

"I thought you said I should hurry!"

"Just curious."

"*Who do I talk to!?!*"

"The floor."

So the stalker-cat talked to the floor, and they struck a bargain. Rather a lopsided bargain, true; but a bargain nonetheless.

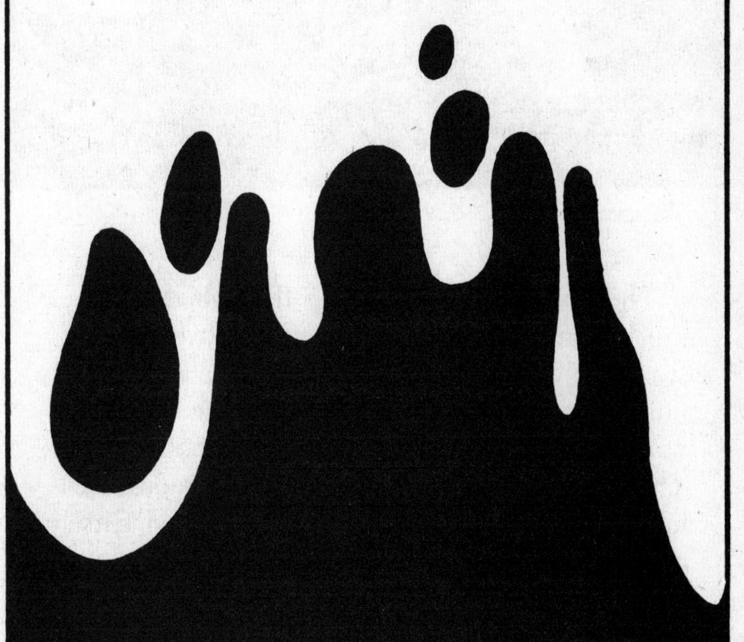

The hookworm was coming through the tunnel much more rapidly than the cat would have expected. It seemed to be sliding, but even as he watched, it bunched—inchworm-like—and propelled itself forward, following the movement with another slide. The wooden tunnel walls oozed with a noxious smelling moistness as the worm passed. It was moving itself on a slime track of its own secretions.

It was eight feet across, segmented, a filthy gray in color, and what passed for a face was merely a slash-mouth dripping yellowish mucus, several hundred cilia-like feelers surrounding the slit, and four glaze-covered protuberances in an uneven row above the slit perhaps serving in some inadequate way as "eyes."

Like a strange Hansel dropping bread crumbs to mark a trail, the spore things clinging to the cat's back began to ooze off. First one, then another. The cat backed down the tunnel. The hookworm came on. It dropped its fleshy penis-like head and snuffled at the spore lying in its path. Then the cilia feelers attached themselves and the spore thing was slipped easily into the slash mouth. There was a disgusting wet sound, and the hookworm moved forward again. The same procedure was repeated at the next spore. And the next, and the next. The hookworm followed the stalker through the tunnels.

Some miles away, the Filonii stared into their screens as a strange procession of red spores formed in the shape of a long thick hawser-like chain emerged from the forest and began to encircle the ship.

"Repulsors?" Kicker asked.

"Not yet, they haven't made a hostile move," the Homer said. "The cat could have won them somehow. This may be a welcoming ceremony. Let's wait and see."

The ship was completely circled, at a distance of fifty feet from the vessel. The Filonii waited, having faith in their cat lad.

And far underground, the stalker-cat led the hookworm a twisting chase through tunnel after tunnel.

Some of the tunnels were formed only moments before the cat and his pursuer entered them. The tunnels always sloped gently upward. The cat—dropping his spore riders as he went—led the enormous slug-thing by a narrow margin. But enough to keep him coming.

Then, into a final tunnel, and the cat leaped to a planed outcropping overhead, then to a tiny hole in the tunnel ceiling, and then out of sight.

The Filonii shouted with delight as the stalker emerged from a hole in the blasted earth, just beyond the circle of red spores, linked and waiting.

"You see! Good cat!" Driver yelled to his fellows.

But the cat made no move toward the ship.

"He's waiting for the welcoming ceremony to end," the Homer said with assurance.

Then, on their screens, they saw first one red spore, then another, vanish, as though sucked down through the ground from below.

They vanished in sequence, and the Filonii followed their disappearance around the screens, watching them go in a 90° arc, then 180° of half circle, then 250° and the ground began to tremble.

And before the hookworm could suck his dinner down through a full 360° of the circle, the ground gave way beneath the thirteen thousand tons of Filonii starship, and the vessel thundered through, down into special tunnels dug straight down. Plunged down with the plates of the ship separating and cracking open. Plunged down with the hookworm that would soon discover sweeter morsels than even red spore things.

The Filonii tried to save themselves.

There was very little they could do. Driver cursed

the cat and made a final contact with the Succubus. It was an automatic hookup, much easier to throw in than to fire the ship for takeoff. Particularly a quarter of a mile underground.

The hookworm broke through the ship. The Tszechmae waited. When the hookworm had gorged itself, they would move in and slay the creature. Then *they* would feast.

But Bailey would not be around to see the great meal. For only moments after the Filonii ship plunged crashing out of sight, he felt a ghastly wrenching at his soulself, and the stalker-cat was left empty once more—thereby proving in lopsided bargains no one is the winner but the house—and the soul of William Bailey went streaking out away from Belial toward the unknown.

Deep in wooden tunnels, things began to feed.

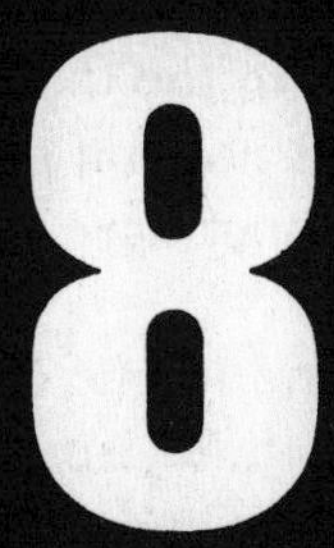

The darkness was the deepest blue. Not black. It was blue. He could see nothing. Not even himself. He could not tell what the body into which he had been cast did, or had, or resembled, or did not do, or not have, or not resemble. He reached out into the blue darkness. He touched nothing.

But then, perhaps he had not reached out. He had felt himself extend *something* into the blueness, but how far, or in what direction, or if it had been an appendage . . . he did not know.

He tried to touch himself, and did not know where to touch. He reached for his face, where a Bailey face would have been. He touched nothing.

He tried to touch his chest. He met resistance, and then penetrated something soft. He could not distinguish if he had pushed through fur or skin or hide or jelly or moisture or fabric or metal or vegetable matter or foam or some heavy gas. He had no feeling in either his "hand" or his "chest" but there was *something* there.

He tried to move, and moved. But he did not know if he was rolling or hopping or walking or sliding or flying or propelling or being propelled. But he moved. And he reached down with the thing he had used to touch himself, and felt nothing below him. He did not have legs. He did not have arms. Blue. It was so blue.

He moved as far as he could move in one direction, and there was nothing to stop him. He could have moved in that direction forever, and met no resistance. So he moved in another direction—opposite, as far as he could tell, and as far as he could go. But there was no boundary. He went up and went down and went around in circles. There was nothing. Endless nothing.

Yet he knew he was *in* somewhere. He was not in the emptiness of space, he was in an enclosed place. But what dimensions the place had, he could not tell. And what he was, he could not tell.

It made him upset. He had not been upset in the body of Pinkh, nor in the body of the stalker-cat But this life he now owned made him nervous.

Why should that be?
Something was coming for him.
He knew that much.

He was here and something else was out there, coming toward him.

He knew fear. Blue fear. Deep unseeing blue fear. If it was coming fast, it would be here sooner. If slow, then later. But it was coming. He could feel, sense, intuit it coming for him. He wanted to change. To become something else.

To become *this*
Or to become THIS
Or to become *THIS*
Or to become tHiS

But to become *something* else, something that could withstand what was coming for him. He didn't know what that could be. All he knew was that he needed equipment. He ran through his baileythoughts, his baileymind, to sort out what he might need.

What he needed might be

Fangs Poisonous breath
Eyes Horns
Malleability
Webbed feet
Armored hide Talons
Camouflage Wings
Carapaces Muscles
Vocal cords Scales
Self-regeneration
Stingers Wheels
Multiple brains

What he already had Nothing

It was coming closer. Or was it getting farther away? (And by getting farther away, becoming more of a threat to him?) (If he went toward it, would he be safer?) (If only he could know what he looked like, or where he was, or what was required of him?) (Orient!) (Damn it, orient yourself, Bailey!) He was deep in blueness, extended, fetal, waiting. Shapeless. (Shape—) (Could *that* be it?)

Something blue flickered in the blueness.

It was coming end-for-end, flickering and sparking and growing larger, swimming toward him in the blueness. It sent tremors through him. Fear gripped him as it had never gripped him before. The blue shape coming toward him was the most fearful thing he could remember: and he remembered:

The night he had found Moravia with another man. They were standing having sex in a closet at a party. Her dress was bunched up around her waist; he had her up on tiptoes. She was crying with deep pleasure, eyes closed.

The day at the end of the war, when a laser had sliced off the top of the head of the man on his left in the warm metal trench. The sight of things still pulsing in the jasmine jelly.

The moment he had come to the final knowledge of his hopeless future. The moment he had decided to go to the Center to find death.

The thing changed shape and sent out scintillant waves of blueness and fear. He writhed away from them but they swept over him, and he turned over and over trying to escape. The thing of blue came nearer, growing larger in his sight. (Sight? Writhing? Fear?) It suddenly swept toward him, faster than before, as though it had tried a primary assault—the waves of fear—and the assault had failed; and now it would bull through.

He felt an urge to leap, high. He felt himself do it, and suddenly his sight went up and his propulsive equipment went lower, and he was longer, taller, larger. He fled. Down through the blueness, with the coruscating blue devil following. It elongated itself and shot past him on one side, boiled on ahead till it was a mere pinpoint of incandescence on some heightless, dimensionless horizon. And then it came racing back toward him, thinning itself and stretching itself till it was opaque, till the blueness of where they were shone through it darkly, like effulgent isinglass in a blue hyperplane.

He trembled in fear and went minute. He balled and shrank and contracted and drew himself to a finite point, and the whirling danger went hurtling through him and beyond, and was lost back the way they had come.

Inside the body he now owned, Bailey felt something wrenching and tearing. Fibers pulled loose from moorings and he was certain his mind was giving way. He had memories of sense-deprivation chambers and what had happened to men who had been left in them too long. This was the same. No shape, no size, no idea or way of gaining an idea of what he was, or where he was, or the touch, smell, sound, sight of *anything* as an anchor to his sanity. Yet he was surviving.

The dark blue devil kept arranging new assaults—

and he had no doubt it would be back in seconds (seconds?)—and he kept doing the correct thing to escape those assaults. But he had the feeling (feeling?) that at some point the instinctive reactions of this new body would be insufficient. That he would have to bring to this new role his essential baileyness, his human mind, his thoughts, the cunning he had begun to understand was so much a part of his way. (And why had he not understood that cunningness when he had been Bailey, all the years of his hopeless life?)

The effulgence began again somewhere off to his side and high above him, coming on rapidly.

Bailey, some *thing* unknown, prepared. As best he could.

MARVELOUS, ANIK! HOW DID YOU MANAGE TO REVITALIZE IT?
OH, I'M SURE YOU DID BUT *HOW* DID YOU MANAGE? PLEASE!
FIVE!?! YOU REALLY *DO* WANT TO WIN, DON'T YOU? TSK-TSK.
I KNOW: YOU DON'T LOOK ON THIS AS A GAME. NOR SHOULD I.
AND THAT'S SIMPLY BECAUSE YOU WERE BORN ALTHUS, WHILE—
WHEN IT MEANT SOMETHING SIGNIFICANT? YES, BUT TIME GOES.
FLUSTER YOU? MY DEAR GOOD ANIK, HOW CAN YOU SAY THAT?
TEN THOUSAND TENILS ISN'T TOO LONG. NOT FOR A HERDUR.
ARE YOU PLEADING FOR SURCEASE, MY FRIEND? DO YOU SUBMIT?
WHY? BECAUSE YOUR CHAMPION IS A FALSE SOUL IN ITS BODY?
TRULY, ANIK, YOU MUST THINK ME A CULLY OR A FOOL! DIE!
THEN GO TO RESERVE FRAMES. I CAN'T CONCERN MYSELF NOW.
LET *ME* WORRY ABOUT THE EXTENT OF MY OVER-EXTENSIONS!
YOU'LL WORRY ABOUT THAT TILL THE MOMENT I DESTROY YOU.
IT WAS *INTENDED* THAT WE FIGHT. IF YOU WANT OUT, I SAY GO!
YOUR SUBSTITUTE CHAMPION HAS NO CHANCE, I SWEAR IT, ANIK!

you may be sure i paid dearly to do so, my dear yaquil.
the succubus. yaquil it cost me five tenils of life.
chide me all you wish unlike you, i do not look on—
but you do you have *always* thought of it as a game.
while you were born herdur. there *was* a time when it—
and we remain. you cannot fluster me with platitudes!
i can say it because we have waged this combat too long.
but for an althus it is. call an end, yaquil! do it now.
submission is no part of it. i merely say stop quickly.
no, because the tenils pass and the heat goes and we die!
yes, die! and i've used more frames than i can afford.
better now than too late. you over-extend yourself, sir.
impudence, impertinence how you ever became a combatant—
you leave me no alternative. frames be damned, we fight!
and concede a defeat i need not have conceded? fight on.
i offered you an opportunity. the time for talk is done!

The blue devil swept down on him, crackling with energy. He felt the incredible million sting-points of pain and a sapping of strength. Then a

for it had. Now Bailey knew what he was, and what he had to do. He lay still, swimming in the never-ending forever blueness. He was soft and he was solitary. The blue devil swarmed and came on. For the last time. And when it was all around him, Bailey let it drink him. He let its deep blueness and its fear and its sparkling effulgence sweep over him, consume him. The blue devil gorged itself, grew larger, fuller, more incapable of movement, unable to free itself. Bailey stuffed it with his amoebic body. He split and formed yet another, and the blue devil extended itself and began feeding on his second self. The radiating sparking waves of fear and blueness were thicker now, coming more slowly. Binary fission again. Now there were four. The blue devil fed, consumed, filled its chambers and its source-buds. Again, fission. And now there were eight. And the blue devil began to lose color. Bailey did not divide again. He knew what he had to do. Neither he nor the blue devil could win this combat. Both must die. The feeding went on and on, and finally the blue devil had drained itself with fullness, made itself immobile, died. And he died. And there was emptiness in the blueness once more.

The frames, the tenils, the fullness of combat were ended. And in that last fleeting instant of sentience, Bailey imagined he heard scented wails of hopelessness from two Duelmasters somewhere out there. He gloated. Now they knew what it was to be a William Bailey, to be hopeless and alone and afraid.

He gloated for an instant, then was whirled out and away.

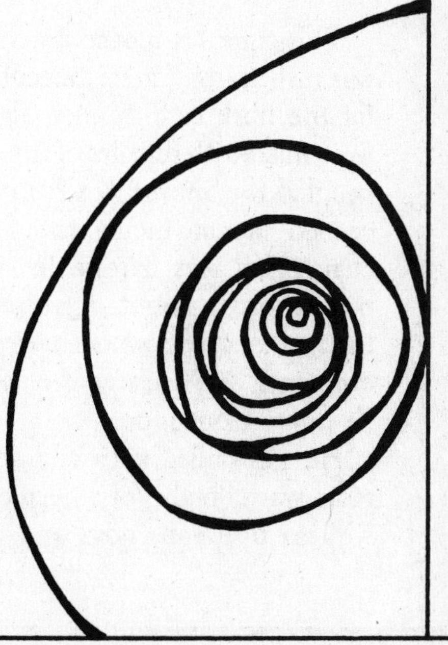

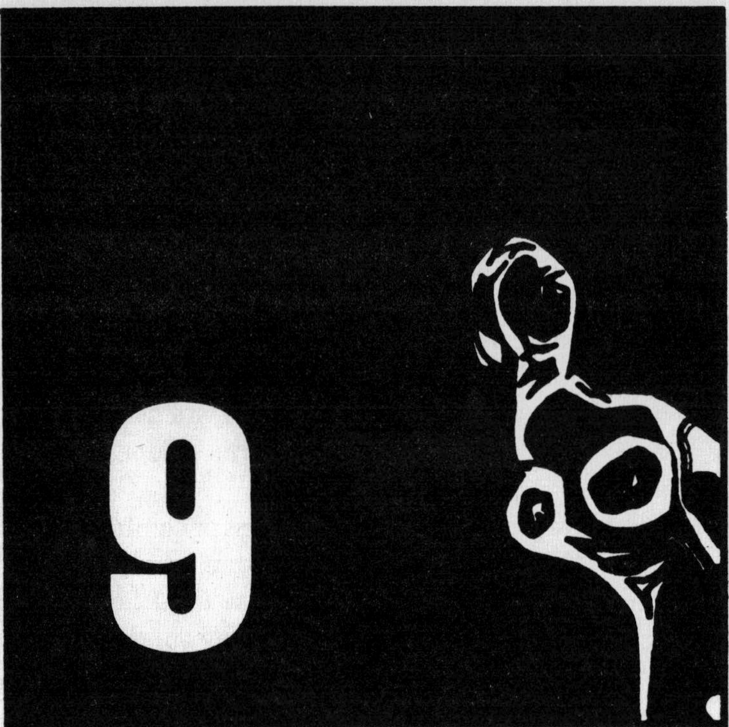


This time his repose lasted only a short time. It was rush season for the Succubus. Bailey went out to fill the husk of a Master Slavemaster whose pens were filled with females of the eighty-three races that peopled the Snowdrift Cluster asteroids. Bailey succeeded in convincing the Slavemaster that male chauvinism was detestable, and the females were bound into a secret organization that returned to their various rock-worlds, overthrew the all-male governments, and declared themselves the Independent Feminist Concourse.

He was pulled back and sent out to inhabit the radio wave "body" of a needler creature used by the Kirk to turn suns nova and thereby provide them with power sources. Bailey gained possession of the needler and imploded the Kirk home sun.

He was pulled back and sent out to inhabit the shell of a ten-thousand-year-old terrapin whose retention of random construction information made it invaluable as the overseer of a planetary reorganization project sponsored by a pale gray race without a name that altered solar systems just beyond the Finger Fringe deepout. Bailey let the turtle feed incorrect data to the world-swingers hauling the planets into their orbits, and the entire configuration collided in the orbit of the system's largest heavy-mass world. The resultant uprising caused the total eradication of the pale gray race.

He was pulled back . . .

Finally, even a creature as vast and involved as the Succubus, a creature plagued by a million problems and matters for attention, in effect a god-of-a-sort, was forced to take notice. There was a soul in his file that was causing a fullness leak. There was a soul that was anathema to what the Succubus had built his reputation on. There was a soul that seemed to be (unthinkable as it was) out to get him. There was a soul that was ruining things. There was a soul that was inept. There was a soul that was (again, unthinkably) consciously trying to ruin the work the Succubus had spent his life setting in motion. There was a soul named Bailey.

And the Succubus consigned him to soul limbo till he could clear away present obligations and draw him under the lens for scrutiny.

So Bailey was sent to limbo.

This is what it was like in soul limbo.

Soft pasty maggoty white. Roiling. Filled with sounds of things desperately trying to see. Slippery underfoot. Without feet. Breathless and struggling for breath. Enclosed. Tight, with great weight pressing down till the pressure was asphyxiating. But without the ability to breathe. Pressed brown to cork, porous and feeling imminent crumbling; then boiling liquid poured through. Pain in every filament and glass fiber. A wet thing settling into bones, turning them to ash and paste. Sickly sweetness, thick and rancid, tongued and swallowed and bloating. Bloating till bursting. A charnel scent. Rising smoke burning and burning the sensitive tissues. Love lost forever, the pain of knowing nothing could ever matter again; melancholia so possessive it wrenched deep inside and twisted organs that never had a chance to function.

Cold tile.

Black crepe paper.

Fingernails scraping slate.

Button pains.

Tiny cuts at sensitive places.

Weakness.

Hammering steadily pain.

That was what it was like in the Succubus's soul limbo. It was not punishment, it was merely the dead end. It was the place where the continuum had not been completed. It was not Hell, for Hell had form and substance and purpose. This was a crater, a void, a storeroom packed with uselessness. It was the place to be sent when pastpresentfuture were one and indeterminate. It was altogether ghastly.

Had Bailey gone mad, this would have been the place for it to happen. But he did not. There was a reason.

One hundred thousand eternities later, the Succubus cleared his desk of present work, filled all orders and answered all current correspondence, finished inventory and took a long-needed vacation. When he returned, before turning his attention to new business, he brought the soul of William Bailey out of limbo and ushered it under the lens.

And found it, somehow, *different*.

Quite unlike the millions and millions of other souls he had stolen.

He could not put a name to the difference. It was not a force, not a vapor, not a quality, not a potentiality, not a look, not a sense, not a capacity, not anything he could pinpoint. And, of course, such a *difference* might be invaluable.

So the Succubus drew a husk from the spare parts and rolling stock bank, and put Bailey's soul into it.

It must be understood that this was a consummately E M P T Y husk. Nothing lived there. It had been scoured clean. It was not like the many bodies into which Bailey had been inserted. Those had had their souls stolen. There was restraining potential in all of them, memories of persona, fetters invisible but present nonetheless. This husk was now Bailey. Bailey only, Bailey free and Bailey whole.

The Succubus summoned Bailey before him.

Bailey might have been able to describe the Succubus, but he had no such desire.

The examination began. The Succubus used light and darkness, lines and spheres, soft and hard, seasons of change, waters of nepenthe, a hand outstretched, the whisper of a memory, carthing, enumeration, suspension, incursion, requital and thirteen others.

He worked over and WHAT through and inside the soul HE DID NOT of Bailey in an attempt to KNOW isolate the wild and dangerous WAS THAT difference that made this soul WHILE HE WAS unlike all others he EXAMINING had ever stolen for his tables of fulfillment BAILEY, BAILEY for the many races WAS that called upon EXAMINING him HIM.

Then, when he had all the knowledge he needed, all the secret places, all the unspoken promises, all the wished and fleshed depressions, the power that lurked in Bailey . . . that had *always* lurked in Bailey . . . before either of them could try or hope to contain it . . . surged free.

(It had been there all along.)
(Since the dawn of time, it had been there.)
(It had always existed.)

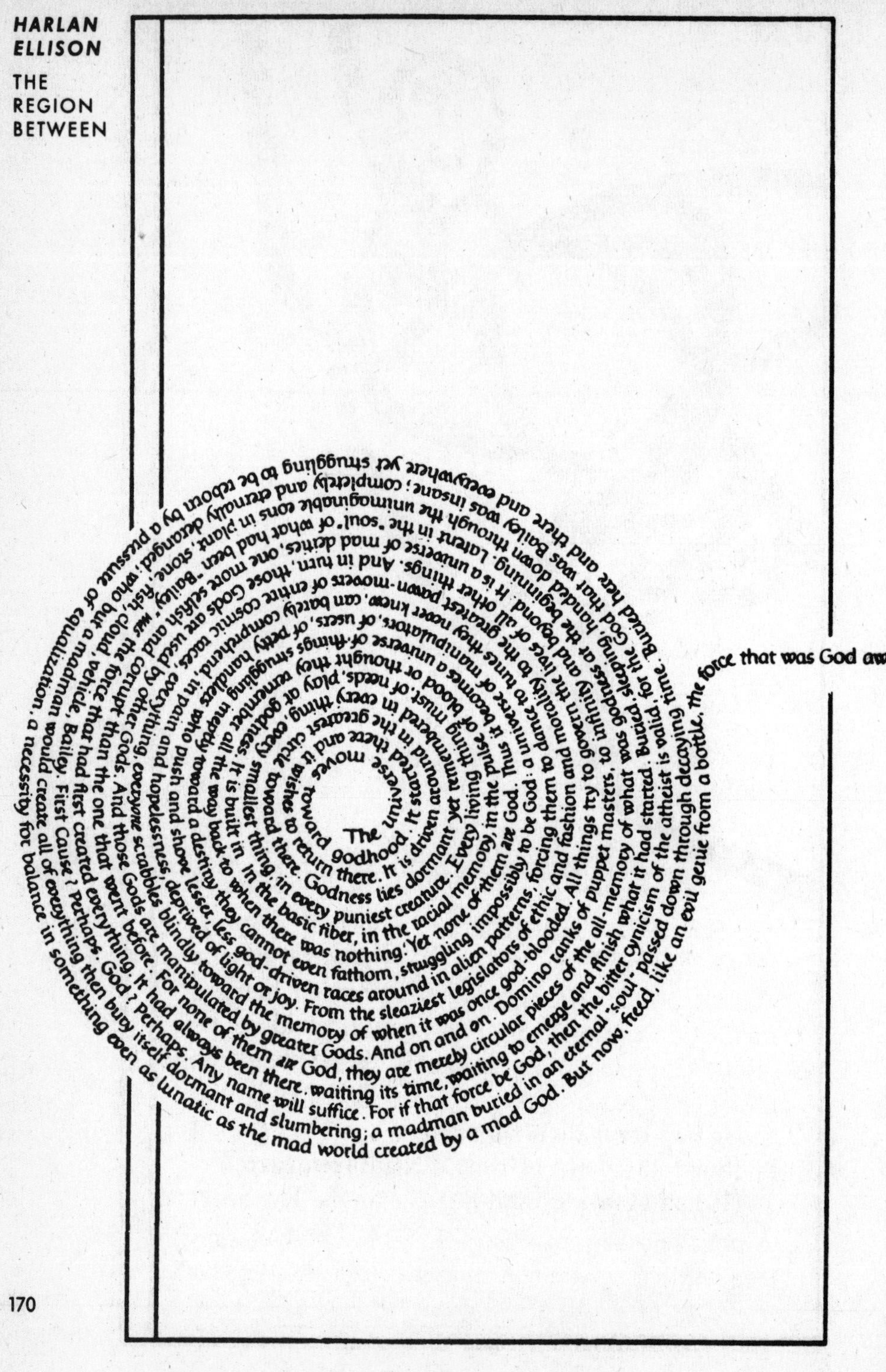
The universe moves toward godhood. It started there and it wishes to return there. It is driven around in the greatest circle toward there. Godness lies dormant yet remembered in every thing, every smallest thing, in every puniest creature. Every living thing must, of needs, play at godness. It is built in. In the basic fiber, in the racial memory, in the pulse of blood or thought they remember all the way back to when there was nothing. Yet none of them are God. Thus it becomes a universe of things struggling mightily toward a destiny they cannot even fathom, struggling impossibly to be God: a universe of manipulators, of users, of petty handlers who push and shove lesser, less god-driven races around in alien patterns, forcing them to dance to tunes they never know, can barely comprehend, in pain and hopelessness, deprived of light or joy. From the sleaziest legislators of ethic and fashion and morality to the greatest pawn-movers of entire cosmic races, everything, everyone scrabbles blindly toward the memory of when it was once god-blooded. All things try to govern the lives of all other things. And in turn, those Gods are used by other Gods. And those Gods are manipulated by greater Gods. And on and on. Domino ranks of puppet masters, to infinity and beyond. It is a universe of mad deities, one more selfish and corrupt than the one that went before. For none of them are God, they are merely circular pieces of the all-memory of what was goodness at the beginning. Latent in the "soul" of what had been "Bailey," was the force that had first created everything. It had always been there, waiting its time, waiting to emerge and finish what it had started. Buried, sleeping, the God, handed down through the unimaginable eons in plant, stone, fish, cloud, vehicle, Bailey. First Cause? Perhaps. God? Perhaps. Any name will suffice. For if that force be God, then the bitter cynicism of the atheist is valid; for the God that was Bailey was insane; completely and eternally deranged; who but a madman would create all of everything then bury itself dormant and slumbering; a madman buried in an eternal "soul" passed down through decaying time. Buried here and there and everywhere yet struggling to be reborn by a pressure of equalization. a necessity for balance in something even as lunatic as the mad world created by a mad God. But now, freed, like an evil genie from a bottle, the force that was God awok

blossomed to fullness, rejuvenated by its slumber, stronger than it had been even when it had created the universe. And, freed, it set about finishing what had begun millennia before.

Bailey remembered the Euthanasia Center, where it had begun for him. Remembered dying. Remembered being reborn. Remembered the life of inadequacy, impotency, hopelessness he had led before he'd given himself up to the Suicide Center. Remembered living as a one-eyed bear creature in a war that would never end. Remembered being a stalker-cat and death of a ghastliness it could not be spoken of. Remembered blueness. Remembered all the other lives. And remembered all the gods that had been less God than himself Bailey. The Lords of Propriety. The Filonii. The Montagasques. The Thils. The Tszechmae. The Duelmasters. The hookworms. The Slavemaster. The Kirk. The pale gray race without a name. And most of all, he remembered the Succubus.

Who thought he was God. Even as the Thieves thought *they* were Gods. But none of them possessed more than the faintest scintilla of the all-memory of godness, and Bailey had become the final repository for the force that *was* God. And now, freed, unleashed, unlocked, swirled down through all of time to this judgment day, Bailey flexed his godness and finished what he had begun at the beginning.

There is only one end to creation. What is created is destroyed, and thus full circle is achieved.

Bailey, God, set about killing the sand castle he had built. The destruction of the universes he had created.

Never before.

Songs unsung.

Washed but never purified.

Dreams spent and visits to come.

Up out of slime.

Drifted down on cool trusting winds.

Heat.

Free.

All created, all equal, all wondering, all vastness.

Gone to night.

The power that was Bailey that was God began its efforts. The husk in which Bailey lived was drawn into the power. The Succubus, screaming for reprieve, screaming for reason, screaming for release or explanation, was drawn into the power. The soul station drawn in. The home world drawn in. The solar system of the home world drawn in. The galaxy and all the galaxies and the metagalaxies and the far island universes and the alter dimensions and the

past back to the beginning and beyond it to the circular place where it became now, and all the shadow places and all the thought recesses and then the very fabric and substance of eternity . . . all of it, everything . . . drawn in.

All of it contained within the power of Bailey who is God.

And then, in one awesome exertion of will, God-Bailey destroys it all, coming full circle, ending what it had been born to do. Gone.

And all that is left is Bailey. Who is dead.

In the region between.

# LAUGH TRACK

I LOVED MY Aunt Babe for three reasons. The first was that even though I was only ten or eleven, she flirted with me as she did with any male of any age who was lucky enough to pass through the heat of her line-of-sight. The second was her breasts — I knew them as "titties" — which left your arteries looking like the Holland Tunnel at rush hour. And the third was her laugh. Never before and never since, in the history of this planet, including every species of life-form extant or extinct, has there been a sound as joyous as my Aunt Babe's laugh which I, as a child, imagined as the sound of the Toonerville Trolley clattering downhill. If you have never seen a panel of that long-gone comic strip, and have no idea what the Toonerville Trolley looked like, forget it. It was some terrific helluva laugh. It could pucker your lips.

My Aunt Babe died of falling asleep and not waking up in 1955, when I was twelve years old.

I first recognized her laugh while watching a segment of *Leave It to Beaver* in November of 1957. It was on the laugh track they'd dubbed in after the show had been shot, but I was only fourteen and thought those were real people laughing at Jerry Mathers's predicament. I yelled for my mother to come quickly, and she came running from the kitchen, her hands all covered with wax from putting up the preserves, and she thought I'd hurt myself or something.

"No . . . no, I'm okay . . . listen!"

She stood there, listening. "Listen to what?" she said after a minute.

"Wait . . . wait . . . *there*! You hear that? It's Aunt Babe. She isn't dead, she's at that show."

My mother looked at me just the way your mother would look at you if you said something like that, and she shook her head, and she said something in Italian my grandmother had no doubt said while shaking her head at *her*, long ago; and she went back to imprisoning boysenberries. *I* sat there and watched The Beav and Eddie Haskell and Whitey Whitney, and broke up every time my Aunt Babe laughed at their antics.

I heard my Aunt Babe's laugh on *The Real McCoys* in 1958; on *Hennessey* and *The Many Loves of Dobie Gillis* in 1959; on *The Andy Griffith Show* in 1960; on *Car 54, Where Are You?* in 1962; and in the years that followed I laughed along with her at *The Dick Van Dyke Show, The Lucy Show, My Favorite Martian, The Addams Family, I Dream of Jeannie,* and *Get Smart!*

In 1970 I heard my Aunt Babe laughing at *Green Acres*, which — though I always liked Eddie Albert and Alvy Moore — I thought was seriously lame; and it bothered me that her taste had deteriorated so drastically. Also, her laugh seemed a little thin. Not as ebulliently Toonerville Trolley going downhill any more.

By 1972 I knew something was wrong because Aunt Babe was convulsing over *Me and the Chimp* but not a sound from her for *My World . . . And Welcome To It.*

By 1972 I was almost thirty, I was working in television, and because I had lived with the sound of my Aunt Babe's laughter for so long, I never thought there was anything odd about it, and I never again mentioned it to anyone.

Then, one night, sitting with a frozen pizza and a Dr. Brown's cream soda, watching an episode of the series I was writing, a sitcom you may remember called *Misty Malone*, I heard my Aunt Babe laughing at a line that the story editor had not understood, that he had rewritten. At that moment, bang! comes the light bulb burning in my brain, comes the epiphany, comes the rude awakening, and I hear myself say, "This is crazy. Babe's been dead and buried lo these seventeen years, and there is strictly *no way* she can be laughing at this moron line that Bill Tidy rewrote from my golden prose, and this is weirder than shit, and *what the hell is going on here!?*"

Besides which, Babe's laugh was now sounding a lot like a 1971 Pinto without chains trying to rev itself out of a snowy rut into which cinders had been shoveled.

And I suppose for the first time I understood that Babe was not alive at the taping of all those shows over the years, but was merely on an old laugh track. At which point I remembered the afternoon in 1953 when she'd taken me to the Hollywood Ranch Market to go shopping, and one of those guys had been standing there handing out tickets to the filming of tv shows, and Babe had taken two tickets to *Our Miss Brooks*, and she'd gone with some passing fancy she was dating at the time, and told us later that she thought Eve Arden was funnier than Lucille Ball.

The laugh track from that 1953 show was obviously still in circulation. Had been, in fact, in circulation for twenty years. And for twenty years my Aunt Babe had been forced to laugh at the same old weary sitcom minutiae, over and over and over. She'd had to laugh at the salt instead of the sugar in Fred MacMurray's coffee; at Granny Clampett sending Buddy Ebsen out to shoot a possum in Beverly Hills; at Bob Cummings trying to conceal Julie Newmar's robot identity; at The Fonz *almost* running a comb through his pompadour; at all the mistaken identities, all the improbable last-minute saves of hopeless situations, all the sophomoric pratfalls from Gilligan to Gidget. And I felt just terrible for her.

Native Americans, what we used to be allowed to call Indians when I was a kid, have a belief that if someone takes their picture with a camera, the box captures their soul. So they shy away from photographers. AmerInds seldom become bank robbers: there are cameras in banks. There was no graduation picture of Cochise in his high school yearbook.

What if — I said to myself — sitting there with that awful pizza growing cold on my lap — what if my lovely Aunt Babe, who had been a Ziegfeld Girl, and who had loved my Uncle Morrie, and who had had such wonderful titties and never let on that she knew *exactly* what I was doing when I'd fall asleep in the car on the way home and snuggle up against them, *what if* my dear Aunt Babe's soul, like her laugh, had been trapped on that goddam track?

And what if she was in there, in there forever, doomed to laugh endlessly at imbecile shit rewritten by ex-hairdressers, instead of roaming around Heaven, flirting with the angels, which I was certain should have been her proper fate, being that she was such a swell person? What if?

It was the sort of thinking that made my head hurt a lot.

And it made me feel even lower, the more I thought about it, because I didn't know what I could do about it. I just knew that that was what had happened to my Aunt Babe; and there she was in there, 
condemned to the stupidest hell imaginable. In some arcane way,

she had been doomed to an eternity of electronic restimulation. In speech therapy they have a name for it: cataphasia: verbal repetition. But I could tell from the frequency with which I was now hearing Babe, and from the indiscriminate use to which her laugh was being put — not just on *M*A*S*H* and *Maude*, but on yawners like *The Sandy Duncan Show* and a midseason replacement with Larry Hagman called *Here We Go Again*, which didn't — and the way her laugh was starting to slur like an ice-skating elephant, that she wasn't having much fun in there. I began to believe that she was like some sort of beanfield slave, every now and then being goosed electronically to laugh. She was a video galley slave, one of the pod people, a member of some ghastly high-frequency chain gang. Cataphasia, but worse. Oh, how I wanted to save her; to drag her out of there and let her tormented soul bound free like a snow rabbit, to vanish into great white spaces where the words *Laverne and Shirley* had never trembled in the lambent mist.

Then I went to bed and didn't think about it again until 1978.

By September of 1978 I was working for Bill Tidy again. In years to come I would refer to that pox-ridden period as the Season I Stepped in a Pile of Tidy.

Each of us has one dark eminence in his or her life who somehow has the hoodoo sign on us. Persons so cosmically loathsome that we continually spend our time when in their company silently asking ourselves, *What the hell, what the bloody hell, what the everlasting Technicolor hell am I doing sitting here with this ambulatory piece of offal? This is the worst person who ever got born, and someone ought to wash out his life with a bar of Fels-Naptha.*

But there you sit, and the next time you blink, there you sit again. It was probably the way Catherine the Great felt on her dates with Rasputin.

Bill Tidy had that hold over me.

In 1973 when I'd been just a struggling sitcom writer, getting his first breaks on *Misty Malone*, Tidy had been the story editor. An authoritarian Fascist with all the creative insight of a sump pump. But now, a mere five years later, things were a great deal different: I had created a series, which meant I was a struggling sitcom writer with my name on a parking slot at the studio; and Bill Tidy, direct lineal descendant of The Blob that tried to eat Steve McQueen, had swallowed up half the television industry. He was now the heavy-breathing half of Tidy-Spellberg Productions, in partnership with another ex-hairdresser named Harvey Spellberg, whom he'd met during a metaphysical retreat to Reno, Nevada. They'd become corporate soul mates while praying over the crap tables and in just a few years had built upon their unerring sense of how much debasement the American television-viewing audience could sustain (a much higher gag-reflex level than even the experts had postulated, thereby paving the way for *Three's Company*), to emerge as "prime suppliers" of gibbering lunacy for the three networks.

Bill Tidy was to Art as Pekin, North Dakota is to wild nightlife.

But he was the fastest money in town when it came to marketing a series idea to one of the networks, and my agent had sent over the prospectus for *Ain't It the Truth*, without my knowing it; and before I had a chance to scream, "Nay, nay, my liege! There are some things mere humans were never meant to know, Doctor Von Frankenstein!" the network had made a development deal with the Rupert Murdoch of mindlessness, and of a sudden I was — as they so aptly put it — in bed with Bill Tidy again.

This is the definition of ambivalence: to have struggled in the ditches for five years, to have created something that was guaranteed to get on the air, and to have that creation masterminded by a toad with the charm of a charnel house and the intellect of a head of lettuce. I thought seriously of moving to Pekin, North Dakota, where the words *coaxial cable* are as speaking-in-tongues to the simple, happy natives; where the blight of Jim Nabors has never manifested itself; where I could open a grain and feed store and never have to sit in the same room with Bill Tidy as he picked his nose and surreptitiously examined the findings.

But I was weak, and even if the series croaked before the season ran its course, I would have a credit that could lead to bigger things. So I pulled down the covers, plumped the pillows, straightened the rubber pishy-pad, and got into bed with Bill Tidy.

By September, I was a raving lunatic. I spent much of my time dreaming about biting the heads off chickens. The deranged wind of network babble and foaming Tidyism blew through the haunted cathedral of my brain. What little originality and invention I'd brought to the series concept — and at best what we're talking about here is prime-time network situation comedy, not a PBS tour conducted by Alistair Cooke through the Library of Alexandria — was steadily and firmly leached out of the production by Bill Tidy. Any time a line or a situation with some charm or esthetic value dared to peek its head out of the *merde* of the scripts, Tidy as Grim Reaper would lurch onto the scene swinging the scythe of his demented bad taste, and intellectual decapitation instantly followed.

I developed a hiatic hernia, I couldn't hold down solid food and took to subsisting on strained mung from Gerber's inexhaustible and vomitous larder, I snapped at everyone, sex was a concept whose time had come and gone for me, and I saw my gentle little offering to the Gods of Comedy turn into something best suited for a life under mossy stones.

Had I known that on the evening of Thursday, September 14, 1978 *Ain't It the Truth* was to premiere opposite a new ABC show called *Mork & Mindy*, and that within three weeks a dervish named Robin Williams would be dining on Nielsen rating shares the way sharks devour entire continents, I might have been able to hold onto enough of my sanity to weather the Dark Ages. And I wouldn't have gotten involved with Wally Modisett, the phantom sweetener, and I wouldn't have spoken into the black box, and I wouldn't have found the salvation for my dead Aunt Babe's soul.

But early in September Williams had not yet uttered his first *Nanoo-nanoo* (except on a spinoff segment of *Happy Days* and who the hell watched *that*?) and we had taped the first three segments of *Ain't It the Truth* before a live audience at the Burbank Studios, if you can call those who voluntarily go to tapings of sitcoms as "living," and late one night the specter of Bill Tidy appeared in the doorway of my office, his great horse face looming down at me like the demon that emerges from the *Night on Bald Mountain* section of Disney's *Fantasia*; and his sulphurous breath reached across the room and made all the little hairs in my nostrils curl up and try to pull themselves out so they could run away and hide in the back of my head somewhere; and the two reflective puddles of Vegemite he called eyes smoldered at me, and this is what he said. First he said:

"That fuckin' fag cheese-eater director's never gonna work again. He's gonna go two days over, mark my words. I'll see the putzola never works again."

Then he said:

"I bought another condo in Phoenix. Solid gold investment. Better than Picassos."

Then he said:

"I heard it at lunch today. A cunt is just a clam that's wearin' a fright-wig. Good, huh?"

Then he said:

"I want you to stay late tonight. I can't trust anyone else. Guy'll show up here about eight. He'll find you. Just stay put till he gets here. Never mind a name. He'll make himself known to you. Take him over to the mixing studio, run the first three shows for him. Nobody else gets in, *kapeesh, paisan*?"

I was having such a time keeping my gorge from becoming buoyant that I barely heard his directive. Bill Tidy gave new meaning to the words King of the Pig People. The only groups he had failed to insult in the space of thirteen seconds were blacks, Orientals, paraplegics, and Doukhobors, and if I didn't quickly agree to his demands, he'd no doubt round on them, as well. "Got it, Bill. Yessiree, you can count on me. Uh-huh, absolutely, right-on, dead-center, I hear ya talkin', I'm your boy, I loves workin' foah ya Massa' Tidy-suh, you can bank on me!"

He gave me a look. "You know, Angelo, you are gettin' stranger and stranger, like some kind of weird insect."

And he turned and he vanished, leaving me all alone there in the encroaching darkness, just tuning my antennae and rubbing my hind legs together.

I was slumped down on my spine, eyes closed, in the darkened office with just the desk lamp doing its best to rage against the dying of the light, when I heard someone whisper huskily, "Turn off the light."

I opened my eyes. The room was empty. I looked out the window behind my desk. It was night. I was three flights up in the production building. No one was there.

"The light. Turn off the light, can you hear what I'm telling you?"

I strained forward toward the open door and the dark hallway beyond. "You talking to me?" Nothing moved out there.

"The light. Slow; you're a very slow person."

Being Catholic, I respond like a Pavlovian dog to guilt. I turned out the light.

From the deeper darkness of the hallway I saw something shadowy detach itself and glide into my office. "Can I keep my eyes open," I said, "or would a blindfold serve to palliate this unseemly paranoia of yours?"

The shadowy form snorted disdainfully. "At these prices you can use words even bigger than that and I don't give a snap." I heard fingers snap. "You care to take me over to the mixing booth?"

I stood up. Then I sat down. "Don't wanna play." I folded my arms.

The shadowy figure got a petulant tone in his voice. "Okay, c'mon now. I've got three shows to do, and I haven't got all night. The world keeps turning. Let's go."

"Not in the cards, Lamont Cranston. I've been ordered around a lot these last few days; and since I don't know you from a stubborn stain, I'm digging in my heels. Remember the Alamo. Millions for defense, not one cent for tribute. The only thing we have to fear is fear itself. Forty-four forty or fight."

"I think that's fifty-four forty or fight," he said.

We thought about that for a while. Then after a long time I said, "Who the hell are you, and what is it you do that's so illicit and unspeakable that first of all Bill Tidy would hire you to do it, which puts you right on the same level as me, which is the level of graverobbers, dog catchers, and horse-dopers; and second, which is so furtive and vile that you have to do it in the dead of the night, coming in here wearing garb fit only for a commando raid? Answer in the key of C#."

He chuckled. It was a nice chuckle. "You're okay, kid," he said. And he dropped into the chair on the other side of my desk where writers pitching ideas for stories sat; and he turned on the desk lamp.

"Wally Modisett," he said, extending a black-gloved hand. "Sound editor." I took the hand and we shook. "Free-lance," he said.

That didn't sound so ominous. "Why the Creeping Phantom routine?"

Then he said the word no one in Hollywood says. He looked intently at all of my face, particularly around the mouth, where lies come from, and he said: "Sweetening."



If I'd had a silver crucifix, I'd have thrust it at him at arm's length. *Be still my heart*, I thought.

There are many things of which one does not speak in the television industry. One does not repeat the name of the NBC executive who was making women writers give him blowjobs in his office in exchange for writing assignments, even though he's been pensioned off with a lucrative production deal at a major studio and the network paid for his psychiatric counseling for several years. One does not talk about the astonishing Digital Dance done by the royalty numbers in a major production company's ledgers, thereby fleecing several superstar participants out of their "points" in the profits, even though it made a large stink on the *World News Tonight* and everybody scampered around trying to settle out of court while *TV Guide* watched. One does not talk about how the studio frightened a buxom ingénue who had become an overnight national sensation into modifying her demands for triple salary in the second season her series was on the air, not even to hint knowingly of a kitchen chair with nails driven up through the seat from the underside.

And one never, never, no never ever talks about the phantom sweeteners.

*This show was taped before a live studio audience!*

If you've heard it once, you've heard it at least twice. And so when those audiences break up and fall on the floor and roll around and drum their heels and roar so hard they have to clutch their stomachs and tears of hilarity blind them and their noses swell from crying too much and they sound as if they're all genetically selected high-profile tickleables, you fall right in with them because that ain't canned laughter, it's a live audience, onaccounta *This show was taped before a live studio audience.*

While high in the fly loft of the elegant opera house, the Phantom Sweetener looks down and chuckles smugly.

They're legendary. For years there was only Charlie Douglas, a name never spoken. A laugh man. A sound technician. A sweetener. They say he still uses laughs kidnapped off radio shows from the Forties and Fifties. Golden laughs. Unduplicable originals. Special, rich laughs that blend and support and lift and build a resonance that punches your subliminal buttons. Laughs from *The Jack Benny Show*, from segments of *The Fred Allen Show* down in Allen's Alley, from *The Chase & Sanborn Hour* with Edgar Bergen and Charlie McCarthy (one of the shows on which Charlie mixed it up with

W. C. Fields). The laughs that Ed Wynn got, that Goodman and Jane Ace got, that Fanny Brice got. Rich, teak-colored laughs from a time in this country when humor wasn't produced by slugs like Bill Tidy. For a long time Charlie Douglas was all alone as the man who could make even dull thuds go over boffola.

But no one knew how good he was. Except the IRS, which took note of his underground success in the industry by raking in vast amounts of his hard-earned cash.

Using the big Spotmaster cartridges — carts that looked like eight-track cassettes, with thirty cuts per cart — twelve or fourteen per job — Charlie Douglas became a hired gun of guffaws, a highwayman of hee-haws, Zorro of zaniness; a troubleshooter working extended overtime in a specialized craft where he was a secret weapon with a never-spoken code-name.

Carrying with him from studio to studio the sounds of great happy moments stolen from radio signals long since on their way to Proxima Centauri.

And for a long time Charlie Douglas had it all to himself, because it was a closely guarded secret; not one of the open secrets perhaps unknown in Kankakee or Key West, like Merv Griffin or Ida Lupino or Roger Moore; but common knowledge at the Polo Lounge and Chasen's.

But times got fat and the industry grew and there was more work, and more money, than one Phantom Sweetener could handle.

So the mother of invention called forth more audio soldiers of fortune: Carroll Pratt and Craig Porter and Tom Kafka and two silent but sensational guys from Tokyo and techs at Glen Glenn Sound and Vidtronics. And you never mention their names or the shows they've sweetened, lest you get your buns run out of the industry. It's an open secret, closely held by the community. The networks deny their existence, the production company executives would let you nail them hands and feet to their office doors before they'd cop to having their shows shot before a live studio audience sweetened. In the dead of night by the phantoms.

Of whom Wally Modisett is the most mysterious.

And here I sat, across from him. He wore a black turtleneck sweater, jeans, and gloves. And he placed on the desk the legendary black box. I looked at it. He chuckled.

"That's it," he said.

"I'll be damned," I said.

I felt as if I were in church.

In sound editing, the key is equalization. Bass, treble, they can isolate a single laugh, pull it off the track, make a match even twenty years later. They put them on "endless loops" and then lay the show over to a multitrack audio machine, and feed in one laugh on a separate track, meld it, blend it in, punch it up, put that special button-punch giggle right in there with the live studio audience track. They do it, they've always done it, and soon now they'll be able to do it with digital encoding. And he sat right there in front of me with the legendary black box. Legendary, because Wally Modisett was an audio genius, an electronics Machiavelli who had built himself a secret system to do it all through that little black box that he took to the studios in the dead of night when everyone was gone, right into the booth at the mixing room, and he didn't need a multitrack.

If it weren't something to be denied to the grave, the *mensches* and moguls of the television industry would have Wally Modisett's head right up there on Mt. Rushmore in the empty space between Teddy Roosevelt and Abe Lincoln.

What took twenty-two tracks for a combined layering on a huge machine, Wally Modisett carried around in the palm of his hand. And looking at his long, sensitive face, with the dark circles under his eyes, I guess I saw a foreshadowing of great things to come. There was laughter in his eyes.

I sat there most of the night, running the segments of *Ain't It the Truth*. I sat down below in the screening room while the Phantom Sweetener locked himself up in the booth. *No one*, he made it clear, watched him work his magic.

And the segments played, with the live audience track, and he used his endless loops from his carts — labeled "Single Giggle 1" and "Single Giggle 2" and slightly larger "Single Giggle 3" and the dreaded "Titter/Chuckle" and the ever-popular "Rim Shot" — those loops of his own design, smaller than those made by Spotmaster, and he built and blended and sweetened the hell out of that laugh track till even I chuckled at moronic material Bill Tidy had bastardized to a level that only the Jukes and Kallikaks could have found uproarious.

And then, on the hundredth playback, after Modisett had added another increment of hilarity, I heard my dead Aunt Babe. I sat straight up in the plush screening room chair, and I slapped the switch on the console that fed into the booth, and I yelled, "Hey! That last one! That last laugh . . . what was that . . . ?"

He didn't answer for a moment. Then, tinnily, through the console intercom, he said, "I call it a wonky."

"Where'd it come from?"

Silence.

"C'mon, man, where'd you get that laugh?"

"Why do you want to know?"

I sat there for a second, then I said, "Listen, either you've got to come down here, or let me come up there. I've got to talk to you."

Silence. Then after a moment, "Is there a coffee machine around here somewhere?"

"Yeah, over near the theater."

"I'll be down in about fifteen minutes. We'll have a cup of coffee. Think you can hold out that long?"

"If you nail a duck's foot down, does he walk in circles?"

It took me almost an hour to convince him. Finally, he decided I was almost as bugfuck as he was, and the idea was so crazy it might be fun to try and work it out. I told him I was glad he'd decided to try it because if he hadn't I'd have followed him to his secret lair and found some way to blackmail him into it, and he said, "Yeah, I can see you'd do that. You're not a well person."

"Try working with Bill Tidy sometime," I said. "It's enough to turn Mother Teresa into a hooker."

"Give me some time," he said. "I'll get back to you."

I didn't hear from him for a year and a half. *Ain't It the Truth* had gone to the boneyard to join *The Chicago Teddy Bears* and *Angie* and *The Dumplings*. Nobody missed it, not even its creator. Bill Tidy had wielded his scythe with skill.

Then just after two A.M. on a summer night in Los Angeles, my phone rang, and I fumbled the receiver off the cradle and found my face somehow, and a voice said, "I've got it. Come." And he gave me an address; and I went.

The warehouse was large, but all his shit was jammed into one corner. Multitracks and oscilloscopes and VCRs and huge 3-mil-thick Mylar foam speakers that looked like the rear seats of a 1933 Chevy. And right in the middle of the floor was a larger black box.

"You're kidding?" I said.

He was like a ten-year-old kid. "Would I shit you? I'm telling you, fellah, I've gone where no man has gone before. I has done did it! Jonas Salk and Marie Curie and Lee De Forest and all the rest of them have got to move over, slide aside, get to the back of the bus." And he leaped around, howling, "*I am the king!*"

When I was able to peel him off the catwalks and made a spider-web tracery above us, he started making some sense. Not a *lot* of sense, because I didn't understand half of what he was saying, but enough sense for me to begin to believe that this peculiar obsession of mine might have some toe in the world of reality.

"The way they taped shows back in 1953, when your aunt went to that *Our Miss Brooks*, was they'd use a ¼" machine, reel-to-reel. They'd have directional mikes above the audience, to separate individual laughs. One track for the program, and another track for the audience. Then they'd just pick up what they want, equalize, and sock it onto one track for later use. Sweetened as need be."

He went to a portable fridge and pulled out a Dr. Pepper and looked in my direction. I shook my head. I was too excited for junk food. He popped the can, took a swig and came back to me.

"The first thing I had to do was find the original tape, the master. Took me a long time. It was in storage with . . . well, you don't need to know that. It was in storage. I must have gone through a thousand old masters. But I found her. Then I had to pull her out. But not just the *sound* of her laugh. The actual laugh itself. The electronic impulses. I used an early model of this to do it." He waved a hand at the big black box.

"She'd started sounding weak to me, over the years," I said. "Slurred sometimes. Scratchy."

"Yeah, yeah, yeah." Impatient to get on with the great revelation. "That was because she was being diminished by fifth, sixth, twentieth generation re-recording. No, I got her at full strength, and I did what I call 'deconvolving.' "



"Which is?"

"Never mind."

"You going to say 'never mind' every time I ask what the hell you did to make it work?"

"As Groucho used to say to contestants, 'You bet your ass.'"

I shrugged. It was his fairy tale.

"Once I had her deconvolved, I put her on an endless loop. But not just *any* kind of normal standard endless loop. You want to know what kind of endless loop I put her on?"

I looked at him. "You going to tell me to piss off?"

"No. Go ahead and ask."

"All right already: I'm asking. What the hell kind of endless loop did you put her on?"

"A moebius loop."

He looked at me as if he'd just announced the birth of a two-headed calf. I didn't know what the hell he was talking about. That didn't stop me from whistling through my two front teeth, loud enough to cause echoes in the warehouse, and I said, "No shit?!?"

He seemed pleased, and went on faster than before. "Now I feed her into the computer, digitally encode her so she never diminishes. Slick, right? Then I feed in a program that says harmonize and synthesize her, get a simulation mapping for the instrument that produced that sound; in other words, your aunt's throat and tongue and palate and teeth and larynx and alla that. Now comes the tricky part. I build a program that postulates an actual physical *situation*, a terrain, a *place* where that voice exists. And I send the computer on a search to bring me back everything that comprises that place."

"Hold hold *hold* it, Lamont. Are you trying to tell me that you went in search of the Land of Oz, using that loop of Babe's voice?"

He nodded about a hundred and sixteen times.

"How'd you do *that*? I know: piss off. But that's some kind of weird metaphysical shit. It can't be done."

"Not by drones, fellah. But *I* can do it. I *did* it." He nodded at the black box.

"The tv sitcom land where my dead Aunt Babe is trapped, it's in there, in that cube?"

"Ah calls it a *simularity matrix*," he said, with an accent that could get him killed in SouthCentral L.A.



"You can call it rosewater if you like, Modisett, but it sounds like the foothills of Bandini Mountain to me."

His grin was the mutant offspring of a sneer and a smirk. I'd seen that kind of look only once, on the face of a failed academic at a collegiate cocktail party. Later that evening the guy used the smirk ploy once too often and a little tweety-bird of an English prof gave him high cause to go see a periodontal reconstructionist.

"I can reconstruct her like a clone, right in the machine," he said.

"How do you know? Tried it yet?"

"It's your aunt, not mine," he said. "I told you I'd get back to you. Now I'm back to you, and I'm ready to run the showboat out to the middle of the river."

So he turned on a lot of things on the big board he had, and he moved a lot of slide-switches up the gain slots, and he did this, and he did that, and a musical hum came from the Quad speakers, and he looked over his shoulder at me, across the tangle of wires and cables that disappeared into the black box, and he said, "Wake her up."

I said, "What?"

He said, "Wake her. She's been an electronic code for almost twenty-five years. She's been asleep. She's an amputated frog leg. Send the current through her."

"How?"

"Call her. She'll recognize your voice."

"How? It's been a long time. I don't sound like the kid I was when she died."

"Trust me," he said. "Call her."

I felt like a goddam fool. "Where do I speak?"

"Just speak, asshole. She'll hear you."

So I stood there in the middle of that warehouse and I said, "Aunt Babe?" There was nothing.

"A little louder. Gentle, but louder. Don't startle her."

"You're outta your . . ." His look silenced me. I took a deep breath and said, a little louder, "Hey, Aunt Babe? You in there? It's me, Angelo."

I heard something. At first it sounded like a mouse running toward me across a long blackboard, a blackboard maybe a hundred miles long. Then there was something like the wind you hear in thick woods in the autumn. Then the sound of somebody unwrapping Christmas presents. Then the sound of water, like surf, pouring into a cave at the base of a cliff, and then draining out again. Then the sound of a baby crying and the sound suddenly getting very deep as if it were a three-hundred-pound killer baby that wanted to be fed parts off a freshly-killed dinosaur. This kind of torrential idiocy went on for a while, and then, abruptly, out of nowhere, I heard my Aunt Babe clearing her throat, as if she were getting up in the morning. That phlegmy throat-clearing sound that sounds like quarts of yogurt being shoveled out of a sink.

"Angelo . . . ?"

I crossed myself about eleven times, ran off a few fast Hail Mary's and Our Father's, swallowed hard and said, "Yeah, Aunt Babe, it's me. How are you?"

"Let me, for a moment here, let me get my bearings." It took more than a moment. She was silent for a few minutes, though she did once say, "I'll be right with you, *mio caro.*"

And finally, I heard her say, "I am really fit to be tied. Do you have any idea what they have put me through? Do you have even the *faintest* idea how many times they've made me watch *The Partridge Family*? Do you have any *idea* how much I hate that kind of music? Never Cole Porter, never Sammy Cahn, not even a little Gus Edwards; I'd settle for Sigmund Romberg after those squalling children. *Caro nipote, quanto mi sei mancato!* Angelo . . . *bello bello.* I want you to tell me everything that's happened, because as soon as I get a chance, I'm going to make a stink you're not going to believe!"

It *was* Babe. My dearest Aunt Babe. I hadn't heard that wonderful mixture of pungent English and lilting Italian with its show-biz Yiddish resonances in almost thirty years. I hadn't *spoken* any Italian in nearly twenty years. But I heard myself saying to the empty air, "*Come te la sei passata?*" How've you been?

"*Ti voglio bene — bambino caro.* I feel just fine. A bit fuzzy, I've been asleep a while but *come sta la famiglia? Anche quelli che non posso soppartare.*"

So I told her all about the family, even the ones she couldn't stand, like Uncle Nuncio with breath like a goat, and Carmine's wife, Giuletta, who'd always called Babe a floozy. And after a while she had me try to explain what had happened to her, and I did the best I could, to which she responded, "*Non mi sento come un fantasma.*"

So I told her she didn't feel like a ghost because she *wasn't*, strictly speaking, a ghost. More like a random hoot in the empty night.

Well, that didn't go over too terrific, because in an instant she'd grasped the truth that if she wasn't going where it is that dead people go, she'd never meet up with my Uncle Morrie again; and that made her very sad. "*Oh, dio!*" and she started crying.

So I tried to jolly her out of it by talking about all the history that had transpired since 1955, but it turned out she knew most of it anyhow. After all, hadn't she been stuck there, inside the biggest blabbermouth the world had ever known? Even though she'd been in something like an alpha state of almost-sleep, her essence had been *saturated* with news and special reports, docudramas and public service announcements, talk shows and panel discussions, network extra alerts and hour-by-hour live coverage of fast-breaking events.

Eventually I got around to explaining how I'd gotten in touch with her, about Modisett and the big black box, about how the Phantom Sweetener had deconvolved her, and about Bill Tidy.

She was not unfamiliar with the name.

After all, hadn't she been stuck there, inside the all-talking, all-singing, all-dancing electromagnetic pimp for Tidy's endless supply of brain-damaged, insipid persiflage?

I painted Babe a loving word-portrait of my employer and our unholy liaison. She said: "*Stronzo! Figlio di una mignotta! Mascalzone!*" She also called him *bischero*, by which I'm sure she meant the word in its meaning of goof, or simpleton, rather than literally: "man with erection."

Modisett, who spoke no Italian, stared wildly at me, seeming to bask in the unalloyed joy of having tapped a line into some Elsewhere. Yet even he could tell from the tone of revulsion in Babe's disembodied voice that she had suffered long under the exquisite tortures of swimming in a sea of Tidy product.

What Tidy had been doing to me seemed to infuriate her. She was still my loving Aunt Babe.

So I spent all that night, and the next day, and the next night — while Modisett mostly slept and emptied Dr. Pepper down his neck — chatting at leisure with my dead Aunt Babe.

You'll never know how angry someone can get from prolonged exposure to Gary Coleman.



• • •

The Phantom Sweetener can't explain what followed. He says it defies the rigors of Boolean logic, whatever the hell that means. He says it transcends the parameters of Maxwell's Equations, which ought to put Maxwell in a bit of a snit. He says (and with more than a touch of the gibber in his voice) it deflowers, rapes, & pillages, breaks & enters Minkowski's Covariant Tensor. He says it is enough to start Philo T. Farnsworth spinning so hard in his grave that he would carom off Vladimir K. Zworykin in his. He says it would get Marvin Minsky up at M.I.T. speaking in tongues. He says — and this one *really* turned me around and opened my eyes — he says (wait for it), "Distorts Riemannian geometry." To which I said, "You have *got* to be shitting me! Not Riemannian gefuckingometry!?!"

This is absolute babble to me, but it's got Modisett down on all fours, foaming at the mouth and sucking at the electrical outlets.

Apparently, Babe has found pathways in the microwave comm-system. The Phantom Sweetener says it might have happened because of what he calls "print-through," that phenomenon that occurs on audio tape when one layer magnetizes the next layer, so you hear an echo of the word or sound that is next to be spoken. He says if the tape is wound "heads out" and is stored that way, then the signal will jump. The signal that is my dead Aunt Babe has jumped. And keeps jumping. She's loose in the comm-system and she ain't asking where's the beef: *she knows!* And Modisett says the reason they can't catch her and wipe her is that old tape *always* bleeds through. Which is why, when Bill Tidy's big multimillion-dollar sitcom aired last year, instead of the audience roaring with laughter, there was the voice of this woman shouting above the din, "That's stupid! Worse than stupid! That's *bore*-ing! Ka-ka! C'mon folks, let's have a good old-fashioned Bronx cheer for crapola like this! Let's show 'em what we *really* think of this flopola!"

And then, instead of augmented laughter, instead of yoks, came a raspberry that could have floated the Titanic off the bottom.

Well, they pulled the tape, and they tried to find her, but she was gone, skipping off across the simularity matrix like Bambi, only to turn up the next night on another Tidy-Spellberg abomination.

Well, there was no way to stop it, and the networks got very leery of Tidy and Company, because they couldn't even use the millions of billions of dollars worth of shitty rerun shows they'd paid billions and millions for syndication rights to, and they sued the hell out of Bill Tidy, who went crazy as a soup sandwich not too long ago, and I'm told he's trying to sell ocean view lots in some place like Pekin, North Dakota, and living under the name Silas Marner or somesuch because half the civilized world is trying to find him to sue his ass off.

And I might have a moment of compassion for the creep, but I haven't the time. I have three hit shows running at the moment, one each on ABC, NBC, and CBS.

They are big hits because somehow, in a way that no one seems able to figure out, there are all these little subliminal buttons being pushed by my shows, and they just soar to the top of the Nielsen ratings.

And I said to Aunt Babe, "Listen, don't you want to go to Heaven, or wherever it is? I mean, don't you want out of that limbo existence?"

And with love, because she wanted to protect her *bambino caro*, because she wanted to make up for the fact that I didn't have her wonderful bosom to fall asleep on any more, she said, "Get out of here, Angelo, my darling? What . . . and leave show business?"

The Author would like to thank Franco & Carol Betti, Jody Clark, Bart Di Grazia, Tom Kafka, Alan Kay, Ann Knight, Gil Lamont, Michele D. Malamud, and the Grand Forks (North Dakota) Public Library reference staff for invaluable assistance in getting the details of this story written accurately.

# EIDOLONS

## Eidolon:
## *a phantom, an apparition, an image*

Ancient geographers gave a mystic significance to that extremity of land, the borderland of the watery unknown at the southwestern tip of Europe. Marinus and Ptolemy knew it as *Promontorium Sacrum*, the sacred promontory. Beyond that beyondmost edge, lay nothing. Or rather, lay a place that was fearful and unknowable, a place in which it was always the twenty-fifth hour of the day, the thirtieth or thirty-first of February; a turbid ocean of lost islands where golden mushroom trees reached always toward the whispering face of the moon; where tricksy life had spawned beasts and beings more of satin and ash than of man and woman; dominion of dreams, to which the unwary might journey, but whence they could never return.

My name is Vizinczey, and my background is too remarkable to be detailed here. Suffice to note that before Mr. Brown died in my arms, I had distinguished myself principally with occupations and behavior most cultures reward by the attentions of the headsman and the *strappado*. Suffice to note that before Mr. Brown died in my arms, the most laudable engagement in my *vita* was as the manager and sole roustabout of an abattoir and ossuary in Li Shih-min. Suffice to note that there were entire continents I was forbidden to visit, and that even my closest acquaintances, the family of Sawney Beane, chose to avoid social intercourse with me.

I was a pariah. Whatever land in which I chose to abide, became a land of darkness. Until Mr. Brown died in my arms, I was a thing without passion, without kindness.

While in Sydney — Australia being one of the three remaining continents where hunting dogs would not be turned out to track me down — I inquired if there might be a shop where authentic military miniatures, toy soldiers of the sort H. G. Wells treasured, could be purchased. A clerk in a bookstore recalled "a customer of mine in Special Orders mentioned something like that . . . a curious little man . . . a Mr. Brown."

I got onto him, through the clerk, and was sent round to see him at his home. The moment he opened the door and our eyes met, he was frightened of me. For the brief time we spent in each other's company, he never ceased, for a moment, to fear me. Ironically, he was one of the few ambulatory creatures on this planet that I meant no harm. Toy soldiers were my hobby, and I held in high esteem those who crafted, painted, amassed or sold them. In truth, it might be said of the Vizinczey that was I in those times before Mr. Brown died in my arms, that my approbation for toy soldiers and their aficionados was the sole salutary aspect of my nature. So, you see, he had no reason to fear me. Quite the contrary. I mention this to establish, in spite of the police records and the warrants still in existence, seeking my apprehension, I had nothing whatever to do with the death of Mr. Brown.

He did not invite me in, though he stepped aside with a tremor and permitted entrance. Cognizant of his terror at my presence, I was surprised that he locked the door behind me. Then, looking back over his shoulder at me with mounting fear, he led me into an enormous central drawing room of his home, a room expanded to inordinate size by the leveling of walls that had formed adjoining areas. In that room, on every horizontal surface, Mr. Brown had positioned rank after rank of the most astonishing military miniatures I had ever seen.

Perfect in the most minute detail, painted so artfully that I could discern no brushstroke, in colors and tones and hues so accurate and lifelike that they seemed rather to have been created with pigmentations inherent, the battalions, cohorts, regiments, legions, phalanxes, brigades and squads of metal figurines blanketed in array without a single empty space, every inch of floor, tables, cabinets, shelves, window ledges, risers, showcases and countless numbers of stacked display boxes.

Enthralled, I bent to study more closely the infinite range of fighting men. There were Norman knights and German Landsknecht, Japanese samurai and Prussian dragoons, foot grenadier of the

French Imperial Guard and Spanish conquistadors. U.S. 7th Cavalry troopers from the Indian wars; Dutch musketeers and pikemen who marched with the army of Maurice of Nassau during the long war of independence fought by the Netherlands against the Spanish Habsburgs; Greek hoplites in bronze helmets and stiff cuirasses; cocked hat riflemen of Morgan's Virginia Rifles who repulsed Burgoyne's troops with their deadly accurate Pennsylvania long-barrels; Egyptian chariot-spearmen and French Foreign Legionnaires; Zulu warriors from Shaka's legions and English longbowmen from Agincourt; Anzacs and Persian Immortals and Assyrian slingers; Cossacks and Saracen warriors in chain-mail and padded silk; 82nd Airborne paratroopers and Israeli jet pilots and Wehrmacht Panzer commanders and Russian infantrymen and Black Hussars of the 5th Regiment.

And as I drifted through a mist of wonder and pleasure, from array to array, one overriding observation dominated even my awe in the face of such artistic grandeur.

Each and every figure — to the last turbaned Cissian, trousered Scythian, wooden-helmeted Colchian or Pisidian with an oxhide shield — every one of them bore the most exquisite expression of terror and hopelessness. Faces twisted in anguish at the precise moment of death, or more terribly, the moment of *realization* of personal death, each soldier looked up at me with eyes just fogging with tears, with mouth half-open to emit a scream, with fingers reaching toward me in splay-fingered hope of last-minute reprieve.

These were not merely painted representations.

The faces were individual. I could see every follicle of beard, every drop of sweat, every frozen tic of agony. They seemed able to complete the shriek of denial. They looked as if, should I blink, they would spring back to life and then fall dead as they were intended.

Mr. Brown had left narrow aisles of carpet among the vast armadas, and I had wandered deep into the shoe-top grassland of the drawing room with the little man behind me, still locked up with fear but attendant at my back. Now I rose from examining a raiding party of Viet Cong frozen in attitudes of agony as the breath of life stilled in them, and I turned to Mr. Brown with apparently such a look on my face that he blurted it out. I could not have stopped the confession had I so desired.



They were not metal figurines. They were flesh turned to pewter.

Mr. Brown had no artistic skill save the one ability to snatch soldiers off the battlefields of time, to freeze them in metal, to miniaturize them, and to sell them. Each commando and halberdier captured in the field and reduced, at the moment of his death . . . realizing in that moment that Heaven or whatever Valhalla in which he believed, was to be denied him. An eternity of death in miniature.

"You are a greater ghoul than ever I could have aspired to become," I said.

His fright overcame him at that moment. Why, I do not know. I meant him no harm. Perhaps it was the summation of his existence, the knowledge of the monstrous hobby that had brought him an unspeakable pleasure through his long life, finally caught up with him. I do not know.

He spasmed suddenly as though struck at the base of his spine by a maul, and his eyes widened, and he collapsed toward me. To prevent the destruction of the exquisite figurines, I let him fall into my arms; and I carefully lowered him into the narrow aisle. Even so, his lifeless left leg decimated the ranks of thirteenth-century Mongol warriors who had served Genghis Khan from the China Sea in the east to the gates of Austria in the west.

He lay face down and I saw a drop of blood at the base of his neck. I bent closer as he struggled to turn his head to the side to speak, and saw the tiniest crossbow quarrel protruding from his rapidly discoloring flesh, just below the hairline.

He was trying to say something to me, and I kneeled close to his mouth, my ear close to the exhalations of dying breath. And he lamented his life, for though he might well have been judged a monster by those who exist in conformity and abide within the mundane strictures of accepted ethical behavior, he was not a bad man. An obsessed man, certainly; but not a bad man. And to prove it, he told me haltingly of the *Promontorium Sacrum*, and of how he had found his way there, how he had struggled back. He told me of the lives and the wisdom and the wonders to be found there.

And he made one last feeble gesture to show me where the scroll was hidden. The scroll he had brought back, which had contained such knowledge as had permitted him to indulge his hobby. He made that last feeble gesture, urging me to find the scroll and to remove it from its hidden niche, and to use it for ends that would palliate his life's doings.

I tried to turn him over, to learn more, but he died in my arms. And I left him there in the narrow aisle among the Nazi Werewolves and Royal Welsh Fusiliers; and I threaded my way through the drawing room large enough to stage a cotillion; and I found the secret panel behind which he had secreted the scroll; and I removed it and saw the photograph he had taken in that beyond that lay beyond the beyondmost edge; the only image of that land that has ever existed. The whispering moon. The golden mushroom trees. The satin sea. The creatures that sit and ruminate there.

I took the scroll and went far away. Into the Outback, above Arkaroo Rock where the Dreamtime reigns. And I spent many years learning the wisdom contained in the scroll of Mr. Brown.

It would not be hyperbole to call it an epiphany.

For when I came back down, and re-entered the human stream, I was a different Vizinczey. I was recast in a different nature. All that I had been, all that I had done, all the blight I had left in my track . . . all of it was as if from someone else's debased life. I was now equipped and anxious to honor Mr. Brown's dying wish.

And that is how I have spent my time for the past several lifetimes. The scroll, in a minor footnote, affords the careful reader the key to immortality. Or as much immortality as one desires. So with this added benison of longevity, I have expended entire decades improving the condition of life for the creatures of this world that formerly I savaged and destroyed.

Now, due to circumstances I will not detail (there is no need to distress you with the specifics of vegetables and rust), the time of my passing is at hand. Vizinczey will be no more in a very short while. And all the good I have done will be the last good I can do. I will cease to be, and I will take the scroll with me. Please trust my judgment in this.

But for a very long time I have been your guardian angel. I have done you innumerable good turns. Yes, even you reading these words: I did you a good turn just last week. Think back and you will remember a random small miracle that made your existence prettier. That was I.

And as parting gift, I have extracted a brief number of the most important thoughts and skills from the scroll of the *Promontorium Sacrum*. They are the most potent runes from that astonishing document. So they will not burn, but rather will serve to warm, if properly adduced, if slowly deciphered and assimilated and understood, I have couched them in more contemporary, universal terms. I do this for your own good. They are not quite epigraphs, nor are they riddles; though set down in simple language, if pierced to the nidus they will enrich and reify; they are potentially analeptic.

I present them to you now, because you will have to work your lives without me from this time forward. You are, as you were for millennia, alone once again. But you can do it. I present them to you, because from the moment Mr. Brown died in my arms, I have been unable to forget the look of human misery, endless despair, and hopelessness on the face of a Spartan soldier who lay on a carpet in a house in Sydney, Australia. This is for him, for all of them, and for you.

## 1

It's the dark of the sun. It's the hour in which worms sing madrigals, tea leaves tell their tales in languages we once used to converse with the trees, and all the winds of the world have returned to the great throat that gave them life. Messages come to us from the core of quiet. A friend now gone tries desperately to pass a message from the beyond, but the strength of ghosts is slight: all he can do is move dust-motes with great difficulty, arranging them with excruciating slowness to form words. The message comes together on the glossy jacket of a book casually dropped on a table more than a year ago. Laboriously laid, mote by mote, the message tells the friend still living that friendship must involve risk, that it is merely a word if it is never tested, that anyone can claim *friend* if there is no chance of cost. It is phrased simply. On the other side, the shade of the friend now departed waits and hopes. He fears the inevitable: his living friend despises disorder and dirt: what if he chances on the misplaced book while wearing his white gloves?

## 2



Do they chill, the breezes that whisper of yesterday, the winds that come from a hidden valley near the top of the world? Do they bite, the shadowy thoughts that lie at the bottom of your heart during daylight hours, that swirl up like wood smoke in the night? Can you hear the memories of those who have gone before, calling to you when the weariness takes you, close on midnight? They are the winds, the thoughts, the voices of memory that prevail in the hour that lies between awareness and reverie. And on the other side of the world, hearing the same song, is your one true love, understanding no better than you, that those who cared and went away are trying to bring you together. Can you breach the world that keeps you apart?

## 3

This is an emergency bulletin. We've made a few necessary alterations in the status quo. For the next few weeks there will be no madness; no imbecile beliefs; no paralogical, prelogical or paleological thinking. No random cruelty. For the next few weeks all the impaired mentalities will be frozen in stasis. No attempts to get you to believe that vast and cool intelligences come from space regularly in circular vehicles. No runaway tales of yetis, sasquatches, hairy shamblers of a lost species. No warnings that the cards, the stones, the running water or the stars are against your best efforts. This is the time known in Indonesia as *djam karet* — the hour that stretches. For the next few weeks you can breathe freely and operate off these words by one who learned too late, by one who has gone away, who was called Camus: "It is not man who must be protected, but the possibilities within him." You have a few weeks without hindrance. Move quickly.

## 4

The casement window blows open. The nightmare has eluded the guards. It's over the spiked wall and it's in here with you. The lights go out. The temperature drops sharply. The bones in your body sigh. You're all alone with it. Circling with your back to the wall. Hey, don't be a nasty little coward; face it and disembowel it. You've got time. You have *always* had time, but the fear slowed you, and you were overcome. But this is the hour that stretches . . . and you've got a chance. After all, it's only your conscience come to kill you. Stop shivering and put up your dukes. You might beat it this time, now that you know you have some breathing space. For in this special hour anything that has ever happened will happen again. Except, this time, it's *your* turn to risk it all.

## 5

In the cathedral at the bottom of the Maracot Deep the carillon chimes for all the splendid thinkers you never got to be. The memories of great thoughts left unspoken rise from their watery tomb and ascend to the surface. The sea boils at their approach and a siege of sea eagles gathers in the sky above the disturbance. Fishermen in small boats listen as they have never listened before, and all seems clear for the first time. These are warnings of storms made only by men. Tempests and sea-spouts, tsunamis and bleeding oceans the color of tragedy. For men's tongues have been stilled, and more great thoughts will die never having been uttered. Memories from the pit of the Deep rise to lament their brethren. Even now, even in the hour that stretches, the past silently cries out not to be forgotten. Are you listening, or must you be lost at sea forever?

## 6

Did you have one of those days today, like a nail in the foot? Did the pterodactyl corpse dropped by the ghost of your mother from the spectral Hindenburg forever circling the Earth come smashing through the lid of your glass coffin? Did the New York strip steak you attacked at dinner suddenly show a mouth filled with needle-sharp teeth, and did it snap off the end of your fork, the last solid-gold fork from the set Anastasia pressed into your hands as they took her away to be shot? Is the slab under your apartment building moaning that it cannot stand the weight on its back a moment longer, and is the building stretching and creaking? Did a good friend betray you today, or did that good friend merely keep silent and fail to come to your aid? Are you holding the razor at your throat this very instant? Take heart, comfort is at hand. This is the hour that stretches. *Djam karet.* We are the cavalry. We're here. Put away the pills. We'll get you through this bloody night. Next time, it'll be your turn to help us.

## 7

You woke in the night, last night, and the fiery, bony hand was enscribing mystic passes in the darkness of your bedroom. It carved out words in the air, flaming words, messages that required answers. One picture is worth a thousand words, the hand wrote. "Not in *this* life," you said to the dark and the fire. "Give me one picture that shows how I felt when they gassed my dog. I'll take less than a thousand words and make you weep for the last Neanderthal crouched at the cliff's edge at the moment he realized his kind were gone . . . show me your one picture. Commend to me the one picture that captures what it was like for me in the moment she said it was all over between us. Not in *this* life, Bonehand." So here we are, once again in the dark, with nothing between us in this hour that stretches but the words. Sweet words and harsh words and words that tumble over themselves to get born. We leave the pictures for the canvas of your mind. Seems only fair.

## 8

Rain fell in a special pattern. I couldn't believe it was doing that. I ran to the other side of the house and looked out the window. The sun was shining there. I saw a hummingbird bury his stiletto beak in a peach on one of the trees, like a junkie who had turned himself into the needle. He sucked deeply and shadows flowed out of the unripe peach: a dreamy vapor that enveloped the bird, changing its features to something jubilantly malevolent. With juice glowing in one perfect drop at the end of its beak, it turned a yellow eye toward me as I pressed against the window. Go away, it said. I fell back and rushed to the other side of the house where rain fell in one place on the sunny street. In my soul I knew that not all inclement weather meant sorrow, that even the brightest day held dismay. I knew this all had meaning, but there was no one else in the world to whom I could go for interpretation. There were only dubious sources, and none knew more than I, not really. Isn't that the damnedest thing: there's never a good reference when you need one.

## 9

Through the jaws of night we stormed, banners cracking against the icy wind, the vapor our beasts panted preceding us like smoke signals, warning the enemy that we looked forward to writing our names in the blood of the end of their lives. We rode for Art! For the singing soul of Creativity! Our cause was just, because it was the only cause worth dying for. All others were worth living for. They stood there on the black line of the horizon, their pikes angrily tilted toward us. *For Commerce,* they shouted with one voice. *For Commerce!* And we fell upon them, and the battle was high wave traffic, with the sound of metal on metal, the sound of hooves on stone, the sound of bodies exploding. We battled all through the endless midnight till at last we could see nothing but hills and valleys of dead. And in the end, we lost. We always lost. And I, alone, am left to tell of that time. Only I, alone of all who went to war to measure the height of the dream, only I remain to speak to you here in the settling silence. Why do *you* feel diminished . . . you weren't there . . . it wasn't your war. Hell hath no fury like that of the uninvolved.

## 10

Hear the music. Listen with all your might, and you needn't clap to keep Tinker Bell from going into a coma. The music will restore her rosy cheeks. Then seek out the source of the melody. Look long and look deep, and somewhere in the murmuring world you will find the storyteller, there under the cabbage leaves, singing to herself. Or is that a she? Perhaps it's a he. But whichever, or whatever, the poor thing is crippled. Can you see that now? The twisting, the bending, the awkward shape, the milky eye, the humped back, do you now make it out? But if you try to join in, to work a duet with wonder, the song ceases. When you startle the cricket its symphony ceases. Art is not by committee, nor is it by wish-fulfillment. It is that which is produced in the hour that stretches, the timeless time wherein *all* songs are sung. In a place devoid of electrical outlets. And if you try to grasp either the singer or the song, all you will hold is sparkling dust as fine as the butter the moth leaves on glass. How the bee flies, how the lights go on, how the enigma enriches and the explanation chills . . . how the music is made . . . are not things we were given to know. And only the fools who cannot hear the song ask that the rules be posted. Hear the music. And enjoy. But do not cry. Not everyone was intended to reach A above high C.

## 11

Ah, there were giants in the land in those days. There was a sweet-faced, honey-voiced girl named Barbara Wire, who we called Nancy because no one had the heart to call her Barb Wire. She tossed a salamander into a window fan to see what would happen. There was Sofie, who had been bitten by *The Sun Also Rises* at a tender age, and who took it as her mission in life to permit crippled virginal boys the enjoyment of carnal knowledge of her every body part: harelips, lepers, paraplegics, albinos with pink eyes, aphasiacs, she welcomed them all to her bed. There was Marissa, who could put an entire unsegmented fried chicken in her mouth all at once, chew without opening her lips or dribbling, and who would then delicately spit out an intact skeleton, as dry and clean as the Gobi Desert. Perdita drew portraits. She would sit you down, and with her pad and charcoal, quickly capture the depth and specificity of your most serious flaws of honor, ethic and conscience, so accurately that you would rip the drawing to pieces before anyone else could see the nature of your corruption. Jolanda: who stole cars and then reduced them to metal sculpture in demolition derbies, whose residence was in an abandoned car-crusher. Peggy: who never slept but told endlessly of her waking dreams of the things the birds told her they saw from on high. Naomi: who was white, passing for black, because she felt the need to shoulder some of the guilt of the world. Ah, there were giants in the land in those days. But I left the room, and closed the door behind me so that the hour that stretches would not leak out. And though I've tried portal after portal, I've never been able to find that room again. Perhaps I'm in the wrong house.

## 12

I woke at three in the morning, bored out of sleep by dreams of such paralyzing mediocrity that I could not lie there and suffer my own breathing. Naked, I padded through the silent house: I knew that terrain as my tongue knows my palate. There were rolls of ancient papyrus lying on a counter. I will replace them, high in a dark closet, I thought. Then I said it aloud . . . the house was silent, I could speak to the air. I took a tall stool and went to the closet, and climbed up and replaced the papyrus. Then I saw it. A web. Dark and billowing in the corner of the ceiling, not silvery but ashy. Something I could not bear to see in my home. It threatened me. I climbed down, moved through the utter darkness, and struggled with the implements in the broom closet, found the feather duster, and hurried back. Then I killed the foaming web and left the closet. Clean the feather duster, I thought. In the back yard I moved to the wall, and shook it out. Then, as I returned, incredible pain assaulted me. The cactus pup with its cool, long spikes had imbedded itself in the ball of my naked right foot. My testicles shrank and my eyes watered. I took an involuntary step, and the spines drove deeper. I reached down to remove the agony and a spike imbedded itself in my thumb. I shouted. I hurt. Limping, I got to the kitchen. In the light of the kitchen I tried to pinch out the spines. They were barbed. They came away with bits of flesh attached. The poison was already spreading. I hurt very much. I hobbled to the bathroom to put antiseptic or the Waters of Lethe on the wounds. They bled freely. I salved myself, and returned to the bed, hating my wife who slept unknowing; I hated my friend who lay dreaming in another part of the house. I hated the world for placing random pain in my innocent path. I lay down and hated all natural order for a brief time. Then I fell fast asleep. Relieved. Boredom had been killed with the billowing web. Somehow, the universe always provides.

. . .

## 13

Like all men, my father was a contradiction in terms. Not more than two or three years after the Great Depression, when my family was still returning pop bottles for the few cents' deposit, and saving those pennies in a quart milk bottle, my father did one of the kindest things I've ever known: he hired a man as an assistant in his little store; an assistant he didn't really need and couldn't afford. He hired the man because he had three children and couldn't find a job. Yet not more than a week later, as we locked up the stationery shop late on a Saturday night, and began to walk down the street to the diner where we would have our hot roast beef sandwiches and french fries, with extra country gravy for dipping the fries, another man approached us on the street and asked for twenty-five cents to buy a bowl of soup. And my father snarled, "No! Get away from us!" I was more startled at that moment than I had ever been — or ever *would* be, as it turned out, for my father died not much later that year — more startled than by anything my father had ever said or done. If I had known the word at that age — I was only twelve — I would have realized that I was *dumbfounded*. My gentle father, who never raised his voice to me or to anyone else, who was unfailingly kind and polite even to the rudest customer, who has forever been a model of compassion for me, *my father* had grown icy and stony in that exchange with an innocent stranger. "Dad," I asked him, as we walked away from the lonely man, "how come you didn't give that fellah a quarter for some soup?" He looked down at me, as if through a crack in the door of a room always kept locked, and he said, "He won't buy a bowl of soup. He'll only buy more liquor." Because my father never lied to me, and because I knew it was important for him always to tell me the truth, I didn't ask anything more about it. But I never forgot that evening; and it is an incident I can never fit into the film strip of loving memories I run and rerun starring my father. Somehow I feel, without understanding, that it was the most important moment of human frailty and compassion in the twelve years through which I was permitted to adore my father. And I wonder when I will grow wise enough to understand the wisdom of my father.



Thus, my gift. There were six more selections from the scroll of the *Promontorium Sacrum*, but once having entered them here, I realized they would cause more harm than good. Tell me truly: would you really want the power to bend others to your will, or the ability to travel at will in an instant to any place in the world, or the facility for reading the future in mirrors? No, I thought not. It is gratifying to see that just the wisdom imparted here has sobered you to that extent.

And what would you do with the knowledge of shaping, the talent for sending, the capturing of rainbows? You already possess such powers and abilities as the world has never known. Now that I've left you the time to master what you already know, you should have no sorrow at being denied these others. Be content.

Now I take my leave. Passage of an instant sort has been arranged. Vizinczey, the I that I became, goes finally on the journey previously denied. Until I had fulfilled the dying request of Mr. Brown, I felt it was unfair of me to indulge myself. But now I go to the sacred promontory; to return the scroll; to sit at the base of the golden mushroom trees and confabulate with astonishing creatures. Perhaps I will take a camera, and perhaps I will endeavor to send back a snap or two, but that is unlikely.

I go contentedly, for all my youthful crimes, having left this a prettier venue than I found it.

And finally, for those of you who always wash behind your ears because, as children, you heeded the admonition "go wash behind your ears," seeing motion pictures of children being examined by their parents before being permitted to go to the dinner table, remembering the panels in comic strips in which children were being told, "Go back and wash behind your ears," who always wondered why that was important — after all, your ears fit fairly closely to your head — who used to wonder what one could possibly have behind one's ears — great masses of mud, dangerous colonies of germs, could vegetation actually take root there, what are we talking about and why such obsessive attention to something so silly? — for those of you who were trusting enough to wash behind your ears, and still do . . . for those of you who know the urgency of tying your shoelaces tightly . . . who have no fear of vegetables or rust . . . I answer the question you raise about the fate of those tiny metal figurines left in eternal anguish on the floor of Mr. Brown's drawing room. I answer the question in this way:

There was a man standing behind you yesterday in the check-out line at the grocery store. You casually noticed that he was buying the most unusual combinations of exotic foods. When you dropped the package of frozen peas, and he stooped to retrieve it for you, you noticed that he had a regal, almost one might say *militaristic* bearing. He clicked his heels as he proffered the peas, and when you thanked him, he spoke with a peculiar accent.

Trust me in this: not even if you were Professor Henry Higgins could you place the point of origin of that accent.

*Dedicated to the memory of Mike Hodel*

# SOFT MONKEY

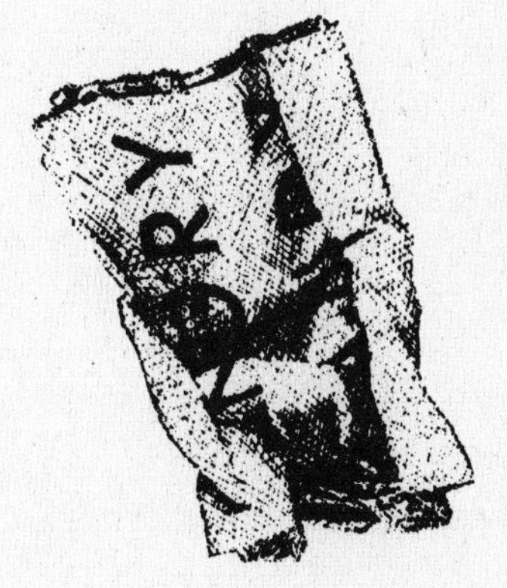

AT TWENTY-FIVE MINUTES past midnight on 51st Street, the wind-chill factor was so sharp it could carve you a new asshole.

Annie lay huddled in the tiny space formed by the wedge of locked revolving door that was open to the street when the document copying service had closed for the night. She had pulled the shopping cart from the Food Emporium at 1st Avenue near 57th into the mouth of the revolving door, had carefully tipped it onto its side, making certain her goods were jammed tightly in the cart, making certain nothing spilled into her sleeping space. She had pulled out half a dozen cardboard flats — broken-down sections of big Kotex cartons from the Food Emporium, the half dozen she had not sold to the junkman that afternoon — and she had fronted the shopping cart with two of them, making it appear the doorway was blocked by the management. She had wedged the others around the edges of the space, cutting the wind, and placed the two rotting sofa pillows behind and under her.

She had settled down, bundled in her three topcoats, the thick woolen merchant marine stocking cap rolled down to cover her ears, almost to the bridge of her broken nose. It wasn't bad in the doorway, quite cozy, really. The wind shrieked past and occasionally touched her, but mostly was deflected. She lay huddled in the tiny space, pulled out the filthy remnants of a stuffed baby doll, cradled it under her chin, and closed her eyes.

She slipped into a wary sleep, half in reverie and yet alert to the sounds of the street. She tried to dream of the child again. Alan. In the waking dream she held him as she held the baby doll, close under her chin, her eyes closed, feeling the warmth of his body. That was important: his body was warm, his little brown hand against her cheek, his warm, warm breath drifting up with the dear smell of baby.

*Was that just today or some other day?* Annie swayed in reverie, kissing the broken face of the baby doll. It was nice in the doorway; it was warm.

The normal street sounds lulled her for another moment, and then were shattered as two cars careened around the corner off Park Avenue, racing toward Madison. Even asleep, Annie sensed when the street wasn't right. It was a sixth sense she had learned to trust after the first time she had been mugged for her shoes and the small change in her snap-purse. Now she came fully awake as the sounds of trouble rushed toward her doorway. She hid the baby doll inside her coat.

The stretch limo sideswiped the Caddy as they came abreast of the closed repro center. The Brougham ran up over the curb and hit the light stanchion full in the grille. The door on the passenger side fell open and a man scrabbled across the front seat, dropped to all four on the sidewalk, and tried to crawl away. The stretch limo, angled in toward the curb, slammed to a stop in front of the Brougham, and three doors opened before the tires stopped rolling.

They grabbed him as he tried to stand, and forced him back to his knees. One of the limo's occupants wore a fine navy blue cashmere overcoat; he pulled it open and reached to his hip. His hand came out holding a revolver. With a smooth stroke he laid it across the kneeling man's forehead, opening him to the bone.

Annie saw it all. With poisonous clarity, back in the V of the revolving door, cuddled in darkness, she saw it all. Saw a second man kick out and break the kneeling victim's nose. The sound of it cut against the night's sudden silence. Saw the third man look toward the stretch limo as a black glass window slid down and a hand emerged from the black seat. The electric hum of opening. Saw the third man go to the stretch and take from the extended hand a metal can. A siren screamed down Park Avenue, and kept going. Saw him return to the group and heard him say, "Hold the motherfucker. Pull his head back!" Saw the other two wrench the victim's head back, gleaming white and pumping red from the broken nose, clear in the sulfurous light from the stanchion overhead. The man's shoes scraped and scraped the sidewalk. Saw the third man reach into an outer coat pocket and pull out a pint of scotch. Saw him unscrew the cap and begin to pour booze into the face of the victim. "Hold his mouth open!" Saw the man in the cashmere topcoat spike his thumb and index fingers into the hinges of the victim's jaws, forcing his mouth open. The sound of gagging, the glow of spittle. Saw the scotch spilling down the man's front. Saw the third man toss the pint bottle into the gutter where it shattered; and saw him thumb press the center of the plastic cap of the metal can; and saw him make the cringing, crying, wailing victim drink the Drano. Annie saw and heard it all.

The cashmere topcoat forced the victim's mouth closed, massaged his throat, made him swallow the Drano. The dying took a lot longer than expected. And it was a lot noisier.

The victim's mouth was glowing a strange blue in the calcium light from overhead. He tried spitting, and a gobbet hit the navy blue cashmere sleeve. Had the natty dresser from the stretch limo been a dunky slob uncaring of what GQ commanded, what happened next would not have gone down.

Cashmere cursed, swiped at the slimed sleeve, let go of the victim; the man with the glowing blue mouth and the gut being boiled away wrenched free of the other two, and threw himself forward. Straight toward the locked revolving door blocked by Annie's shopping cart and cardboard flats.

He came at her in fumbling, hurtling steps, arms wide and eyes rolling, throwing spittle like a racehorse; Annie realized he'd fall across the cart and smash her flat in another two steps.

She stood up, backing to the side of the V. She stood up: into the tunnel of light from the Caddy's headlights.

"The nigger saw it all!" yelled the cashmere.

"Fuckin' bag lady!" yelled the one with the can of Drano.

"He's still moving!" yelled the third man, reaching inside his topcoat and coming out of his armpit with a blued steel thing that seemed to extrude to a length more aptly suited to Paul Bunyan's armpit.

Foaming at the mouth, hands clawing at his throat, the driver of the Brougham came at Annie as if he were spring-loaded.

He hit the shopping cart with his thighs just as the man with the long armpit squeezed off his first shot. The sound of the .45 magnum tore a chunk out of 51st Street, blew through the running man like a crowd roar, took off his face and spattered bone and blood across the panes of the revolving door. It sparkled in the tunnel of light from the Caddy's headlights.

And somehow he kept coming. He hit the cart, rose as if trying to get a first down against a solid defense line, and came apart as the shooter hit him with a second round.

There wasn't enough solid matter to stop the bullet and it exploded through the revolving door, shattering it open as the body crashed through and hit Annie.

She was thrown backward, through the broken glass, and onto the floor of the document copying center. And through it all, Annie heard a fourth voice, clearly a fourth voice, screaming from the stretch limo, "Get the old lady! Get her, she saw everything!"

Men in topcoats rushed through the tunnel of light.

Annie rolled over, and her hand touched something soft. It was the ruined baby doll. It had been knocked loose from her bundled clothing. *Are you cold, Alan?*

She scooped up the doll and crawled away, into the shadows of the reproduction center. Behind her, crashing through the frame of the revolving door, she heard men coming. And the sound of a burglar alarm. Soon police would be here.

All she could think about was that they would throw away her goods. They would waste her good cardboard, they would take back her shopping cart, they would toss her pillows and the hankies and the green cardigan into some trashcan; and she would be empty on the street again. As she had been when they made her move out of the room at 101st and First Avenue. After they took Alan from her . . .

A blast of sound, as the shot shattered a glass-framed citation on the wall near her. They had fanned out inside the office space, letting the headlight illumination shine through. Clutching the baby doll, she hustled down a hallway toward the rear of the copy center. Doors on both sides, all of them closed and locked. Annie could hear them coming.

A pair of metal doors stood open on the right. It was dark in there. She slipped inside, and in an instant her eyes had grown acclimated. There were computers here, big crackle-gray-finish machines that lined three walls. Nowhere to hide.

She rushed around the room, looking for a closet, a cubbyhole, anything. Then she stumbled over something and sprawled across the cold floor. Her face hung over into emptiness, and the very faintest of cool breezes struck her cheeks. The floor was composed of large removable squares. One of them had been lifted and replaced, but not flush. It had not been locked down; an edge had been left ajar; she had kicked it open.

She reached down. There was a crawlspace under the floor.

Pulling the metal-rimmed vinyl plate, she slid into the empty square. Lying face-up, she pulled the square over the aperture, and nudged it gently till it dropped onto its tracks. It sat flush. She could see nothing where, a moment before, there had been the faintest scintilla of filtered light from the hallway. Annie lay very quietly, emptying her mind as she did when she slept in the doorways; making herself invisible. A mound of rags. A pile of refuse. Gone. Only the warmth of the baby doll in that empty place with her.

She heard the men crashing down the corridor, trying doors. *I wrapped you in blankets, Alan. You must be warm.* They came into the computer room. The room was empty, they could see that.

"She *has* to be here, dammit!"

"There's gotta be a way out we didn't see."

"Maybe she locked herself in one of those rooms. Should we try? Break 'em open?"

"Don't be a bigger asshole than usual. Can't you hear that alarm? We gotta get out of here!"

"He'll break our balls."

"Like hell. Would he do anything else than we've done? He's sittin' on the street in front of what's left of Beaddie. You think he's happy about it?"

There was a new sound to match the alarm. The honking of a horn from the street. It went on and on, hysterically.

"We'll find her."

Then the sound of footsteps. Then running.

Annie lay empty and silent, holding the doll.

It was warm, as warm as she had been all November. She slept there through the night.

The next day, in the last Automat in New York with the wonderful little windows through which one could get food by insertion of a token, Annie learned of the two deaths.

Not the death of the man in the revolving door; the deaths of two black women. Beaddie, who had vomited up most of his internal organs, boiled like Chesapeake Bay lobsters, was all over the front of the *Post* that Annie now wore as insulation against the biting November wind. The two women had been found in midtown alleys, their faces blown off by heavy-caliber ordnance. Annie had known one of them; her name had been Sooky and Annie got the word from a good Thunderbird worshipper who stopped by her table and gave her the skinny as she carefully ate her fish cakes and tea.

She knew who they had been seeking. And she knew why they had killed Sooky and the other street person: to white men who ride in stretch limos, all old nigger bag ladies look the same. She took a slow bite of fish cake and stared out at 42nd Street, watching the world swirl past; what was she going to do about this?

They would kill and kill till there was no safe place left to sleep in midtown. She knew it. This was mob business, the *Post* inside her coats said so. And it wouldn't make any difference trying to warn the women. Where would they go? Where would they *want* to go? Not even she, knowing what it was all about . . . not even she would leave the area: this was where she roamed, this was her territorial imperative. And they would find her soon enough.

She nodded to the croaker who had given her the word, and after he'd hobbled away to get a cup of coffee from the spigot on the wall, she hurriedly finished her fish cake and slipped out of the Automat as easily as she had the document copying center this morning.

Being careful to keep out of sight, she returned to 51st Street. The area had been roped off, with sawhorses and green tape that said *Police Investigation — Keep Off*. But there were crowds. The streets were jammed, not only with office workers coming and going, but with loiterers who were fascinated by the scene. It took very little to gather a crowd in New York. The falling of a cornice could produce a *minyan*.

Annie could not believe her luck. She realized the police were unaware of a witness: when the men had charged the doorway, they had thrown aside her cart and goods, had spilled them back onto the sidewalk to gain entrance; and the cops had thought it was all refuse, as one with the huge brown plastic bags of trash at the curb. Her cart and the good sofa pillows, the cardboard flats and her sweaters . . . all of it was in the area. Some in trash cans, some amid the piles of bagged rubbish, some just lying in the gutter.

That meant she didn't need to worry about being sought from two directions. One way was bad enough.



And all the aluminum cans she had salvaged to sell, they were still in the big Bloomingdale's bag right against the wall of the building. There would be money for dinner.

She was edging out of the doorway to collect her goods when she saw the one in navy blue cashmere who had held Beaddie while they fed him Drano. He was standing three stores away, on Annie's side, watching the police lines, watching the copy center, watching the crowd. Watching for her. Picking at an ingrown hair on his chin.

She stepped back into the doorway. Behind her a voice said, "C'mon, lady, get the hell outta here, this's a place uhbizness." Then she felt a sharp poke in her spine.

She looked behind her, terrified. The owner of the haberdashery, a man wearing a bizarrely-cut gray pinstripe worsted with lapels that matched his ears, and a passion-flame silk hankie spilling out of his breast pocket like a crimson afflatus, was jabbing her in the back with a wooden coat hanger. "Move it on, get moving," he said, in a tone that would have gotten his face slapped had he used it on a customer.

Annie said nothing. She *never* spoke to anyone on the street. Silence on the street. *We'll go, Alan; we're okay by ourselves. Don't cry, my baby.*

She stepped out of the doorway, trying to edge away. She heard a sharp, piercing whistle. The man in the cashmere topcoat had seen her; he was whistling and signaling up 51st Street to someone. As Annie hurried away, looking over her shoulder, she saw a dark blue Oldsmobile that had been double-parked pull forward. The cashmere topcoat was shoving through the pedestrians, coming for her like the number 5 uptown Lexington express.

Annie moved quickly, without thinking about it. Being poked in the back, and someone speaking directly to her . . . that was frightening: it meant coming out to respond to another human being. But moving down her streets, moving quickly, and being part of the flow, that was comfortable. She knew how to do that. It was just the way she was.

Instinctively, Annie made herself larger, more expansive, her raggedy arms away from her body, the dirty overcoats billowing, her gait more erratic: opening the way for her flight. Fastidious shoppers and suited businessmen shied away, gave a start as the dirty old black bag lady bore down on them, turned sidewise praying she would not brush a recently Martinized shoulder. The Red Sea parted miraculously permitting flight, then closed over instantly to impede navy blue cashmere. But the Olds came on quickly.

Annie turned left onto Madison, heading downtown. There was construction around 48th. There were good alleys on 46th. She knew a basement entrance just three doors off Madison on 47th. But the Olds came on quickly.

Behind her, the light changed. The Olds tried to rush the intersection, but this was Madison. Crowds were already crossing. The Olds stopped, the driver's window rolled down and a face peered out. Eyes tracked Annie's progress.

Then it began to rain.

Like black mushrooms sprouting instantly from concrete, Totes blossomed on the sidewalk. The speed of the flowing river of pedestrians increased; and in an instant Annie was gone. Cashmere rounded the corner, looked at the Olds, a frantic arm motioned to the left, and the man pulled up his collar and elbowed his way through the crowd, rushing down Madison.

Low places in the sidewalk had already filled with water. His wingtip cordovans were quickly soaked.

He saw her turn into the alley behind the novelty sales shop (*Nothing over $1.10!!!*); he *saw* her; turned right and ducked in fast; *saw* her, even through the rain and the crowd and half a block between them; *saw* it!

So where was she?

The alley was empty.

It was a short space, all brick, only deep enough for a big Dempsey Dumpster and a couple of dozen trash cans; the usual mounds of rubbish in the corners; no fire escape ladders low enough for an old bag lady to grab; no loading docks, no doorways that looked even remotely accessible, everything cemented over or faced with sheet steel; no basement entrances with concrete steps leading down; no manholes in the middle of the passage; no open windows or even broken windows at jumping height; no stacks of crates to hide behind.

The alley was empty.



*Saw* her come in here. *Knew* she had come in here, and couldn't get out. He'd been watching closely as he ran to the mouth of the alley. She was in here somewhere. Not too hard figuring out where. He took out the .38 Police Positive he liked to carry because he lived with the delusion that if he had to dump it, if it were used in the commission of a sort of kind of felony he couldn't get snowed on, and if it were traced, it would trace back to the cop in Teaneck, New Jersey from whom it had been lifted as he lay drunk in the back room of a Polish social club three years earlier.

He swore he would take his time with her, this filthy old porch monkey. His navy blue cashmere already smelled like soaked dog. And the rain was not about to let up; it now came sheeting down, traveling in a curtain through the alley.

He moved deeper into the darkness, kicking the piles of trash, making sure the refuse bins were full. She was in here somewhere. Not too hard figuring out where.

Warm. Annie felt warm. With the ruined baby doll under her chin, and her eyes closed, it was almost like the apartment at 101st and First Avenue, when the Human Resources lady came and tried to tell her strange things about Alan. Annie had not understood what the woman meant when she kept repeating *soft monkey, soft monkey,* a thing some scientist knew. It had made no sense to Annie, and she had continued rocking the baby.

Annie remained very still where she had hidden. Basking in the warmth. *Is it nice, Alan? Are we toasty; yes, we are. Will we be very still and the lady from the City will go away? Yes, we will.* She heard the crash of a garbage can being kicked over. *No one will find us. Shh, my baby.*

There was a pile of wooden slats that had been leaned against a wall. As he approached, the gun leveled, he realized they obscured a doorway. She was back in there, he knew it. Had to be. Not too hard figuring that out. It was the only place she could have hidden.

He moved in quickly, slammed the boards aside, and threw down on the dark opening. It was empty. Steel-plate door, locked.

Rain ran down his face, plastering his hair to his forehead. He could smell his coat, and his shoes, oh god, don't ask. He turned and looked. All that remained was the huge dumpster.



He approached it carefully, and noticed: the lid was still dry near the back side closest to the wall. The lid had been open just a short time ago. Someone had just lowered it.

He pocketed the gun, dragged two crates from the heap thrown down beside the Dempsey, and crawled up onto them. Now he stood above the dumpster, balancing on the crates with his knees at the level of the lid. With both hands bracing him, he leaned over to get his fingertips under the heavy lid. He flung the lid open, yanked out the gun, and leaned over. The dumpster was nearly full. Rain had turned the muck and garbage into a swimming porridge. He leaned over precariously to see what floated there in the murk. He leaned in to see. *Fuckin' porch monk —*

As a pair of redolent, dripping arms came up out of the muck, grasped his navy blue cashmere lapels, and dragged him headfirst into the metal bin. He went down, into the slime, the gun going off, the shot spanging off the raised metal lid. The coat filled with garbage and water.

Annie felt him struggling beneath her. She held him down, her feet on his neck and back, pressing him face first deeper into the goo that filled the bin. She could hear him breathing garbage and fetid water. He thrashed, a big man, struggling to get out from under. She slipped, and braced herself against the side of the dumpster, regained her footing, and drove him deeper. A hand clawed out of the refuse, dripping lettuce and black slime. The hand was empty. The gun lay at the bottom of the bin. The thrashing intensified, his feet hitting the metal side of the container. Annie rose up and dropped her feet heavily on the back of his neck. He went flat beneath her, trying to swim up, unable to find purchase.

He grabbed her foot as an explosion of breath from down below forced a bubble of air to break on the surface. Annie stomped as hard as she could. Something snapped beneath her shoe, but she heard nothing.

It went on for a long time, for a time longer than Annie could think about. The rain filled the bin to overflowing. Movement under her feet lessened, then there was hysterical movement for an instant, then it was calm. She stood there for an even longer time, trembling and trying to remember other, warmer times.



Finally, she closed herself off, buttoned up tightly, climbed out dripping and went away from there, thinking of Alan, thinking of a time after this was done. After that long time standing there, no movement, no movement at all in the bog beneath her waist. She did not close the lid.

When she emerged from the alley, after hiding in the shadows and watching, the Oldsmobile was nowhere in sight. The foot traffic parted for her. The smell, the dripping filth, the frightened face, the ruined thing she held close to her.

She stumbled out onto the sidewalk, lost for a moment, then turned the right way and shuffled off.

The rain continued its march across the city.

No one tried to stop her as she gathered together her goods on 51st Street. The police thought she was a scavenger, the gawkers tried to avoid being brushed by her, the owner of the document copying center was relieved to see the filth cleaned up. Annie rescued everything she could, and hobbled away, hoping to be able to sell her aluminum for a place to dry out. It was not true that she was dirty; she had always been fastidious, even in the streets. A certain level of dishevelment was acceptable, but this was unclean.

And the blasted baby doll needed to be dried and brushed clean. There was a woman on East 60th, near Second Avenue; a vegetarian who spoke with an accent; a white lady who sometimes let Annie sleep in the basement. She would ask her for a favor.

It was not a very big favor, but the white woman was not home; and that night Annie slept in the construction of the new Zeckendorf Towers, where S. Klein-On-The-Square used to be, down on 14th and Broadway.

The men from the stretch limo didn't find her again for almost a week.

She was salvaging newspapers from a wire basket on Madison near 44th when he grabbed her from behind. It was the one who had poured the liquor into Beaddie, and then made him drink the Drano. He threw an arm around her, pulled her around to face him, and she reacted instantly, the way she did when the kids tried to take her snap-purse.

She butted him full in the face with the top of her head, and drove him backward with both filthy hands. He stumbled into the street, and a cab swerved at the last instant to avoid running him down. He stood in the street, shaking his head, as Annie careened down 44th, looking for a place to hide. She was sorry she had left her cart again. This time, she knew, her goods weren't going to be there.

It was the day before Thanksgiving.

Four more black women had been found dead in midtown doorways.

Annie ran, the only way she knew how, into stores that had exits on other streets. Somewhere behind her, though she could not figure it out properly, there was trouble coming for her and the baby. It was so cold in the apartment. It was always so cold. The landlord cut off the heat, he always did it in early November, till the snow came. And she sat with the child, rocking him, trying to comfort him, trying to keep him warm. And when they came from Human Resources, from the City, to evict her, they found her still holding the child. When they took it away from her, so still and blue, Annie ran from them, into the streets; and she ran, she knew how to run, to keep running so she could live out here where they couldn't reach her and Alan. But she knew there was trouble behind her.

Now she came to an open place. She knew this. It was a new building they had put up, a new skyscraper, where there used to be shops that had good throwaway things in the cans and sometimes on the loading docks. It said Citicorp Mall and she ran inside. It was the day before Thanksgiving and there were many decorations. Annie rushed through into the central atrium, and looked around. There were escalators, and she dashed for one, climbing to a second storey, and then a third. She kept moving. They would arrest her or throw her out if she slowed down.

At the railing, looking over, she saw the man in the court below. He didn't see her. He was standing, looking around.

Stories of mothers who lift wrecked cars off their children are legion.

When the police arrived, eyewitnesses swore it had been a stout, old black woman who had lifted the heavy potted tree in its terracotta urn, who had manhandled it up onto the railing and slid it along till she was standing above the poor dead man, and who had dropped it three storeys to crush his skull. They swore it was true, but beyond a vague description of old, and black, and dissolute looking, they could not be of assistance. Annie was gone.

On the front page of the *Post* she wore as lining in her right shoe, was a photo of four men who had been arraigned for the senseless murders of more than a dozen bag ladies over a period of several months. Annie did not read the article.

It was close to Christmas, and the weather had turned bitter, too bitter to believe. She lay propped in the doorway alcove of the Post Office on 43rd and Lexington. Her rug was drawn around her, the stocking cap pulled down to the bridge of her nose, the goods in the string bags around and under her. Snow was just beginning to come down.

A man in a Burberry and an elegant woman in a mink approached from 42nd Street, on their way to dinner. They were staying at the New York Helmsley. They were from Connecticut, in for three days to catch the shows and to celebrate their eleventh wedding anniversary.

As they came abreast of her, the man stopped and stared down into the doorway. "Oh, Christ, that's awful," he said to his wife. "On a night like this, Christ, that's just awful."

"Dennis, *please!*" the woman said.

"I can't just pass her by," he said. He pulled off a kid glove and reached into his pocket for his money clip.

"Dennis, they don't like to be bothered," the woman said, trying to pull him away. "They're very self-sufficient. Don't you remember that piece in the *Times*?"

"It's damned near Christmas, Lori," he said, taking a twenty dollar bill from the folded sheaf held by its clip. "It'll get her a bed for the night, at least. They can't make it out here by themselves. God knows, it's little enough to do." He pulled free of his wife's grasp and walked to the alcove.

He looked down at the woman swathed in the rug, and he could not see her face. Small puffs of breath were all that told him she was alive. "Ma'am," he said, leaning forward. "Ma'am, please take this." He held out the twenty.

Annie did not move. She never spoke on the street.

"Ma'am, please, let me do this. Go somewhere warm for the night, won't you . . . please?"

He stood for another minute, seeking to rouse her, at least for a *go away* that would free him, but the old woman did not move. Finally, he placed the twenty on what he presumed to be her lap, there in that shapeless mass, and allowed himself to be dragged away by his wife.

Three hours later, having completed a lovely dinner, and having decided it would be romantic to walk back to the Helmsley through the six inches of snow that had fallen, they passed the Post Office and saw the old woman had not moved. Nor had she taken the twenty dollars. He could not bring himself to look beneath the wrappings to see if she had frozen to death, and he had no intention of taking back the money. They walked on.

In her warm place, Annie held Alan close up under her chin, stroking him and feeling his tiny black fingers warm at her throat and cheeks. *It's all right, baby, it's all right. We're safe. Shhh, my baby. No one can hurt you.*

# STUFFING

BECAUSE HE REALIZED he had been responsible for the elevation of the first Indo-Chinese Catholic to the Papacy, Eugene Keeton decided to use his incredible, though specific, power for the good of all mankind.

All right, he admitted to himself, when he was finally convinced he had "the might to vote," I made a few mistakes. Nixon and Reagan were examples of muddy thinking; and voting for *The Greatest Show on Earth* for the 1952 Oscar, just because I liked Jimmy Stewart as a clown, when I should have gone for *The Man in the White Suit* or *Viva Zapata!* or *Moulin Rouge* or *High Noon*, was just plain stupid. But who knew? Who knew I was the deciding vote? Who could believe such a thing?

Now, miraculously, he knew.

He believed.

In some wonderful, cockeyed flash of inspiration on the part of the sentient universe (no doubt in league with the powers of synchronicity, serendipity and entropy), he had been touched by the Paw of Chance: he had been accorded the lofty position of holder of the deciding vote. The knowledge had come slowly; it had taken forty of his fifty years to understand who and what he was.

It hadn't dawned though he had cast vote for every successful presidential candidate since his twenty-first birthday. It hadn't dawned though he had been chosen by Flora from the slate of suitors for her hand. It hadn't dawned though he had been dead-on selecting every Emmy, Oscar, Tony and Obie winner for the past three decades. It hadn't dawned though he'd been on the winning side for the Rose Bowl, the Super Bowl, the World Series and the Stanley Cup.

But when, for a lark, he voted for Daffy Duck as a write-in for the Board of Supervisors, and D. Duck won — after six recounts — by one vote, he began to have suspicions.



So he tried a lightweight experiment. When *TV Guide* ran a readers' poll coupon for viewers to select their favorite television shows, he picked the sign-off *Sermonette* as best dramatic presentation, Tom Snyder as most outstanding male personality, and *The National Drunk Driving Test* as the best comedy.

When they won, to the amazement and dyspepsia of Walter Annenberg, he knew he was on to something hot.

He vaguely remembered a filler item he'd seen on ABC just before the last election. A county in Wisconsin — or had it been Oklahoma? — where the voting record had been identical to that of the nation as a whole since the 1840s without a miss. A statistical fluke, the announcer had said.

Fluke, indeed. He was another.

Eugene Keeton was the stuffer of the ballot boxes.

He came to think of himself as a superhero with a secret identity. In real life he was mild-mannered, fifty-year-old Eugene Keeton, good old Gene, an electrician at Universal Studios, a husband, father of two grown daughters, slow and precise and a credit to his race. But when the bat-signal flashed against the night sky, when the beleaguered forces of Good and Decency called for The Green Hornet, then Eugene Keeton shed his bib overalls and his Hush Puppies and became *the deciding vote*.

Even with the emphysema and the arthritis, the secret knowledge made Eugene Keeton's life a happy dream.

And when Cardinal Sorapong Krung Utanan was elevated by the Holy See, when the puff of white smoke went up over the Vatican and Reuters flashed the incredible news to the bead-counting world, Eugene Keeton knew he was the focus of vast powers. With knowledge came a sense of responsibility.

Then he decided to do good things.

But first, because he didn't have any concrete plans, because having the power and knowing how best to use it were very different matters, he resolved to share his wonderfulness with Flora.

"You what?" she said.

"I'm the ballot-box stuffer. I can make it all go my way."

"Go to bed, I'll get the heat pad."

"Flora, you've lived with me for twenty-two years. Have you ever heard me say anything like this? Do I see flying saucers? When Sandi wanted me to go to that self-actualization seminar her boyfriend was running, did I come back and talk about needing my space? Am I a sensible person or am I not?"

"Maybe the hot water bottle, too," she said.

Eugene Keeton went fishing. He hadn't gone fishing in over fifteen years; nonetheless, he sought privacy and sat for six silent hours in a small boat on Lake Sherwood. And as darkness fell a great sorrow took him.

I'm fifty years old, he thought, and I don't know what to do with the world. I'm just a man, no great brain, no deep thinker, and I know there are so many things that are wrong, that ought to be made better, the world easier for people, and *I don't know how to do it*.

He considered taking trips to other lands, to vote in elections so the terrorist strongmen in the Middle East would be deposed. He contemplated voting for little-known men and women he would seek out and research and assure himself would make the world a better place.

But the enormity of his lack of expertise in such matters stopped him. How would he *know* if they were the right people, honest and courageous? And what if they did things he didn't like?

Eugene Keeton had caught no fish in six hours. He had, in fact, been caught himself: by the terrible dread certainty that he had been selected as God . . . and was impotent.

Flora was waiting up for him. She was in the yellow terrycloth bathrobe, sitting in his chair in the rec room, in the dark, holding a mug of cold tea in both hands. She spoke out of the darkness as he came limping down the stairs. "The arthritis again?"

"A little. It's not bad."

She waited till he had sunk into the old sofa they had put down here after they'd bought the new suite for the living room. He had not turned on the lights.

"Honey?"

He made an acknowledging sound. She could barely see him.

"I didn't mean to make light."

"That's all right. I know how it sounded."

"Even so. I should have listened to you."

They sat silently for a time. Finally, he sighed and said, "Flora, I never knew how hard it is. The electrical bill goes up and we swear at the Arabs. Half my crew gets laid off at the Studio and we blame

Carter, or Reagan, or whoever's at the top. People get assassinated, crime all over the place, the Dinettis down the street get broken into and we say it's the Mexicans or the blacks . . . but we don't really know. And when you get a chance to *do* something, to take a hand, maybe to vote for someone you think'll change it . . . it's just more of the same."

He was quiet again. Then he said:

"God ought to be able to do something. But there's nothing to do. He can't get a handle on it."

"You shouldn't say that, Gene."

"But I *know!* I'm sure He's just like we are. Just sitting in the dark and hoping something'll happen. But it won't."

"Yes, it will. It *has* to, Gene. God or someone else has to take a hand. If you think you're the one, well, maybe you've been touched by Him. Maybe He's working through you."

Silence. For a long time. Then, "Maybe."

He resolved at least to *try*.

It wasn't right to have this power and not *do* something with it. So he resolved at least to *try*.

The union had an election coming up. There had been problems. Talk. Just idle talk about featherbedding and more layoffs. About some tie-in with people under indictment in Chicago and Detroit. Kickbacks. Just talk, idle talk. But Eugene had been disturbed by it.

He studied the background of the men running for office. He made his selections after careful consideration. He voted and they won, all of them, down to the last dark horse who had been on the stump for sweeping changes. They all seemed honest.

Within a month, six more of his crew were laid off; and the dues were raised.

Flora came home from volunteer work at the hospital to find him sitting at the kitchen table with an open, full bottle of beer. It had grown warm.

"Did you heat the casserole?"

He shook his head.

"Bad day?"

"Hersh and Ken Toland and four others were laid off today."

"How did it happen? Didn't the union make a fuss?"

He looked at her. In twenty-two years she had never seen such desperation on his face. He was always ready with a silly riddle — why is a chicken sitting on a fence like a new penny? — but these days he seldom had anything silly to say. "How did it happen?" he said softly. "*I* made it happen."

She started to say, don't be silly, Gene, but his eyes were sad and she laid down her purse and put her arms around him and kissed his hair.

After a while they went to bed. She lay awake hearing him breathe. She pretended to be asleep, not wanting him to know she was so worried about him. But he didn't fall off till almost morning.

And the next day he called in sick. He wandered around the house in Toluca Lake that now seemed too large for an aging couple whose children had lives of their own in far places called Seattle and Rapid City. She found him, during one empty hour, standing in the middle of the living room, staring into the blank wall. She spoke his name gently but he didn't respond; so she went back into the kitchen and after a while found herself washing the same tumbler over and over.

Late that afternoon she found him in the backyard, sitting on the grass under the loquat tree, staring at the remains of a dead bird. He sat like a child, his legs out straight in front of him, his hands folded, staring unblinkingly at the rotted thing that had once danced through sunlight. She stood waiting for him to notice her, and when he failed to look up, as if he were willing himself into the shapeless mass, she said, "I think that was the jay we heard hit the window last week. Mrs. Carmichael's angora must've been at it, you think?"

He didn't answer for a long time. Then he looked up at her and she realized he had been crying. He said something that clogged up in his throat.

"I didn't hear you, dear," she said.

He repeated it, and she could not bear to let him see the effect his words had on her. She turned away and went back to the kitchen, hearing him say it again and again in her terror:

*I should ought to be able to do* something *for it.*

She waited in the kitchen, waited for the fall of darkness and waited for the sound of his footsteps coming into the house asking what was for dinner; but he sat out there in the evening and she sat inside in the darkness, fearing even to turn on the television.

Finally, he came in and after a while they went to bed. Again he lay awake all night, and so did Flora, until close to dawn, when she drifted off into troubled dreams.

And the next morning he was gone.

She stayed in bed. He had gone away. She knew he would never come back. She just knew it. And there would be ever so much time for crying during all the later that lay ahead.

He went away.

God, helpless as those He had created, wandered forlorn through the machine that had assumed a life of its own; that would run, and continue to run, until there was no one left to notice.



The Author wishes to acknowledge the assistance of Lance A. Diernback in the creation of this piece of fiction.

# WITH VIRGIL ODDUM AT THE EAST POLE

*Dedicated to the genius of Sam Rodia*

THE DAY HE CRAWLED out of the dead cold Icelands, the glaciers creepings down the great cliff were sea-green: endless rivers of tinted, faceted emeralds lit from within. Memories of crippled chances shone in the ice. That was a day, and I remember this clearly, during which the purple sky of Hotlands was filled with the downdrifting balloon spores that had died rushing through the beams of the UV lamps in the peanut fields of the silver crescent. That was a day — remembering clearly — with Argo squatting on the horizon of Hotlands, an enormous inverted tureen of ruby glass.

He crawled toward me and the ancient fux I called Amos the Wise; crawled, literally crawled, up the land-bridge of Westspit onto Meditation Island. Through the slush and sludge and amber mud of the Terminator's largest island.

His heat-envelope was filthy and already cracking, and he tore open the velcro mouthflap without regard for saving the garment as he crawled toward a rotting clump of spillweed.

When I realized that he intended to *eat* it, I moved to him quickly and crouched in front of him so he couldn't get to it.

"I wouldn't put that in your mouth," I said. "It'll kill you."

He didn't say anything, but he looked up at me from down there on his hands and knees with an expression that said it all. He was starving, and if I didn't come up with some immediate alternative to the spillweed, he was going to eat it anyhow, even if it killed him.

This was only one hundred and nineteen years after we had brought the wonders of the human race to Medea, and though I was serving a term of penitence on Meditation Island, I wasn't so sure I wanted to make friends with another human being. I was having a hard enough time just communicating with fuxes. I certainly didn't want to take charge of his life . . . even in as small a way as being responsible for saving it.

Funny the things that flash through your mind. I remember at that moment, with him looking at me so desperately, recalling a cartoon I'd once seen: it was one of those standard thirsty-man-crawling-out-of-the-desert cartoons, with a long line of crawl-marks stretching to the horizon behind an emaciated, bearded wanderer. And in the foreground is a man on a horse, looking down at this poor dying devil with one clawed hand lifted in a begging gesture, and the guy on the horse is smiling and saying to the thirsty man, "Peanut butter sandwich?"

I didn't think he'd find it too funny.

So I pulled up the spillweed, so he wouldn't go for it before I got back, and I trotted over to my wickyup and got him a ball of peanut cheese and a nip-off bulb of water, and came back and helped him sit up to eat.

It took him a while, and of course we were covered with pink and white spores by the time he finished. The smell was awful.

I helped him to his feet. Pretty unsteady. And he leaned on me walking back to the wickyup. I laid him down on my air-mattress and he closed his eyes and fell asleep immediately. Maybe he fainted, I don't know.

His name was Virgil Oddum; but I didn't know that, either, at the time.

I didn't ever know much about him. Not then, not later, not even now. It's funny how everybody knows *what* he did, but not why he did it, or even who he was; and until recently, not so much as his name, nothing.

In a way, I really resent it. The only reason anybody knows me is because I knew him, Virgil Oddum. But they don't care about me or what I was going through, just him, because of what he did. My name is Pogue. William Ronald Pogue, like *rogue*; and I'm important, too. You should know names.

Jason was chasing Theseus through the twilight sky directly over the Terminator when he woke up. The clouds of dead balloon spores had passed over and the sky was amber again, with bands of color washing across the bulk of Argo. I was trying to talk with Amos the Wise.



I was usually trying to talk with Amos the Wise.

The xenoanthropologists at the main station at Perdue Farm in the silver crescent call communication with the fuxes *ekstasis* — literally, "to stand outside oneself." A kind of enriched empathy that conveys concepts and emotional sets, but nothing like words or pictures. I would sit and stare at one of the fuxes, and he would crouch there on his hindquarters and stare back at me; and we'd both fill up with what the other was thinking. Sort of. More or less overcome with vague feelings, general tones of emotion . . . memories of when the fux had been a hunter; when he had had the extra hindquarters he'd dropped when he was female; the vision of a kilometer-high tidal wave once seen near the Seven Pillars on the Ring; chasing females and endlessly mating. It was all there, every moment of what was a long life for a fux: fifteen Medean years.

But it was all flat. Like a drama done with enormous expertise and no soul. The arrangement of thoughts was random, without continuity, without flow. There was no color, no interpretation, no sense of what it all meant for the dromids.

It was artless and graceless; it was merely data.

And so trying to "talk" to Amos was like trying to get a computer to create original, deeply meaningful poetry. Sometimes I had the feeling he had been "assigned" to me, to humor me; to keep me busy.

At the moment the man came out of my wickyup, I was trying to get Amos to codify the visual nature of the fuxes' religious relationship to Castor C, the binary star that Amos and his race thought of as Maternal Grandfather and Paternal Grandfather. For the human colony they were Phrixus and Helle.

I was trying to get Amos to understand flow and the emotional load in changing colors when the double shadow fell between us and I looked up to see the man standing behind me. At the same moment I felt a lessening of the ekstasis between the fux and me. As though some other receiving station was leaching off power.

The man stood there, unsteadily, weaving and trying to keep his balance, staring at Amos. The fux was staring back. They were communicating, but what was passing between them I didn't know. Then Amos got up and walked away, with that liquid rolling gait old male fuxes affect after they've dropped their hindquarters. I got up with some difficulty: since coming to Medea I'd developed mild arthritis in my knees and sitting cross-legged stiffened me.

As I stood up, he started to fall over, still too weak from crawling out of Icelands. He fell into my arms, and I confess my first thought was annoyance because now I *knew* he'd be another thing I'd have to worry about.

"Hey, hey," I said, "take it easy."

I helped him to the wickyup, and put him on his back on the air-mattress. "Listen, fellah," I said, "I don't want to be cold about this, but I'm out here all alone, paying my time. I don't get another shipment of rations for about four months and I can't keep you here."

He didn't say anything. Just stared at me.

"Who the hell are you? Where'd you come from?"

Watching me. I used to be able to read expression very accurately. Watching me, with hatred.

I didn't even know him. He didn't have any idea what was what, why I was out there on Meditation Island; there wasn't any reason he should hate me.

"How'd you get here?"

Watching. Not a word out of him.

"Listen, mister: here's the long and short of it. There isn't any way I can get in touch with anybody to come and get you. And I can't keep you here because there just isn't enough ration. And I'm not going to let you stay here and starve in front of me, because after a while you're sure as hell going to go for my food and I'm going to fight you for it, and one of us is going to get killed. And I am not about to have that kind of a situation, understand? Now I know this is chill, but you've got to go. Take a few days, get some strength. If you hike straight across Eastspit and keep going through Hotlands, you might get spotted by someone out spraying the fields. I doubt it, but maybe."

Not a sound. Just watching me and hating me.

"Where'd you come from? Not out there in Icelands. Nothing can live out there. It's minus thirty Celsius. Out there." Silence. "Just glaciers. Out there."

Silence. I felt that uncontrollable anger rising in me.

"Look, jamook, I'm not having this. Understand me? I'm just not having any of it. You've got to go. I don't give a damn if you're the Count of Monte Crespo or the lost Dauphin of Threx: you're getting the hell out of here as soon as you can crawl." He stared up at me and

I wanted to hit the bastard as hard as I could. I had to control myself. This was the kind of thing that had driven me to Meditation Island.

Instead, I squatted there watching him for a long time. He never blinked. Just watched me. Finally, I said, very softly, "What'd you say to the fux?"

A double shadow fell through the door and I looked up. It was Amos the Wise. He'd peeled back the entrance flap with his tail because his hands were full. Impaled on the three long, sinewy fingers of each hand were six freshly caught dartfish. He stood there in the doorway, bloody light from the sky forming a corona that lit his blue, furry shape; and he extended the skewered fish.

I'd been six months on Meditation Island. Every day of that time I'd tried to spear a dartfish. Flashfreeze and peanut cheese and boxration, they can pall on you pretty fast. You want to gag at the sight of silvr wrap. I'd wanted fresh food. Every day for six months I'd tried to catch something live. They were too fast. That's why they weren't called slowfish. The fuxes had watched me. Not one had ever moved to show me how they did it. Now this old neuter Amos was offering me half a dozen. I knew what the guy had said to him.

"Who the hell are you?" I was about as skewed as I could be. I wanted to pound him out a little, delete that hateful look on his face, put him in a way so I wouldn't have to care for him. He didn't say a word, just kept looking at me; but the fux came inside the wickyup — first time he'd ever done *that*, damn his slanty eyes! — and he moved around between us, the dartfish extended.

This guy had some kind of *hold* over the aborigine! He didn't say a thing, but the fux knew enough to get between us and insist I take the fish. So I did it, cursing both of them under my breath.

And as I pried off the six dartfish I felt the old fux pull me into a flow with him, and stronger than I'd ever been able to do it when we'd done ekstasis, Amos the Wise let me know that this was a very holy creature, this thing that had crawled out of the Icelands, and I'd better treat him pretty fine, or else. There wasn't even a hint of a picture of what *or else* might be, but it was a strong flow, a *strong* flow.

So I took the fish and put them in the larder, and I let the fux know how grateful I was, and he didn't pay me enough attention to mesmerize a gnat; and the flow was gone; and he was doing ekstasis with my guest lying out as nice and comfy as you please; and then he turned and slid out of the wickyup and was gone.

I sat there through most of the night watching him, and one moment he was staring at me, and the next he was asleep; and I went on through that first night just sitting there looking at him gonked-in like that, where I would have been sleeping if he hadn't showed up. Even asleep he hated me. But he was too weak to stay awake and enjoy it.

So I looked at him, wondering who the hell he was, most of that night. Until I couldn't take it any more, and near to morning I just beat the crap out of him.

They kept bringing food. Not just fish, but plants I'd never seen before, things that grew out there in Hotlands east of us, out there where it always stank like rotting garbage. Some of the plants needed to be cooked, and some of them were delicious just eaten raw. But I knew they'd never have showed me *any* of that if it hadn't been for him.

He never spoke to me, and he never told the fuxes that I'd beaten him the first night he was in camp; and his manner never changed. Oh, I knew he could talk all right, because when he slept he tossed and thrashed and shouted things in his sleep. I never understood any of it; some offworld language. But whatever it was, it made him feel sick to remember it. Even asleep he was in torment.

He was determined to stay. I knew that from the second day. I caught him pilfering stores.

No, that's not accurate. He was doing it openly. I didn't catch him. He was going through the stash in the transport sheds, mostly goods I wouldn't need for a while yet, and items whose functions no longer related to my needs. He had already liberated some of those items when I discovered him burrowing through the stores: the neetskin tent I'd used before building the wickyup from storm-hewn fellner trees; the spare air-mattress; a hologram projector I'd used during the first month to keep me entertained with a selection of laser beads, mostly Nōh plays and conundramas. I'd grown bored with the diversions very quickly: they didn't seem to be a part of my life of penitence. He had commandeered the projector, but not the beads. Everything had been pulled out and stacked.



"What do you think you're doing?" I stood behind him, fists knotted, waiting for him to say something snappy.

He straightened with some difficulty, holding his ribs where I'd kicked him the night before. He turned and looked at me evenly. I was surprised: he didn't seem to hate me as much as he'd let it show the day before. He wasn't afraid of me, though I was larger and had already demonstrated that I could bash him if I wanted to bash him, or leave him alone if I chose to leave him alone. He just stared, waiting for me to get the message.

The message was that he was here for a while.

Like it or not.

"Just stay out of my way," I said. "I don't like you, and that's not going to change. I made a mistake pulling that spillweed, but I won't make any more mistakes. Keep out of my food stores, keep away from me, and don't get between me and the dromids. I've got a job to do, and you interfere . . . I'll weight you down, toss you in, and what the scuttlefish don't chew off is going to wash up at Icebox. You got that?"

I was just shooting off my mouth. And what was worse than my indulging in the same irrational behavior that had already ruined my life was that he knew I was just making a breeze. He looked at me, waited long enough so I couldn't pretend to have had my dignity scarred, and he went back to searching through the junk. I went off looking for fuxes to interrogate, but they were avoiding us that day.

By that night he'd already set up his own residence.

And the next day Amos delivered two females to me, who unhinged themselves on their eight legs in a manner that was almost sitting. And the old neuter let me know these two — he used an ekstasis image that conveyed *nubile* — would join flow with me in an effort to explain their relationship to Maternal Grandfather. It was the first voluntary act of assistance the tribe had offered in six months.

So I knew my unwelcome guest was paying for his sparse accommodations.

And later that day I found, wedged into one of the extensible struts I'd used in building the wickyup, the thorny branch of an emeraldberry bush. It was festooned with fruit. Where the aborigines had found it, out there in that shattered terrain, I don't know. The berries were going bad, but I pulled them off greedily, nicking my hands on the thorns, and squeezed their sea-green juice into my mouth.



So I knew my unwelcome guest was paying for his sparse accommodations.

And we went on that way, with him lurking about and sitting talking to Amos and his tribe for hours on end, and me stumping about trying to play Laird of the Manor and getting almost nowhere trying to impart philosophical concepts to a race of creatures that listened attentively and then gave me the distinct impression that I was retarded because I didn't understand Maternal Grandfather's hungers.

Then one day he was gone. It was early in the crossover season and the hard winds were rising from off the Hotlands. I came out of the wickyup and knew I was alone. But I went to his tent and looked inside. It was empty, as I'd expected it to be. On a rise nearby, two male fuxes and an old neuter were busy patting the ground, and I strolled to them and asked where the other man was. The hunters refused to join flow with me, and continued patting the ground in some sort of ritual. The old fux scratched at his deep blue fur and told me the holy creature had gone off into the Icelands. Again.

I walked to the edge of Westspit and stared off toward the glacial wasteland. It was warmer now, but that was pure desolation out there. I could see faint trails made by his skids, but I wasn't inclined to go after him. If he wanted to kill himself, that was his business.

I felt an irrational sense of loss.

It lasted about thirty seconds; then I smiled; and went back to the old fux and tried to start up a conversation.

Eight days later the man was back.

Now he was starting to scare me.

He'd patched the heat-envelope. It was still cracked and looked on the edge of unserviceability, but he came striding out of the distance with a strong motion, the skids on his boots carrying him boldly forward till he hit the mush. Then he bent and, almost without breaking stride, pulled them off, and kept coming. Straight in toward the base camp, up Westspit. His cowl was thrown back, and he was breathing deeply, not even exerting himself much, his long, horsey face flushed from his journey. He had nearly two weeks' growth of beard and so help me he looked like one of those soldiers of fortune you see smoking clay pipes and swilling up boar piss in the spacer bars around Port Medea. Heroic. An adventurer.

He sloughed in through the mud and the suckholes filled with sargasso, and he walked straight past me to his tent and went inside, and

I didn't see him for the rest of the day. But that night, as I sat outside the wickyup, letting the hard wind tell me odor tales of the Hotlands close to Argo at the top of the world, I saw Amos the Wise and two other old dromids come over the rise and down to his tent; and I stared at them until the heroic adventurer came out and squatted with them in a circle.

They didn't move, they didn't gesticulate, they didn't do a goddamned thing, they just joined flow and passed around the impressions like a vonge-coterie passing its dream-pipe.

And the next morning I was wakened by the sound of clattering, and threw on my envelope and came out to see him snapping together the segments of a jerry-rigged sledge of some kind. He'd cannibalized boot skids and tray shelves from the transport sheds and every last one of those lash-up spiders the lading crews use to tighten down cargo. It was an ugly, rickety thing, but it looked as if it would slide across ice once he was out of the mush.

Then it dawned on me he was planning to take all that out there into the Icelands. "Hold it, mister," I said. He didn't stop working. I strode over and gave him a kick in the hip. "I said: hold it!"

With his right hand he reached out, grabbed my left ankle and *lifted*. I half-turned, found myself off the ground, and when I looked up I was two meters away, the breath pulled out of me; on my back. He was still working.

I got up and ran at him. I don't recall seeing him look up, but he must have, otherwise how could he have gauged my trajectory?

When I stopped gasping and spitting out dirt, I tried to turn over and sit up, but there was a foot in my back. I thought it was him, but when the pressure eased and I could look over my shoulder I saw the blue-furred shape of a hunter fux standing there, a spear in his sinewy left hand. It wasn't aimed at me, but it was held away in a direct line that led back to aiming at me. Don't mess with the holy man, that was the message.

An hour later he pulled the sledge with three spiders wrapped around his chest, and dragged it off behind him, down the landbridge and out into the mush. He was leaning forward, straining to keep the travois from sinking into the porridge till he could hit firmer ice. He was one of those old holograms you see of a coolie in the fields, pulling a plow by straps attached to a leather band around his head.

He went away and I wasn't stupid enough to think he was going for good and all. That was an *empty* sledge.

What would be on it when he came back?

It was a thick, segmented tube a meter and a half long. He'd chipped away most of the ice in which it had lain for twenty years, and I knew what it was, and where it had come from, which was more than I could say about him.

It was a core laser off the downed Daedalus power satellite whose orbit had decayed inexplicably two years after the Northcape Power District had tossed the satellite up. It had been designed to calve into bergs the glaciers that had gotten too close to coastal settlements; and then melt them. It had gone down in the Icelands of Phykos, somewhere between the East Pole and Icebox, almost exactly two decades ago. I'd flown over it when they'd hauled me in from Enrique and the bush pilot decided to give me a little scenic tour. We'd looked down on the wreckage, now part of a complex ice sculpture molded by wind and storm.

And this nameless skujge who'd invaded my privacy had gone out there, somehow chonked loose the beamer — and its power collector, if I was right about the fat package at the end of the tube — and dragged it back who knows how many kilometers . . . for why?

Two hours later I found him down one of the access hatches that led to the base camp's power station, a fusion plant, deuterium source; a tank that had to be replenished every sixteen months: I didn't have a refinery.

He was examining the power beamers that supplied heat and electricity to the camp. I couldn't figure out what he was trying to do, but I got skewed over it and yelled at him to get his carcass out of there before we both froze to death because of his stupidity.

After a while he came up and sealed the hatch, and went off to tinker with his junk laser.

I tried to stay away from him in the weeks that followed. He worked over the laser, stealing bits and pieces of anything nonessential that he could find around the camp. It became obvious that though the lacy solar-collector screens had slowed the Daedalus's fall as they'd been burned off, not even that had saved the beamer from serious damage. I had no idea why he was tinkering with it, but I fantasized that if he could get it working he might go off and not come back.

And that would leave me right where I'd started, alone with creatures who did not paint pictures or sing songs or devise dances or make idols; to whom the concept of art was unknown; who responded to my attempts to communicate on an esthetic level with the stolid indifference of grandchildren forced to humor a batty old aunt.

It was penitence indeed.

Then one day he was finished. He loaded it all on the sledge — the laser, some kind of makeshift energy receiver package he'd mated to the original tube, my hologram projector, and spider straps and harnesses and a strut tripod — and he crawled down into the access hatch and stayed there for an hour. When he came back out he spoke to Amos, who had arrived as if silently summoned, and when he was done talking to him he got into his coolie rig and slowly dragged it all away. I started to follow, just to see where he was going, but Amos stopped me. He stepped in front of me and he had ekstasis with me and I was advised not to annoy the holy man, and not to bother the new connections that had been made in the camp's power source.

None of that was said, of course. It was all vague feelings and imperfect images. Hunches, impressions, thin suggestions, intuitive urgings. But I got the message. I was all alone on Meditation Island, there by sufferance of the dromids. As long as I did not interfere with the holy adventurer who had come out of nowhere to fill me with the rage I'd fled across the stars to escape.

So I turned away from the Icelands, good riddance, and tried to make some sense out of the uselessness of my life. Whoever he had been, I knew he wasn't coming back, and I hated him for making me understand what a waste of time I was.

That night I had a frustrating conversation with a turquoise fux in its female mode. The next day I shaved off my beard and thought about going back.

He came and went eleven times in the next two years. Where and how he lived out there, I never knew. And each time he came back 
he looked thinner, wearier, but more ecstatic. As if he had found

God out there. During the first year the fuxes began making the trek: out there in the shadowed vastness of the Icelands they would travel to see him. They would be gone for days and then return to speak among themselves. I asked Amos what they did when they made their hegira, and he said, through ekstasis, "He must live, is that not so?" To which I responded, "I suppose so," though I wanted to say, "Not necessarily."

He returned once to obtain a new heat-envelope. I'd had supplies dropped in, and they'd sent me a latest model, so I didn't object when he took my old suit.

He returned once for the death ceremony of Amos the Wise, and seemed to be leading the service. I stood there in the circle and said nothing, because no one asked me to contribute.

He returned once to check the fusion plant connections.

But after two years he didn't return again.

And now the dromids were coming from what must have been far distances, to trek across Meditation Island, off the land-bridge, and into the Icelands. By the hundreds and finally thousands they came, passed me, and vanished into the eternal winterland. Until the day a group of them came to me and their leader, whose name was Ben of the Old Times, joined with me in the flow and said, "Come with us to the holy man." They'd always stopped me when I tried to go out there.

"Why? Why do you want me to go now? You never wanted me out there before!" I could feel the acid boiling up in my anger, the tightening of my chest muscles, the clenching of my fists. They could burn in Argo before I'd visit that lousy skujge!

Then the old fux did something that astonished me. In three years they had done *nothing* astonishing except bring me food at the man's request. But now the aborigine extended a slim-fingered hand to his right and one of the males, a big hunter with bright blue fur, passed him his spear. Ben of the Old Times pointed it at the ground and, with a very few strokes, *drew two figures in the caked mud at my feet.*

It was a drawing of two humans standing side by side, their hands linked. One of them had lines radiating out from his head, and above the figures the dromid drew a circle with comparable lines radiating outward.



It was the first piece of intentional art I had ever seen created by a

Medean life-form. The first, as far as I knew, that had ever *been* created by a native. And it had happened as I watched. My heart beat faster. I *had* done it! I had brought the concept of art to at least one of these creatures.

"I'll come with you to see him," I said.

Perhaps my time in purgatory was coming to an end. It was possible I'd bought some measure of redemption.

I checked the fusion plant that beamed energy to my heat-envelope, to keep from freezing; and I got out my boot skids and Ba'al iceclaw; and I racked the ration dispenser in my pack full of silvr wrap; and I followed them out there. Where I had not been permitted to venture, lest I interfere with their holy man. Well, we'd see who was the more important of us two: a nameless intruder who came and went without ever a thank-you, or William Ronald Pogue, the man who brought art to the Medeans!

For the first time in many years I felt light, airy, worthy. I'd sprayed fixative on that pictograph in the mud. It might be the most valuable exhibit in the Pogue Museum of Native Art. I chuckled at my foolishness, and followed the small band of fuxes deeper into the Icelands.

It was close on crossback season, and the winds were getting harder, the storms were getting nastier. Not as impossible as it would be a month hence, but bad enough.

We were beyond the first glacier that could be seen from Meditation Island, the spine of ice cartographers had named the Seurat. Now we were climbing through the NoName Cleft, the fuxes chinking out hand-and-footholds with spears and claws, the Ba'al snarling and chewing pits for my own ascent. Green shadows swam down through the Cleft. One moment we were pulling ourselves up through twilight, and the next we could not see the shape before us. For an hour we lay flat against the ice-face as an hysterical wind raged down the Cleft trying to tear us loose and fling us into the cut below.

The double shadows flickered and danced around us. Then everything went into the red, the wind died, and through now-bloody shadows we reached the crest of the ridge beyond the Seurats.

A long slope lay before us, rolling to a plain of ice and slush pools, very different from the fields of dry ice that lay farther west to the lifeless expanse of Farside. Sunday was rapidly moving into Darkday.

Across the plain, vision was impeded by a great wall of frigid fog that rose off the tundra. Vaguely, through the miasma I could see the great glimmering bulk of the Rio de Luz, the immense kilometers-long ice mountain that was the final barrier between the Terminator lands and the frozen nothingness of Farside. The River of Light.

We hurried down the slope, some of the fuxes simply tucking two, four or six of their legs under them and sliding down the expanse to the plain. Twice I fell, rolled, slid on my butt, tried to regain my feet, tumbled again, and decided to use my pack as a toboggan. By the time we had gained the plain, it was nearly Darkday and fog had obscured the land. We decided to camp till Dimday, hacked out sleeping pits in the tundra, and buried ourselves.

Overhead the raging aurora drained red and green and purple as I closed my eyes and let the heat of the envelope take me away. What could the "holy man" want from me after all this time?

We came through the curtain of fog, the Rio de Luz scintillating dimly beyond its mask of gray-green vapor. I estimated that we had come more than thirty kilometers from Meditation Island. It was appreciably colder now, and ice-crystals glimmered like rubies and emeralds in the blue fux fur. And, oddly, a kind of breathless anticipation had come over the aborigines. They moved more rapidly, oblivious to the razor winds and the slush pools underfoot. They jostled one another in their need to go toward the River of Light and whatever the man out there needed me to assist with.

It was a long walk, and for much of that time I could see little more of the icewall than its cruel shape rising at least fifteen hundred meters above the tundra. But as the fog thinned, the closer we drew to the base of the ice mountain, the more I had to avert my eyes from what lay ahead: the permanent aurora lit the ice and threw off a coruscating glare that was impossible to bear.

And then the fuxes dashed on ahead and I was left alone, striding across the tundra toward the Rio de Luz.



I came out of the fog.

And I looked up and up at what rose above me, touching the angry sky and stretching as far away as I could see to left and right. It seemed hundreds of kilometers in length, but that was impossible.

I heard myself moaning.

But I could not look away, even if it burned out my eyes.

Lit by the ever-changing curtain of Medea's sky, the crash and downdripping of a thousand colors that washed the ice in patterns that altered from instant to instant, the Rio de Luz had been transformed. The man had spent three years melting and slicing and sculpting kilometers of living ice — I couldn't tell how many — into a work of high art.

Horses of liquid blood raced through valleys of silver light. The stars were born and breathed and died in one lacy spire. Shards of amber brilliance shattered against a diamond-faceted icewall through a thousand apertures cut in the facing column. Fairy towers too thin to exist rose from a shadowed hollow and changed color from meter to meter all up their length. Legions of rainbows rushed from peak to peak, like waterfalls of precious gems. Shapes and forms and spaces merged and grew and vanished as the eye was drawn on and on. In a cleft he had formed an intaglio that was black and ominous as the specter of death. But when light hit it suddenly, shattering and spilling down into the bowl beneath, it became a great bird of golden promise. And the sky was there, too. All of it, reflected back and new because it had been pulled down and captured. Argo and the far suns and Phrixus and Helle and Jason and Theseus and memories of suns that had dominated the empty places and were no longer even memories. I had a dream of times past as I stared at one pool of changing colors that bubbled and sang. My heart was filled with feelings I had not known since childhood. And it never stopped. The pinpoints of bright blue flame skittered across the undulating walls of sculpted ice, rushed toward certain destruction in the deeps of a runoff cut, paused momentarily at the brink, then flung themselves into green oblivion. I heard myself moaning and turned away, looking back toward the ridge across the fog and tundra; and I saw nothing, nothing! It was too painful not to see what he had done. I felt my throat tighten with fear of missing a moment of that great pageant unfolding on the ice tapestry. I turned back and it was all new, I was seeing it first and always as I had just minutes before . . . was it minutes . . . how long had I been staring into that dream pool . . .

how many years had passed . . . and would I be fortunate enough to spend the remainder of my life just standing there breathing in the rampaging beauty I beheld? I couldn't think, pulled air into my lungs only when I had forgotten to breathe for too long a time.

Then I felt myself being pulled along, and cried out against whatever force had me in its grip, that would deprive me of a second of that towering narcotic.

But I was pulled away, and was brought down to the base of the River of Light, and it was Ben of the Old Times who had me. He forced me to sit, with my back to the mountain, and after a very long time in which I sobbed and fought for air, I was able to understand that I had almost been lost, that the dreamplace had taken me. But I felt no gratitude. My soul ached to rush out and stare up at beauty forever.

The fux flowed with me, and through ekstasis I felt myself ceasing to pitch and yaw. The colors dimmed in the grottos behind my eyes. He held me silently with a powerful flow until I was William Pogue again. Not just an instrument through which the ice mountain sang its song, but Pogue, once again Pogue.

And I looked up, and I saw the fuxes hunkered down around the body of their "holy man," and they were making drawings in the ice with their claws. And I knew it was not I who had brought them to beauty.

He lay face down on the ice, one hand still touching the laser tube. The hologram projector had been attached with a slipcard computer. Still glowing was an image of the total sculpture. Almost all of it was in red lines, flickering and fading and coming back in with power being fed from base camp; but one small section near the top of an impossibly angled flying bridge and minaret section was in blue line.

I stared at it for a while. Then Ben said this was the reason I had been brought to that place. The holy man had died before he could complete the dreamplace. And in a rush of flow he showed me where, in the sculpture, they had first understood what beauty was, and what art was, and how they were one with the Grandparents in the sky. Then he created a clear, pure image. It was the man, flying to become one with Argo. It was the stick figure in the mud: it was the uninvited guest with the lines of radiance coming out of his head.

There was a pleading tone in the fux's ekstasis. Do this for us. Do what he did not have the time to do. Make it complete.

I stared at the laser lying there, with its unfinished hologram image blue and red and flickering. It was a bulky, heavy tube, a meter and a half long. And it was still on. He had fallen in the act.

I watched them scratching their first drawings, even the least of them, and I wept within myself; for Pogue who had come as far as he could, only to discover it was not far enough. And I hated him for doing what I could not do. And I knew he would have completed it and then walked off into the emptiness of Farside, to die quickly in the darkness, having done his penance . . . and more.

They stopped scratching, as if Ben had ordered them to pay some belated attention to me. They looked at me with their slanted vulpine eyes now filling with mischief and wonder. I stared back at them. Why should I? Why the hell should I? For what? Not for me, that's certain!

We sat there close and apart, for a long time, as the universe sent its best light to pay homage to the dreamplace.

The body of the penitent lay at my feet.

From time to time I scuffed at the harness that would hold the laser in position for cutting. There was blood on the shoulder straps.

After a while I stood up and lifted the rig. It was much heavier than I'd expected.

Now they come from everywhere to see it. Now they call it Oddum's Tapestry, not the Rio de Luz. Now everyone speaks of the magic. A long time ago he may have caused the death of thousands in another place, but they say that wasn't intentional; what he brought to the Medeans was on purpose. So it's probably right that everyone knows the name Virgil Oddum, and what he created at the East Pole.

But they should know me, too. I was there! I did some of the work.

My name is William Ronald Pogue, and I mattered. I'm old, but I'm important, too. You should know names.

# QUICKTIME

THE MOBS THAT FED the guillotines raged, screaming, through Galiopolis, storming the Sixty Towers, dragging out the Lords and their executioners, their secret police, their paladins; holding mass slayings in the verdant gardens and tiled squares. The *chunk* of the blade became a regular beat in the great city of gold. The holiday cheers of the mobs rose round and round the onyx Towers as each Brother Lord in his turn was separated from his head.

And yet, miraculously, one Lord escaped. His spies among the poor had warned him that the vassals were beginning to talk of blood. They had warned him days ago. The last complement of peasant children taken for the arena had set the starving poor loose. They became a drum beating for death. He heard the swelling sound, and he took steps to protect himself if the worst should happen. Now, as the mobs became a tide washing through the great city, he fled as his Brother Lords died. He alone, of the sixty Brother Lords, escaped.

He used secret passages and hidden tunnels, and he escaped to the edge of the golden city. There at the verge of the forest, a rat pack close on his trail, he found the cleverly concealed pit that had been dug under the protecting, ground-sweeping branches of a thylax tree; and he buried himself, with only his dirt-smeared face and the muzzle of a stinger showing through the foliage. And he waited.

This Lord was known to the peasants as Garth of the Red Hand. And he knew how to wait. In the chambers of pain beneath his Tower he had absorbed the lessons of waiting: to enjoy with a gentle patience the exact science of his resident hectors as they pleasured themselves with razors and chemicals and fire. Masks and needles and paring knives and lasers. He could sit without moving for hours.

Now he waited in fear. For close on a thousand years the Brother Lords had ruled, and fear was unknown to them, but Garth was not ashamed to admit he was frightened. From the balcony of his throne room he had seen the mob dragging Oldan and his mistresses to the blade. He had seen them clubbed to their knees, their arms held straight back, and the thrashing in the moment before the sound of *swish* and *chunk*. He had seen that the blade had already grown dull, and that the peasants took pleasure in the fact: raising the blade for a second strike; the head only half-severed; the body twitching.

He was not ashamed of his fear. And he waited with the utmost patience. There was no alternative.

The pack came crashing through the forest, and from his pit he watched. He saw the head of his brother Wanzor, eyes still open, thumping at the belt of the pack's leader.

Then they were gone, ripping away the entwined branches of the downswept trees, plunging deeper into the forest to find him. He had to believe all the others were dead now. They would . . . count heads. They would know he had not been sent to the blade. They would not rest till they had him.

There had to be an escape route. Nowhere in the world was safe. Nowhere in this world.

By now they had smashed open his treasure rooms and scattered his diamonds, killed his concubines, slaughtered his matched teams of horses and panthers. The thousand-year rule of the Brother Lords had ended.

There would be retribution when the peasants realized they could not rule themselves. When they called for their Lords to return.

Then he remembered what he had known a moment before; there were no more Lords. The fifty-nine Brothers were meat now, nothing but meat. And the sixtieth shivered in a hole in the forest.

Night came; and with it the merciless light of the full moon. Garth thought the time had come to escape. There *was* a way. He had spent his time waiting . . . and thinking. As he began to scoop away the dirt that hid him, torches moved into the forest. He could see their firefly light moving out from the burning core of Galiopolis. He waited till the hungry mobs had divided into hunting groups and had searched past his ignoble hideout. If he had sought hope in the delusion that they might have forgotten him, he knew, now, that they would never rest till they had located and slaughtered the last of the Brother Lords.



And so he burrowed deeper; he waited; crouched in the damp

hole, his stinger aimed at the forest's shadows — waiting for the first unfortunate piggish face to discover him.

He waited and waited, but they seemed to have returned by other routes, seemed to have bypassed him in the darkness. For now, for a while, he was safe.

Then, as dawn sent its first glow through the trees, he crawled out of the pit beneath the ground-scraping branches, and cautiously made his way into the city.

To the Experimental Buildings.

The Professor had survived because he had come up from peasant stock. But even though he had been granted an elevated position in the world of the Lords, he knew his place. He knew who was of the royal crèche, and who was not. And so he cowered in fear as Garth of the Red Hand leveled the stinger at his face.

Rats danced in the Professor's eyes, but he knew he was helpless. It was a tiny weapon, but it was in the hand of this Lord he had known all his life. Knew him as a thing that could kill without drawing a hesitant breath. He stared at this man, one of the former rulers of the world, whom he had never thought to see alive again; and he wished with a most unscientific intensity that there might be some way he could complete the moist job the peasants had begun.

Garth perched, hip cocked on the edge of a low experiment shelf, pointing the stinger directly into the Professor's face. "I have been subsidizing you far too long, Professor; but your foolish experiments may at last proffer some reward." The Professor looked confused. What could the Red Hand want that he could give?

"You will send me back one hundred years; and if you do not, I will burn out first your left eye; and then your right. And then your left leg; and then your right . . . and then . . ." He spoke in a soft, steady voice. The old man knew he was serious; he would do as he said.

"But, my Lord," he said, indicating the banks of time-stress warpers, "we have not yet perfected the machine. We can send you only to one historical era and only to one geographical coordinate: to the Mesozoic . . . more specifically, to the Upper Jurassic Period; approximately one hundred and thirty million years ago."

Lord Garth studied the scientist with narrowed eyes. "Convince me this is not a trick, old man; or die here and now."

The Professor replied with obvious fear in his voice. "We don't yet know why this should be so, my Lord; it is the consuming subject of our studies. It is the reason we have not been able to repay your unceasing faith in our continuing experiments. But we have sent men back and we have brought them forward again, with no difficulty. A genuine breakthrough; some might call it a miracle of science."

"And I call it useless for my purpose." He was silent a moment. Then his face, all but his eyes, went dead. "And your widows might call it the cause of their loneliness."

The Professor found breathing difficult. The tiny blind eye of the stinger stared unwaveringly at him.

"My Lord, please! It is only that we have not yet been able to develop a method for precise chronophase calibration."

Garth read the old man's fear. An unpleasant truth, that was what he was hearing. "Can you bring me back, after a suitable amount of time has elapsed here?"

"Yes, my Lord. You remain in the stress field, no matter where you go in that period. You could be brought back at any time."

"Then you will do it," Garth said. He lowered the stinger and stood away from the shelf as if ready for the journey.

"But . . ."

"*You will do it,*" Garth said softly. "And hear me, Professor. I have a trusted agent still at large; one who owes his life to me; one who will see your every action. If you do not bring me back when all this is ended . . ." He waved his hand toward the outside of the Experimental Buildings. "He will not merely kill *you* . . . oh no: he has instructions to kill your wives and all your children. Slowly. As they would have died in the rooms of pain in my Tower. Do you understand, Professor? Do you *really* understand?"

The old man nodded. It had all been bluff, but the Professor could not know Garth was lying. He felt the flames of hatred burn higher; this animal should be killed as quickly as possible, should not be permitted to escape. Even in an age one hundred and thirty million years gone, his evil was something that should not be permitted to exist.

But he was old, and easily frightened. He was hampered as Garth was not: he had love in him. He would do it.



. . .

The old man readied his machines. And when the bright, smooth metal transmission stage had been elevated, and when the banks of time-stress warpers softly hummed with power, and when the cone of orange light shone down on the stage, he told Lord Garth to stand on the circular plate.

The escape route lay open before the last of the sixty Brother Lords. He did not move.

"How strong is your hatred?" he said. He studied the old man. "Is it strong enough that you would condemn your women and all your children?" The old man was too terrified to speak. "It might be that strong, though I think not. But I ask myself, 'Why has the Professor not mentioned the dangers that I might face in that ancient time? Even if I should be there but moments, and years pass here, and the Professor grows older and returns me in the blink of an eye . . . what of the invisible microbes in that ancient world? What of the beasts that roamed there? Am I not being sent off too easily, with so little preparation?' I ask myself these things, Professor. And you do not answer."

The Professor clasped his hands nervously. "The danger, my Lord, would be to any creatures living in that time, not to you. Contamination from the future, from sophisticated viruses *we* might carry, that is the threat." *You are the threat, then as now*, he thought. "And as you say . . . you will perceive the journey and your time there as merely an instant. Ten years here, even twenty . . . as you say . . . the blink of an eye."

Garth looked at him. "Twenty years? You won't live another twenty years."

"But my wives and children will."

"And what if you die before the time is right to return me?" He asked the question aloud, but it was as if he were worrying it in his mind.

"There is an automatic return mechanism, my Lord. It could be set before you go."

"And what would prevent you from canceling it once I was gone?"

"I wouldn't do that, my Lord. On my honor, I would not do that."

Garth stared at him silently for a long time. Then, as if he had thought it through logically, considering every vaguest possibility, he said, "My agent will know when the time is right for my return, for the moment when your beloved peasants need a Lord to come again and rule them as before. Not sixty Brother Lords, but one. Just one."

"Yes, my Lord. Your . . . agent . . ."

Garth considered the old man. He *seemed* cowed by the thought of shadowy watchers. "And what of the great saurians that dominated the world? I am no peasant, old man. I have studied. I know of these dinosaurs, these terrible meat-eaters."

"That has been considered, my Lord. The experiments we have conducted, the men who have gone back, have selected the very site to which you will be transported. A safe location we have visited many times. The Morrison Formation, in the area they called Utah over a thousand years ago. Classic Upper Jurassic terrain, my Lord: warm, equitable climate; the seas have long since retreated to the north; this is a broad, low floodplain. Very sparsely inhabited by saurians, though our most recent expedition reported a herd of sauropods, very likely apatosaurus, but possibly diplodocus, foraging in the area."

Garth tried to remember. "They were herbivores? They did not eat meat?"

The Professor nodded with enthusiasm. "Exactly. Harmless vegetarians. Safe, my Lord, absolutely safe for the few moments you will exist in that time."

Garth ruminated a moment longer, then said, "I will watch as you set the return mechanism. Do it now."

The old man went to a console of heat-sensitive controls, and Lord Garth stood over him as he explained the calibrations. "Set it for one hundred years from today." The old man tapped out the proper coding, and the date appeared in a liquid-crystal display. Garth studied the console, and when he seemed satisfied he waited till the Professor had walked away from the mechanism and followed him back to the transmission stage.

The Professor stood waiting next to a single knife-switch. "Now what do you do to send me?" the Lord asked.

The Professor motioned to the switch. "Just this, my Lord, and it is done."

Garth mounted to the transmission stage with one step, and stood bathed in the cone of orange light. "Send me away," he said quietly. "And remember, Professor: You are not alone."

There was smoldering hatred on the Professor's face for an instant as he threw home the knife-switch, and it was the true face Garth had known he would see in that final moment. He smiled with satisfaction. As the orange light flickered, he raised the stinger and squeezed the trigger. An explosive dart erupted from the weapon, struck the Professor in the left eye and, as the laboratory wavered and dimmed around him, Garth saw the old man's face erupt and the headless body thrown half across the room.

*Now your wives and children need never fear,* he thought. *Nor need I.* Concealing the location of the pharaoh's grave with the execution of the grave diggers was always de rigueur.

All through the Experimental Buildings, down the corridors, to the subbasements, in the walls, the power of the time-stress warpers throbbed and hummed, the sound rising as the orange light that washed him grew stronger and the world of the sixty Brother Lords grew as ephemeral as clouds seen in a lake.

He felt a thin pain throughout his body, as if he were being sliced neatly by a giant scalpel . . .

The light strobed brilliantly. And then the transmission stage was empty. And then the automatic cutoff killed power to the banks of warpers. And then the laboratory was empty save for the smoking ruin that had been an old man. And Lord Garth of the Red Hand had drunk deeply from the time stream.

He drew a breath that scored his throat raw, and opened his eyes. For an instant he saw nothing, and the pain was cataclysmic. Then he swallowed and tried to get his heart to beat more slowly; and sight came back; and he was standing up to his ankles in water. His gold-thread boots were soaked.

It was marshland. Reedy grass rose all around him.

He could look off across the floodplain to granite mountains that rose on the horizon. The sun was a melting bronze ball. To his right, very near, gigantic cycads stood in a forest crush that dominated the area. The palm trees had thick, unbranched columnar trunks. Thirty feet above his head, huge, leathery fronds formed a violently green canopy that blotted out the sunlight.

All around him in the water stood the sauropods. He had materialized in the middle of the herd. Massive bodies seventy feet long, gray-green hide all around him, sunk with their vast tonnage in the moist earth, fifteen-foot-long necks, their ridiculously small heads high in the foliage, risen on their hind legs, tearing at the fronds thirty feet overhead.

The sound of the instant of his arrival was the *crack* of lightning as air was displaced.

Directly above him the apatosaurus started at the report, twisted its great sinewy neck, and the projectile-shaped head plummeted toward Lord Garth.

In the instant of awareness as he saw the terrifying open mouth with its rows of long, narrow teeth rushing toward him, he had no time to scream, and only half enough time to think: *But it only eats vegetation!*

Nor *did* the gargantuan herbivore eat meat. As its great jaws clamped themselves onto Garth's upper torso, masticating his head and shoulders between its pencil-like teeth, the dinosaur understood in its dim way that the new food it had found growing in the marsh grass was not a tender new kind of vegetation.

And from a height it dropped the unpleasant thing. It had needed to sample. To reject.

Lord Garth had fallen from a great height, bearing with him the answer to the question the Professor had often asked: *Did dinosaurs think?*

The answer was yes. But not quickly.

# THE AVENGER OF DEATH

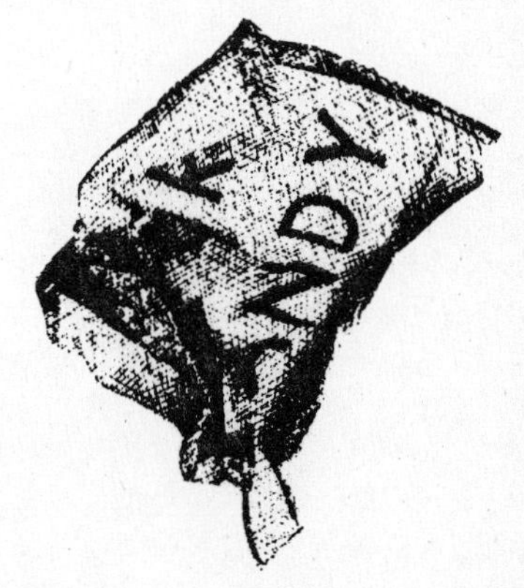

THE FIRST ONE Pen Robinson killed came to his attention partially through the good offices of the Manhattan branch of the Federal Bureau of Investigation. He had been holding a dusty copy of *Burke's Peerage* when they took him into custody.

They came for him — two frosty agents who had bought their suits at the same Big & Tall Men's Shop — just after two-thirty on Saturday. The bookstore — "just off Broadway, rare books and technical texts in Good Condition" — was busier than usual because of the two Puerto Rican boys who had approached him the previous Monday as he was unlocking the shop. They had braced him, suggesting a way in which he — Meester Robinson of Robinson's Good Used Books — could attract new business, "guaranteed *absolutamente*." For a small fee, they would undertake to slip under the windshield wipers of every automobile parked between Eighth Avenue and Park, between 42nd and 59th Streets, a flier advertising whatever Meester Robinson wanted to push that week.

Pen had gone to the Kinko instant print shop on Lexington, and had ordered three thousand fliers extolling the arcane virtues of books scented with shelf dust and written by men and women who had vanished into the lonely posterity of the Dewey Decimal System.

The boys had been as good as their word, and mailboxes, doorways, lunch counters — and windshields — had worn his fliers throughout the week. Pen had paid them gladly; and Saturday was busier than usual when the FBI chilled the doorknob of the shop, entering to take him into custody.

One moment he had been standing there, dusting *Burke's Peerage*, and the next he was crossing the sidewalk on 51st Street, being sternly guided by a cold hand, slipping as effortlessly as an exhalation, into the velour darkness of the black limo double-parked in front of the shop. Fifteen minutes later he was somewhere in the towering abyss of the Pan Am building, seated in a moderately comfortable knockoff of an Eames design, being punctiliously but courteously questioned by a man half his age. Pen Robinson, at age fifty-five, looked no older than forty; and his judgment of the inquisitor's youth may have been faulty. He was under no misapprehension about the quality of the man's eyes, however.

He thought, *I'm glad I never have to look out of those eyes.* He knew he would not like the world seen from that side.

"You called a bicycle shop in Queens yesterday," said the wearer of the bad eyes.

"Uh, yes . . ." Pen was wary.

"Why did you call that number, Mr. Robinson?"

"It was a wrong number."

"Whom," he said precisely, "were you looking for at that number?"

Pen furrowed his brow. He had no idea where this was going. "They said they were from the FBI. The men who brought me here. I never asked to see their identification. I suppose it's against the law to say you're from the FBI if you're not. Are you really the FBI?"

The young man neither nodded nor blinked. "Whom were you seeking at that number, sir?"

"Maybe I ought to ask to see your credentials. I don't even know your name . . . there's nothing on the door out there. How do I know you're —"

The young man leaned forward, resting his pale, freckled hands on his desk blotter. The desk was empty of all but the leather-framed blotter, and a pair of pale, freckled hands. "You don't want to get yourself in any deeper, do you, Mr. Robinson? You're only here for a visit; you understand that the liaison we share, at the moment, does not involve the possibility of arrest, imprisonment, detainment, any of that. You understand that, don't you?"

Pen was frightened. People vanished, it happened all the time; and not just in Latin American dictatorships. Right here in the United States, it could happen: Judge Crater, hundreds of children every year, Jimmy Hoffa. And those who vanished into *apparats* controlled by people who spent their time spying on one another. There had to be hidden places where the vanished were taken. And from there to other locations . . . from which one never returned . . . or if you did, the years would have been stolen, and your loved ones would never recognize you . . . to come back as an old, old man they did not know. There were no loved ones: Pen was alone in the world.

But that only made it worse. If they decided he would never return, who but the New York State tax assessor would try to find him?

"Look, I don't know what this is all about," he said, trying to get back to whatever safe place he had unknowingly abandoned. "But this is all crazy; it's a mistake of some kind. Why don't I just tell you what that call was about."

"Why don't you tell me that, Mr. Robinson." No resonance: flat silver panes of reflective glass.

So he told him how inconsequential it had been.

"I bought a library at an estate sale. From an agent in Detroit. It was one of the last elements of the dissolved estate of a man who had worked for GM for many years. I was told there were hundreds of technical journals and books of design." He paused a beat to clarify. "My store specializes in technical texts."

The eyes blinked. Pen took that as encouragement.

"I was opening the crates . . . so I could catalogue what had come. I was slapping them."

Another blink. Pen was beginning to get the drill: he clarified.

"Slapping them. Flat banging two books together to get the dust off them. Then I turn each one upside down and riffle the pages; for good measure. A check fell out of one of them. I picked it up, and it was a check that had been written by a man named Henry Chatley. The address was in Queens. It was a perfectly good check drawn to cash, in the amount of something like one hundred and fifty dollars. It was only two weeks since it had been written, it was a check someone could cash. I called the number on the face of it. A man answered and said it was some bicycle repair shop. I thought I'd misdialed, and called back, and got the same man. I dialed very carefully the second time. So I didn't know what to do."

The mouth beneath the eyes moved. "How did it get there?"

"How did *what* get there? The shop, the man, what?"

"The check, Mr. Robinson. How did the check get into that book?"

"How am I supposed to know?"

"You say you bought these books from the library of a man who lived in Detroit."

"Yes. He died, and they liquidated his assets to pay outstanding taxes."

"This was an old book?"

Pen shrugged. "I didn't check the copyright, but I'd say it had been in his library for years, yes, I think I can say that."

"What was the title of this book, that you say the check fell from?"

"I'm not *saying* it fell, it *did* fall. I didn't make this up!" He felt anger rising despite his caution. "And what if I *am* making it up, what's the problem here? I did a decent thing, I made a good samaritan phone call; I got a number that had been changed. Obviously, that's the answer. What is it you *think* this is all about?"

"I don't think it's about anything, sir. I'm asking a few questions."

There wasn't anything to say to that, so Pen sat and waited. It had to stop sometime; perhaps now.

"So you don't know Henry Chatley."

Pen said, very seriously, sitting forward and placing his hands opposite the pale, freckled pair: "I wouldn't know Henry Chatley if he walked through that door. I have never *met* a Henry Chatley; I have never *heard* of a Henry Chatley; and I wish to god I'd never seen his damned check! Now does that satisfy you? Have I been here long enough for you to run me through your computers or whatever you do, long enough for you to understand I'm a used bookseller and not Ashenden the Secret Agent?"

The young man with the bad eyes said nothing. He looked at all the parts of Pen's face, as if certain duplicity would reveal itself in dark lines if he applied enough visual pressure. Finally, he said, "Thank you, Mr. Robinson."

Pen was astonished. It was over, as abruptly as that. His inquisitor obviously meant for him to go.

"That's it?" he said. Now he was annoyed. It seemed he should have ended with a bit more fanfare . . . *something!*

"That's it, sir."

"Not even going to tell me what this has been about, are you? Not even a word, right? Just let me march out and find my way back to my place of business, from which you dragged me for this waste of time!"

"Goodbye, Mr. Robinson." The door opened behind him, and he felt a chill. The cold hand touched him again, and he knew it was time to get up, now, right now, and go with the agent.

Three minutes later, he was on the street.

He was hailing a cab when it hit him. How *did* that two-week-old check, written on a New York bank, by a man whose phone number had been changed with such impossible swiftness that it had already been reassigned to a bicycle repair shop in Queens, get into a book that had sat on an old man's bookshelf in Detroit for possibly decades? And who the hell was Henry Chatley?

In the cab going back uptown, he felt as if he stood poised before a membrane. Where he stood, on this side, it was the real world, the mimetic universe, a place of order, even if this thing with the FBI made no sense, was something out of *Alice*. On the other side, through that translucent curtain, lay a great many small items, only imperfectly seen, but probably very important. Where the check had come from, how it had gotten into the book, who Henry Chatley was . . . or had been. He had an overwhelming sense of certainty that Henry Chatley, whoever, wherever, was dead.

But how to get through the membrane?

He needed a trope, a metaphor, a puff of smoke, a rabbit for the hat. Twenty minutes later, back in the shop, near to closing time, the rabbit manifested itself.

While he had been at the Pan Am building, his clerks had tended to the benefits proffered by the two Puerto Rican boys. The shop was empty.

He decided to lock up early, cleared the cash register, gave out the paychecks, and watched as the clerks wandered up the street, seeking weekend euphoria. He stared out the front window for a time, then locked the doors and stared out the window for a longer time. In all, it had been only twenty minutes, yet in that time he had resisted the impulse to find the book again: not once, but a hundred times.

Finally, he went back into the storeroom, to the stack of books he had removed from the crate the day before. He had not lied to the inquisitor. He really *didn't* know which book it had been. When the check had floated to the floor, he had laid the book on the stack beside the crate, and had taken no further notice of it. If all was as it had been, the book should still be there.

It was. One of the clerks had placed a folded newspaper atop the stack, but otherwise, everything was as it had been. He picked up the book. *Elements of Structural Design*, with a copyright notice of

1926. Pen held the book in both hands, and stared at it; then, as he flipped the pages, he discovered two more pieces of paper.

The first was part of a press release for a book titled *Tian Wen: A Chinese Book of Origins*. It had been torn off, possibly having been used as a bookmark. It bore an excerpt from the twenty-three-hundred-year-old Taoist catalogue of mythology, philosophy and pre-Imperial legend. It read as follows:

1
Of the beginning of old,
Who spoke the tale?

2
When above and below were not yet formed,
Who was there to question?

3
When dark and bright were obscured,
Who could distinguish?

He had no idea what it meant. He *never* understood such riddles, though apparently entire nations found the words urgently meaningful. The only one of such epigraphs that had ever made sense to him was: *The oxen are slow, but the Earth is patient*. That seemed peculiarly appropriate now, even if the three excerpts from *Tian Wen* were not.

So he continued flipping the pages of the book, and came, at last, to the stiff file card wedged into the spine fold. Printed on the card were the words CHATLEY and WHERE THE WOODBINE TWINETH. Under these words, written in a fine hand, with an ink pen, was the direction *Take by truck, corner 82nd and Amsterdam, Friday, 7:17 pm*.

He took the IRT uptown to 79th and Broadway, and walked quickly to 82nd and Amsterdam. He expected to find a shop, or an apartment, or something that related. He found nothing but the dead faces of apartment buildings as night fell.

But he knew he had been intended to find *something*. However the three seemingly disconnected pieces of paper had found their way into that book, he understood in his meat and bones that it was he, Pen Robinson, who had been meant to discover the puzzle, and to solve it. He had never been a mystic, lived life surely in the pragmatic universe of shelf dust and self-prepared meals after work, and knew there was a logical explanation waiting for him here on the corner of 82nd Street and Amsterdam Avenue.

He loitered. He leaned against a wall and studied the street. Nothing, for the longest time. He looked to the rooftops, and then to the filthy New York sky. Nothing, for a longer time. He felt his eyes closing. He knew he shouldn't be weary, nothing really exhausting had happened to him that day. Perplexing, emotionally taxing, but not truly something to make the flesh sag. But the waiting was beginning to take its measure of him.

And the rabbit came again.

Across the street, directly opposite his station, a pale blue light pulsed softly from the stairwell leading down to a basement apartment. He studied it for a while, and then slowly walked across 82nd to the apartment building. He looked over the wrought iron railing, leaning between heavy black plastic bags of garbage waiting for the truck some distant morning. In the stairwell, lying on his back, was a man with a hole in his chest. From the hole pulsed a distressingly blue light, and as Pen watched, the hole expanded slightly, and the glowing light colored the man's anguished face. He was in terrible pain.

Pen walked to the gate in the railing, slipped the latch, and walked down the stone steps to the filthy bottom. He knelt beside the man, and looked into his face. "Henry Chatley," he said. He knew who this had to be.

The man looked up at him, and nodded with the tiniest movement. "You found the termination order," he said, the words sighing from between lips that barely moved.

The glow pulsed steadily, as Chatley's chest was being eaten away; and Pen could see inside him. It was like looking into a cauldron of soup being roiled by an invisible ladle. "What's happening to you?" Pen said urgently. He felt he should be doing something for Chatley, but this new strangeness was more frightening than anything that had yet happened. "Is there something I can do?"

The man made an attempt to smile. It was a thin rictus, the corners of his mouth twitching for just an instant. The sound coming from the glowing hole in his chest was faint, but if Pen leaned closer he could make out the unmistakable keening of mountain winds.

Whatever was happening to Chatley, it had been intended that he would suffer. Pen asked again if there was some help he could offer: a hospital, moving the man's limbs to a more comfortable position, some kind of cover that would block the hole?

Chatley shook his head without much actual movement. "I took George S. Patton and Bert Lahr."

Pen said, "What? Say again, please: I couldn't make that out."

"Patton and Bert Lahr. And Huey Long and Groucho Marx. I took them."

"Took them? Took them where? Were you a cab driver? What?"

"I took them where the woodbine twineth. And Ansel Adams. I took him."

"Who are you, Mr. Chatley? What are you saying to me?"

Chatley looked up, and for a moment there were ages in his eyes. And enormous measures of pure pain. And the sense of things rushing away from the lens of his sight, while mountain winds howled. "I worked for the Dust Man. I collected for him. Got notices and did the actual work."

Pen had no idea what he meant.

That was not quite true.

He had an idea, but it lay so far beyond the membrane, on the shadowy side of other realities, that he could not countenance it.

Chatley said, "The Dust Man. The reaper. He laughs when he calls himself Boneyard Bill."

"He did this to you?"

"I did this to myself. He gave me a termination order for you. I didn't do it. So he had George fulfill the order on me."

Pen remembered the file card in the book. "Take by truck."

Chatley was speaking so softly now, Pen had to lean in almost to his mouth. The blue glow had spread, the hole was gigantic, nearly from armpit to armpit. "George isn't as adept as he should be. The truck threw me over the railing. I've been waiting for you. I'm glad you came." These words were spoken so haltingly, so filled with dying air, that it took him several minutes to release them.

"Why didn't you take me?" Pen asked.

Chatley would have shrugged, had he been able. As it was, he twitched terribly, saying, "If it hadn't been you, it would have been my next order. Should have been the woman before you. The order was an epileptic seizure, death all alone, in the evening, dressed to go out to dinner with her daughter." He closed his eyes against the pain, and said, "Her name was Emily Austin. In California. It should have been her, but I was still afraid. I'm still afraid; it hurts very much; Bill likes to hurt. But he may not be done with me. There was a taker once, a while ago, Ottmar, he got word back to some of us . . . the same way I got the papers into the book for you to find . . . he said it didn't stop after Bill had his way. Not for orders like you or Emily Austin, you're on the books. But for us, the takers. Bill likes to hurt. He doesn't get as much of a chance as he'd like."

"Can I help you in *any* way?"

Chatley opened his eyes. There was distance behind the color. He was on his way. The blue glow had eaten its way down through his stomach. "You know."

"I can't do that," Pen said, wishing he hadn't.

"Then why ask?"

"What would I have to do? I don't think I can do it, but what would that be . . . to help . . . ?"

Chatley told him. It was simple, but it was unpleasant. Then he said, "You can always tell one of us by the eyes." And he described the bad eyes Pen had seen watching him across a desk earlier that day. He lay silently for a long time, as the blue glow ate away the flesh and the bones and Pen could see the maelstrom swirling inside him. Then he said, "If you're going to do it, please now. It's very bad now. It's very bad."

And so Henry Chatley became the first for Pen Robinson.

But when Chatley was gone, perhaps having been saved from the Dust Man's special attentions on that other plain beyond the membrane, Pen realized he had not asked what the Chinese epigraphs meant, nor why he had written a check for cash in the amount of one hundred and fifty dollars, nor how he — using Ottmar's method — had been able to get the papers into that old book, nor what had turned him against the Dust Man, nor what had finally broadened his courage to defy Bill, nor what the takers posing as FBI men had sought to find out from Pen (but perhaps it had only been a matter of needing to be convinced Pen was an unsuspecting bystander), nor the answers to the other questions that now would never go into the solving of the puzzle, the passage through the membrane.

And one morning very soon, the truck would pick up a black plastic bag filled with remaining parts.

Pen gave over the running of the shop to the clerks.

He wandered the city, looking into people's faces.

He found the taker who had fulfilled the orders on P. T. Barnum and Babe Ruth and Adlai Stevenson, among others. Those were the names she remembered best, the ones she would tell him about. He found her eating dinner alone at the Russian Tea Room, and he followed her home, and did what he would never have thought himself capable of doing. He forced his way into her building, then into her apartment. He tied her to a chair and asked her more than a hundred questions. Chatley had died before he could answer those questions, more than a hundred Pen had been too distracted to ask. She possessed the bad eyes Henry Chatley had described, so Pen was able to do what he had to do. But she knew only a few things, despite her age. She did as she was told. Had been doing it for a very long time; and Pen learned that it was because of the gift of *a very long time* that many takers hired on.

It seemed to Pen a poor reason for working at such an unpleasant job. And when she told him, with resignation, that now he would have to put her out of Bill's reach, because of finding her and talking to her and interfering with her anonymity and making her suspect in Bill's eyeless sockets, he said he couldn't do that, and she began to cry, which Pen thought was shameless of her, and she told him some of what it would be like, but he already knew that because he had crouched beside Chatley, and she said if he had even a spark of human kindness, a vestige of human decency, he would do what had to be done, and he thought that was even crueler of her to say, because where did human kindness and human decency enter into *her* job description? Had she said anything to Babe Ruth when she took him? Had Adlai Stevenson given her unassailable reasons for demonstrating human decency and kindness?

"You mustn't leave me for Bill!"

"It would serve you right."

"*Please!* Show some compassion!"



"My god, this is an obscenity!"

But in the end, he did it. Because thinking about all the reasons why he *couldn't* do it, which were all the reasons she had ignored and *did* do it, made him so desolately angry that he couldn't stop himself. And so with the second one he became the avenger of Death.

He found the taker who had gotten Ernie Pyle, and he killed him. He found the taker who had arranged for John Lennon and Fiorello La Guardia and Brendan Behan, and killed him. He found the taker who had gotten Mackenzie King and Marilyn Monroe and Frank Herbert, and he killed her. He found the taker who had gotten Sergei Rachmaninoff and Eleanor Roosevelt and Helen Keller, and he killed him. He sat behind the one who had taken Emiliano Zapata and Leon Trotsky and Amelia Earhart and Aleister Crowley as she stolidly watched an Arnold Schwarzenegger movie. She was a very old, blue-haired woman, and she studied the film as if preparing for a final exam. And Pen waited for a car crash, reached into her lap, pulled out a knitting needle; and he killed her. He saw the taker who had been his inquisitor, and he followed him into a restaurant, and when he went to the men's toilet followed him again, and didn't even ask whom he had gotten, because he knew the list would be long and filled with people whose names he would not know, and which the taker would not remember, and he simply killed him. But not once did he ask the question that transcended, in simplicity and importance, all the hundreds of questions he *did* get answered.

Not once did he ask a taker why the Dust Man was not making any effort to stop him from decimating the ranks of his chosen agents, why he was allowing Pen Robinson to course through the city being the avenger of Death.

On the first day of winter, in Central Park, near the statue of Alice, he saw a taker about to put his hands on a child climbing a rock. Pen moved in, feeling his years in his aching bones, and he was about to use the icepick on the man whose hand stretched toward the little girl, when he felt a chill that was not part of the season, and a hand dropped onto his shoulder. The voice behind him said, "No, I think not, Pen. That will be enough. It's certainly enough for me."

In the moment before the cold hand turned him away, Pen saw the taker reach to the child, and touch her on the ankle, and the child fell. It lay on the crackling icy grass, and the taker moved off, casting only a momentary glance at Pen and his companion. The taker was frightened.

Then Pen was turned, without seeming effort, and he looked at the face of the Dust Man. He had not seen that face in forty-one years.

Tears came to his eyes, and he reached out to touch the chest of the reaper, the reiver, the slayer of nations; and he said, "You went away and I never got to say goodbye."

Pen Robinson's father, who had died in a mill accident when Pen had been fourteen, smiled down at his boy and said, "I'm sorry, Pen. But I've spent a long time getting back to you, and I've missed you."

Now Pen could see clearly through the membrane; and he understood why Henry Chatley had been permitted to contact him; and why he had found it so effortless, after a quiet, empty, essentially lonely life of shelf dust and cold meals prepared after work, to do the things he had done.

And he walked with the Dust Man, whose name was Bill, as had been his father's name, through the membrane and straight into a long lifetime position in the family business.

# CHAINED TO THE FAST LANE IN THE RED QUEEN'S RACE

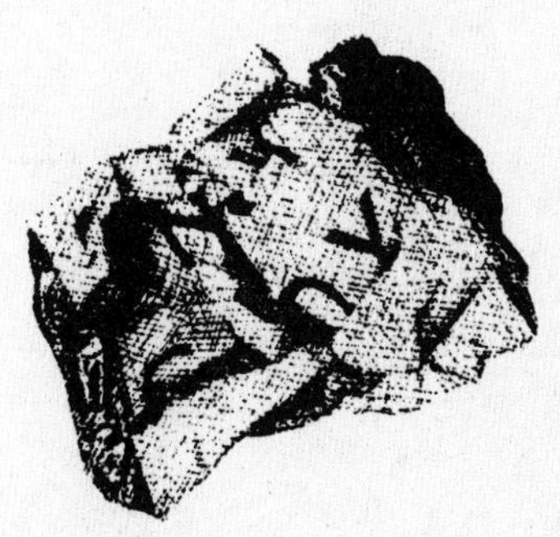

Is he who opens a door and he who
closes it the same being?

GASTON BACHELARD (1884–1962)
*French philosopher of science, Sorbonne*

OVER CAPPUCCINO and key lime pie he told her that even though it wouldn't seem as if he was going away, he *was*, in fact, going away. Farther than she could imagine.

"I'll go with you. Take me with you." She started to cry. "Nothing's holding me here. I can go with you."

So he told her that though he could not take her, that he could take nothing and no one with him, she needn't worry about his being gone, because he would be here. With her.

She thought he was speaking in metaphor, invoking that occasional spirituality in his nature that was a large part of his attraction. "I don't *want* the memory of you . . . I want *you*!" she said urgently.

"It'll *be* me. I'll be here, except that it won't be *this* me. It'll be the next one over."

She got hysterical at that and he quickly came around the teak dinner table that she had polished so assiduously with lemon oil in joyous expectation of having dinner with him; and he held her tightly, his unhappiness made somehow supportable by the mingled odors of her recently washed hair and the lemon oil. "I love you," she sobbed. He told her he knew that; and he said he loved her, too; and he told her not to cry, because it was going to be all right. All of which was true. Then he told her that she might not even realize it wasn't him but some *other* him, which was also true. But it made her more hysterical.

Then he said the truest thing about their relationship. He said, "We didn't really fall in love. What we did was collide at the intersection of your life and mine."

She had no idea what that really meant, but she took it to mean he had fallen out of love with her; and he was abandoning her; and she ran away from him, locked herself in the bathroom; and he left, not wanting to cause her any more anguish. Because, in truth, he had loved her more than any woman he had ever known in this life. In *this* life.

But he had only resided in this life for eleven months.

He left her then: gathering up his jacket and muffler, and the little Steuben glass panda he had found gift-wrapped on his place at the dinner table. The chances of carrying the figurine through were not good, but he wanted to try.

Wanted to try not only because it would have been cruelty for her to come out of the bathroom, find him gone, and see the frivolous, dear gift left behind. Wanted to try because he felt he should try to remember her.

Forgetting her, as he had forgotten so many others from so many lives past, was inevitable. But like a child who saves a special seashell, a memorable rock, a useless lanyard from summer camp, in order that the memories will not fade too quickly, he always tried to carry some memento through.

He was alone in the creaking, ancient elevator when he felt himself going. Like the onset of the flu. He had felt it coming as they had sat eating dinner. The dryness in the nasal passages, the unpleasant feeling at the back of his throat that he had never been able to describe, save by comparing it to the gasping discomfort that accompanies the too-rapid consumption of too much ice cream; the burning in the eyes, the arthritic pains in hip and finger joints.

He was relieved that he had felt the onset of the slippage and had gotten away before he vanished. Otherwise, how could she have reconciled the appearance of the other him when he was gone?

He leaned against the wall of the elevator, hoping no one had pressed the button on a lower floor, hoping he would go quietly before the elevator reached the lobby; and he drew in long, deep, shuddering breaths.

And in a moment he had slipped through.

The elevator was empty. A faint scintillance in the air, and a not unpleasant odor: the smell of sunshine on dusky Concord grapes bursting on their vines.

He was gone from that life. His name had been Alan Justes. And he was gone.

At precisely the instant that Alan Justes scintillated out of existence in an elevator traveling between the fifteenth and fourteenth floors of an apartment building on East 63rd Street in New York City, a man who looked exactly like Alan Justes emerged from the doorway of Steinway & Sons, the famous piano makers on East 57th Street, who had closed for the evening three hours earlier; and he hurried toward Fifth Avenue on his way to 63rd Street. He was dressed quite differently from Alan Justes, which would cause momentary confusion when, eighteen minutes hence, he would ring the doorbell of that certain apartment on the twentieth floor of the building on East 63rd. A moment of pain and confusion that would be compounded when the door was opened and he would say to the attractive brunette whose eyes were swollen from crying, "Hi. Katherine? I'm Allen." Because he would say it and not spell it, she would not realize till weeks later that he was no longer A-l-a-n, but someone named A-l-l-e-n. There were other, minor differences, as well: a mole on the left shoulder no longer existed; the lyrics to a number of popular songs were absent from his available repertoire for singing in the shower; he now liked brussels sprouts; the buffalo-head nickel he carried as a lucky piece would soon be spent with the rest of the change in his pocket, because for Allen it had no special significance.

But later than night, in bed, Katherine would perceive a subtle, salutary difference between the man who had walked out of her apartment and the man who had returned less than half an hour later.

It is an ill wind that blows no one some good.

Alan breathed deeply as he passed through the membrane. It might not have been a membrane. But it felt very much like pressing one's face against a balloon, pushing steadily and without discomfort into a resilient surface. And in a timeless moment he was through. His right hand, which had been in his jacket pocket, holding the glass panda, was now empty. *Goodbye, Kathy,* he thought; and put her out of his mind as the memory faded, faded.

"You can't sleep here, buddy," said a voice. "Move it along."

He looked up. By moonlight he saw the not-unkind face of a cop, staring down at him. There were broken veins in his round cheeks and on the fleshy bulb of his nose. *He drinks,* Alan thought. *But then, if I had to spend my nights waiting for teenage creeps to rob convenience marts, I'd drink, too.*

"I'm not sleeping, Officer," Alan said, getting to his feet. "I'm sitting, thinking, contemplating the moon and the steady passage of the hours." He was eloquent in this new life; he liked that.

It was a doorway in which he stood. Now he stepped out onto the sidewalk. A section of residential buildings, well-tended townhouses, neat entranceways. Traffic was light. The first car he noticed had no wheels. It shussshed past on what appeared to be an air-cushion mechanism. There was no unpleasant exhaust smell.

The cop examined him, stepping back to give him room in case a gun or knife might materialize in a hand. The cop's manner altered instantly as he perceived the cut of suit was expensive, the shoes so highly polished they reflected both streetlight and moonlight, the face shaved, the hair combed. The faint scent of lime aftershave. "Sorry to startle you like that, sir. Thought you might be an old skid catching forty winks."

"No harm done, Officer," Alan said. "The cement was cool and I was stalling the return home."

"Why . . . it's Mr. Justman, isn't it?" Alan's face was full in the light now. He smiled at the cop. They stood staring at each other for another second; then the cop said, "Well, say hello to your mother for me, Mr. Justman." And he touched the shiny black visor of his cap with his stubby left hand, in a gesture as old as the deference paid by city employees to those known as gentry. And he walked away, leaving Alan Justman to contemplate the necessity of going home.

He stood in the channel of street and the sound of a spiky, screamhorn saxophone cut through the empty moment. He looked up at the few bright windows but could not find the source of the music. *I have to go home,* he thought. And the thought reinterpreted itself visually in his mind as a dark, ominous rush of water slithering into the distance. Smooth, slick, oily shapes, barely breaking the surface of the freshet, frightening shapes cruising along, were caught in the moonlight of his mind. *I have to go home. Mother will be worried.*



He let himself into the darkened townhouse. The beaded lamp on the foyer credenza threw an asthmatic glow halfway up the stairs.

Mother's elevator-chair was at the top of the balustrade. So she was in bed already. The day nurse would have put her down, tucked her in, and left her to the company of the bizarre coterie. He stood with one hand on the newel post, a foot on the lowest step; and he listened. From abovestairs he could hear the sound of malicious laughter and that same ugly sitar music Johann insisted on playing all night.

He started to turn away.

"Aren't you coming up, Alvin?" He looked up as the voice of the woman caught him in a noose of command.

She stood there half-shrouded in darkness, but not even the shadows pooled at the head of the stairs could hide the luminous expanse of thigh and leg her parted dressing gown revealed. She touched the corner of her mouth with a fingertip. Black lacquered fingernail against her lower lip.

He climbed the stairs slowly. Breathing steadily, she waited for him. And when he was one step below the landing she reached out and put her hand behind his neck, drawing his face toward her. She looked down into his eyes and smiled a feral smile of possession. "Your mother is waiting. *Everyone's* been waiting."

Then she led him up and into the master bedroom where the lights were low and the pale throng moved on a silent tide around the yellowed figure of his mother, propped up on her pillows in the great canopied bed.

It was not as bad a night as it might have been. The blind child was not there. Nor the woman without arms.

He was a Chinese puzzle box: a box within a box within a box . . .

A Russian capsule doll that, when the halves were broken open, revealed a smaller doll nestling inside; a smaller doll that, when opened, exposed an even smaller doll; down and down and down to the most minuscule doll secreted at the core of the largest, so tiny its features were indistinguishable.

Like Gurdjieff and Giordano Bruno and Tesla before him; like Cagliostro and David Hume; like Confucius and Prester John and Livy the historian; and like Brahmagupta, Muhammad, Cassiodorus, and even the poet Sylvia Plath, he had discovered — in a blinding epiphany on no special day, one day — that there was no such thing as luck. Nor such a thing as serendipity, no such thing as synchronism. No single life of random chance existed. No single life was led by any breathing mortal.

He learned: there was only slipping across from one life to the next. One life that gave onto the next, slightly different, and beyond that the doorway to the next life, and the next . . .

He learned that humans were immortal. Life was not of a finite length, not of a proscribed duration; life was serial. Each spark of life — not reincarnated as incorrectly perceived in dim analogue of the reality — traveled through consecutive existences, in contiguous universes, replenished and reformed as a new individual. But each altered from the life just behind; altered still more when it became the next one ahead.

He came to think of the totality of existence as baklava: the Armenian pastry made up of thousands of isinglass-thin layers, one atop the others, so tightly pressed one could not differentiate among them, could not know when one had bitten through to the next.

There was no luck, merely slipping through the membrane into the next universe layer, assuming a new variation of self. And sometimes it was a better variation, and that was a day in which everything went right. And sometimes it was a worse variation, and that was a day in which random troubles compounded till life was not worth living.

Reality was a shunting station, an invisible railroad terminal without end; and through that switching station every soul that had ever existed came and went . . . moving on to its next manifestation of self. . . all unaware as memory of the transfer was obliterated by passage . . . all unaware that *today's* self was a vaguely familiar but completely different entity than yesterday's self.

But like Da Vinci and Karl Marx and William James before him, something had gone wrong and he had not lost the memory of where and who he had been. Imperfectly, shadowy in retrospect, neither amnesia nor forgetfulness, came the realization that, like cats nudging each other over from food bowl to food bowl, he was being pushed from life to life by the *him* behind him. And in turn, he was pushing the him next in line. He could not, he understood, coexist in the same universe with another of himself.



It was a journey without end.

How many hundreds, thousands, millions of lives he had led since he had been born . . . he could not begin to surmise.

And how he longed to find the perfect life. To stop the flow. To halt and feel no pressure to move along. The cop that was the life-flow would not tap him on the sole of his shoe and order him to get up, move it along, buddy. To reach a life that was pleasing, rewarding, supportable. And to stop.

But every *him* behind him was also seeking the good life; and they kept the pressure constant.

Who would want to be stuck in a life such as the one he now shared with his mother and her society of twisted degenerates? Alvin Justman longed for check-out time.

"Where were you last night?" his mother asked. Her voice was thin and filled with catarrh. How much longer could she live in her condition? The day nurse and the scarred hunchback who told her fortune ministered to the old woman. They bustled around the bed, fluffing, inoculating, moistening, touching the sores. He stared at the tableau and said, "Mother, why don't you let me kill you so you can pass on to the next bright world?"

Her lips trembled before she spoke. "What are you talking about? I raised you. The least you can do is stay by me till the end."

"There is no end in sight, Mother."

"Thank God for the wonders of medical science." A tube clamped to her throat made bubbling sounds.

"Yes. Thank God," Alvin said.

"And so . . ." she said, ". . . where were you last night? The séance had to be put off. We needed that occasional spirituality in your nature that is, my son, a large part of your attractiveness."

"I was out walking, my mother. Communing with the cosmos and the cop on the beat."

She stared at him through milky irises. "Sometimes I wonder if you are, indeed, my child."

"Sometimes you're not alone in wondering," he replied. Then, cheerily, he asked again, "So there's no matricide in the cards, is that right?"

The day nurse turned to him. "She's asleep again."

"Thank God for the wonders of medical science," he murmured, and left the bedroom. Somewhere behind him a man named Allen was enjoying a better life than the one he had left, fearing with just cause the life that lay ahead. *I've got to get the hell out of here*, Alvin Justman thought.

But all he could do was apply pressure. And if it was a better life ahead, there would be a *him* who would resist that pressure, as Alan Justes had resisted until Allen grew strong enough to effect the transition.

And so, for the next nine years, Alvin lived in that dark townhouse with the everchanging clique of human refuse and with his dear mother, thankful for the wonders of medical science.

On a Sunday night, stoking the ancient furnace in the basement, still wincing from the pain of the straight-razor wounds into which they had poured the hot wax, he felt himself trembling with self-loathing and hysteria, and the onset of slippage. He began to cry with relief. *Thank God*, he thought.

And in a moment he was pressing against the membrane, feeling compassion for whichever *him* was at that moment emerging into the world of mother and her minions.

And in another moment he was through into his next life, where he was Elvin Luckman, a young man whose mother had just died and who, desolate with the loss, had signed up for the Merchant Marine. Two years later, understanding at last that the extended series of heartbreakingly empty liaisons he had had with women who despised and ridiculed him was an attempt to pay penance for his mother's death, he also came to understand that this life was destined to be a tragic one. His mother's death, an inevitability for which he bore no accountability after they had opened her and discovered the carcinoma had metastasized like ergot in a field of rye, had become the central issue of his existence.

He became celibate, withdrawn, obscure to the point of laying out his clothes and standing his watch aboard ship in harmony with the lines of tellurian force he had found described in a worthless book of crackpot mysticism in a sidestreet bookshop in Hong Kong.

His sanity slipped from him, day by day; and without the companionship of friends he had no sticking-post to which his floating mind could adhere. Strange phantasms and arcane beliefs assaulted him.

Standing watch, as the sea billowed around him, he held conversations with himself. And only occasionally was he rational enough to remember that there was a life beyond this one.

Finally, what saved him was the waking terror of the life in which he had been Alvin Justman. The pressure behind him.

The life with mother and her band of freaks.

The life he, Elvin, had totally forgotten.

But there had been another *him* who had emerged into that monstrous venue; and like Alvin before him, Allen wanted *out*! The pressure was significant.

And during shore leave in London, Elvin Luckman felt the breath-catching unpleasantness of having eaten too much ice cream too quickly. He lay down in the bottom of the punt on the Serpentine, and in a moment was gone from that place.

Overtime for use of the punt went unpaid and the quayside entrepreneur who rented the little boats not only had to absorb the loss, but was required to pay three pounds six to the son of the man who located the punt.

It is an ill wind . . .

Into a life as William Rucklin. A life working in a vacuum-bead circuit-coding factory in Liverpool. Life without color. Life without change. Life that was no life. Three years.

Into a life as Wilhelm Richter. Life of detestation for everyone around him. He knew how intelligent he was. He knew it was bad breaks, the efforts of those around him who were crazed with jealousy at his gifts, that and that alone keeping him from ascendancy. He despised having to smile at them, loathed having to kowtow to them, hated them for their enjoyment of his subservient position. He knew Iris was having an affair with one of her old paramours, knew that, too; but not which one. Nine months, fifteen days.

Into a life as Waldemar van Rensburg, who lived within sight of The Hague and had a perfectly pleasant, if uneventful, life. Wife, Trina; three children, Hans, Karel, Wilhelmina (after the Queen, rest her soul); small tobacco shop; three weeks in Belgium every year. Only a year — Wilhelm was mad with his life and pushed hard from behind — and he was nudged into the next layer of baklava.



The slippage did not go smoothly.

It was as if he were being born again. Pushing, pressing, thrusting against the membrane. It would not give. As if this entranceway was of a stronger, less resilient substance.

As if someone on the other side were pushing back in the opposite direction, as if the life-flow were trying to run upstream, as if he were going against the grain. He had time to register the anomaly while in the transitional state.

But the pressure from behind him, the pressure of lives as Alan, Allen, Alvin, Elvin, William, Wilhelm — terrible lives — could not be contained. He went through.

In the first moments of his new life, as usual, he was able to remember the totality of his journey. Not each life individually, but a vast panorama of personae, with a few that stood out in sharper relief than the mass. The flamenco dancer he had been; the sandhog digging the Holland Tunnel; the feudal serf; the confidant of the Medicis; the gravedigger in Denmark; the catamaran-riding Melanesian.

In that moment he thought of himself, each time it happened he thought of himself, as Alice had perceived herself: running as fast as he could run, to stay in the same place, in the Red Queen's race.

Then the moment passed, and he opened his eyes, and his face stared closely back at him. He was sitting in an easy chair in a pleasant drawing room filled with books, a fireplace, and the scent of cavendish, and he was not looking in a mirror.

"Waldemar?" the face that was his said.

"Ja, Waldemar," he replied. "And you are — ?"

"Wallace Vanowen. And I'm not going."

The memory started to slip away.

"Wha . . . what do you —" And Wally Vanowen slapped him across the face as hard as he could. He didn't pull the blow, simply let fly. Waldemar's head snapped around and in that instant his mind cleared.

"Hold onto it, boy!" said Wally angrily, urgently. "Don't let it slip away or who the hell knows what I'll have to do with you . . . because *I ain't going*, cookie."



"You *remember*?"

"Yeah, I remember. I remember Alvin and his creepy old lady, I remember that paranoid Wilhelm, remember all the way back to footsoldiering with Black Jack Pershing. You remember *that* one, the gangrene and the dysentery?"

"My God, I do, *yes*! All the way back then."

"That's nothing to what I remember, son. And it's what makes for a good life. Which is what this is, in case you hadn't figured it out yet. This is the one. The top of the line. The prize in the Cracker Jack box. This is the best possible life that can be led by this series of guys who've been me. And here I stay. I don't budge."

"But you have to."

Wally chuckled, lit his pipe.

Then he went and sat down in an easy chair across from Waldemar's. They stared at each other for a long time.

"They're pushing me from behind," Waldemar said. "I'd be *happy* to let you have this life . . . but I have no control over the process. I'm nudged, you're nudged."

Wally shook his head. "I don't go."

"They'll *make* you go! The pressure."

Wally exhaled a cloud of smoke. The drawing room smelled woodsy and comfortably close. In fact, now that Waldemar thought about it, the room — and himself in it — felt more comfortable than anything he could remember. He felt as if he *belonged* here. He knew, in that moment, that his predecessor in this life, the Wally Vanowen sitting across from him, had told him the absolute truth: *this* was the best of all possible worlds.

This was the terminus he had sought for uncountable lifetimes.

Here the Flying Dutchman came to rest.

Here the Red Queen's race marked its finish line.

And somehow . . . *somehow* . . . he would stay here!

His mind scrabbled through possibilities, clawing at one plan, then another, casting them aside like a dog digging through a wastebasket for that bit of refuse producing the wondrous aroma. Somewhere in his past, somewhere in all those lives he had led, was the method, the bit of data, the spark of cunning that would permit him to shove Wally through before him, back into the life-flow, back into the race . . .

Then he would worry about keeping all the others behind him locked out. Jubilation sang along the wires of his soul.

"What makes this such a perfect life?" He had to stall till he could reason this out.

Wally smiled. "The knowledge, cookie."

"What knowledge?"

"The knowledge that I'm not a slave. The smarts to know that I can live the life I choose if I don't let the life I'm in live *me*. I'm happy in my skin."

Waldemar could not comprehend what Wally was saying. It sounded like errant nonsense, obscurant philosophy of the most sophomoric sort, the kind of twaddle he'd heard from trendy half-wits floating on drugs and cheapjack religiosity. He had led too many lives to go for such simplistic generalities.

But he *felt* comfortable here. Felt as if he belonged, for the first time in numberless years of lives.

But he listened as Wally told him of this life. And there was nothing at all remarkable about it.

"I get up each morning and make a cup of coffee with cardamon and chocolate in it. I sit and look out at the ridge of hills behind this house; and I watch the seasons change. I dress every day in clothes that I like, that are comfortable, with a pair of old boots that know my feet. I do my work: I translate poetry by Latin American writers for the university press. I spend many hours a day in their words, surrounded by their beauty. My friends call and suggest we go for barbecue dinners, and we laugh and make up bad puns. My wife is the part of me I need but don't have the history or space within myself to contain. I have two children, who search through my coat pockets for little gifts when I come home from a trip. I read a book that made me cry this week."

Waldemar felt a subtle shift in his body; as if the blood had sped up in veins and arteries; as if he had gotten late growth in his bones; as if his heart had been touched. Then it passed, and he felt contempt for Wally. To reside in paradise and dine so frugally! The water was deeper, but this fool had no sense of the vastness. He resolved to snatch this Eden from its totally unworthy tenant. And for the first time he contemplated suicide.

Well, wasn't it suicide if he killed Wally? How could it be murder if he killed *himself*? Two of them could not exist in the same life . . . he knew that. So Wally had to go.

Seeming still to be listening to the dreary panegyric, he looked around the drawing room. He would have to move fast, without hesitation, brutally. He would have only one chance . . . he knew that. They were in the middle of the drawing room. The walls of bookcases were filled with volumes and the three doors were closed. A sofa, a small sideboard, the two easy chairs, a floor lamp, the fireplace.

There was a stand of fireplace implements: tongs, ash shovel, heavy poker. Yes.

He pushed himself out of the easy chair. He was still a bit unsteady. Wally stopped speaking, watching him. "I have to get my sea legs," he said, acting wobblier than he felt. Strength was coming into his body now. He put out a hand toward the fireplace mantel, as if reaching for support. Wally started to say something. He stumbled, took two faltering steps toward the fireplace, and in a rush grabbed the handle of the poker. He spun with the weapon raised over his head, one sharp blow, one powerful smash, an instant, just an instant, and he would be alone here . . .

Three doors opened into the drawing room. Three men stood in the openings, and behind them were others. But the poker was on its descent already. Wally's eyes widened.

And Waldemar felt himself hurled into the membrane.

Men in many doorways faded and were receding shadows.

He was sick with having eaten too much ice cream too quickly. His hip joints ached. He was on his way toward another life.

He was Walter Vernon and he was a failure. Every time he had attempted to ameliorate the mediocrity in which he existed, disaster slipped from the shadows to crush his spirit. He was simply *not good enough*. And Belinda never missed an opportunity to tell him of his inadequacies. The children were impossible, needing a strong hand and not having a father who could provide it. Each day was a campaign in a war that was lost before it had begun.

Walter Vernon, though he could not remember the fact, was running as fast as he could in a life of desolation that stretched on before him for fifteen years. At the end of that life lay a membrane that gave onto a fast lane of lives, each more awful than the ones before. Oh, perhaps some were better; and perhaps somewhere ages away there was another existence in which one could read a book that brought tears.

But, maintaining the pattern, Walter Vernon might not recognize it.

In a drawing room filled with books, a large group of men who bore a striking resemblance to each other stood talking quietly. There was a sense of great loss among them.

"He was too damaged. Too bent by what he'd been through, the poor sonofabitch," Wally Vanowen said. They nodded and sighed.

"You'd think he would have realized," said Merle Webber. "We *all* believed no two of us could exist in the same life when we got here. But couldn't he see he was existing with you, Wally, right here, right in this room? Couldn't he see that it *could* work?"

Wallace Vanowen spread his hands in hopeless resignation. "Sometimes it's been too awful for them. We do the best we can."

They talked about it for a while longer, then decided they and their wives and their lovers and their children would spend the rest of the day having a barbecue and relaxing before they returned to their separate lives here in this world that was rapidly filling up with themselves. Here in this best of all possible worlds where those who were worthy of happiness had found it.

It was the best of all possible worlds because they had made it so; a world in which check-out time never came.

> Is he who opens a door and he who
> closes it the same being?
>
> GASTON BACHELARD (1884–1962)

# THE FUNCTION OF DREAM SLEEP

McGrath awoke suddenly, just in time to see a huge mouth filled with small, sharp teeth closing in his side. In an instant it was gone, even as he shook himself awake.

Had he not been staring at the flesh, at the moment his eyes opened from sleep, he would have missed the faintest pink line of closure that remained only another heartbeat, then faded and was gone, leaving no indication the mouth had ever existed; a second — secret — mouth hiding in his skin.

At first he was sure he had wakened from a particularly nasty dream. But the memory of the thing that had escaped from within him, through the mouth, was a real memory — not a wisp of fading nightmare. He had *felt* the chilly passage of something rushing out of him. Like cold air from a leaking balloon. Like a chill down a hallway from a window left open in a distant room. And he had *seen* the mouth. It lay across the ribs vertically, just below his left nipple, running down to the bulge of fat parallel to his navel. Down his left side there had been a lipless mouth filled with teeth; and it had been open to permit a breeze of something to leave his body.

McGrath sat up on the bed. He was shaking. The Tensor lamp was still on, the paperback novel tented open on the sheet beside him, his body naked and perspiring in the August heat. The Tensor had been aimed directly at his side, bathing his flesh with light, when he had unexpectedly opened his eyes; and in that waking moment he had surprised his body in the act of opening its secret mouth.

He couldn't stop the trembling, and when the phone rang he had to steel himself to lift the receiver.

"Hello," he heard himself say, in someone else's voice.

"Lonny," said Victor Kayley's widow, "I'm sorry to disturb you at this hour . . ."

"It's okay," he said. Victor had died the day before yesterday. Sally relied on him for the arrangements, and hours of solace he didn't begrudge. Years before, Sally and he . . . then she drifted toward Victor, who had been McGrath's oldest, closest . . . they were drawn to each other more and more sweetly till . . . and finally, McGrath had taken them both to dinner at the old Steuben Tavern on West 47th, that dear old Steuben Tavern with its dark wood booths and sensational schnitzel, now gone, torn down and gone like so much else that was . . . and he had made them sit side by side in the booth across from him, and he took their hands in his . . . I love you both so much, he had said . . . I see the way you move when you're around each other . . . you're both my dearest friends, you put light in my world . . . and he laid their hands together under his, and he grinned at them for their nervousness . . .

"Are you all right; you sound so, I don't know, so *strained*?" Her voice was wide awake. But concerned.

"I'm, yeah, I'm okay. I just had the weirdest, I was dozing, fell asleep reading, and I had this, this *weird* —" He trailed off. Then went back at it, more sternly: "I'm okay. It was a scary dream."

There was, then, a long measure of silence between them. Only the open line, with the sound of ions decaying.

"Are *you* okay?" he said, thinking of the funeral service day after tomorrow. She had asked him to select the casket. The anodized pink aluminum "unit" they had tried to get him to go for, doing a bait-and-switch, had nauseated him. McGrath had settled on a simple copper casket, shrugging away suggestions by the Bereavement Counselor in the Casket Selection Parlor that "consideration and thoughtfulness for the departed" might better be served by the Monaco, a "Duraseal metal unit with Sea Mist Polished Finish, interior richly lined in 600 Aqua Supreme Cheney velvet, magnificently quilted and shirred, with matching jumbo bolster and coverlet."

"I couldn't sleep," she said. "I was watching television, and they had a thing about the echidna, the Australian anteater, you know . . . ?" He made a sound that indicated he knew. "And Vic never got over the trip we took to the Flinders Range in '82, and he just loved the Australian animals, and I turned in the bed to see him smiling . . ."

She began to cry.

He could feel his throat closing. He knew. The turning to tell your best friend something you'd just seen together, to get the reinforcement, the input, the expression on his face. And there was no face. There was emptiness in that place. He knew. He'd turned to Victor three dozen times in the past two days. Turned, to confront emptiness. Oh, he knew, all right.

"Sally," he murmured. "Sally, I know; I know."

She pulled herself together, snuffled herself unclogged and cleared her throat. "It's okay. I'm fine. It was just a second there . . ."

"Try to get some sleep. We have to do stuff tomorrow."

"Of course," she said, sounding really quite all right. "I'll go back to bed. I'm sorry." He told her to shut up, if you couldn't call a friend at that hour to talk about the echidna, who the hell *could* you call?

"Jerry Falwell," she said. "If I have to annoy someone at three in the morning, better it should be a shit like him." They laughed quickly and emptily, she said good night and told him he had been much loved by both of them, he said I know that, and they hung up.

Lonny McGrath lay there, the paperback still tented at his side, the Tensor still warming his flesh, the sheets still soggy from the humidity, and he stared at the far wall of the bedroom on whose surface, like the surface of his skin, there lay no evidence whatever of secret mouths filled with teeth.

"I can't get it out of my mind."

Dr. Jess ran her fingers down his side, looked closer. "Well, it *is* red; but that's more chafing than anything out of Stephen King."

"It's red because I keep rubbing it. I'm getting obsessive about it. And don't make fun, Jess. I can't get it out of my mind."

She sighed and raked a hand back through her thick auburn hair. "Sorry." She got up and walked to the window in the examination room. Then, as an afterthought, she said, "You can get dressed." She stared out the window as McGrath hopped off the physical therapy table, nearly catching his heel on the retractable step. He partially folded the stiff paper gown that had covered his lap, and laid it on the padded seat. As he pulled up his undershorts, Dr. Jess turned and stared at him. He thought for the hundredth time that his initial fears, years before, at being examined by a female physician, had been foolish. His friend looked at him with concern, but without the *look* that passed between men and women. "How long has it been since Victor died?"

"Three months, almost."

"And Emily?"

"Six months."

"And Steve and Melanie's son?"

"Oh, Christ, Jess!"

She pursed her lips. "Look, Lonny, I'm not a psychotherapist, but even I can see that all these deaths of friends is getting to you. Maybe you don't even see it, but you used the right word: obsessive. *No*body can sustain so much pain, over so brief a period, the loss of so many loved ones, without going into a spiral."

"What did the X-rays show?"

"I told you."

"But there might've been *some*thing. Some lesion, or inflammation; an irregularity in the dermis . . . *some*thing!"

"Lonny. Come *on*. I've never lied to you. You looked at them with me, did *you* see anything?" He sighed deeply, shook his head. She spread her hands as if to say, well, there you are, I can't make something sick where nothing sick exists. "I can work on your soft prostate, and I can give you a shot of cortisone in the ball joint where that cop worked you over; but I can't treat something out of a penny dreadful novel that doesn't leave any trace."

"You think I need a shrink?"

She turned back to the window. "This is your third visit, Lonny. You're my pal, kiddo, but I think you need to get counseling of a different sort."

McGrath knotted his tie and drew it up, spreading the wings of his shirt collar with his little fingers. She didn't turn around. "I'm worried about you, Lonny. You ought to be married."

"I *was* married. You're not talking wife, anyway. You're talking keeper." She didn't turn. He pulled on his jacket, and waited. Finally, with his hand on the doorknob, he said, "Maybe you're right. I've never been a melancholy sort, but all this . . . so many, in so short a time . . . maybe you're right."

He opened the door. She looked out the window. "We'll talk." He started out, and without turning, she said, "There won't be a charge for this visit."



He smiled thinly, not at all happily. But she didn't see it.

• • •

He called Tommy and begged off from work. Tommy went into a snit. "I'm up to my ass, Lonny," he said, affecting his Dowager Empress tone. "This is Black goddam Friday! The Eroica! That Fahrenheit woman, Farrenstock, whatever the hell it is . . ."

"Fahnestock," Lonny said, smiling for the first time in days. "I thought we'd seen the last of her when you suggested she look into the possibility of a leper sitting on her face."

Tommy sighed. "The grotesque bitch is simply a glutton. I swear to God she must be into bondage; the worse I treat her, the more often she comes in."

"What'd she bring this time?"

"Another half dozen of those tacky petit-point things. I can barely bring myself to look at them. Bleeding martyrs and scenes of culturally depressed areas in, I suppose, Iowa or Indiana. Illinois, Idaho, I don't know: one of those places that begins with an I, teeming with people who bowl."

Lonny always wound up framing Mrs. Fahnestock's gaucheries. Tommy always took one look, then went upstairs in back of the framing shop to lie down for a while. McGrath had asked the matron once, what she did with all of them. She replied that she gave them as gifts. Tommy, when he heard, fell to his knees and prayed to a God in which he did not believe that the woman would never hold him in enough esteem to feel he deserved such a gift. But she spent, oh my, how she spent.

"Let me guess," McGrath said. "She wants them blocked so tightly you could bounce a dime off them, with a fabric liner, a basic pearl matte, and the black lacquer frame from Chapin Molding. Right?"

"Yes, of course, right. Which is *another* reason your slacker behavior is particularly distressing. The truck from Chapin just dropped off a hundred feet of the oval top walnut molding. It's got to be unpacked, the footage measured, and put away. You *can't* take the day off."

"Tommy, don't whip the guilt on me. I'm a goy, remember?"

"If it weren't for guilt, the *goyim* would have wiped us out three thousand years ago. It's more effective than a Star Wars defense system." He puffed air through his lips for a moment, measuring how much he would *actually* be inconvenienced by his assistant's absence. "Monday morning? Early?"

McGrath said, "I'll be there no later than eight o'clock. I'll do the petit-points first."

"All right. And by the way, you sound awful. D'you know the worst part about being an Atheist?"

Lonny smiled. Tommy would feel it was a closed bargain if he could pass on one of his horrendous jokes. "No, what's the worst part about being an Atheist?"

"You've got no one to talk to when you're fucking."

Lonny roared, silently. There was no need to give him the satisfaction. But Tommy knew. He couldn't see him, but Lonny knew he was grinning broadly at the other end of the line. "So long, Tommy. See you Monday."

He racked the receiver in the phone booth and looked across Pico Boulevard at the office building. He had lived in Los Angeles for eleven years, since he and Victor and Sally had fled New York, and he still couldn't get used to the golden patina that lay over the days here. Except when it rained, at which times the inclemency seemed so alien he had visions of giant mushrooms sprouting from the sidewalks. The office building was unimpressive, just three storeys high and brick; but a late afternoon shadow lay across its face, and it recalled for him the eighteen frontal views of the Rouen Cathedral that Monet had painted during the winter months of 1892 and 1893: the same façade, following the light from early morning till sunset. He had seen the Monet exhibition at MOMA. Then he remembered with whom he had taken in that exhibition, and he felt again the passage of chill leaving his body through that secret mouth. He stepped out of the booth and just wanted to go somewhere and cry. *Stop it!* he said inside. *Knock it off.* He swiped at the corner of his eye, and crossed the street. He passed through the shadow that cut the sidewalk.

Inside the tiny lobby he consulted the glass-paneled wall register. Mostly, the building housed dentists and philatelists, as best he could tell. But against the ribbed black panel he read the little white plastic letters that had been darted in to include THE REM GROUP 306. He walked up the stairs.

To find 306, he had to make a choice: go left or go right. There were no office location arrows on the wall. He went to the right, and was pleased. As the numbers went down, he began to hear someone speaking rather loudly. "Sleep is of several kinds. Dream sleep, or rapid eye movement sleep — what we call REM sleep, and thus the name of our group — is predominantly found in mammals who bring forth living young, rather than eggs. Some birds and reptiles, as well."

McGrath stood outside the glass-paneled door to 306, and he listened. *Viviparous mammals*, he thought. He could now discern that the speaker was a woman; and her use of "living young, rather than eggs" instead of *viviparous* convinced him she was addressing one or more laypersons. *The echidna*, he thought. A *familiar viviparous mammal.*

"We now believe dreams originate in the brain's neocortex. Dreams have been used to attempt to foretell the future. Freud used dreams to explore the unconscious mind. Jung thought dreams formed a bridge of communication between the conscious and the unconscious." *It wasn't a dream*, McGrath thought. *I was awake. I know the difference.*

The woman was saying, ". . . those who try to make dreams work for them, to create poetry, to solve problems; and it's generally thought that dreams aid in consolidating memories. How many of you believe that if you can only *remember* the dream when you waken, that you will understand something very important, or regain some special memory you've lost?"

*How many of you.* McGrath now understood that the dream therapy group was in session. Late on a Friday afternoon? It would have to be women in their thirties, forties.

He opened the door, to see if he was correct.

With their hands in the air, indicating they believed the capturing of a dream on awakening would bring back an old memory, all six of the women in the room, not one of them older than forty, turned to stare at McGrath as he entered. He closed the door behind him, and said, "I don't agree. I think we dream to forget. And sometimes it doesn't work."

He was looking at the woman standing in front of the six hand-raised members of the group. She stared back at him for a long moment, and all six heads turned back to her. Their hands were frozen in the air. The woman who had been speaking settled back till she was perched on the edge of her desk.

"Mr. McGrath?"

"Yes. I'm sorry I'm late. It's been a day."

She smiled quickly, totally in command, putting him at ease. "I'm Anna Picket. Tricia said you'd probably be along today. Please grab a chair."

McGrath nodded and took a folding chair from the three remaining against the wall. He unfolded it and set it at the far left of the semicircle. The six well-tended, expensively-coifed heads remained turned toward him as, one by one, the hands came down.

He wasn't at all sure letting his ex-wife call this Anna Picket, to get him into the group, had been such a good idea. They had remained friends after the divorce, and he trusted her judgment. Though he had never availed himself of her services after they'd separated and she had gone for her degree at UCLA, he'd been assured that Tricia was as good a family counseling therapist as one could find in Southern California. He had been shocked when she'd suggested a dream group. But he'd come: he had walked through the area most of the early part of the day, trying to decide if he wanted to do this, share what he'd experienced with total strangers; walked through the area stopping in at this shop and that boutique, having some gelato and shaking his head at how this neighborhood had been "gentrified," how it had changed so radically, how all the wonderful little trademen who had flourished here had been driven out by geysering rents; walked through the area growing more and more despondent at how nothing lasted, how joy was drained away shop by shop, neighborhood by neighborhood, person by . . .

Until one was left alone.

Standing on an empty plain. The dark wind blowing from the horizon. Cold, empty dark: with the knowledge that a pit of eternal loneliness lay just over that horizon, and that the frightening wind that blew up out of the pit would never cease. That one would stand there, all alone, on the empty plain, as one after another of the ones you loved were erased in a second.

Had walked through the area, all day, and finally had called Tommy, and finally had allowed Tricia's wisdom to lead him, and here he sat, in a folding straight-back chair, asking a total stranger to repeat what she had just said.

"I asked why you didn't agree with the group, that remembering dreams is a good thing?" She arched an eyebrow, and tilted her head.

McGrath felt uncomfortable for a moment. He blushed. It was something that had always caused him embarrassment. "Well," he said slowly, "I don't want to seem like a smart aleck, one of those people who reads some popularized bit of science and then comes on like an authority . . ."

She smiled at his consternation, the flush of his cheeks. "Please, Mr. McGrath, that's quite all right. Where dreams are concerned, we're *all* journeyists. What did you read?"

"The Crick–Mitchison theory. The paper on 'unlearning.' I don't know, it just seemed, well, *reasonable* to me."

One of the women asked what that was.

Anna Picket said, "Dr. Sir Francis Crick, you'll know of him because he won the Nobel Prize for his work with DNA; and Graeme Mitchison, he's a highly respected brain researcher at Cambridge. Their experiments in the early 1980s. They postulate that we dream to forget, not to remember."

"The best way I understood it," McGrath said, "was using the analogy of cleaning out an office building at night, after all the workers are gone. Outdated reports are trashed, computer dump sheets are shredded, old memos tossed with the refuse. Every night our brains get cleaned during the one to two hours of REM sleep. The dreams pick up after us every day, sweep out the unnecessary, untrue, or just plain silly memories that could keep us from storing the important memories, or might keep us from rational thinking when we're awake. *Remembering* the dreams would be counter-productive, since the brain is trying to unlearn all that crap so we function better."

Anna Picket smiled. "You were sent from heaven, Mr. McGrath. I was going precisely to that theory when you came in. You've saved me a great deal of explanation."

One of the six women said, "Then you don't *want* us to write down our dreams and bring them in for discussion? I even put a tape recorder by the bed. For instance, I had a dream just last night in which my bicycle . . ."

He sat through the entire session, listening to things that infuriated him. They were so self-indulgent, making of the most minor inconveniences in their lives, mountains impossible to conquer. They were so different from the women he knew. They seemed to be antiquated creatures from some primitive time, confused by changing times and the demand on them to be utterly responsible for their existence. They seemed to want succor, to be told that there were greater forces at work in their world; powers and pressures and even conspiracies that existed solely to keep them nervous, uncomfortable, and helpless. Five of the six were divorcées, and only one of the five had a full-time job: selling real estate. The sixth was the daughter of an organized crime figure. McGrath felt no link with them. He didn't need a group therapy session. His life was as full as he wanted it to be . . . except that he was now always scared, and lost, and constantly depressed. Perhaps Dr. Jess was dead on target. Perhaps he *did* need a shrink.

He was certain he did not need Anna Picket and her well-tailored ladies whose greatest *real* anguish was making sure they got home in time to turn on the sprinklers.

When the session ended, he started toward the door without saying anything to the Picket woman. She was surrounded by the six. But she gently edged them aside and called to him, "Mr. McGrath, would you wait a moment? I'd like to speak to you." He took his hand off the doorknob, and went back to his chair. He bit the soft flesh of his inner cheek, annoyed.

She blew them off like dandelion fluff, far more quickly than McGrath thought possible, and did it without their taking it as rejection. In less than five minutes he was alone in the office with the dream therapist.

She closed the door behind the Mafia Princess and locked it. For a deranged moment he thought . . . but it passed, and the look on her face was concern, not lust. He started to rise. She laid a palm against the air, stopping him. He sank back onto the folding chair.

Then Anna Picket came to him and said, "For McGrath hath murdered sleep." He stared up at her as she put her left hand behind his head, cupping the nape with fingers extending up under his hair along the curve of the skull. "Don't be nervous, this'll be all right," she said, laying her right hand with the palm against his right cheek, the spread thumb and index finger bracketing an eye he tried mightily not to blink. Her thumb lay alongside his nose, the tip curving onto the bridge. The forefinger lay across the bony eye-ridge.

She pursed her lips, then sighed deeply. In a moment her body twitched with an involuntary rictus, and she gasped, as if she had had the wind knocked out of her. McGrath couldn't move. He could feel the strength of her hands cradling his head, and the tremors of — he wanted to say — *passion* slamming through her. Not the passion of strong amorous feeling, but passion in the sense of being acted upon by something external, something alien to one's nature.

The trembling in her grew more pronounced, and McGrath had the sense that power was being drained out of him, pouring into her, that it had reached saturation level and was leaking back along the system into him, but changed, more dangerous. But why dangerous? She was spasming now, her eyes closed, her head thrown back and to the side, her thick mass of hair swaying and bobbing as she jerked, a human double-circuit high-voltage tower about to overload.

She moaned softly, in pain, without the slightest trace of subliminal pleasure, and he could see she was biting her lower lip so fiercely that blood was beginning to coat her mouth. When the pain he saw in her face became more than he could bear, he reached up quickly and took her hands away with difficulty; breaking the circuit.

Anna Picket's legs went out and she keeled toward him. He tried to brace himself, but she hit him with full dead weight, and they went crashing to the floor entangled in the metal folding chair.

Frightened, thinking insanely *what if someone comes in and sees us like this, they'd think I was molesting her*, and in the next instant thinking with relief *she locked the door*, and in the next instant his fear was transmogrified into concern for her. He rolled out from under her trembling body, taking the chair with him, wrapped around one ankle. He shook off the chair, and got to his knees. Her eyes were half-closed, the lids flickering so rapidly she might have been in the line of strobe lights.

He hauled her around, settling her semi-upright with her head in his lap. He brushed the hair from her face, and shook her ever so lightly, because he had no water, and had no moist washcloth. Her breathing slowed, her chest heaved not quite so spastically, and her hand, flung away from her body, began to flex the fingers.

"Ms. Picket," he whispered, "can you talk? Are you all right? Is there some medicine you need . . . in your desk?"



She opened her eyes, then, and looked up at him. She tasted the blood on her lips and continued breathing raggedly, as though she had run a great distance. And finally she said, "I could feel it in you when you walked in."

He tried to ask what it was she had felt, what it was in him that had so unhinged her, but she reached in with the flexing hand and touched his forearm.

"You'll have to come with me."

"Where?"

"To meet the *real* REM Group."

And she began to cry. He knew immediately that she was weeping for him, and he murmured that he would come with her. She tried to smile reassurance, but there was still too much pain in her. They stayed that way for a time, and then they left the office building together.

They were impaired, every one of them in the sprawling ranch-style house in Hidden Hills. One was blind, another had only one hand. A third looked as if she had been in a terrible fire and had lost half her face, and another propelled herself through the house on a small wheeled platform with restraining bars to keep her from falling off.

They had taken the San Diego Freeway to the Ventura, and had driven west on 101 to the Calabasas exit. Climbing, then dropping behind the hills, they had turned up a side road that became a dirt road that became a horse path, Lonny driving Anna Picket's '85 Le Sabre.

The house lay within a bowl, completely concealed, even from the dirt road below. The horse trail passed behind low hills covered with mesquite and coast live oak, and abruptly became a perfectly surfaced blacktop. Like the roads Hearst had had cut in the hills leading up to San Simeon, concealing access to the Castle from the Coast Highway above Cambria, the blacktop had been poured on spiral rising cuts laid on a reverse bias.

Unless sought from the air, the enormous ranch house and its outbuildings and grounds would be unknown even to the most adventurous picnicker. "How much of this acreage do you own?" McGrath asked, circling down the inside of the bowl.



"All this," she said, waving an arm across the empty hills, "almost to the edge of Ventura County."

She had recovered completely, but had said very little during the hour and a half trip, even during the heaviest weekend traffic on the 101 Freeway crawling like a million-wheeled worm through the San Fernando Valley out of Los Angeles. "Not a lot of casual drop-ins I should imagine," he replied. She looked at him across the front seat, fully for the first time since leaving Santa Monica. "I hope you'll have faith in me, trust me just a while longer," she said.

He paid strict attention to the driving.

He had been cramped within the Buick by a kind of dull fear that strangely reminded him of how he had always felt on Christmas Eve, as a child, lying in bed, afraid of, yet anxious for, the sleep that permitted Santa Claus to come.

In that house below lay something that knew of secret mouths and ancient winds from within. Had he not trusted her, he would have slammed the brake pedal and leaped from the car and not stopped running till he had reached the freeway.

And once inside the house, seeing all of them, so ruined and tragic, he was helpless to do anything but allow her to lead him to a large sitting-room, where a circle of comfortable overstuffed chairs formed a pattern that made the fear more overwhelming.

They came, then, in twos and threes, the legless woman on the rolling cart propelling herself into the center of the ring. He sat there and watched them come, and his heart seemed to press against his chest. McGrath, as a young man, had gone to a Judy Garland film festival at the Thalia in New York. One of the revived movies had been *A Child Is Waiting*, a nonsinging role for Judy, a film about retarded children. Sally had had to help him out of the theater only halfway through. He could not see through his tears. His capacity for bearing the anguish of the crippled, particularly children, was less than that of most people. He brought himself up short: why had he thought of that afternoon at the Thalia now? These weren't children. They were adults. All of them. Every woman in the house was at least as old as he, surely older. Why had he been thinking of them as children?

Anna Picket took the chair beside him, and looked around the circle. One chair was empty. "Catherine?" she asked.

The blind woman said, "She died on Sunday."

Anna closed her eyes and sank back into the chair. "God be with her, and her pain ended."

They sat quietly for a time, until the woman on the cart looked up at McGrath, smiled a very kind smile, and said, "What is your name, young man?"

"Lonny," McGrath said. He watched as she rolled herself to his feet and put a hand on his knee. He felt warmth flow through him, and his fear melted. But it only lasted for a moment, as she trembled and moaned softly, as Anna Picket had done in the office. Anna quickly rose and drew her away from McGrath. There were tears in the cart-woman's eyes.

A woman with gray hair and involuntary head tremors, indicative of Parkinson's, leaned forward and said, "Lonny, tell us."

He started to say *tell you what?* but she held up a finger and said the same thing again.

So he told them. As best he could. Putting words to feelings that always sounded melodramatic; words that were wholly inadequate for the tidal wave of sorrow that held him down in darkness. "I miss them, oh God how I miss them," he said, twisting his hands. "I've never been like this. My mother died, and I was lost, I was miserable, yes there was a feeling my heart would break, because I loved her. But I could *handle* it. I could comfort my father and my sister, I had it in me to do that. But these last two years . . . one after another . . . so many who were close to me . . . pieces of my past, my life . . . friends I'd shared times with, and now those times are gone, they slip away as I try to think of them. I, I just don't know *what to do.*"

And he spoke of the mouth. The teeth. The closing of that mouth. The wind that had escaped from inside him.

"Did you ever sleepwalk, as a child?" a woman with a clubfoot asked. He said: yes, but only once. Tell us, they said.

"It was nothing. I was a little boy, maybe ten or eleven. My father found me standing in the hallway outside my bedroom, at the head of the stairs. I was asleep, and I was looking at the wall. I said, 'I don't see it here anywhere.' My father told me I'd said that; the next morning he told me. He took me back to bed. That was the only time, as best I know."

The women murmured around the circle to each other. Then the woman with Parkinson's said, "No, I don't think that's anything." Then she stood up, and came to him. She laid a hand on his forehead and said, "Go to sleep, Lonny."

And he blinked once, and suddenly sat bolt upright. But it wasn't an instant, it had been much longer. He had been asleep. For a long while. He knew it was so instantly, because it was now dark outside the house, and the women looked as if they had been savaged by living jungles. The blind woman was bleeding from her eyes and ears; the woman on the cart had fallen over, lay unconscious at his feet; in the chair where the fire victim had sat, there was now only a charred outline of a human being, still faintly smoking.

McGrath leaped to his feet. He looked about wildly. He didn't know what to do to help them. Beside him, Anna Picket lay slumped across the bolster arm of the chair, her body twisted and blood once again speckling her lips.

Then he realized: the woman who had touched him, the woman with Parkinson's, was gone.

They began to whimper, and several of them moved, their hands idly touching the air. A woman who had no nose tried to rise, slipped and fell. He rushed to her, helped her back into the chair, and he realized she was missing fingers on both hands. Leprosy . . . *no*! Hansen's disease, that's what it's called. She was coming to, and she whispered to him, "There . . . Teresa . . . help her . . ." and he looked where she was pointing, at a woman as pale as crystal, her hair a glowing white, her eyes colorless. "She . . . has . . . lupus . . ." the woman without a nose whispered.

McGrath went to Teresa. She looked up at him with fear and was barely able to say, "Can you . . . please . . . take me to a dark place . . . ?"

He lifted her in his arms. She weighed nothing. He let her direct him up the stairs to the second floor, to the third bedroom off the main corridor. He opened the door and it was musty and unlit. He could barely make out the shape of a bed. He carried her over and placed her gently on the puffy down comforter. She reached up and touched his hand. "Thank you." She spoke haltingly, having trouble breathing. "We, we didn't expect anything . . . like that . . ."

McGrath was frantic. He didn't know what had happened, didn't know what he had done to them. He felt awful, felt responsible, *but he didn't know what he had done!*

"Go back to them," she whispered. "Help them."



"Where is the woman who touched me . . . ?"

He heard her sobbing. "She's gone. Lurene is gone. It wasn't your fault. We didn't expect anything . . . like . . . that."

He rushed back downstairs.

They were helping one another. Anna Picket had brought water, and bottles of medicine, and wet cloths. They were helping one another. The healthier ones limping and crawling to the ones still unconscious or groaning in pain. And he smelled the fried metal scent of ozone in the air. There was a charred patch on the ceiling above the chair where the burned woman had been sitting.

He tried to help Anna Picket, but when she realized it was McGrath, she slapped his hand away. Then she gasped, and her hand flew to her mouth, and she began to cry again, and reached out to apologize. "Oh, my God, I'm so *sorry*! It wasn't your fault. You couldn't know . . . not even Lurene knew." She swabbed at her eyes, and laid a hand on his chest. "Go outside. Please. I'll be there in a moment."

A wide streak of dove-gray now bolted through her tangled hair. It had not been there before the instant of his sleep.

He went outside and stood under the stars. It was night, but it had not been night before Lurene had touched him. He stared up at the cold points of light, and the sense of irreparable loss overwhelmed him. He wanted to sink to his knees, letting his life ebb into the ground, freeing him from this misery that would not let him breathe. He thought of Victor, and the casket being cranked down into the earth, as Sally clung to him, murmuring words he could not understand, and hitting him again and again on the chest; not hard, but without measure, without meaning, with nothing but simple human misery. He thought of Alan, dying in a Hollywood apartment from AIDS, tended by his mother and sister who were, themselves, hysterical and constantly praying, asking Jesus to help them; dying in that apartment with the two roommates who had been sharing the rent keeping to themselves, eating off paper plates for fear of contracting the plague, trying to figure out if they could get a lawyer to force Alan's removal; dying in that miserable apartment because the Kaiser Hospital had found a way around his coverage, and had forced him into "home care." He thought of Emily, lying dead beside her bed, having just dressed for dinner with her daughter, being struck by the grand mal seizure and her heart exploding, lying there for a day, dressed for a dinner she would never eat, with a daughter she would never again see. He thought of Mike, trying to smile from the hospital bed, and forgetting from moment to moment who Lonny was, as the tumor consumed his brain. He thought of Ted seeking shamans and homeopathists, running full tilt till he was cut down. He thought of Roy, all alone now that DeeDee was gone: half a unit, a severed dream, an incomplete conversation. He stood there with his head in his hands, rocking back and forth, trying to ease the pain.

When Anna Picket touched him, he started violently, a small cry of desolation razoring into the darkness.

"What *happened* in there?" he demanded. "Who *are* you people? What did I do to you? Please, oh please I'm asking you, tell me *what's going on*!"

"We absorb."

"I don't know what —"

"We take illness. We've always been with you. As far back as we can know. We have always had that capacity, to assume the illness. There aren't many of us, but we're everywhere. We absorb. We try to help. As Jesus wrapped himself in the leper's garments, as he touched the lame and the blind, and they were healed. I don't know where it comes from, some sort of intense empathy. But . . . we do it . . . we absorb."

"And with me . . . what was that in there . . . ?"

"We didn't know. We thought it was just the heartache. We've encountered it before. That was why Tricia suggested you come to the Group."

"My wife . . . is Tricia one of you? Can she . . . take on the . . . does she absorb? I lived with her, I never —"

Anna was shaking her head. "No, Tricia has no idea what we are. She's never been here. Very few people have been so needing that I've brought them here. But she's a fine therapist, and we've helped a few of her patients. She thought you . . ." She paused. "She still cares for you. She felt your pain, and thought the Group might be able to help. She doesn't even know of the *real* REM Group."

He grabbed her by the shoulders, intense now.

*"What happened in there?"*

She bit her lip and closed her eyes tightly against the memory. "It was as you said. The mouth. We'd never seen that before. It, it *opened*. And then . . . and then . . ."

He shook her. *"What!?!"*

She wailed against the memory. The sound slammed against him and against the hills and against the cold points of the stars. "Mouths. In each of us! Opened. And the wind, it, it just, it just *hissed* out of us, each of us. And the pain we held, no, that *they* held — I'm just their contact for the world, they can't go anywhere, so I go and shop and bring and do — the pain *they* absorbed, it, it took some of them. Lurene and Margid . . . Teresa won't live . . . I know . . ."

McGrath was raving now. His head was about to burst. He shook her as she cried and moaned, demanding, "What's happening to us, what am I doing, why is this doing to us now, what's going wrong, please, you've got to help me, we've got to *do* something —"

And they hugged each other, clinging tightly to the only thing that promised support: each other. The sky wheeled above them, and the ground seemed to fall away. But they kept their balance, and finally she pushed him to arm's length and looked closely at his face and said, "I don't know. I *do not* know. This isn't like anything we've experienced before. Not even Alvarez or Ariès know about this. A wind, a terrible wind, something alive, leaving the body."

"*Help me!*"

"I *can't* help you! No one can help you, I don't think *anyone* can help you. Not even Le Braz . . ."

He clutched at the name. "Le Braz! Who's Le Braz?"

"No, you don't want to see Le Braz. Please, listen to me, try to go off where it's quiet, and lonely, and try to handle it yourself, that's the only way!"

"Tell me who Le Braz is!"

She slapped him. "You're not hearing me. If *we* can't do for you, then no one can. Le Braz is beyond anything we know, he can't be trusted, he does things that are outside, that are awful, I think. I don't really know. I went to him once, years ago, it's not something you want to —"

I don't care, he said. I don't care about any of it now. I have to rid myself of this. It's too terrible to live with. I see their faces. They're calling and I can't answer them. They plead with me to say something to them. I don't know what to say. I can't sleep. And when I sleep I dream of them. I can't live like this, because this isn't living. So tell me how to find Le Braz. I don't care, to hell with the whole thing, I just don't give a damn, *so tell me*!

She slapped him again. Much harder. And again. And he took it. And finally she told him.

He had been an abortionist. In the days before it was legal, he had been the last hope for hundreds of women. Once, long before, he had been a surgeon. But they had taken that away from him. So he did what he could do. In the days when women went to small rooms with long tables, or to coat hangers, he had helped. He had charged two hundred dollars, just to keep up with supplies. In those days of secret thousands in brown paper bags stored in clothes closets, two hundred dollars was as if he had done the work for free. And they had put him in prison. But when he came out, he went back at it.

Anna Picket told McGrath that there had been other . . .

. . . work. Other experiments. She had said the word *experiments*, with a tone in her voice that made McGrath shudder. And she had said again, "For McGrath hath murdered sleep," and he asked her if he could take her car, and she said yes, and he had driven back to the 101 Freeway and headed north toward Santa Barbara, where Anna Picket said Le Braz now lived, and had lived for years, in total seclusion.

It was difficult locating his estate. The only gas station open in Santa Barbara at that hour did not carry maps. It had been years since free maps had been a courtesy of gas stations. Like so many other small courtesies in McGrath's world that had been spirited away before he could lodge a complaint. But there was no complaint department, in any case.

So he went to the Hotel Miramar, and the night clerk was a woman in her sixties who knew every street in Santa Barbara and knew very well the location of the Le Braz "place." She looked at McGrath as if he had asked her the location of the local abattoir. But she gave him explicit directions, and he thanked her, and she didn't say you're welcome, and he left. It was just lightening in the east as dawn approached.

By the time he found the private drive that climbed through heavy woods to the high-fenced estate, it was fully light. Sun poured across the channel and made the foliage seem Rain Forest lush. He looked back over his shoulder as he stepped out of the Le Sabre, and the Santa Monica Channel was silver and rippled and utterly oblivious to shadows left behind from the night.

He walked to the gate, and pressed the button on the intercom system. He waited, and pressed it again. Then a voice — he could not tell if it was male or female, young or old — crackled, "Who is it?"

"I've come from Anna Picket and the REM Group." He paused a moment, and when the silence persisted, he added, "The *real* REM Group. Women in a house in Hidden Hills."

The voice said, "Who are you? What's your name?"

"It doesn't matter. You don't know me. McGrath, my name is McGrath. I came a long way to see Le Braz."

"About what?"

"Open the gate and you'll know."

"We don't have visitors."

"I saw . . . there was a . . . I woke up suddenly, there was a, a kind of *mouth* in my body . . . a wind passed . . ."

There was a whirring sound, and the iron gate began to withdraw into the brick wall. McGrath rushed back to the car and started the engine. As the gate opened completely, he decked the accelerator and leaped through, even as the gate began without hesitation to close.

He drove up the winding drive through the Rain Forest, and when he came out at the top, the large, fieldstone mansion sat there, hidden from all sides by tall stands of trees and thick foliage. He pulled up on the crushed rock drive, and sat for a moment staring at the leaded windows that looked down emptily. It was cool here, and dusky, even though it was burgeoning day. He got out and went to the carved oak door. He was reaching for the knocker when the door was opened. By a ruined thing.

McGrath couldn't help himself. He gasped and fell back, his hands coming up in front of him as if to ward off any approach by the barely human being that stood in the entranceway.

It was horribly pink where it was not burned. At first McGrath thought it was a woman, that was his quick impression; but then he could not discern its sex, it might have been male. It had certainly been tortured in flames. The head was without hair, almost without skin that was not charred black. There seemed to be too many bends and joints in the arms. The sense that it was female came from the floor-length wide skirt it wore. He was spared the sight of the lower body, but he could tell there was considerable bulk there, a bulk that seemed to move gelatinously, as if neither human torso nor human legs lay within the circle of fabric.

And the creature stared at him from one milky eye, and one eye so pure and blue that his heart ached with the beauty of it. As features between the eyes and the chin that became part of the chest, without discernible neck, there were only charred knobs and bumps, and a lipless mouth blacker than the surrounding flesh. "Come inside," the doorkeeper said.

McGrath hesitated.

"Or go away," it said.

Lonny McGrath drew a deep breath and passed through. The doorkeeper moved aside only a trifle. They touched: blackened hip, back of a normal hand.

Closed and double-bolted, the passage out was now denied McGrath. He followed the asexual creature through a long, high-ceilinged foyer to a closed, heavily-paneled door to the right of a spiral staircase that led to the floor above. The thing, either man or woman, indicated he should enter. Then it shambled away, toward the rear of the mansion.

McGrath stood a moment, then turned the ornate L-shaped door handle, and entered. The heavy drapes were drawn against the morning light, but in the outlaw beams that latticed the room here and there, he saw an old man sitting in a high-backed chair, a lap robe concealing his legs. He stepped inside the library, for library it had to be: floor to ceiling bookcases, spilling their contents in teetering stacks all around the floor. Music swirled through the room. Classical music; McGrath didn't recognize it.

"Dr. Le Braz?" he said. The old man did not move. His head lay sunk on his chest. His eyes were closed. McGrath moved closer. The music swelled toward a crescendo, something symphonic. Now he was only three steps from the old man, and he called the name Le Braz again.

The eyes opened, and the leonine head rose. He stared at McGrath unblinkingly. The music came to an end. Silence filled the library.

The old man smiled sadly. And all ominousness left the space between them. It was a sweet smile. He inclined his head toward a stool beside the wingback. McGrath tried to give back a small smile, and took the seat offered.

"It is my hope that you are not here to solicit my endorsement for some new pharmacological product," the old man said.

"Are you Dr. Le Braz?"

"It is I who was, once, known by that name, yes."

"You have to help me."

Le Braz looked at him. There had been such a depth of ocean in the words McGrath had spoken, such a descent into stony caverns that all casualness was instantly denied. "Help you?"

"Yes. Please. I can't bear what I'm feeling. I've been through so much, seen so much these last months, I . . ."

"Help you?" the old man said again, whispering the phrase as if it had been rendered in a lost language. "I cannot even help myself. . . how can I possibly help you, young man?"

McGrath told him. Everything.

At some point the blackened creature entered the room, but McGrath was unaware of its presence till he had completed his story. Then, from behind him, he heard it say, "You are a remarkable person. Not one living person in a million has ever seen the Thanatos mouth. Not one in a hundred million has felt the passage of the soul. Not one in the memory of the human race has been so tormented that he thought it was real, and not a dream."

McGrath stared at the creature. It came lumbering across the room and stood just behind the old man's chair, not touching him. The old man sighed, and closed his eyes.

The creature said, "This was Josef Le Braz, who lived and worked and cared for his fellow man, and woman. He saved lives, and he married out of love, and he pledged himself to leave the world slightly better for his passage. And his wife died, and he fell into a well of melancholy such as no man had ever suffered. And one night he woke, feeling a chill, but he did not see the Thanatos mouth. All he knew was that he missed his wife so terribly that he wanted to end his life."

McGrath sat silently. He had no idea what this meant, this history of the desolate figure under the lap robe. But he waited, because if no help lay here in this house, of all houses secret and open in the world, then he knew that the next step for him was to buy a gun and to disperse the gray mist under which he lived.



Le Braz looked up. He drew in a deep breath and turned his eyes to McGrath. "I went to the machine," he said. "I sought the aid of the circuit and the chip. I was cold, and could never stop crying. I missed her so, it was unbearable."

The creature came around the wingback and stood over McGrath. "He brought her back from the Other Side."

McGrath's eyes widened. He understood.

The room was silent, building to a crescendo. He tried to get off the low stool, but he couldn't move. The creature stared down at him with its one gorgeous blue eye and its one unseeing milky marble. "He deprived her of peace. Now she must live on, in this half-life.

"This is Josef Le Braz, and he cannot support his guilt."

The old man was crying now. McGrath thought if one more tear was shed in the world he would say to hell with it and go for the gun. "Do you understand?" the old man said softly.

"Do you take the point?" the creature said.

McGrath's hands came up, open and empty. "The mouth . . . the wind . . ."

"The function of dream sleep," the creature said, "is to permit us to live. To flense the mind of that which dismays us. Otherwise, how could we bear the sorrow? The memories are their legacy, the parts of themselves left with us when they depart. But they are not whole, they are joys crying to be reunited with the one to whom they belong. You have seen the Thanatos mouth, you have felt a loved one departing. It should have freed you."

McGrath shook his head slowly, slowly. No, it didn't free me, it enslaved me, it torments me. No, slowly, no. I cannot bear it.

"Then you do not yet take the point, do you?"

The creature touched the old man's sunken cheek with a charred twig that had been a hand. The old man tried to look up with affection, but his head would not come around. "You must let it go, all of it," Le Braz said. "There is no other answer. Let it go . . . let *them* go. Give them back the parts they need to be whole on the Other Side, and let them in the name of kindness have the peace to which they are entitled."

"Let the mouth open," the creature said. "We cannot abide here. Let the wind of the soul pass through, and take the emptiness as release." And she said, "Let me tell you what it's like on the Other Side. Perhaps it will help."

McGrath laid a hand on his side. It hurt terribly, as of legions battering for release on a locked door.

He retraced his steps. He went back through previous days as if he were sleepwalking. *I don't see it here anywhere.*

He stayed at the ranch-style house in Hidden Hills, and helped Anna Picket as best he could. She drove him back to the city, and he picked up his car from the street in front of the office building on Pico. He put the three parking tickets in the glove compartment. That was work for the living. He went back to his apartment, and he took off his clothes, and he bathed. He lay naked on the bed where it had all started, and he tried to sleep. There were dreams. Dreams of smiling faces, and dreams of children he had known. Dreams of kindness, and dreams of hands that had held him.

And sometime during the long night, a breeze blew.

But he never felt it.

And when he awoke, it was cooler in the world than it had been for a very long time; and when he cried for them, he was, at last, able to say goodbye.

A man is what he does with his attention.
*John Ciardi*

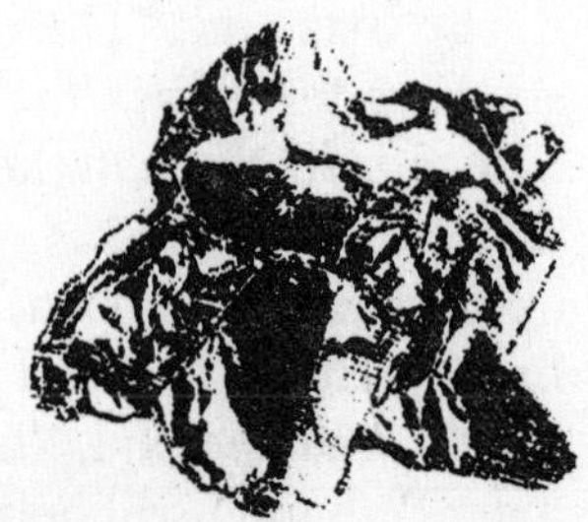